DANGER IN

Jeff Cape has been kicking around Indonesia as an oil geologist, and now he's ready for home. But before his boat sails from Bali, he stops for a drink where he meets Nicole Balashov, a bewitching White Russian trying to smuggle information out to the U.S. Cape agrees to take it with him but after Nicole leaves, he sees a large, bald man rush out after her. Alarmed for her safety, Cape takes off after the man and misses his boat. Now every shady character on the island seems to be after him, including Mr. Chu and his mysterious serindit bird, and Regina Williams, a seductive American woman. Then there's the fat man himself, Apollo Fry, who will certainly kill anyone who gets in his way. All Cape wants to do is find Nicole again— before it's too late!

MALAY WOMAN

Eden has been found murdered and Jock is the only suspect. Stowing away in a ship bound for Kuala Tang, he overhears a plot to kill a young woman named Kay Allison, the widowed owner of a rubber plantation. Jock tries to warn her. But the task is anything but a simple one, because Jock finds himself immediately attracted to her—yet he can't tell her who he is. When the ship lands, matters only become more complicated when he decides to hide out at the home of his best friend, Gabriel Wing. Jock soon finds out that Gabb's restless wife Monique has her own plans for him!

Danger in Paradise

Malay Woman

By A. S. Fleischman

STARK HOUSE

Stark House Press • Eureka California

DANGER IN PARADISE / MALAY WOMAN

Published by Stark House Press
2200 O Street
Eureka, CA 95501, USA
Griffinskye3@sbcglobal.net
www.starkhousepress.com

ISBN: 1-933586-28-1

Text set in Figural. Heads set in Behemoth Semi Condensed.
Cover design and layout by Mark Shepard, SHEPGRAPHICS.COM
Proofreading by Rick Ollerman

First Stark House Press Edition: August 2010

Reprint Edition

Now Watch Closely...
THE WORLDS OF
A.S. FLEISCHMAN

by David Laurence Wilson

"*I put my greatest faith in chaos.*" SID FLEISCHMAN

It was an inauspicious start for one of America's most beloved novelists: *He was a man of unusually large frame in a blue chalk-striped suit.*

Then this beginner added a place, an action, and an attitude:

He crossed San Diego's Fifth Street against the signal and turned in from the gray morning sidewalk to the Verlaine Building. The elevator operator was a skinny red-head with more lipstick than lips. "Well, Mr. Brindle," she said. "You're an early-bird this morning."

"I've got a date with a worm."

"You look like you've already had one," she smiled, and flapped her dimestore eyelashes.

O.K. You have to admit the guy had instincts. He knew how to write the lighter side of hard-boiled. As it turned out, he was able to write just about anything.

The year was 1948, the novel was *The Straw Donkey Case* and the publisher was Phoenix Press, a rather peculiar prize at the end of the crime fiction rainbow. This was one of the lowest rungs on the road to book-length publication, the bottom of the word-chain. These were books that were designed not for purchase but for rent at lending libraries, usually for three cents a day. They were hardcover, in many categories, and the art on their dust jackets was low-key, sometimes ugly. Among the writers who sold their first books to Phoenix were Harry Whittington and Edward S. Aarons.

Have you ever heard the phrases "five cents a word" or "$1000 a novel?" Phoenix stayed in business by offering its' writers $150 a book.

The name of this new Phoenix writer, the creator of the "chalk-striped" suit, was A. S. Fleischman, initials instead of a first name, a device that conveyed a certain veneer of authority and age that "Sid," or "Sidney," perhaps, did not.

The detective was named Brindle because Fleischman had a dog with brindle colored hair.

"When I was a kid we'd go down to Tijuana," Fleischman explained. "Do you remember the straw donkeys they used to sell along the border? I thought that somebody could smuggle something in one of those donkeys. So I started with the title, *The Straw Donkey Case*. I knew you had to have a detective, and a crime.

"I didn't know the murderer until I finished the book. I could have created a rationale for any one of my surviving characters being the murderer. Even today, I never know my endings ahead of time."

Albert Sidney Fleischman was a man of many hats, including a top hat and a yarmulke. He wrote under a wide canopy of experience, using many means to tell his stories, including screenplays, adult suspense and novels for children. If things didn't work out there would always be magic. Before he became a writer on paper, Fleischman was a storyteller on stage, a magician during the last days of vaudeville.

Fleischman was born in 1920 in New York City, where his father worked as a tailor. Two years later his family moved to San Diego, California. In the fifth grade Sid saw his first magician, a moment that would generate a lifelong love of illusion. His hero became Harry Houdini (Eric Weisz), another working-class Jew. Nearly eighty years later he would write a biography of the magician.

As a teenager, Fleischman became a voracious reader of magic manuals. Fleischman and his friend Buddy Ryan billed themselves as "The Mirthful Magicians" and tried to pass themselves off as brothers, Irish and Jewish. They hopped in a car with a couple suitcases filled with tricks and toured the small mining towns of Northern California. When they weren't performing they tried gold mining.

Fleischman graduated high school and broke into vaudeville at the Hippodrome Theater in Los Angeles. As "Al Sidney" he toured with a Spook Show for two years, with magic tricks and luminous props. At first he was underage—too young to officially perform magic—but he managed to grow a mustache and pass as an adult. Then he returned to San Diego and spent two years at San Diego State.

Fleischman's first publications were in the realm of magic. *Between Cocktails: With a Packet of Matches* (1939) was written in high school and sold for $50, for all rights, in perpetuity. To be exact, that was $50 in trade... not in cash. Two years before he could actually legally drink a cocktail he was already a suave customer: "Well, now let's do a couple of tricks between cocktails!" he wrote. The book featured thirty-four pages of close-up magic tricks illustrated by photographs of the author's hands. In 2009 the book was still in print.

Ready, Aim, Magic! Tricks for the Magician in Uniform (1942), *Call the Witness* (1943), *The Blue Bug: A Manual of Sorcery with Cigarette Papers* (1947), and *Top Secrets* (1947) were all written with Fleischman's friend Bob Gunther, a magician who would also contribute illustrations to the booklets and would later become an artist at Disney. In 1953 Fleischman wrote *Magic Made Easy*, with a rare pseudonym (Carl March) and a cover featuring more photographs of Fleischman's hands manipulating cards, coins and spools. He completed his magic books with *Mr. Mysterious's Secrets of Magic* (1975) and *The Charlatan's Handbook* (1993).

Fleischman also contributed sixty or seventy articles for magic magazines like *The Genii* and *The Sphinx*. All of these explained new tricks or new angles on old tricks. Magicians, it seems, like the how-tos: "Few magic books deal with theory," Fleischman noted. "Virtually all explain fresh secrets. That seems to be all that magicians seek or will pay money for. A few exceptions, of course."

When Fleischman began writing fiction he was following in the footsteps of the magicians turned writers Walter Gibson (1897-1985), creator of *The Shadow,* and Clayton Rawson (1906-1971). Gibson's magician-detectives included Norgil, Valdor, and Ardini. Rawson created The Great Merlini (also Rawson's own onstage name) and Don Diavolo.

Gibson wrote scores of books on magic and card tricks, beginning with *After Dinner Tricks,* in 1921 and including collaborations with the master magicians Houdini, Thurston, and Dunninger. Rawson wrote his own handful of magic books, including *How To Entertain Children*

With Magic (1962) and *The Golden Book of Magic* (1964).

There must have been something special or unusual about the air—or perhaps the water—in San Diego during the late nineteen forties. Four students from San Diego State—Oakley Hall, Sid Fleischman, and the team of Bob Wade and Bill Miller—returned to school after their lives were interrupted by four years of World War II service. All of them would write novels featuring San Diego Private Eyes, including *The Deadly Weapon* (1946, by Wade Miller) and *Murder City* (1949, by O.M. Hall). Suddenly trench coats were in fashion and four new writers were going on to exceptional success.

In 1942 Fleischman married his girl, Betty Taylor, a Spanish-language major. Betty would remain a supportive spouse until her death of cancer in 1993.

After service on a Navy Destroyer Escort in the South Pacific and Far East, Fleischman was back in San Diego in an apartment with Betty. They reupholstered the back seat of a sedan for a living room couch, a comfortable piece of furniture that would last them for years. Fleischman could still perform as a magician, but the best jobs—vaudeville and nightclub acts—seemed to have dried up during the war. It didn't feel like a profession anymore. Fleischman retired as a performer but as he moved through life, he never completely gave up on the magic trade. He was often at his most at ease when he was surrounded by magicians.

Before his overseas duty Fleischman had sold a love story to *Liberty* magazine. Now he was going to try freelance writing on Betty's portable red typewriter while she began working for the Veterans Administration. In the next year and a half Sid wrote dozens of short stories and sold five of them, to the Sunday supplement *This Week*, *Rexall's Magazine*, *Family Circle* and the *Toronto Star Weekly*. With the $300 he received from Phoenix for *The Straw Donkey Case*, written in three weeks, and its sequel, *Murder's No Accident* (1949), also with the Private Eye Max Brindle, Fleischman made a total of $470. Even when *The Straw Donkey Case* went into a paperback edition, it earned him no additional income.

After sizing up the $470 Fleischman returned to San Diego State under the G. I. Bill. He contributed to the student newspaper, *The Aztec*. He graduated at the age of 29 and a few months later, Jane, the first of his three children, was born, to be followed by Paul and Anne. Fleischman began work as a copyboy on the *San Diego Daily Journal*, also contributing a couple of feature articles. Two weeks later he was transferred to the rewrite desk, where he spent a year rearranging words. Later he was freed from copy-editing, taking on the paper's political beat, just as Richard Nixon was making his first run for the U.S. Senate.

"I once wrote an entire column on the boneless Nixon handshake," Fleischman noted in his delightful 1996 autobiography, *The Abracadabra Kid*. "It was like wrapping your fingers around a squid."

When the Journal went out of business he joined a group that established an alternative journal, *Point*, later purchased by *San Diego Magazine*.

The fiction angels continued to look favorably upon Sid Fleischman. When Fawcett began its Gold Medal series, Donald McCampbell, an agent who had serviced the rental publishers and placed *Magic Made Easy* asked Fleischman if he'd like to submit a story for the new line. Gold Medal paid a $2,000 advance. As quickly as he could, Fleischman crafted together a story and sent it to McCampbell, a manuscript titled *The Man Who Died Laughing* (later renamed *Shanghai Flame*), set in postwar China.

Fawcett's accounting and policies had finally made it possible for a generation of ink stained wretches to earn a living. They featured action, suspense and adventure and they were geographically democratic. They were as willing to feature a murder in the jungle, swamp, or desert, as they were to stick to urban streets. Fleischman's specialty was the Far East. His novels were set in China, Bali, Macao and the British colonies that would become Malaysia. What he didn't know personally he convincingly researched.

The novels were hard work. If he could write two books a year he was on a good pace. "Actually, when I get to about 220, 240 pages, I'm glad to see the end," Fleischman said.

For the readers of Fleischman's children's fiction it might be a shock to discover that he had also written fiction for adults. There was sex and violence and unnecessary characters were quickly dispatched under the most gruesome of circumstances. His characters were tough but it was not so much a coarseness of character but of situation. He didn't go in for the moody confusion of many of his contemporaries. There is a clarity and completeness in his writing that is distinct from the fog of noir.

Fleischman enjoyed wordplay, appreciating a fortuitous turn of phrase as much as he enjoyed turning over a card.

For example:

"I felt like a guy who wandered on the stage of a puppet show and discovered someone attaching strings to him. It's a weird feeling, and makes you want to run like hell." ...from *Look Behind You, Lady* (1952) and...

"There were three stand up customers and I made four. Fish net was hung from the ceiling and the floor was covered with beach sand. The place was a kind of narrow ash tray with a liquor license." ...from *The Venetian Blonde* (1963) and...

"Finally, miles from anywhere and with night coming on, there rose up a narrow, slab-sided building with a tall false front at the edge of the road. It didn't seem to belong there. It looked like a building that had wandered away from town and got lost." ...from *Humbug Mountain* (1978)

In *Look Behind You, Lady*, Fleischman's hero is a magician hacking out his act in Macao. In *The Venetian Blonde* his characters are the denizens of sleight-of-hand: a seductive medium and a cardsharp who can tell the manufacturer of a playing card by the way it feels in his hand. These two novels were reprinted by Stark House in 2006.

The collection that you now hold in your hands, including *Malay Woman* and *Danger in Paradise*, is witness to the exotic, when European and American powers could impose themselves on cultures they did not understand. In these pages you'll find Bali and Malaysia, freighters, rubber trees, quinine, Java, Sumatra, terrorists and the C.I.A., multi-lingual heroes, sarongs, whiskey and gin, fried dragonflies and the smell of drying fish.

In other words, magic and surprise.

In a life of 89 years a span of four years can seem like a single adventure, a long weekend. This moment of suspense writing, from 1951 to 1954, resulted in six paperback originals, five for Fawcett and one manuscript sold to Ace. All of these Fawcett novels were set in the Far East, China Macao, Bali and Singapore.

There are gems all over these tales of secret tunnels and exotic cafes. Fleischman's stories were filled with local color, personality and lingo. It seems that Fleischman would be an ideal companion around the Sankoochan jetty, or the shacks of Singapore's Lavender Street. He researched as he wrote, though he never returned to China or the rest of the Far East.

"I was enchanted with my experience in China and the whole former colonial East," Fleischman said. "For Gold Medal, this was my address. Others had staked out the rest of the world.

"I had never been to Bali but right after I finished *Danger in Paradise*, I was on a freighter and there was a woman aboard, a world traveler, and she had been there. I pretended I had also been there and found that I knew infinitely more, street by street, hotel by hotel, theater name by theater name, than she did. It was then I realized... research is not so bad."

Fleischman's heroes on these Far East mean streets are reminiscent of other defenders of an old Anglo empire, with echoes of Kipling, John Buchan and George Orwell. Local insurgencies, random killings and deceit are part of the background, activities in the periphery of our vision. In *Malay Woman* Fleischman's characters drive through jungles while the locals mob their cars, a menace but not yet a threat.

Fleischman's heroes could make a happy ending seem possible, though really... for how long? There were bigger forces at work. Continental drift. Birth rates and famine. All along Asia was becoming more Asian. American know-how was only going to work for so long.

In 1954 Fleischman's most recent manuscript, *Counterspy Express*, had been set in Europe, and it featured his trademarks—including a special familiarity of time and place. You could almost unfold the novel and use it as a map. *Counterspy Express* had also been Fleischman's first novel rejected by Fawcett.

For his next suspense novel Fleischman would return his characters to China and the Formosa Straits. Fawcett's editor, Dick Carroll, was a friend of Robert Fellows, a partner with John Wayne in the production company, Batjac. He'd arranged for Batjac to see a copy of *Blood Alley*, the story of an American trying to spirit a whole town of Chinese, including livestock and relics, out from under the Communists to shelter in Hong Kong.

A week later Fleischman received a call from Batjac. They wanted to purchase the film rights before publication. They offered $5,000, enough, Fleischman figured, to support his family for a year. Days later he heard from director William "Wild Bill" Wellman, who had directed WINGS (1927), winner of the first Academy Award for Best Picture. Wellman wanted him to write the screenplay.

Before this Fleischman had never even looked at a screenplay. Now he was the sole writer on a two million dollar picture with one of the motion picture industry's biggest-drawing stars, Robert Mitchum. Fleischman and Wellman would go over the book and the script, page by page. They met three or four times every week, and spoke by phone daily.

Wellman liked to keep an advocate for the story in tow, and he liked a writer to be on hand for sudden, intuitive changes. It also seemed that he just liked to hang out with writers. Wellman, a loner, was 59, twenty-five years and a few days older than Fleischman. They got along well.

On the first day of the shoot, Mitchum, after a night out with a group of stuntmen, got into an altercation with the production's Head Driver and knocked him off a gangplank into the chilly waters of San Francisco Bay. Batjac settled with Mitchum and sent him home. Gregory Peck then turned down the role, followed by Humphrey Bogart who wanted a cool half million in salary. Wayne himself took over as lead after Warner Brothers threatened to pull out of their distribution deal.

BLOOD ALLEY would be regarded as a broadly-painted anti-communist fable. Fleischman didn't think that either he or Wellman was trying to produce an anti-Red movie, but that the Chinese setting was simply a good one for an adventure story.

Fleischman was reconciled to accepting credit for the BLOOD ALLEY script, a first effort and an embarrassment, he said, that he had to watch "every ten seconds, it seems, on a television."

Fleischman recalled this turn in his career: "Wellman had an uncanny eye. To begin with, he was a great gambler with talent. A man in his position, with all the great films he made, he should have been working with major, best-selling novels. But he wasn't that kind of man. He liked to throw the dice and take a chance."

Their second film as collaborators, GOODBYE MY LADY (1956), had the distinction of offering Walter Brennan his favorite role. In a sly piece of foreshadowing, The Daughters of the American Revolution gave it their award for the best children's picture of the year.

After GOODBYE MY LADY Batjac cut its costs by laying off most of its staff. Wellman stayed on at Warner Brothers, where he would work on DARBY'S RANGERS (1958), and then on another dream project, LAFAYETTE ESCADRILLE (1958).

For Fleischman, who received sole screenplay credit for Wellman's story, LAFAYETTE ESCADRILLE was a difficult, frustrating effort. They didn't have enough money or the right kind of actors.

As far as his work in movies, Fleischman remonstrated, "It paid the rent."

This was when another writer and aspiring director would appear in Fleischman's life: Harry Whittington. In 1958, Warner's had purchased Whittington's western novel *Trouble Rides Tall* (1958). For three months Whittington would work with producer Roy Del Ruth on a never-filmed screenplay. Whittington numbered Fleischman among his handful of Hollywood friends.

Fleischman was younger but more experienced—and more success-ful—in the ways of the studios. The two writers met and the Whit-tingtons came to dinner.

"He was a lovely guy, just the sweetest, nicest Southern gentleman," Fleischman said. "He had nice manners, and he was a caring, affec-tionate person. A professional acquaintance who I really liked."

Over the years they exchanged Christmas cards, and if Whittington was in Los Angeles they'd meet for lunch. When Whittington returned to Florida and attempted to make his own films, he had hopes that Fleischman could produce some of the screenplays. Fleischman tried to help Whittington find distribution for THE FACE OF THE PHANTOM (1960), the single film produced by Harry Whittington Productions.

Fleischman was undoubtedly the only one in the world who had seen films made by both the Wade Miller writing team and Harry Whittington. What did he think of the vanished Whittington film, the tawdry Holy Grail: THE FACE OF THE PHANTOM?

"He sent out the film and it was just a home movie with amateur actors. I couldn't believe how amateurish it was. The story had holes in it. Harry had lost control of himself. He caught the Hollywood bug. He mortgaged his house, he got into a lot of debt over that picture. He had to write nurse novels to pull himself out of it."

The three films Fleischman made with Wellman represented one third of his film credits. *Counterspy Express* (as SPY IN THE SKY, 1958), *By the Great Horn Spoon* (as THE ADVENTURES OF BULLWHIP GRIF-FIN, 1967), *Yellowleg* (as THE DEADLY COMPANIONS, 1961) and *Ghost in the Midday Sun* were all filmed, and Fleischman received screenplay credit for SCALAWAG (1975). He used the name of his San Diego detective, Brindle, for his screenplay for THE WHIPPING BOY (1995) because he was unhappy with changes to his script.

Among the efforts that never met a clapboard or camera was SON OF THE CRIMSON PIRATE, a sequel to the Burt Lancaster film THE CRIMSON PIRATE. When Fleischman found this half finished script, in 2009, he couldn't even remember the short-term project, though he found pay stubs from the Harold Hecht-Lancaster production compa-ny that had made the original film.

He worked on FRENCHTOWN, a screenplay for Maureen O'Hara and a musical at MGM. He wrote a screenplay and a sequel for his novel *Jingo Django* (1971) but his producer couldn't get backing.

Yellowleg (1960), originally a screenplay, was also rewritten as a novel, a revenge story with a particularly gruesome premise, that of a former Union soldier searching for a scarred man who has scalped him.

"Every writer wants to try a Western," Fleischman said.

It was then that Fleischman began writing a story for his children, turning from the sex and violence of his suspense novels to draw upon his early background as a touring magician. He invented Mr. Mysterious, a frontier magician who outwits both outlaws and Native Americans. He named the characters after his children and read each chapter to them, soliciting their opinions.

Though he hadn't written the book for publication, he sent it to his agent, along with a note of apology. It was purchased overnight. Fleischman entered the world of juvenile fiction and there he would remain. After writing about murder, prostitution, international intrigue and con-men, now he was writing for kids.

Fleischman intended to return to adult suspense, but he soon decided that children's books were a more comfortable niche. Historical fiction became his specialty. He wrote with an energy reminiscent of the comic novelettes of Ellis Parker Butler.

By the Great Horn Spoon (1963), Fleischman's second novel for young readers, is a near-classic, the story of the scion of a once prosperous Boston family and his butler who join the California gold rush. It is an odyssey echoing Fleischman's own experiences digging for gold in Northern California. Through clever and whimsical schemes, fortunes are saved, outlaws are reformed, and gold is found and then lost. The book is filled with solid information and history about early California and gold mining.

Fleischman was not an undiscovered genius, nor a bitter noir poet. He received the fruits of his labor during his lifetime. One of the sweetest among them was when he watched his son Paul take home the John Newbery Medal for *Joyful Noise: Poems for Two Voices*, judged "the most distinguished contribution to American children's literature" in 1989. This was just two years after Sid had received his own Newbery for *The Whipping Boy* (1987).

For children of a certain age Fleischman was their Seuss, their Lewis Carroll or Twain. His books became bestsellers. It was not unusual for him to have over 20 books in print. He received thousands of fan letters and he replied to all of them. He spoke at schools and book conventions and there are at least two books about his children's books.

He was nominated for a National Book Award for *Humbug Mountain* (1978).

Fleischman considers perhaps his greatest contribution to be his work in the "tall tale" tradition. Fleischman told his fibs in the McBroom series published by Norton Books, including *McBroom Tells the Truth* (1966), *McBroom the Rainmaker* (1973) and *McBroom Tells a Lie* (1976).

The first time I met Fleischman was in 1975 in Santa Monica, at the house bought by *Blood Alley*. In his home near the beach we could both hear the ocean and the traffic in a never-ending war that would not be won during either of our lives. I was there to talk about Wellman. Fleischman had been there during the end of a long, fabulously combative Hollywood career. At the time I knew little about Sid's own history.

And what was Fleischman like? Have you ever seen a sloppy magician? Well in this case, you'll have to keep looking. Sid had presence. He looked like a performer: stylish, angular and youthful at fifty-five. He seemed to possess an unusual awareness of his movements, a rare precision. He was about five-foot-eight, the kind of guy who always photographs well. As a twenty-two year old rookie measuring a professional, it was hard for me to judge his height. Bigger than me, it seemed.

I was also defenseless. He could have hidden a card anywhere he wanted. I didn't want to buy a used car from this persuasive gent.

He spoke, low key and comfortable. He was a man who worked with his hands: writing, typing, sleight of hand and a five-year flirtation with classical guitar. He didn't want to wear them out by talking with them too.

By 1998 Fleischman's old suspense novels had been rediscovered. He attended Paperback Conventions in Mission Hills, California, where he would also lunch with his old friend Bob Wade, who would come up from San Diego. He'd been surprised by the reactions of the collectors and the new readers.

That was when he told me that he never worked ahead, never outlined or knew what was going to happen before he sat down at the typewriter. "I was just dying to find out what was going to happen," he said. "I'm not alone in working like this. Henry James wrote this way. Saroyan wrote this way. Lots of authors have written this way. I'm anxious to get to the typewriter each day because I don't know how the characters are going to get out of the jam I put them in yesterday. I want to find out what's going to happen.

"I put my characters in a scene and I think, 'How's this character going to talk? How does this character react? Does he have any habits? How does he dress?' Little by little I carve them out of the darkness.

"You know, each writer, over a period of time, finds his own best way of working. You do what works for you. I have bad writing habits but they have worked for me. I don't do a rough draft. I spend a lot of time working on the first page. I improvise daily, but I develop a sense of direction for the book, and I keep it on track.

"I developed the habit of writing it right the first time. If that page isn't right, do it over again, do it over again. Page two, page three, page four... so that by the time I get to the end of what I'd done, I've wasted a lot of paper. That became my way of working. When I wrote fast and sloppy it took too long to clean it up. I might as well have written it right the first time.

"My hours are flexible. I'll work until I get tired or stuck, and I need to walk it off and figure out what's going to happen next. Or I'll get hungry. Maybe I'll only write two or three hours a day. It depends upon what stage of the book I'm on.

"In the early stages I wear myself out. The first chapter is a killer. You have to set up the characters, the background, the relationships and the plot, and it's all got to be done gracefully, without any strain. You have to set your style and the tone, how your characters talk. You have to find out all these things in the first couple of chapters. That's really tough.

"When I'm coming down the homestretch I'm writing in the morning, in the afternoon and evening, after a nap. I can't stay away from it."

Sid looked like he could still hide a few cards. What did he consider the highlights of his career?

"That wonderful feeling of triumph when you've finished a book. Nothing beats that.

"Some of it happens every day. I can get so thrilled about a scene, when I really get it right! It's a wonderful, wonderful experience but it doesn't last for long. The next day you're back in the stew.

"I'll give you another feeling of triumph... to still have my wits about me. To be able to think my way through a plot, with all the characters, to conceive of the scenes. It's one of those youthful, athletic, mentally athletic things that you do when you're a young writer."

That was Sid in 1998. Even sweeter then, to be still going over those new galleys in 2009.

After fifty or sixty years the paper mounts up. By 2009 Fleischman had written over fifty novels, over sixty books altogether. "It's easy when you're as old as I am," he said. Opportunities had pulled him down several unexpected avenues. "I've improvised my life as I have my novels," he said.

Fleischman hadn't expected to become a nonfiction writer but while we prepared this volume he was also preparing a biography of Charles Chaplin. A new novel, *The Dream Stealer*, would be published later in 2009. He was featured on the internet, on the website for Scholastic Books, and I recommend a visit for everyone reading these words. You can see Sid there, talking about his career and offering tips about the writing trade. Fleischman looked "professorial," "distinguished," "venerable"—the best words we have to honor grace and past achievement. It's a consolation that Sid remains a presence in a new century and really, when has anyone come closer to publishing in three centuries?

Fleischman's career might be *the* case study in the department of nice guys who finish well. He dedicated *The Abracadabra Kid*: "For the cast of players in these pages, each and every one, with gratitude and affection."

Schedules and distance having their impact, we crossed emails and made a date for 2020, long enough for another seven or eight books and a new trick or three. Sid doesn't plan to stop. By 2020 we might finally try a story about that big subject we didn't talk about, the elephant in the room, the one rolling around his floor, the long run of books that have provoked so many oohs and ahhs from young readers and their mothers.

In 2020 Fleischman will be 100 and with luck, there will be new books to talk about. It will be time for another update on this living, breathing, monument of words, a writer who has always added a little magic to his prose.

DOWNIEVILLE, CA
OCTOBER 2009

Sid Fleischman, 1920-2010

"The less you know, the easier the writing." Sid Fleischman, 2009

For me, Sid Fleischman was a key, a ubiquitous advisor in the background. He knew Bill and Dottie Wellman, he knew Harry Whittington, his wife Kathyrn, and Day Keene. When I tried to write about these people Sid was the connection I needed, a confirmation that these men had truly walked the earth. They had died too early. Fleischman, at 90, hadn't lived long enough. He was still engaged in the present, fielding interviews, reading galleys, preparing his magic. Well into his 'eighties, Fleischman remained a kind and vital man.

After Sid's death, the publisher of this volume wrote to say he was sorry that Sid would not receive a copy of the book. It would be published after his death. Sid had seen the introduction, he'd made a couple corrections, and he marveled at events he had forgotten. He was a gracious man.

With Sid it was the process that intrigued and challenged him. He'd been writing for 70 years. For at least the past ten years he was thrilled that he hadn't lost it, that spark, the interest and the skill to continue. While we worked on this volume Sid was also preparing two more books: a new novel for young readers and a biography of Charlie Chaplin. He didn't pretend to be annoyed about any of the details. Far better to enjoy even the drudgery and delays of the book-making process, like savoring a last taste of cafeteria food.

After this there would undoubtedly be another book. There always had been. His suspense writing was far away from him now but as a writer of children's books, he was a hero for two generations. The books would go on as long as Sid could go on.

I wrote to him about my experience with cancer: Stage 3-B Melanoma at the age of 52. Fleischman shared his own cancer story, a recent diagnosis. He intended to be lucky.

And he was, lucky and successful. Success had come easily to him. The same guy who could saw a kid in half could also make a reader sweat or laugh.

I never saw him do a magic trick. Once a month, magicians gathered at his home "to fool each other," he wrote. "We've become a geriatric pack, but I can still manipulate playing cards and do that famous rabbit and hat trick.... But who has a hat these days."

I never asked him about Writer's Block. He might have had a cure. "A Methuselah age needn't necessarily mummify a writer," he told me.

He had not been forgotten. He had never gone into eclipse. He was a social man and an entertainer and he always had time for others, though he had become more jealous of that time. His moments were more valuable now, each day worth a King's ransom.

In an obituary you should try to be brief, but to honor someone correctly, you also want to sneak in as many words as you can. You think of people differently, when they're gone. There's a summing up that you wouldn't otherwise attempt. The subject of the piece has to share the moment, however unwillingly, with the verb, which is death.

I hadn't been in contact with Fleischman since the New Year. The book was done; we were in a holding pattern. He had read a longer version of the introduction.

"What a tenacious researcher you are!" he wrote. "Can't believe you dug up so much on my early magic life. I'm immensely impressed. I am, of course, delighted with the entire 49 pages. But isn't it a bit long for the casual reader?"

So I cut it — there's a lot less Wellman. I also added a couple things, just enough that it would still read fresh when the book came out. This would be the most thorough, if not the most labored study of Fleischman's many careers.

In March I spent a Sunday at the Paperback Convention in Mission Hills, where Fleischman and Bob Wade had signed books and met for lunch. Now neither of them were in attendance, just their books. One of the booksellers said something about Sid's passing, an unwelcome surprise that no one else could confirm.

As I drove home I wondered if I could arrange a signing party with Sid in Santa Monica at a new bookstore a few miles from his home.

That night I found a notice in the L.A. Times. Sid had died on Wednesday.

Fleischman labored at his writing. I'll always delight in his description of the craft, "carving a book out of a block of marble".

And from time to time I'll go back and read *The Venetian Blonde*.

DOWNIEVILLE, CA
APRIL 2010

Introduction

by Sid Fleischman

When I sat down to write *Danger in Paradise* and *Malay Woman*, I was living in a San Diego cliffside bungalow with an unobstructed view of the Pacific Ocean. In fact, if I stood on a rock I could see clear to Bali and Singapore, where these novels are set.

That was more than half a century ago. The long second World War had ended. The U.S. Navy no longer needed my doubtful services and threw me to the curb of civilian life.

Before the war, I had eked out a living as a magician, working in vaudeville and night clubs. But now both were vanishing quicker than the eye.

I was still able to deal cards from the bottom of the deck (and still can). But it was my misfortune to be too confounded honest and squaretoed to cheat at cards.

What was I to do now that I was obliged to make an honest living for my wife and child?

I had tried my hand at writing short stories in the navy, with spotty success. Meanwhile, with great prescience, the war had brought me to Shanghai.

Why not write a novel set in the Far East?

Little did I suspect that I was dooming myself to everlasting labor, for writers never retire.

A quirky thought came to me out of thin air. What if an American girl voyaged to the island of Bali and went native? A topless heroine? I was the right age for such youthful fantasies and years ahead of Las Vegas, who was yet to invent the topless review.

Voila, from that bit of thin air emerged an entire novel. Sold a couple of hundred thousand copies in the blink of an eye.

I was minding my own business when thin air rescued me again. A curious situation flashed across my mind. What if a stowaway were hiding somewhere on a Singapore freighter and overhears villains planning a great crime?

That's the sort of premise a writer dreams of: a story idea with a burning fuse.

It's the rare book that writes itself. But *Malay Woman* tried, and it was all I could do to keep up. But at other times, I had to give the tale a prod or lay in a few land mines to keep my characters in peril.

In the decades since these adventures in the tropics, I have discarded my initials and used my middle name—Sid. I have written a couple of shelves of books—some 65 volumes. They are mostly novels, for children as well as adults; insider magic books for sleight of hand buffs and, recently, biographies of Houdini, Mark Twain and Charlie Chaplin. And a lot of movies.

Aspiring writers consider me prolific. I consider myself slow. If I have a secret it arose when I was a newspaperman and the publisher confided in me that you couldn't accomplish much on a 40-hour week.

My daily writing habit is as fixed as breathing. The pages stack up on my desk until—behold! I have another book.

I may take a siesta of a few weeks, but before long I'm reaching back into thin air. Is there another story idea lurking up there?

SANTA MONICA, CALIFORNIA
AUGUST 2009

Danger in Paradise

By A. S. Fleischman

Chapter One

As the *prau* neared the jetty I could see along the main drag, and it looked hot and dusty. Wiry palms fringed the town and corrugated tin roofs reflected the midafternoon heat like smudged mirrors. It looked like any backwater port in the tropics, but it would have a few bars and that's all I was going ashore for. A drink. A quick one. The freighter was pulling out at four, and that gave me time only for a quick one.

I glanced back sourly at the *Timor Lady*, tugging at her anchor chain in the stiff offshore current. I had paid my fare and gone aboard yesterday in Java, and now I wondered how I was going to bear up under another forty or fifty days. Crossing the Pacific with a crazy Australian captain who didn't even keep liquor aboard for medicinal purposes wasn't going to be easy.

This was the last cargo stop before San Pedro and I thought I'd better stock up while I was at it. This was Bali, and I was Jefferson Cape, and let's get together for a quick one.

The boatman let the *prau* rub up against the splintered piles of the jetty. I paid him off and grabbed hold of the ladder.

"Has this place got a name?" I asked.

"Buleléng."

"Is there a good bar in Buleléng?"

"Father Jan's. Very high class, tuan."

"I'll be back in less than an hour. Stick around if you want to earn taxi fare back to the ship."

"Yes, yes, tuan."

I wiped the perspiration off my face and started down the jetty to the street. The air was foul with the odor of copra being loaded aboard a lugger flying the new flag of Indonesia. The overcast sky seemed to enclose the island in its own perspiration.

This was really the end, I thought suddenly. As an oil geologist, I'd made good money in this part of the world, but I'd spent it even faster. Now I was going home. I was going to get rid of this hot-weather crew cut and this Asiatic tan. I was through drinking arrack and taking quinine. I had a couple of hundred dollars in my wallet and two suitcases on the ship. My worldly possessions. The memories don't count, I decided bitterly. The races in Shanghai and the house parties on the Peak in Hong Kong. Ancient history. The world has changed and so have you. Forget it. Grab that drink and get the hell back to the ship.

I went looking for Father Jan's.

It was a small bar halfway up the hill behind town, and it wasn't doing any business. I took a table by the window, where I could watch the *Timor Lady* in the harbor below. As usual, I had trouble with my knees under the table, and put my legs out in front of me. A squat Hollander roused from the back of the bar. He was naked to the waist; he wore khaki shorts and tennis shoes without socks. A white man gone to pot in the tropics, I thought. Father Jan. But at least I had the place to myself and I couldn't get into any trouble.

"You want a drink?" he asked indifferently.

"That's the general idea," I said. "Gin and tonic."

He shook his head. "I have only warm beer or arrack. You are lucky you have a choice, *mijnheer.* Some days I don't have even warm beer."

I sopped up the sweat on the back of my neck with an already moist handkerchief. I'd better change bars before my time ran out. But my throat was dry and I decided to wet it. I told him to get the arrack.

"You won't like my arrack, *mijnheer.* I make it myself and it tastes like petrol."

"Look—even if it tastes like crude oil, *bring* it."

He pursed his lips contemptuously and wandered off to his bottles behind the bar. I lit a cigarette. There was a small fan on the table, a toy-like contraption you wound by hand. Made in China. I wound it up. The light breeze it threw off smelled of machine oil, and it didn't help.

When I looked up, there was a woman standing in the doorway.

Daylight was behind her, and all I saw for a moment was the slim figure, the coral dress and the wide-brimmed straw hat. She hesitated, as though trying to make up her mind whether or not to come in. Then she looked at me, looked hard. She made up her mind. She came in, and settled herself at my table.

"Hello," she said uneasily.

She looked somewhere in her twenties. Her dress had an open collar; her lines were sophisticated rather than spectacular. Her eyes looked me over a little nervously, pale blue and somehow determined. I tried to get my knees in under the table, and wished she'd go away. She seemed to know exactly what she was doing, and I began to feel crowded.

"Beat it," I said. Where was my drink?

She put the words to me very softly. "You're off the *Timor Lady*, aren't you?"

I stared at her uncomfortably. What sort of come-on was this? "That's right," I said.

"I followed you here. I—"

Father Jan set a bottle and glass on the table, and she waited until he moved away. I watched her. She kept glancing through the window at the road as though she expected to see someone out there. She lit a cigarette. Her chin and forehead were polished by the heat, and I wondered how she still managed to look quite beautiful. She wore little gold earrings shaped like temple bells, and they jingled softly every time she glanced out the window. As she sat there the determination seemed to leave her manner, and I began to sense an atmosphere of fright that hung about her like musk. It made me angry. I didn't have time for anyone's troubles but my own. I filled my glass.

"O.K., I'll bite," I said. "You followed me here. Why?"

"Would you take something aboard for me?"

"Is this a gag?"

"It's not a gag."

"Is there any reason why *you* can't take it aboard?"

"Obviously."

"It may be obvious," I said. "But not to me."

"Please." Her voice kept lowering so that I could hardly pick out the words. She was apparently worried about Father Jan, who had returned to his newspaper at the back of the bar. At first glance I had taken her for an American, but I was catching inflections in her voice now that told me she wasn't. "There were men at the jetty—waiting for me."

I had started out with the feeling she had marked me for a sucker, but the dead seriousness about her began to bother me. "All right," I said. "Keep talking."

"I was watching from my hotel room. I saw them. And I saw you leave the ship and come ashore. I decided to ask you to help me."

"How do you know you can trust me?"

"I don't. But I'm willing to take the chance."

"You must be getting desperate."

"Yes." She crushed her half-smoked cigarette and lit another. The earrings murmured. She was looking out the window again.

"What do you want taken aboard?" I asked. I made it sound casual. I wasn't committing myself. I liked her looks, but not her story. The little fan ran down, and I rewound it.

"Something very small—and important."

"Is that all the answer I get?"

She hesitated. "Yes."

"No dice."

Anxiety filled her eyes. She stared at me and her expression turned bitter. "You'll be in no danger."

"That's not the point. You're Russian, aren't you?"

"White Russian. There's a difference."

"Sometimes. What's your name?"

Her eyes began to avoid me. She removed her hat and set it on the table. Her hair was black and cropped boyishly short. Her skin was deeply tanned and I figured she had been in the tropics a long time. "Nicole Balashov," she muttered finally.

I looked at my watch and I looked at the *Timor Lady* in the harbor. I really ought to get going. But I sat there.

"Who are the guys waiting for you to show up at the water front?"

"They won't suspect you," she said. "They'll let you go back to the ship."

"You haven't answered my question."

She inhaled deeply on her cigarette. "All right. How long have you been in Indonesia?"

"I just finished two years in Java. And when the Dutch owned the islands, a year in Sumatra."

"Then you know about the terrorists."

"Naturally."

"These men are part of an organization selling them guns. American guns."

I rubbed the sweat off my eyelids. American guns. The terrorist problem had gotten so mean in Java that you couldn't use the roads at night without risking your neck. The same reports came in from all the main islands of Indonesia, even little Bali. They were mostly guerillas left over from the independence war, but guys who had sided with the Dutch were no longer welcome in their villages. Outcasts with guns in their hands. And lately they had begun showing signs of political organization.

"You're doing better," I said. "What do you want me to take aboard?"

"Information for your government. Once you reach the States, turn it over to the Central Intelligence Agency. But we must hurry. I may have been followed here."

"You haven't told me where you fit in."

"There isn't time."

"You're really quite beautiful."

Her eyebrows arched a little desperately. Was I in or out?

"Sure," I said unhappily. "I'm in. Hand it over."

Vaguely, I felt like a sucker. But what did I have to lose? Her story seemed to make sense, and even if it didn't, I could take care of myself.

She lit a fresh cigarette, studying me all the while, and then shoved a box of Japanese matches across the table. Not far, just enough to let me know I was to pick them up. I wanted to laugh. The moment was melodramatic and unbelievable. But I didn't laugh. I looked at Father Jan, who hadn't stirred from the back of the bar. He didn't look up from his newspaper. He wasn't interested in us.

I left the box of matches on the table. "What about you?" I muttered.

She shrugged her shoulders gently, and picked up her hat. "I'll be all right."

"You don't sound very convincing."

"You'll miss your ship."

"I have twenty-five minutes. I'd like to see you again."

"That's impossible."

"I know. Too bad."

There was a wild honking down the road and the yapping of dogs. A bus was coming and she rose quickly. She started for the door, but stopped and turned.

"I forgot to ask your name."

"Jeff. Jefferson Cape."

"*Bon voyage.*"

Her blue eyes seemed suddenly very feminine, the brittleness gone, and I could almost imagine she was sorry it had to be this way. We should have met in a café on Shanghai's Bubbling Well Road, before the Reds, when there was time for gaiety, not in a steaming water front town on the Java Sea with the East dizzily going to hell. Too bad. The earrings jingled and she hurried to the side of the road.

The bus came up the hill swinging a tail of pariah dogs. I stood at the window and watched. The last I saw of her was a beautiful stretch of leg as she stepped up the platform. Nice legs. Very nice. Then the door closed after her, and the bus took off. There were a bunch of chicken cages tied to the roof, and the chickens squawked back to the dogs.

I looked at the box of matches on the table. I bounced it on my palm and dropped it into my coat pocket. I hadn't touched the glass of arrack, but I drained it quickly now. I wasn't going to have time for another drink in another bar.

I turned to Father Jan. "Look, I'm in a hurry. I'd like to take a bottle of something good aboard ship with me. If you've got something put away for a rainy day, name your price."

His interest rallied. "Two hundred rupiahs, *ja?*"

"What are you selling?"

"Schnapps, *mijnheer.*"

"Go get it. I'll pay in American money."

The newspaper crackled as he rose and waddled through a doorway into the adjoining house. Almost twenty American dollars was a hell of a price to pay for a bottle of gin, but there was no time to bargain.

He was gone a couple of minutes and I kept an eye on the *Timor Lady*. I got my money ready. He reappeared proudly with the bottle of schnapps and wrapped it in his newspaper.

I paid up and hooked it under my arm. "If anyone comes in asking questions about that girl, play dumb. Say she didn't show up here."

He smiled unctuously, and I got the idea. I got a ten out of my wallet, tossed it on the table and walked out.

A pony cart was joggling down the hill toward town and I hopped on. I fought back an impulse to take out the box of matches and examine it. There would be time for that later.

We hadn't gone more than fifty yards from the bar when I saw a glistening black touring car heading up the hill. I got a feeling about it, and I was right. It stopped at Father Jan's.

I kept watching. A man got out of the car, a big man in a white tropical suit with a cigar stuck in his mouth. He stopped to look over the bar. He took off his hat long enough to wipe the sweat off his head, and walked in. His bald head had seemed, during that uncovered moment, waxed.

I thought of the ten dollars I had left to keep Father Jan's mouth shut, and wondered if it was enough. Hell, I decided, stop imagining the worst. A bar was a bar. This guy was probably up to nothing more than a drink.

We were halfway to town, and I looked at my watch. It was a quarter to four. I had fifteen minutes, and a bottle under my arm. I was set.

But I kept glancing behind to the bar. I began to feel on edge, and it made me angry. Still, what if that baldheaded baboon had traced Nicole Balashov to the bar? Twenty bucks would open Father Jan's mouth. Overtaking that bus wouldn't be any trick. For that matter, he might get wise and take out after me.

I saw him hurry out of the bar, pause only a moment to peer along the road toward town, and get in the car. It kicked up a cloud of dust and made a sharp U-turn.

My heart started pounding. He was wise. Father Jan didn't have to give much of a description of me—just a dark-haired, lanky American in a white suit, and carrying a bottle. Hell, he'd probably noticed me on the pony cart as he steamed up the hill.

And he was coming down. Fast.

The pony cart had entered the edge of town. I jumped off, clutched my bottle and ran.

I had reached the far side of a Chinese temple when I heard brakes squeal on the road. I turned for only a glance, and saw the big guy half out of the car before it came to a stop. I held onto the bottle. If I had to, I'd brain him with it.

I hurried into a dirt lane banked with wooden shops and infested with dogs. They added their barks to music blaring from a phonograph store at the end of the passage. I made for it, and they trailed me. Batiks and porcelainware and colored drinks flashed by. I reached the end of the lane and turned right. The barking pack behind me became a pandemonium in my ears, and the leaders began nipping at my ankles. All the stray dogs in the district seemed to have joined the chase before I had gone another block in the tangle of lanes. Hell, I had to get rid of this long, yapping tail! I might as well leave bread crumbs for the big guy to follow.

I passed startled Arab and Chinese shopkeepers, and Balinese sitting on their haunches, grinning. I must have made a hell of a spectacle, but I kept running. Then I saw a meat shop a few doors beyond, grabbed a white slab of bacon hanging from a string in a cloud of flies and tossed it into the pack. The dogs piled up around it, and I kept running.

Once I was free of them I glanced around for some point of reference. I had to get to the water front fast, but suddenly I wasn't sure where it was, even though I knew it had to be very close. I stopped. I felt like a mouse that had been chased into a maze.

I looked at my watch. It was ten to four.

I kept going and a moment later came out onto the deserted market place. I seemed to be getting in deeper. It wasn't market day, and I got past the stalls quickly.

I started along a lane cutting off to the left and walked up a couple of rotting steps to an open jewelry shop. A Balinese with a *udeng* elaborately pleated on his head was working a strand of filigree silver over a flame.

"*Tabé,*" I muttered quickly. I hadn't expected to need Malay again, but I used it now. "Which way is the jetty?"

He pointed to my right. I gripped the bottle tightly and started for the steps. I got a flash of a white suit approaching from the end of the lane, and stepped back quickly. There was only a little native traffic in the lane, but enough so that I was sure he hadn't spotted me.

I looked around the bare box of a room I was in, the front completely open. No back door.

The Balinese recognized the sudden alarm on my face.

"*Baniak susa,*" I said. "Much trouble."

I saw a stack of sleeping pallets on the floor. I did the only thing I could think of. I got under them.

He passed. I lay on my stomach, raised the ends of the mats a crack, and from the raised level of the floor, got a good look at him. He had stopped running. Perspiration streaked down his heavy face. He was big and fat and the back of his neck was red with prickly heat. He wore glasses with heavy black rims. I saw him stop at the near end of the lane, look around dismally at the empty fruit and vegetable stalls of the market place, and start back. I saw then that his driver had been following close behind, a native with copperish cheekbones, and they met almost in front of me.

I saw that the big guy's glasses had steamed up from body heat, and he looped his fat thumbs under the lenses and cleared them. His breath came quick and wheezy, but his voice had gravel in it. "Tell them at the jetty... to stop this guy... understand?"

The driver nodded. "O.K., Tuan Fry."

"He must be off that ship in the harbor. If he misses it, get some more men up here. Go over... every inch of town."

"We find him. Sure thing, tuan."

"The girl took the bus to Den Pasar. I'll take the car and pick her up. She'll pay for this."

The native grinned. Then he turned and started back down the lane at a trot.

My left arm lay flat on the floor near my head and the ticking of my wrist watch sounded clear and quick. But the big guy just stood there catching his breath.

In another moment we heard it, off to the right—the thick blast of a ship's whistle. I closed my eyes in quiet desperation. The *Timor Lady* was pulling out.

That damned Australian captain was leaving me behind.

I thought of the bottle beside me. It was all I could do to keep from grabbing it by the neck and busting it.

Chapter Two

I lay under the pallets trying to think. All I had was the suit on my back, my passport, and a couple of hundred dollars in my wallet. It might be days before another ship touched this port. It might be weeks. I had to get out of town. I had to get off the island.

Fry stood out in the lane and lit a cigar.

I lay in my own sweat, thinking of Nicole Balashov and hating her. I was an oil geologist, not a tin-horn hero.

Why did she have to pick on me?

The big guy finally moved off down the lane. He was going after her, and I had seen the murder in his little, snapping eyes. Even hating her, I had a crazy impulse to get to her first, to warn her, to head him off.

I shoved the pallets off my back and got to my feet. Forget it, I thought grimly. There's your own neck to worry about. I felt for the box of matches. There was *that* to worry about.

But I couldn't shake the idea. She would step off the bus into Fry's arms. She obviously knew too much about gun running. He would kill her.

The Balinese grinned at me over his flame. He hadn't given me away; he seemed amused by my antics. Did he think I was *mabu?* Sure, the white men were always drunk.

"Where can I buy a gun?"

He continued working the strand of silver. "It is outlawed, *jero.*"

"I know. I'll pay a good price."

"Perhaps Ismail will have such a thing to sell."

Ismail turned out to be an Arab coffee merchant at the far end of the lane, and for fifty American dollars he had a gun. It was an old, scabrous Ivor Johnson revolver and the only place it would fit was under my belt. I buttoned my coat over it, and knew I'd have to keep it buttoned even in this heat.

I kept moving, and I kept thinking about Nicole Balashov. I could still hear the small tinkle of her earrings as she faced me, that last moment, from the door, and I remembered that wistful look that came into her eyes.

In another moment I came out under the arcade of the main street and looked around for an island taxi. I clamped my teeth and made up my mind. I was hooked and I knew it. I was going to get to Nicole Balashov first.

I saw a taxi parked under an enormous shade tree across the way. I whistled. The jetty was a block to my left and there were a half dozen figures hanging around. Beyond, I could see the *Timor Lady* swinging out to sea, gray smoke trailing from her stack.

I held on to my bottle and whistled again. The taxi driver took his time starting up the engine and cut across the street to me.

"Den Pasar," I snapped.

I climbed in and the driver faced me curiously. "Den Pasar?"

"Yes."

"But it is over a hundred kilometers, tuan. On the south coast of the island."

"I forgot to tell you," I said. "Step on it."

He began to hassle. Night would fall before we got there, and it was dangerous on the mountain roads at night. I glanced through the rear windows at the jetty, and hoped I hadn't been spotted. Then I did the only thing I could think of to get the driver going. I pulled the gun.

The car had guts, and he used them. In a matter of seconds we passed Father Jan's high-class bar. I glanced at my bottle and the newspaper wrapping had disintegrated at the neck from the sweat of my hand. I tore off the paper, pulled the cork and had a drink. Then I tossed the bottle out the window. It shattered against a mud wall.

That, I thought bitterly, was that.

The clouds were darkening on the horizon, and I hoped it wouldn't rain. The road steepened, but I kept the gun in my hand and the driver kept his foot on the accelerator. We passed flooded rice fields that shimmered in their terraces. The driver knew the twists and turns in the road and drove like hell. I wasn't sure what I was going to do, but there was a good chance that we would overtake Fry. Unless he knew the road as well as this Balinese, his foot would go easy on the turns.

I got out the matchbox, shook it gently, and pushed open the drawer. It was almost full of matches. I emptied them in my palm, and saw something white wedged in the bottom.

I dug it out. A business card folded in half.

The back was tightly packed with small, neat handwriting in indelible ink, but I couldn't read a word of it. The words were Russian.

I turned the card over. *Scrap Metals Export Co. San Francisco. Singapore. Apollo Fry, Pres.*

I wanted to smile. Apollo Fry. The big guy with prickly heat on his neck was a junk dealer.

I folded the card and debated about returning it to the matchbox. Instead, I replaced the matchsticks and dropped the box in my pocket. I got out my handkerchief and looked at the hem. There were openings at each corner. I rolled up the card as tightly as I could and fed it into the hem. I worked it almost to the middle of one side, and put the handkerchief away.

I felt a little better, but not much.

We had been climbing steadily and abruptly left the rice fields behind as we entered a forest. Almost at once the driver slammed on his brakes after making a turn and the taxi swerved all over the road. I saw it too, up ahead—a black touring car on its side, two wheels still spinning.

It was half off the road and we came to a stop just behind it. It was Apollo Fry's car, and I couldn't help wishing he had broken his neck.

I kept the gun in my hand and got out. The air was strangely quiet. The two wheels were losing their momentum and spun noiselessly. I saw a lizard clinging to the bark of a tree very close, and he seemed to be watching.

The car lay on the driver's side, propped at an angle against the embankment. I climbed up and looked in.

Fry was in there behind the wheel, his glasses hanging from one ear, and he was either dead or unconscious. We'd have needed a derrick to lift him out.

The Balinese was behind me, looking confused and a little frightened.

"All right," I said. "Let's get the car back on its wheels."

We could have used more manpower, but no cars came along in either direction, and we got the job done by ourselves. In another moment I had Fry laid out on the road. He was breathing. He looked big and fat and harmless, but I didn't kid myself. I opened his coat and saw a shoulder holster, and it had a gun in it. I emptied the chamber and threw the gun into the trees. I folded his glasses, stuck them in his pocket, and we got him loaded into the taxi. I paid off the driver and told him to rush Fry back to Buleléng and find him a doctor fast.

In another moment I was standing there alone.

I got into Fry's car and tried to start it. The starter worked, but the engine wouldn't turn over. It was going to get dark soon, and I kept playing with it. I didn't like the idea of getting stuck up here in the mountains at night.

I lost another ten minutes on the car, and decided to walk. There might be a village somewhere up ahead. At least I was out of Buleléng and the tension I had developed during the last hour began to slacken.

I had walked about two hundred yards when a car made the turn and came up the road toward me. It slowed, passing Fry's stalled car, but began picking up speed again. I threw out my thumb. It glided by, a sleek Cadillac. Then the tires whined as a sort of afterthought and the car settled in a cloud of dust in the middle of the road. I tossed away my cigarette and ran after it.

Despite the heat of the day, the windows were up except for an inch at the top. I saw a figure in the back seat, an Oriental. I opened the door and looked at him.

"Thanks," I said. "Going to Den Pasar?"

"Exactly. Won't you join me?"

There was an uneasy smile on his face. He was a stocky Chinese with a leathery face, and he needed a head shave. A gray-black stubble was beginning to show. He wore a white suit that looked baggy from traveling, and a black string tie. I got in and shut the door. The driver, a native boy, got the car under way again.

"My car broke down," I said. "Thanks for the lift."

He said nothing, he just smiled more broadly, and I knew what he was thinking. There were mechanics in Buleléng and Den Pasar was a long way off. We let the matter drop, and I saw that his hands were cupped together, as though he was holding something.

"I see you are an American," he said.

"Yes," I said. "It must stick out all over."

He grinned. "The thumb. It is an American custom, I believe, to show the thumb to a passing car. You are an uninhibited race, Mr.—"

"Cape. Jeff Cape."

The car was stuffy with the windows up, but I didn't say anything. I tried to relax in a corner and hoped he wouldn't expect me to keep up a running conversation. I wanted to think.

"I have never been to America," he said. He sat stiffly, his hands firmly cupped, and I began to wonder about the closed windows.

"You speak the language fine," I said. "A little on the British side, but fine."

"Ah, you are too charitable. My early years I spent on the Continent. And England. Now my home is in Sumatra. Do you know Sumatra?"

"I worked there once, before the Dutch war."

"It is a land of big opportunity today, Mr. Cape. Do you mind driving with the windows up?"

"It's your car."

He raised his cupped hands. "May I introduce myself? Mr. Chu. And this is my traveling companion. Do you enjoy birds?"

He lifted one of his hands carefully as I watched. A powder blue serindit flecked with white was nested in his lower palm.

"This is Jong."

"How do you do?" I said.

"We Chinese, you know, are quite sentimental about birds. Jong is a most intelligent bird." He tossed his palm and the serindit accepted its freedom. It began circling the interior of the car and I ducked.

"I often take Jong for long drives. In a car he has something of the sensation of being loose, what with the passing scenery. You are long in Bali, Mr. Cape?"

"I just got in."

The serindit settled itself on Mr. Chu's shoulder. "Jong and I arrived last week. By plane. On business."

My interest rallied. "Where is the airfield?"

"A few miles from Den Pasar."

He kept talking, and I nodded as though I were listening. It might be easy, I thought. Beat that bus to Den Pasar, pick up Nicole Balashov and the both of us could fly out of this island trap before Fry regained consciousness.

"Tell your driver to step on it," I said.

"I beg your pardon?"

The serindit leaped onto my shoulder, and I wanted to brush it away. "These mountains are full of terrorists," I said quickly. "It might be a good idea to hurry."

He grinned. "Of course."

Jungle crowded the edges of the highway and we seemed to be swinging along the inside rim of an old crater. Mr. Chu saw the sweat roll off me, put Jong in his cage and turned down the windows. He did a lot of talking and seemed polite in the questions he put to me. He had lived in Shanghai during the war and until the Reds took over, when he escaped to Sumatra. They had a price on his head, but it didn't worry him. Sumatra was opening up new territories and Mr. Chu busied himself in the archipelago contracting workers for the new plantations. He didn't expect to do well in Bali. "The Balinese won't leave home, you know. A strange people, Mr. Cape. They are afraid of the sea. Mountains are sacred and the sea is evil."

It turned dark suddenly, as though someone had blown out a match. It had been a quick, magical twilight. The damned tropics. I thought back to the long, Montana twilights when I was a kid. What the hell was I doing in this part of the world, anyway?

Almost at once the rain hit us, sweeping across open country as we left the jungle. The driver turned on the windshield wipers, and they squeaked.

I lit a fresh cigarette.

With the windows rolled up against the rain, Jong was let loose again. Would I like to hear Jong talk?

Jong was coaxed onto my shoulder, and he spoke a few words of English. Jong couldn't pronounce his l's.

"Ah, Mr. Cape, Jong likes you. Jong is a dependable judge of men. I rely on him."

I sat there trying not to hear the thin screech of the windshield wipers, trying to ignore a bilingual bird nesting on my shoulder and trying to forget Mr. Chu's grin that seemed to shine even in the dark. I watched the headlights cut through the rain. At least, I thought, no guerrilla in his right mind would be out cutting throats on a night like this.

The wipers stropped the windshield like razors. Suddenly a wavering red dot appeared in the road ahead. The downpour streaked across the headlights, and at first I wasn't sure. The red smudge of light crystallized as we gained on it. A taillight.

The heavy, tropical rain thudded on the roof and washed over the sides. I straightened and Jong flew from my shoulder in sudden fright. My eyes focused on the wet bulk ahead on the road. Our headlights illuminated the swaying chicken cages on the roof. It was the bus. The chickens were probably drowning.

My jaws clenched as the Cadillac pulled out to pass with a long, steady blast on the horn. I wanted a look at Nicole Balashov sitting in that bus, but the interior lights were off. We overtook it quickly and all I could see was the faint movement of an occasional cigarette coal.

I'd meet the bus in town. It couldn't be far.

I turned for a last look. Its headlights flickered weakly, and one of them looked like it would go out any minute.

Mr. Chu was comforting the serindit in Chinese. I leaned forward to talk to the driver.

"How much longer to Den Pasar?"

"Perhaps fifteen minutes, tuan."

"Where does the bus get in?"

"The *alun-alun*. "

The central square. That would make it easy. "I'd like to get off there," I said.

"Yes, tuan. We stop at the Bali Hotel. The *alun-alun* is across from it."

I settled back in the seat, and I could feel Mr. Chu's eyes on me.

"The bus, Mr. Cape, holds a great interest, eh?"

I didn't answer. It was none of his business.

He went on talking. "I always enjoy the company of an American. I am staying at the Bali Hotel. Perhaps we can have tiffin together. Tomorrow, eh?"

"I expect to be tied up," I said. "Thanks, anyway."

"You will be stopping there, of course. The service is excellent. It is the only good hotel on the island."

"No," I said. "I won't be stopping there."

The headlights picked out the mud walls of native compounds on the edge of town, and occasional lights appeared ahead. We went by a few outlying stucco buildings with tiled roofs and a moment later entered the business district. Two giant banyan trees, rolling under the force of the storm, stood at the corner where we turned onto the main drag. The street was badly lit. I saw an empty market place, a narrow movie theater and congested little shops closing for the night. The car pulled over to the sidewalk, and across the way I saw a sweeping driveway that led to the lights of the Bali Hotel, set back from the street.

In the muddy darkness to my right would be the *alun-alun*. I opened the door and wished I had brought my raincoat ashore. Mr. Chu was grinning. "Thanks for the lift," I said.

Jong was cupped in his hands again. It was a pleasure.

There was no point in worrying about it—I was going to get drenched. I stepped out into the black downpour and slammed the door quickly. The Cadillac turned left into the hotel driveway and I watched it go. Mr. Chu and Jong. I wasn't sure which had made me feel more uncomfortable. I tried to shrug off the uneasy feeling that somehow I had let him make a fool of me.

My face was dripping before I reached the nearest awning. There seemed to be almost no life in town and the central square was dark and silent. I walked toward the corner and made out a few cars and taxis huddled together, waiting for the bus to pull in. I fell into a doorway to wait, but by then my clothes were soaked. The gun along my groin felt icy.

There'd be no plane flying out of Bali tonight, I thought, not in this damned rain. By morning Fry might be on the ball again, flashing orders like a two-bit executive. But at least I'd have a chance to warn Nicole Balashov that Den Pasar was too hot for her. We'd have to figure out something fast.

I tried to light a cigarette, but my pack was soaked. There was no sense trying to kid myself. I hadn't come to Den Pasar only to warn her. I wanted to see her again. Because of her I had missed my ship home, but it didn't seem important any more. She was in trouble, and she had passed it on to me like an infection and standing here in the rain I didn't give a damn. I had a gun and she was going to get off that bus and we'd figure out something.

The bus crawled into sight about five minutes later, one headlight blacked out and the other jiggling crazily. I threw up the collar of my jacket and crossed to the open corner of the square. The bus dragged itself to a stop and the driver killed the remaining headlight. His human cargo began to unload and I moved closer to the door. There was only the yellow step light burning and I wondered how Nicole Balashov would react when she saw me standing there.

They came out, all ducking as they stepped into the downpour. They were mostly Balinese, the women in blouses or breast-cloths and a few village types with their firm, pointed breasts bare; a couple of native soldiers and an occasional seedy-looking white. The bus was emptying fast and I began to grow anxious. Hell, she might have figured that Fry would trace her to the Den Pasar bus. And a mile or so beyond Father Jan's bar, she might have hopped off again. And that would leave me standing here in the rain.

The last passenger stepped out of the door. It wasn't Nicole Balashov.

I stood there and got sore. I had made a fool of myself. I had run after her like a punk when I should have been doping out what to do about my own neck. Nicole Balashov could take care of herself. She had told me so herself.

Something hard and pointed pressed into my back.

"Don't you know enough to come in out of the rain, mister?"

My back muscles stiffened. I knew the voice, and I knew it was a gun in my back. I turned my head and made out a huge, wet shoulder, and that was enough. Apollo Fry might have a headache, but he was conscious, and he had gotten to Den Pasar. And he was holding a gun in my back.

Chapter Three

The driver shut the doors in my face, and the bus started off for the garage. The passengers seemed to have dissolved in the rain. We were alone.

I had tossed Fry's gun away earlier; he might be faking with something in my back. His voice, hoarse and gravelly, came out in crisp bursts.

"She stood us up, mister. Let's go. I'll take care of her later. You now."

I had a gun. And my coat was buttoned over it. "You're calling the shots," I said. "Let's go."

"Smart. You get the idea, mister."

I twisted and swung on him.

My fist rocked his jaw, but he came back fast. It wasn't a gun in his hand, it must have been a wrench. It came down hard against my neck, and then again at the side of my head. My skull seemed to crack and the sound of the rain cut out in my ears. It was fast and painless.

"Come in," she said.

I stood in the doorway. I knew I must look a wet, bruised mass, but she showed no alarm. Through the uneasy focus of my eyes I took her for a native girl, but I knew that wasn't right. Her skin was dark, but her hair was ash blonde and upswept.

I didn't know where I was, but it didn't seem to matter. I had awakened with the bitter taste of mud on my lips, my wrists tied behind me and a throbbing in my head. But the rain had washed the mud off me. I had tried to see the lights of the Bali Hotel across the way, but they weren't there. Nothing was there but coco palms flapping in the wind.

Fry had turned my pockets inside out. With my wrists freed, I saw that he had used a handkerchief to bind them. I had quickly gone around the hem. My handkerchief and I had felt vaguely victorious. He had missed what he was looking for.

I had pawed around in the mud and turned up my passport and my wallet. And I had begun to walk through the trees, but the lights of Den Pasar were gone. Fry had taken me for a ride and dumped me. He must have come to after I loaded him in that taxi, gotten the driver to turn around and head for Den Pasar instead of Buleléng. He had missed Nicole Balashov, but not me. At least, I was still alive. After going through my pockets he might have begun to think he had made a mistake, and dumped me alive. I might

not be the same American he had hunted through the streets of Buleléng.
After a few moments I had stumbled onto a deserted road and spotted a
light set far back in the trees on the other side. I had headed for it.

"You look drowned," she said.

"It's raining out."

"I told you to come in. And shut the door."

I shut the door and stood there dripping water on a polished teakwood
floor. "I could use a couple of aspirins."

She sat in a rattan chair across the room from me, and she had what
looked like a highball glass in her hand. She called to someone. Someone
called Madé, and Madé turned out to be a houseboy and he went for the
aspirins. I knew I hadn't stumbled onto a native shack, although it was
built along native lines. It was more like a jungle villa, but still there was
something wrong. She sat with her legs crossed under a tight sarong, a
black coral bracelet on her wrist and her deeply tanned breasts bare. "You
always go around like that?" I asked.

"I decided to go native this year," she replied casually. "It breaks the
monotony."

"I was hoping you'd have a good excuse," I said.

"I don't need excuses."

Madé came with the aspirins and a shot of whisky to wash them down.
I washed them down.

"My name is Regina Williams," she said. "How's the aspirin?"

"Got quite a kick."

Madé took the shot glass back and went away. I looked at Regina
Williams again and wished to hell she'd cover up. The sarong was bright
scarlet with thin stripes of golden thread; her feet were bare and she had
painted her toenails black.

She seemed to enjoy my discomfort. "You're an American, like me," she
said. "And you're shocked."

"I suppose I am," I said.

My eyes began to avoid her, and I started wandering around. She gave
me the willies, but I didn't feel like walking back into the rain. Not yet, not
until I caught my breath. The room was big enough to play baseball in.
Intricately carved posts supported a low, sweeping ceiling of *lalang* grass
and coconut leaves. The furniture was either rattan or carved Asiatic
wood, and there were silver pieces around that gave the whole place a lux-
urious ornamentation. She had dough, that much was obvious.

"You could do me a favor," I said. "Tell me where the hell I am."

"Ever hear of Sanur?"

"No."

"You're just outside of Sanur, but don't go 'way."

"Where's Sanur?"

"Just beyond Den Pasar. You're poking around like you expect the house detective to pop out of a corner."

"Nice place," I said. "Don't you have a husband or something?"

"I have a husband or something. What's your name?"

I told her and found some cigarettes in a silver box. "O.K. if I help myself?"

A light smile crossed her lips and she recrossed her legs the other way. "Why not? Would you like Madé to fix you a stengah? He makes a wonderful stengah."

"Maybe your husband wouldn't like me drinking up his whisky."

"My husband won't be back until tomorrow. Please relax."

"Light on the soda," I said.

She called Madé again and rattled off the order in Malay. I lit the cigarette and decided to take it easy. If she wanted to run around half naked that was her business. It was nice to be out of the rain, to have Madé fix me a drink and to smoke her cigarettes. Nicole Balashov had gotten under my skin for a couple of hours, but maybe I was over that. She had been smart enough to keep a couple of jumps ahead of Fry, which is more than Jeff Cape could say for himself. At least, Fry was off my back and maybe he was out in the rain somewhere trying to get a line on another lanky American in a white suit. I still had the report Nicole Balashov had passed me, so maybe I was doing all right. Tomorrow I'd find some way off the island. There was nothing to do tonight but find a place to sleep, and maybe I'd found it.

"You been on the island long?" I asked when Madé had gone.

"Three years. Headache better?"

"A little."

"What happened to you, Jeff, wherever you came from?"

"Let's not go into it," I said.

"All right." She smiled. "I like mysterious men."

"I think you just like men."

"I don't like my husband. He's a man." She sipped her drink and watched me over the rim of the glass. "I wish you'd look at me. You make me feel indecent."

I looked at her. "Your husband give a damn that you run around at half-mast?"

"It infuriates him. That's why I do it."

"I see."

"You don't see. It's really quite complicated."

The roof whispered under the pummeling of the rain, and for a moment we didn't say anything. A black fly was buzzing around the ceiling and I saw a gecko clinging up there waiting for it to land. The fly must have been blind. The lizard pounced, and I looked away.

"Would you like to change into dry clothes?"

I faced her again. "You seem to have everything a stranger could want."

"Yes," she muttered. "Everything."

"Dry clothes would be swell. Also something to eat. I'm starving."

Madé came in with my drink, but all I got was one sip. After a couple of words from Regina Williams he led me along a hall and into a bedroom. He got me a fresh towel. I stripped and rubbed myself dry, and he came back with my change of clothes. A sarong.

"Is that the best you can do?"

He didn't answer. He retired with a smile, leaving the sarong across the bed. I wrapped it around myself and checked in the wall mirror. At least no one would mistake me for a woman. I had hair on my chest.

I picked up my wet trousers from the floor and got out my handkerchief. I didn't want Madé fussing around with it, in case he went through my pockets. I tucked it out of sight at my waist. Hell, I thought suddenly, I'm getting jumpy. Madé wasn't going to go through my pockets, and even if he did the handkerchief wouldn't mean anything to him. Still, I felt better carrying it with me. Ditto my wallet. Ditto my passport.

I went back into the living room in my bare feet, but I was dry and clean, and starting to feel human again.

She sipped another highball and watched me eat. Madé had served me cold rice and turtle meat barbecued on the ends of bamboo sticks, like lollipops, with a spicy sauce to dip them in. Regina Williams told me the Balinese name was *saté lembat* and that Madé had caught dragonflies that afternoon and would fry them crisp for me in coconut oil. I excused myself on the grounds that I hadn't yet gone native.

"But you're enchanting in a sarong."

I tried to change the subject. "Tell me about your husband."

"Does he worry you?"

"Of course."

She laughed. "He's not important. We hardly speak to each other any more. He plays the stock market and I just play. He won't give me a divorce."

"Any particular reason?"

"I have too much money."

"You could leave him."

"But why? I have too much fun making him miserable. Really, Jeff, I think you're quite silly about women. But I'm glad you came along tonight. I'm always having fits of loneliness during the wet monsoon."

Madé came back with a platter of jackfruit, bananas, mangosteens and grapes, and disappeared again. I began to wish he'd make a little more noise as he moved around the house. I looked up and saw that the gecko was still on the ceiling, waiting for another fly.

I glanced back to Regina Williams. "Don't the terrorists give you any trouble? I mean, living out here away from things."

The question seemed to carry a charge. "They leave me alone," she said quickly. I was puzzled by her unexpected reaction, but I let the matter drop when she picked up the conversation as though it had never faltered. And she remembered to smile. "Tomorrow, if it stops raining, we'll go swimming. The beach isn't far. Would you like that, Jeff?"

"Are you planning to put me up for the night?"

"Have you any place better to go?"

"No," I said. "No place better."

"Then it's settled. My husband won't be back until late tomorrow. That's very convenient, isn't it?"

It was very convenient. I took over fixing the stengahs, and we killed a couple of idle hours. Rain streamed off the eaves of the veranda in a tinkling clatter and I thought, I could have done worse. Tomorrow I'll get on my way. What money I had left wasn't going to get me to the States, but it would get me far off the island and out of Fry's reach. He had found a gun on me, and taken it, and there was the chance that he might want to go over me for a second look. Tomorrow. If the rain stopped I could fly back to Java. I had friends there. I could raise enough money to start back home once again.

The hell with Nicole Balashov. I wasn't going to kill any more time chasing after her.

"Would you like to see me dance?"

"More native stuff?"

"Very native," Regina Williams said. "I'm really an expert on Balinese culture."

"Let's see you dance."

She opened the radio-phonograph and put a record on the turntable. "I'll do Rangda for you. She's my favorite. She's a *leyak*. And *very* bloodthirsty."

"A what?"

"A witch. She eats children and she's very old and full of black magic. I love her." The record began to spin, but she held the arm above it. "Of course, you'll have to imagine the costume. My head is in flames. I have wonderful crooked fangs, and my breasts hang down to my hips—isn't that delightful? I'm quite horrible and I live on a volcano, the tallest mountain in Bali, the sacred Gunung Agung. Got it?"

"Got it," I muttered uncomfortably.

The needle touched the record and by the time she reached the center of the mat the room was jangling with a crossfire of cymbals and gongs and drums. She poised her arms above her head, and then she began to dance. Not fast, but in jerky, stylized movements. I watched, and put down my glass and began getting a little angry. She was a sex wagon and she knew it and she was trying to run me over. She made sudden thrusts toward me against the weird, exotic embroidery of sound. The sounds and smells and colors beat at me and my jaws locked. This wasn't for me. She wasn't for me. She started to smile as she danced, her flesh shivering with each movement. It wasn't a smile, it was an invitation. She came very close, dancing almost over me as I sat there so that I had to look up at her, and then the cymbals crashed. Her head darted down at me, like a snake's, and she bit my ear. She drew back, laughing, and I got up. I lifted the arm off the record and shut off the machine. Outside, the rain cut in with a hiss.

"It won't work, baby," I said. "Sorry."

She stared at me, fury rising in her eyes. She came close and her hand lashed out across my cheek. "Get out!"

The roof rustled under a violent burst of wind and rain. I found my glass where I had left it on the floor, and emptied it. "Relax, baby. I'm sticking around for a while. If I develop an interest in witches, I'll let you know."

I went down the hall to the room where I'd changed clothes. The light was on, and the bed was made up. I closed the door and waited. She didn't show up, and after a moment I heard a door slam. I lit a cigarette and sat on the edge of the bed smoking it. Imagine Jeff Cape walking away from something as well stacked as that. Maybe I'd been out East longer than was good for me, but I wasn't so far gone that I jumped when anything well stacked whistled. I had to do my own chasing. Sorry, baby, that's the way I was put together. But you get an A for effort. I turned off the light, stowed my stuff under the pillow and got out of the sarong. I stood there a moment in the dark and wondered where on the island Nicole Balashov had pulled in out of the rain. I'd probably never run into her again, and I tried to tell myself I didn't give a damn. I shrugged my shoulders and climbed into bed.

Almost at once a throaty little voice started chanting from the ceiling above me. *Gecko! Gecko! Gecko!*

It was that damned lizard. I let it *gecko* me to sleep.

Chapter Four

I awoke to the babble of rain. The morning light pressed raw and gray through the jalousies. Rain. My first thought depressed me. If the weather didn't break I might be stuck on the island another day waiting for a plane. I looked up and saw that the gecko was gone. Then I saw that my clothes were gone. There was only the rust-colored sarong, draped across the foot of the bed.

I wasn't feeling like a native this morning, but I got into it, collected my stuff from under the pillow and went into the hall.

"Madé!"

There was no answer. I seemed to be alone in the house. I walked into the other bedrooms looking for Regina. I found her room, but she wasn't in bed. I don't know why I noticed the folded newspaper on the night table; maybe I was just beginning to gather my suspicions and notice everything. I could see from across the room that Regina had marked an article in red. I walked over and picked up the paper. She had circled a one-column picture and the story under it. I couldn't read a word of the story; it was printed in what I took for Balinese. The picture got a reaction from me.

It was Nicole Balashov's face.

I stared at it, and tried to understand, but I didn't understand anything. Her expression had that fixed, humorless passport look. Her hair was different. It had been cropped short when I met her yesterday, but in the news photo it was shoulder length.

I didn't like the idea that Regina Williams had been interested enough to circle the whole works.

I folded the paper over and started through the house. There had to be someone around. But there wasn't. From the living room I looked out onto a long, wide sweep of citronella grass with frangipani and breadfruit trees planted within the low wall. Beyond was only a thick, rolling mass of palms.

I crossed to the back of the house and discovered servants' quarters separated from the main bungalow. Madé, at least, must be there. I laid the paper aside and walked out into the rain to find him.

The courtyard behind the house was mud. There was a swimming-pool-size lily pond almost in the center, and it looked strangely peaceful even under the pocks of the rain.

"Jeff!"

The voice seemed to come from far off. I turned. It was Regina Williams.

She was standing under the protection of the eaves at one corner of the house. I hurried over.

"What the hell are you doing?" I snapped.

"Taking a shower, Jeff. It's something you'll learn to do when it rains, if you hang around the tropics for a while."

I didn't bother to correct the impression that I was a stranger to the tropics. She was working a bar of soap along her tanned arm. She had stripped off everything, except the black coral bracelet. This kid was a primitive. A primitive with a bank account. If I stuck around much longer, I was going to start feeling pretty primitive myself.

"Sleep well?" she asked.

"Fine."

"Want the soap?"

"No, thanks. I want to talk to you. I want my clothes."

We stood there within the waterfall from the roof, and she went on working up a lather. "It's early," she shouted against the crashing cascade off the eaves. "I didn't think you'd get up this early."

"What happened to my clothes?"

"Madé has them drying. You don't want to leave yet, do you?"

"Yes."

"If the rain keeps up my husband might never get back. He's in Hong Kong."

"Let's cut out the act."

"What?"

"There's a girl's picture in the paper," I yelled. "You marked it. I want to know why."

"Know her?"

"That's my business."

"I'm sorry if you knew her."

"I'll bet."

"She's dead."

I stopped breathing. Then Regina darted through the waterfall to wash off in the rain. I went after her and caught her shoulders in my hands.

"What do you mean—she's dead?"

"That's what the paper says. I was hoping you weren't interested."

"I'm plenty interested. When did it happen?"

"You made me drop the soap in the mud."

"Never mind the soap."

"That's yesterday's paper. Her body was found on the road near Tabanan the day before."

The cold rain pricked my bare shoulders and back. "That doesn't make sense."

"Really?"

"I saw her alive yesterday."

"Did you, Jeff?"

"The paper is wrong. You know something about it!"

"You're hurting me."

"What else did the paper say?"

Her blonde hair clung in wet tendrils to her neck and shoulders. She wrestled loose. "The paper says there's guerrilla activity near Tabanan. The paper says she was killed by terrorists." She picked up the soap and let the rain wash it off clean. "I'm going in."

I caught her wrist. "I want to know where you fit in. You and Apollo Fry and Nicole Balashov."

"I just happen to know her. Something wrong in that, Jeff?"

"Maybe there is."

"I'm getting cold. Are you going to keep me out here all morning?"

I let go of her wrist and watched her walk to the back porch. She turned on the step and washed the mud off her feet, glanced at me once and disappeared into the house.

I stood where I was, letting the rain wash over me, and let my suspicions come to a boil. It wasn't mere chance that Apollo Fry had unloaded me across the road from this place. He knew I'd head for the only light around—Regina Williams' place. He was counting on her to work me over in her own, feminine way. To find out what I knew. To go over my clothes seam by seam. To keep me on ice. And it had worked.

But Madé wouldn't find anything in my suit.

And I was sure Nicole Balashov hadn't been killed by terrorists two days ago.

She was alive, because I met her yesterday.

I went back into the house.

"More coffee, Jeff?"

"Tell Madé to bring back my suit," I said.

It had been a breakfast without table talk. She had tied up her hair in a kerchief. She wore black coolie slacks and a white silk shirt with the sleeves rolled up. "You can't go anywhere in this rain. My husband might not be home for days now. Why don't you make yourself at home?"

"I'm not worried about your husband any more." I refilled my own coffee cup. "Madé. Tell him."

"I could keep you here." She smiled. "I could tell Madé to hide your clothes."

"Maybe you already have. That's what you're supposed to do, isn't it? Keep me here."

"Maybe I like you so well I'd do that, Jeff. You wouldn't go anywhere dressed like a native, would you?"

I stared at her. "You're real cute, aren't you? How do you fit into this thing?"

"I wish you wouldn't be so sullen. You remind me of my husband when you're sullen."

I lit one of her cigarettes. "Shall we run through it once, just for laughs? Apollo Fry came here last night. After he dumped me, he came here and told you to put out the welcome mat for me."

She was the type that could smile at breakfast. "Yes," she said, taking a light off my cigarette. "I suppose he did."

"You're real buddy-buddy, you two."

"In a business way."

"What did I come under—file for future reference?"

She watched me through a breath of smoke, and her eyes became very frank. "You've got it *almost* right, Jeff. Mr. Fry stopped in last night and told me Nicole Balashov had turned up alive and it looked like she'd met an American agent in Buleléng and passed him some information. That's not good, Jeff. Not for Mr. Fry and not for me. Are you an American agent, Jeff?"

"No. Just a dumb American."

"But handsome. You have beautiful eyelashes, Jeff. Very long for a man."

"Stow it."

She laughed. "You're afraid of me, aren't you?"

"Scared stiff."

"Well... Mr. Fry told me he'd worked over a guy, but hadn't found what he was looking for. Maybe this guy was an innocent bystander. Would I take him in and work him over in my own way? The guy would come to across the road and he was sure to head for my place. You did."

"Yes."

"Would you believe it, Jeff, I told Fry to go to hell? He's really a detestable person. But when you stumbled up the veranda and I got a look at you, I changed my mind. You make a charming first impression. Even when you're dripping rain, Jeff."

"Was the sex act Fry's idea too?"

"I get ideas of my own, Jeff. Sex is *always* my own idea."

"What about Fry's outfit—the Scrap Metals Export Company? Where do you fit in?"

She blew the ash off her cigarette. "Scrap metals fascinate me this year."

"Sounds romantic as hell. What about Nicole Balashov?"

"She's half owner in Fry's export firm. Didn't you know?"

I didn't answer. I sat there trying to make sense out of that, and I sat there getting sore about it. If Nicole Balashov was Fry's partner, what sort of double cross had she waltzed me into? I had a sudden impulse to toss Regina my handkerchief, tell her to look in the hem, and waltz myself right out of the whole mess. And yet something didn't fit, Nicole and Fry didn't fit, and I wondered suddenly how much of what Regina Williams was saying I ought to believe. She had a stake in this somewhere, and that seemed to fit least of all.

"You know what I was hoping, Jeff? I was hoping you were the wrong guy. I was hoping Fry had made a mistake about you. Do you really have that information Nicole got on him?"

"Why don't you ask Madé?" I snapped. "He's gone through my stuff."

"Madé couldn't find a thing."

"Tough."

"There's the stuff you carry in the sarong, Jeff."

I stared at her. Behind the bantering tone and smiling eyes I recognized her for what she was, a cold, ruthless female. What Regina Williams was doing mixed up in gunrunning I couldn't guess, and I stopped trying. It was clear that Apollo Fry trusted her and was sure to be back to pick up his merchandise. Me. I had to hand it to him, he was smart. The way he had set it up Regina Williams hadn't had to keep me at home with the point of a gun. I'd stuck around of my own free will. "Do me a favor," I said. "After I'm gone, tell your business associate in the junk business I'm so dumb I walked right into his little trap. Tell him to lay off me. Tell him I'm getting real mad."

"I'll tell him, Jeff. Shall I drive you back to town?"

"No, thanks."

There was a spark of amusement in her eyes; we both knew she wasn't going to drive me anywhere. Then she called Madé from the pantry and spoke to him in effortless Malay. Smiling. She told him to get my suit and she told him to get her a gun.

I watched him go and said nothing.

She got up, and her expression was a study in innocence. "It's stopped raining, Jeff. God, I hate it when it rains. I'm going to get changed."

She left me sitting there and I realized that the roof was quiet again. It *had* stopped raining.

Madé came out of nowhere with my suit draped over his arm. It looked surprisingly clean, and he had pressed it. My eyes hurried over his sarong, but there were no bulges and I decided he hadn't yet gone for the gun. I took the suit and walked into my room. I changed quickly and transferred my wallet, passport and handkerchief to pockets. I made sure the door was locked, opened the jalousies and stuck my head out. A driveway bordered the house on my side and led to a two-car garage. One car was sitting there, a red Buick convertible. I saw no signs of life, climbed out and let myself drop to the ground. Low, misty clouds were breaking up under a blue sky; water straggled from the thatched eaves. Behind me in the house, I heard a gentle knock at the bedroom door. Regina. With a gun. The mud wall ran about forty feet from the bungalow, across a stretch of citronella grass, and I raced for it.

"Jeff!"

As I reached the wall the noise of a car turning onto the driveway from the road startled me. I vaulted the wall. I was sure I hadn't been seen. I turned long enough to watch the car start up the driveway, and I heard Regina's voice again, in fury, only now she was yelling for Madé.

The car stopped beside the veranda. A guy stepped out of the back seat. An Oriental with a bird cage in one hand and a grin on his face. Mr. Chu.

I turned and made off through the palms.

Chapter Five

I had kept away from the road, cutting off where coco and betel-nut palms grew dense. The wild grove had continued for what seemed miles to me, and I was muddy to the knees. I had long ago slowed to a tired walk. I didn't know where Den Pasar was, but I knew I wanted to head for it.

I came out of the trees at the foot of a slope and a wide, muddy rice field stretched out before me. At one end, in the distance, natives were already bent at work. Beyond I saw a small village.

I didn't like exposing myself to cross the field, and held back. The sudden presence of Mr. Chu had rattled me. What the hell, was every foreigner in Bali mixed up in this affair?

I was sure Regina had sent Madé off into the trees after me, and for all I knew Mr. Chu had been quickly filled in and might have joined the chase. Whatever Nicole Balashov had given me, it apparently had everyone jumping. I scanned the open rice field again, about three-quarters of a mile of flat country, and decided to risk it. If anyone had tried to follow me, he should have given up long ago.

I took off my shoes, threw away my socks and started along one of the low, clay dams. Barefooted, I made good time. On either side, the little dykes curved and crossed to divide the flooded field into a thousand ponds. Off to my right I saw a young Balinese clacking bamboo sticks to frighten away a flock of birds.

In the village, I thought, I could find some sort of transportation to Den Pasar. I'd go to the airport. Once on board a plane I'd be out of this mess. I was sick of running away; I was out of my depth and I knew it. I was an oil geologist, not an errand boy, and I didn't like being ganged up on.

Mud made a little sucking sound through my toes. Not far off a crane settled to the field with a gentle flapping of its white, starched wings. The peacefulness and quiet of the place came over me, and I seemed to relax as I walked. As I got well out into the field the sun broke through, warm but not yet hot. Brown paddies around me began to glisten, and almost in front of me an eel slithered off the dyke into the muddy water. Scarecrows stood about as resting places for little flocks of birds.

A pistol shot cracked out over the field, and I spun around. Far behind, at the edge of the palms, stood Mr. Chu. He fired again and started out on the network of dykes. Balinese popped up under their mushroom hats and began to yell. The mud sucked at my feet as I tried to run.

My leg muscles were stiff, but I forced them to work. I slipped, picked myself up and looked back. Chu fired again.

I felt a sharp sting on my left arm. I turned and kept running. I saw a thatched granary up ahead at the edge of the village, and made for it almost mechanically. My feet kept slipping off the mud banks and I finally cut into the rice shoots. A misty heat seemed to envelop my head as I stumbled along. I knew I'd been hit, but my legs worked and that was all that mattered. When I reached the granary and got behind it, I heard another shot on my near right, from the village walls. I glanced at the rice field and saw Mr. Chu dive flat. He had stopped shooting at me—someone was shooting at *him!* I stood catching my breath, and saw him continue again along the dyke until the next explosion. He flattened himself and stayed there.

I edged along the village walls; the place was silent and deserted. I worked my arm around, and it functioned. I couldn't be hit bad.

Then I spotted the road leading out of town and the red Buick convertible parked in the middle of it.

I heard another near explosion and a moment later found Regina Williams standing under a carved stone gateway. She was watching Mr. Chu out in the muddy field, and she had a gun in her hand.

I walked toward her, and she gave me a crazy grin. "I really ought to kill him," she said. "If he gets up again, maybe I will."

She was standing in leather sandals and an orange sarong and nothing else, but it didn't seem to matter any more. "I told you I was a dumb American," I said. "I thought all along Madé got you that gun to point at me."

Mr. Chu was staying down, and she faced me squarely. "I'm pointing it at you now, Jeff."

"So I see. I was sure you and the Chinese had common interests."

"We have. At the moment, it's you. You're it, Jeff."

"I see. Just a harmless double cross between pals."

"Something like that." Her expression altered. "You're bleeding."

I looked down at my sleeve. I was bleeding, but I didn't think I was carrying around the bullet. "What made you come here?"

"We'd better do something about your arm." Her concern seemed genuine, and it made me angry. I didn't want her feeling sorry for me, I didn't want her feeling anything for me.

"I asked you a question."

"You were sure to come out into the valley. You were sure to head for the village. I came. I'll drive you to a doctor."

"I don't need a doctor."

Beside her in the car I stripped off my coat and looked at my arm. My flesh was ripped, it bled and it burned, but I knew I wasn't bad off. She started the engine and once we had picked up speed she put the gun out of sight on her left, between the seat and the door.

I got out my handkerchief, felt for the card in the hem and placed it around my arm in a position where I thought it wouldn't get bloody. Then I tied the ends with one hand and my teeth.

"Anyway," I said as an afterthought, "thanks for stopping Mr. Chu back there. His aim was getting better toward the end."

"So was mine."

"You can let me off in Den Pasar."

"I want that report, Jeff. You have it, don't you?" Her tone was as casual and confident as though she were asking for a cigarette.

"Did Fry tell you I had it?"

"He wasn't sure. But I think you have it. That's why you ran out on me."

"Maybe Fry was kidding you."

"Maybe. But Fry doesn't kid. When in doubt he kills. He's going to kill Nicole Balashov. He said he'd be back this morning to take care of you. I don't want him to kill you, Jeff."

"Thanks."

"Did I tell you? You have wonderful eyelashes."

"You told me. I don't have the report. Sorry, baby. Give it up."

Her eyes shot my way and impatience sprang into her voice. "I'm trying to give you a chance. You can get out of this now. Clean. Give me the report and you're out. You *must* have it."

The car rattled over a wooden bridge and the road began following a stream. I tossed my wallet and passport to her lap. "You've gone through everything else. Look for yourself. I don't have the report. I could use a cigarette."

"In the glove compartment."

She picked up the wallet, and holding it against the steering wheel, she fingered through it. Greenback by greenback, card by card. I lit a cigarette and watched her, a half-nude blonde with intense fingers and impatient eyes.

"Watch the road," I snapped.

"I am."

She finished with the wallet and started in on my passport. When she had turned every page, she threw it at me. I put it back in my coat.

"Where are you taking me?"

"Den Pasar."

"Thanks. I'll drop you a postcard when I get to San Pedro."

She began stepping on it, her lips set and the humor gone from her eyes. I glanced at her evenly tanned skin.

"I thought your going native was a gag."

"Did you?"

"At breakfast you wore a blouse. I liked you better that way. Stop the car."

"What?"

"I said stop. If you're going to take me to town, you're going to wear my coat."

Her mood changed quickly, and she laughed. "Really, Jeff, you're funny. You're trying to reform me. It's impossible."

"Put it on," I said. "At least out in public. For me. Because I'm funny."

She stopped the car and got into my coat. I picked up my shoes from the floor boards, and watched her button up. The coat didn't do much good. "Wait for me," I said. "I'm going down to the stream and wash the mud off my feet."

I opened the door and started down the bank. The stream was chocolate with silt washed down from the hills. I got in up to my knees and washed off. Behind me, the Buick idled. I couldn't quite believe Regina was giving me up so easily, but I hadn't been able to make much sense out of her earlier, and I decided not to worry about it now. My shoes were wrapped in mud and I washed them. Still standing in water, I tore off a handful of pandanus leaves growing at the bank, laid them out to stand on and got back into my shoes without getting my feet muddy. Wet, my shoes felt like lead weights.

I was tying them when I heard the Buick scrape gears and the engine race. I looked up as Regina took off down the road.

I clambered up the bank.

"Hey!"

The road turned, and a moment later the Buick was out of sight.

I stood there swearing. I didn't know what had gotten into her, but she was wearing my coat and my passport was in the pocket.

Chapter Six

The sign said Den Pasar, two kilometers, and I kept walking. Regina Williams had tied a neat little string to me. She had my passport, and she knew I would have to come back to get it. But I wasn't going back to Sanur—not yet. I was going to Den Pasar and I was going to find out when I could get a plane off the island. She had mentioned that Fry was going to return for me, and I felt no urge to be there in the house when he walked in. Maybe she was smart. Maybe she wanted to give me enough string to tie myself in knots. She might have decided I had hidden the report somewhere on the island and would head for it. But always I would have to come back to Sanur. For my passport.

An old Balinese with a bright hibiscus flower over one ear came along on a bicycle and he gave me a lift to Den Pasar.

The town was larger than Buleléng, lined with little shops and sidewalk stalls and set here and there with European-style houses. Pony carts moved nervously through the streets, clanging their bells. The sun had already dried the red tile roofs of government buildings flying the Indonesian flag and turned the walls a blinding white. Overhead, a flock of pigeons swarmed around the town square to the screech of bamboo whistles tied to their tail feathers to frighten off hawks. The rain had washed mosquitoes into the air. In another hour it would be hot.

I decided to stay away from the Bali Hotel. I found a Chinese drugstore and asked to use the phone. I called the airport. Garuda Indonesian Airways had a flight scheduled at 1600. To Jogjakarta, Java. Was there a seat available. There was. My name is Jefferson Cape. Hold it.

I hung up. Four o'clock this afternoon was a long time to hang around. But as I stood there, I got an idea. I wouldn't have to go to Sanur for my passport. I would bring Regina Williams to me.

The blood on my shirt sleeve caught the druggist's eyes, and we got together in Malay. He disinfected the flesh wound and wrapped a clean bandage around my arm. I examined the handkerchief and saw that the bulge in the hem was clear of blood. I put the handkerchief away. I bought myself a white shirt in a nearby shop, changed into it, and set out to look for a photographer.

He was a fat Japanese on a side street, and the walls of his shop were a gallery of Balinese weddings and funerals and bull races. He sucked through his teeth as he nodded me into the place and he spoke English.

"I want something photographed," I said.

"This humble one is at your service, tuan."

I saw a pair of scissors, got out my handkerchief and cut the hem. I would have him photograph both sides of the card, keep the negatives and trade the original to Regina for my passport. But I'd make it look good. I'd tell her I wanted to sell out. The passport was incidental. I wanted money, all she could lay hands on within a couple of hours.

I kept my back turned to the Japanese for the moment it took to operate on the handkerchief. There was no sense arousing his curiosity. With the card in my hand, wet from rain but still a rolled tube, I discarded the handkerchief and turned.

"I want you to take close-ups of both sides of this card," I said. "Immediate service?"

"Ah, quite immediate, tuan."

I unrolled the card, wet and limp. He reached out for it, but I held back and my heart began to throb. Something was wrong. The face of the card said Scrap Metals

Export Company—*but the back of the card was white and blank!*

I stared at it, and got mad. This didn't make sense, and I was tired of all the things that didn't make sense. I had seen the back of that card covered with Russian words, and now they weren't there. The ink hadn't run, it was indelible. I examined the back of the card now in a sort of desperation, as though my sanity depended on it. The surface had obviously *never* been written on. It was clean, untouched, blank.

Either a switch had been pulled or I had had a hallucination somewhere along the line.

"There is something wrong, tuan?"

I crushed the card in my fist. "Forget it."

I walked out and went looking for a bar.

The clock over the bottles said ten-thirty, and that was crazy too. It seemed more like a dozen hours since I had found Regina bathing at dawn in the rain, but it was only ten-thirty. I had been threatened, shot at, provisionally abandoned and my senses bewitched since dawn. It had been a hell of a morning.

I drank gin and tonic and thought of Nicole Balashov. What had she said? "You'll be in no danger." That was a laugh, but it wasn't funny. It wasn't funny that I had risked my life for a card that had gone blank. I checked my movements all the way back to the moment Nicole Balashov had passed me the matchbox. Somehow, somewhere, someone had pulled a switch on me. In a way, that put me out of the running. Someone had wiped my hands of the whole mess and maybe I ought to thank him—or her.

Him. It had to be Fry. No one else fitted. He put me to sleep with a wrench and tied my wrists with my handkerchief. He must have come across the bulge in the hem. He could have substituted one of his own business cards. But if he was kill happy, why hadn't he killed me on the spot? I was the guy, I had the goods on me. Instead, he had dumped me into Regina's saronged lap and led her to believe the report hadn't yet been found. Where did he expect that to get him?

I wondered what Nicole Balashov could have written on the back of a card that could have everyone jumping. She had mentioned illegal American guns, but where did it go from there?

Well, I was out of it. Forget the whole thing. I could call Regina on the phone and tell her how I had been outfoxed and ask her real nice to give me back my passport. I could tell her Fry was pulling some sort of double cross on her, and she might be able to make some sense out of it. It might work. I would need my passport to check off the island.

I sat there drinking by myself, and my mind kept wandering back to Nicole Balashov. Why must she be so damned beautiful and scared? The paper had listed her as dead, but I knew the paper was wrong. So did Fry and so did Regina Williams. She was alive somewhere on the island and she probably thought I was safely out at sea on the *Timor Lady*. I got the feeling that nothing else mattered to her. If she believed the report was beyond Fry's reach, she could tell him to go to hell. Even if he found her and killed her, she could tell him to go to hell.

Somewhere on the street the horn of a car got stuck and blared out over the town. I kept remembering the way Nicole turned in the doorway that last time, the little temple bells jingling from her ears, and the look of trust and regret in her eyes. Blue eyes. Pale blue, and sort of wistful. She had trusted me because there was no one else around to trust and I had resented the whole thing once the chips were down. I still resented it. I didn't like responsibility, that was the way I was made, and I had faced it years ago. And I had gotten along fine. Why did Nicole Balashov have to look at me that way?

The horn began to weaken, like a sick animal, and then nose-dived to silence. I played with my glass, thinking. I wondered suddenly if she had planned to catch the *Timor Lady* out of Bali. She knew where it was heading and when it was sailing. She *must* have been trying to get off the island. But Fry had been at the jetty, and she knew there wasn't a chance of her getting through. It fitted. She had watched me come in on the *prau*. She could have quickly made out a thumbnail report on the back of a card. Fry's card. If she could get me to deliver it to a Central Intelligence Agency in the States, she would have doubled the chances of getting the information out of Bali. And that fitted. If either she or the card got through, Fry was apparently licked.

Well, I had been licked. Fry had found the card and probably destroyed it. That left Nicole Balashov, and for all I knew he might have found her too.

My glass was empty. I was on the verge of ordering a refill, when anger caught up with me and I walked out of the place. I couldn't fade out of this thing, not yet. Nicole's report was gone, but there was still Nicole. Whatever was missing from my make-up, I had enough pride to build up a quick head of steam. I could try finding her, and I could try getting her off the island. She might still be somewhere in Buleléng; I'd start with the bus driver. I'd find out where she hopped off the bus.

I asked questions and found my way to a Chinese garage on a side street where the bus had gone for the night. I found it still there, no one around but a Chinese kid who was gassing it up.

"When does this thing start for Buleléng?" I asked.

"Noon."

"Where's the driver?"

He pointed to the back door and I started across the dirt floor. I heard the excitement of Malay voices. It sounded like an argument starting up behind the garage.

When I stepped through the back door I saw a close ring of Balinese men on their haunches in the yard. The babble died down suddenly, but not because of me. Two roosters with long steel gaffs on their legs were being aroused and the betting had stopped. It was a cockfight, and I knew I would have to wait.

The handlers released their birds and almost at once there was an explosion of feathers in the air. I waited impatiently, but I didn't have to wait long. Spurs flashed, and the fight was over. One cock lay in his own blood, squawking helplessly. The men began exchanging money.

"I'm looking for the driver of the Buleléng bus," I said.

A lithe young Balinese in a common batik *kain* and an old army shirt looked up curiously, but he was smiling. He had won on the cockfight and got to his feet jiggling silver coins in his hand.

"I am the one."

I got him to one side and described Nicole Balashov to him. I reminded him that she had stopped his bus outside Father Jan's place. He remembered.

"I'm trying to find her," I said. "She got off again there in Buleléng, didn't she?"

He kept bouncing the money in his hand. "If you are looking for the girl you describe, you will not find her in Buleléng. She came all the way to Den Pasar."

I stared at him, and tried to retrace my thinking. Another fight was starting, and he excused himself to lay another bet. She hadn't been on the bus when it rolled in last night, I was sure of it. I had also been certain that she left the bus a little while after boarding it. A trick. A blind.

The driver came back, but he kept his eyes on the arena.

"*Béh!* I remember her well." He grinned. "When I came to the garage, out she came from behind a seat. She looked very frightened."

My heart was beating a little faster. She must have spotted Fry waiting at the door of the bus and hidden herself. "O.K., she was frightened," I said. "Where did she go from the garage? Do you know?"

Two roosters were being provoked, and his attention strayed.

"I said where did she go?"

His eyes came back to me impatiently. "You ask the same question as the other man. But he gave me fifty rupiahs for the answer, tuan."

The cocks were being let loose for the attack. I caught hold of his shirt front to keep him there. "What other man?" I snapped. "A big guy built like a mountain?"

"No, tuan."

"What did he look like?"

"As tall as you, but without your flesh. His sun helmet was very dirty."

"All right—to hell with him." I'd heard enough to know I'd never seen him before. "Where did the girl go?"

There was a whirr of feathers, but I pulled him up tighter.

"Sutra was bringing in his taxi for the night. She made him take her away. That Sutra is very superstitious."

"*Where!*"

"To the little harbor. Benua. When he came back he said she is a *leyak*. He saw her picture in the paper. She is dead, Sutra said, and he was afraid not to do what a *leyak* told him. Today he is sick in bed, that superstitious Sutra."

"Never mind Sutra. How long ago was the guy here asking questions?"

"Less than an hour ago, tuan."

The cockfight was over with a fresh burst of voices, and the men began to break up.

"How far is Benua?"

"Ten kilometers."

I let go of his shirt and mumbled my thanks on the run.

Chapter Seven

There was the smell of drying fish in the air as we came into Benua. I saw at once that the harbor was deserted, except for a few scattered fishing *praus*. A marsh spread out in front of town like a dirty apron, and a long, narrow breakwater ran out to a jetty in deeper water. The main drag was an assortment of shops and tiny restaurants, and a couple of old hotels.

"Stop here," I said.

I got out of the taxi, and told the driver to wait. He waited, and I went into the hotel. I described Nicole Balashov to the clerk and got nowhere. Back on the street, I asked the driver to follow me with the taxi.

I tried the other hotel, thinking she'd be a fool to register in a hotel, but maybe she had been a fool. I could only be following in the footsteps of Apollo Fry's man. There was no other explanation for the guy in the dirty sun helmet.

The desk was unattended, and I rang the bell. When no one came, I bounced it hard.

"You're wasting your time, *mijnheer.*"

I glanced around the narrow lobby. A potbellied Dutchman in shapeless duck trousers, his bare feet in sandals, sat lazily by the window. He looked like he might be the village beachcomber, and he looked talkative.

"The *mevrouw* is having another fight with her husband in the back," he explained, sizing me up. "*Ja,* they won't answer your bell if you ring it till noon."

I walked toward him. "Been in the lobby long?"

"For years, *mijnheer.*"

"Do you remember if a girl in a straw hat and a—"

"*Ja,* I do."

My pulse quickened. I didn't have to describe her. He knew. "The skinny guy in a sun helmet's been here, hasn't he?"

"The one with the Malacca cane?"

"Maybe."

"*Ja, ja.* He has been here," he replied with detached amusement.

"Where is he?"

"In her room."

I began tightening up. "Know what room she's in?"

"It is possible I know." He reached to the floor beside his chair and picked up an empty whisky bottle. He stared at me with a rheumy twinkle in his eyes. I could take a hint, but I didn't.

"Build a ship in it," I snapped. "I asked you what room she's in!"

He wiped his nose unhappily, shifting his eyes to the bottle. "You have no sense of charity, *mijnheer?*"

I envisioned Apollo Fry's man working Nicole over while this thirsty bum held me back over the price of a bottle of whisky. I snapped it out of his hands; he must have thought I was going to beat his brains out with it.

He volunteered the information quickly. "She is not upstairs in the room," he said.

"Checked out?"

"No. She went for a walk to the pier a few minutes before the other man came in asking for her, *mijnheer.* I watched her through the window."

"Did you tell him?"

"He didn't ask me, *mijnheer.* The *mevrouw* was here You should buy me a drink for not telling him, *ja?*"

I hurried into the street.

The breakwater began at the foot of the main drag, traveling out across the marsh to the jetty. I ran. I could make out a couple of tiny figures out there, like pencil marks on the horizon. A brisk, salty wind tugged at my clothes.

Halfway along the breakwater, I slowed to a trot. I could see only a single fishing *prau* tied to the jetty. A man, who seemed to be bare-backed. A woman.

The marsh, lonely and deserted, stretched out on either side of the breakwater. The whole picture kept jarring before my eyes, and my ears filled with the sounds of my own breathing. The rickety pier, the girl and a man. A native. I could tell that much now. And the woman was carrying a hat. Then a second native, climbing up out of his boat.

The hat. She carried it to save it from the breeze. She stood facing the breakwater, watching me, her legs set apart. Suddenly I was sure. The coral dress hugged her body against the wind. And she was beginning to recognize me.

It was Nicole Balashov.

I reached the end of the breakwater and moved out onto the wooden jetty. I slowed my steps. The two natives at one side were struggling to get a sea turtle up from their boat.

Nicole Balashov stared at me with calm, resolute blue eyes. There was no surprise on her face, and no surrender in the way she held herself.

I stopped a few feet short of her, catching my breath as my eyes traveled over her.

She looked very beautiful. Her hair was cut short, almost boyishly, just right for the wind. The bright dress fluttered against her legs, molding itself to her skin. God, I thought, how beautiful she is at this moment, and how strangely desirable. Suddenly everything seemed worth while. I was glad I had come. There was no point in kidding myself. I knew I had found someone I could fall deeply in love with. It would be easy.

We traded glances, and we both must have felt a little awkward standing there like strangers with a nightmare in common. She held her legs apart against the sea wind in a sort of poised independence that I liked. And I liked her eyes as she stared at me, alive and very pale against the warm tan of her face. But still, the moment seemed off center. I felt vaguely that something was wrong. There was no expression of surprise or satisfaction on her face. Her eyes were wide and still. It was as though she had been expecting me, but didn't really want to see me at all.

"Small island," I said finally. "Remember me?"

She didn't answer. She just stared at me.

"I missed my ship," I said.

"Yes. I know."

"I figured you ought to be glad to see me."

"Did you?"

"Yes."

"Are you trying to be funny, Mr. Cape?"

There was a brittle edge to her voice, and my temper began to react. "If I said anything funny, let me in on the joke, will you, baby? Did I grow horns or something overnight?"

"Let's not kid each other, Mr. Cape. *Please.*"

My jaws tightened. "Look, sweetheart. I missed my ship back to the States. I've been cracked on the head and I've been shot at. It's been great fun, but not for me. I'm sorry as hell you're not glad to see me, but it really doesn't matter."

"Must you make a speech?"

"I must. A couple of minutes ago I was thinking God, she's beautiful and how nice it's going to be falling in love with her. That's your cue to laugh if you need one. Shows you what a half-witted guy you nailed yesterday. But this is today, and today I'm busy as hell. I've got a plane to catch and some drinking to catch up on and a passport to chase down. Me, I'm busy as hell. If I weren't so busy I'd shake you down for some answers, like what's that newspaper story about your being dead and where does Regina Williams fit in and what the hell is really going on anyway? But I'm too damned busy."

She stood there hating me, quietly hating me on sight, and I wanted to slap her. "Tell Mr. Fry I compliment him," she said. "He's very good at buying up men. He buys them like stocks and bonds, doesn't he? Easy. All you need is the price. What was your price, Mr. Cape?"

I stared at her, and loathed her. Did she actually believe I had sold out to Fry? What sort of low-grade heel did she take me for? "I wasn't expensive," I snapped. "He promised me a box of five-cent cigars when it's all over."

The jetty swayed gently on its spindly piles as the tide tugged at them. She half turned, impatience and contempt in her eyes. "I saw you waiting at the bus last night—both of you waiting for me to get off."

"Swell," I said. "That proves you keep your eyes open."

"Yes."

"Did you also see him holding a gun in my back? It turned out to be a wrench and he creased my skull with it. Pay day."

She turned back to me and her lips parted. The idea seemed to startle her, but she said nothing. She just looked at me. Behind her, the natives had the turtle on the planks of the jetty and watched it flap its paddles in a useless rage. I felt a rage of my own, because she seemed to think I was making a bid for sympathy, and I hadn't meant that.

"Did I tell you?" I said. "I'm busy. You told me you could take care of yourself, and I should have had sense enough to believe you. See you around, baby."

"Jeff—"

I wheeled, but I was still talking. "It's *Mr.* Cape. You had it right the first time." I had a last look at her, and the wind was making her hair dance. I tried to force the whole, quick picture of her out of my mind.

I sensed that she had taken a step forward, and I thought she was going to catch my arm, but she didn't. She let me walk away.

I walked. I had lost my temper, and even though I knew this wasn't what I wanted, I walked. The jetty traveled out in front of me to the breakwater, and it seemed a mile long. My legs felt loose at the knees and long and awkward. A couple of sea gulls were standing nearby and I kicked at them and they took off. I think maybe I wanted her to come after me and stop me and tell me she had been a fool. There was only a silence behind me, growing longer with every step I took. I could feel her eyes on me, watching me. What was she thinking?

And then I stopped. I couldn't go on. Deep down I knew I hadn't come after her only because I thought she needed me. I needed her. I wanted her. It was easy to walk out on trouble, but I couldn't walk out on her, or myself. She was alone and they were hunting her and I wasn't helping by sounding off and deserting her. I touched my pockets for a cigarette, and remembered I was out.

I turned.

She was still standing where I had left her, the hat in her hand and the wind tugging and snapping familiarly at her dress. But her face seemed different. The contempt was gone, and the chill and the anger were gone.

I could almost detect the regret I wanted so much to see in her eyes.

The hell I couldn't fall in love with her.

I walked. Back.

Then we stood facing each other, a few feet apart, and the wind tinkled the earrings, like a distant bell buoy.

When her voice came it was very soft and a little shy. "Hello, Jeff."

"I need a cigarette," I said.

She opened her purse and reached for her pack. I caught her wrist tightly and pulled her against me. Under the high sun and wind her body felt warm and soft and alive. My pulse pounded, but I just held her.

"Oh, Jeff, I'm terribly sorry for what I thought. I—"

I flicked her chin with my knuckles, raising it, and then I found her lips. I kissed her hard and long, because I had to. And I wanted to. And she wanted me to. Nearby, we heard the two fishermen laugh, but it didn't matter. I went on kissing her.

She turned out of my arms a moment later, smiling uncomfortably. What the hell, we were little more than strangers, weren't we?

"I'm dealing myself back in," I said.

She put a cigarette between my lips and found her matches. "You told me you were too busy today, remember?"

"You kissed me like you meant it."

"Impulse." She cupped her long fingers around a match and I lit up.

"You always follow your impulses?"

She shrugged her shoulders. It was a feminine answer. Beyond her, I saw one of the fishermen get the turtle to his back. He started off with an open grin toward the breakwater and shore. The other dropped to the *prau* and began to untie it. We were left alone in the wind. For a moment there were only the little snapping sounds of her dress. Then she turned away from me.

"You had followed me to Den Pasar last night," she muttered, "on your own."

"Yes."

"I was a little fool. I was frightened when I saw you come out here. You have a right to be angry—"

"Don't make a speech. I'm not angry."

She faced me suddenly, and the words came out as though she couldn't hold them in any longer. "I *am* glad to see you. Terribly glad. When you walked away a moment ago, it hurt. Believe me, Jeff?"

"Sure. Relax. We'd better get off this pier."

"Do you hate me for getting you into this mess?"

"I tried real hard. What were you going to do out here? Jump in and swim away?"

She lit a cigarette of her own. "I thought I could get one of the fishermen to take me to Lombok. It's the next island."

"Any luck?"

"No luck. A freighter is due in late tomorrow."

"And that's a long time for you to wait."

"Yes."

"I'd better warn you," I said. "There's something about you that makes me want to fall in love with you."

It brought a faint smile to her eyes, as though she'd been warned by a thousand other guys. "Thanks. But I'm sure you'll be able to talk yourself out of it if it happens." She glanced at the bandage around my arm and raised an eyebrow to ask the question.

I ignored it. She was right. I'd go on trying to talk myself out of falling in love with her, and maybe it would work. Vaguely, I wanted it to work. I'd been in love before and I had the old scars to prove it. I tossed my cigarette into the water. "Look, Fry found the goods on me and has probably destroyed that little report you wrote. That leaves you and what you have tucked away in your head, doesn't it? Let's get off this damned jetty and get you off the island. Come on."

I reached for her hand, but she held back.

"Jeff, there are things about me—"

"I know. You're Fry's partner. O.K. There's no time now, fill me in later. Later I'm going to be full of questions and you'd better be full of answers."

She stood there, her mood shifting to something cold and oddly professional. "It won't work. I'm sorry, Jeff."

Exasperation cut into my voice. "There's a plane out of here at four o'clock. There's an even chance we can be on it."

"No. It's not as simple as that, Jeff, for me. Fry has had the airport watched for days. And he meets the ships. He'll meet this one tomorrow. I've stopped kidding myself. I'm trapped. I'm really sorry I got you into this. I want you to go, Jeff. Don't worry about me. I'll make out. I always have."

She turned away, but I caught her shoulders and pulled her around. Her eyes flared for a moment, as though I had no right to touch her. My voice turned into a harsh, angry whisper. "I dealt myself back in and I meant it. Listen to me. There's no time to stand and argue."

"Jeff—"

"I said listen to me. Someone else picked up your trail to Benua. He's waiting right now in your hotel room. A skinny guy. Pith helmet. And he carries a Malacca cane. Does all that mean anything to you?"

Her earrings jingled. "No."

"You don't know who he is?"

She shrugged her shoulders with an indifference that maddened me. She seemed like a sophisticated savage. All she needed was a cocktail glass in her hand and we might have been discussing the latest bedroom gossip. The wind molded the thin dress to her body as she stood there. Her fresh beauty seemed out of place and her changing moods didn't quite mesh with the shifting dangers that faced her. "Fry must have sent him," she said.

"I figured that much out for myself. Doesn't that worry you any more?"

"Of course, Jeff."

"Then let's go. It was a crazy idea to come out on this pier."

She looked up, her eyes suddenly hesitant and uncertain. "Why should you want to help me? I'm not sure it makes sense, Jeff. You could catch that plane and be free."

"Don't you want me around?"

She smiled. "I didn't say that."

"This isn't the place for a song and dance. But don't expect me to make sense any more. I like your earrings—let's leave it at that."

"Jeff?"

"Come on, baby!"

"Jeff, I think I'm going to like having you around."

We started back, but we didn't go far. We both saw it at once, a lumbering figure already halfway along the breakwater and coming toward us. We stopped. He was still too far away to make out details, but a moment later they sharpened. The sun helmet. The cane he swung as he walked. And probably a gun in his pocket.

I glanced quickly at the ruffled waters surrounding the jetty. There was no way off.

Chapter Eight

The guy had a rangy body in loose-fitting whites. He strode toward us on long, jaunty legs. He had us trapped and he knew it.

I turned to Nicole. "Do you have a gun in your bag?"

"No."

"Fine thing."

"I'm sorry..."

"Stay here," I muttered impatiently. "I'll go meet him. Maybe he hasn't been filled in on me. He might not have sense enough to duck."

I walked away from her and started off the jetty to the breakwater. The sun was overhead, stark and broiling, and I moved with no shadow. I didn't run, I walked. I wasn't sure how I could head him off, but I preferred to face him alone. He didn't seem to be carrying a gun out on the breakwater. Not in his hand.

It was three or four minutes before we were close enough to size each other up. We kept moving toward each other. The marsh stretched out on either side, lonely and desolate.

He carried a dark green raincoat over one arm and the pith helmet was tipped back jauntily against the oppressive noon heat. His nose was prominent but thin, and his face had a parboiled color as though it had simmered for years in the tropics without ever tanning. His eyes swept over me in a critical glance. He walked with the self-assurance of an Englishman down to his last quid, but about to make a killing. He continued his stride, resting the Malacca cane idly against his shoulder.

I stopped in front of him, blocking the way.

"Got a match?" I muttered.

His eyes settled resentfully on me. "That's a hoary one, commissioner. Very old, it is."

"I'm new at the game."

"Step aside, commissioner."

"Where do you think you're going?" I said. "Fishing?"

The cane dropped from his shoulder. "Say now, if you're looking for a bit of trouble, I suppose I can accommodate you."

"Lately trouble just keeps coming my way. Tell Fry he's too damn accommodating to suit me."

"I'll tell him, commissioner."

"Now get the hell off the breakwater and hide somewhere so I can't find you. Go back to the hotel. I won't look there."

I watched the cane, but he didn't seem ready to let it fly. "You frighten a man, you do. I wouldn't want to go anywhere without the young lady, would I?"

"I don't think she'd like your company."

"Oh, I'm a real lady's man, commissioner."

"Blow," I said. "Get going, or swing that cane. I hate to beat up on a guy unless he asks for it."

His lips, chapped and flaking, parted in a grin. "Say, now, you're a decent one, you are. You wouldn't be the chap that was asking questions of that rummy in the hotel? For a fact, I haven't been told where you fit in the picture."

"Next time you see Fry, ask him."

"Fair enough, commissioner."

I watched his hand and saw that he wasn't going to swing the cane. He moved back idly, twisting it near the head—but I didn't wait for the weapon to show. I stepped in and threw a fist that caught him smack on the ear. He staggered to one side, to a thin knee, but by that time he had the cane apart.

The knife was more like an ice pick—a long, flashing spike.

He rolled his head against the ringing I must have set up in his ear. The helmet had tumbled off and his hair was sticky with perspiration. He flung the raincoat off his arm and rose slowly, his eyes steady on me. He took his time. He knew I wasn't going to rush him, not with that spike waiting to impale me.

"I didn't like that, commissioner. Not a bit, I didn't."

My pulse was beating fast. The spike looked at least nine inches long and I had a feeling he knew how to use it. The grin was coming back to his face; he felt in command again. "Sorry," I muttered. "Sorry I didn't knock you all the way into the swamp."

We stood about four feet apart and he began to circle around me. He kept his back hunched and the grin grew wider. I moved, my muscles rigid, waiting for him to spring. In a moment I was facing the jetty and I saw that Nicole was coming toward us.

"What are you waiting for?" I snapped.

"Don't like to kill a man, I don't." He smiled. "Takes a bit of extra courage. If you were smart, commissioner, you'd run while you had the chance."

His raincoat was almost at my feet now.

"Jeff!"

His eyes flicked toward Nicole, less than a hundred yards away.

I bent quickly and straightened with the raincoat in my hands. He lunged on instinct and the spike ripped through the material near my arm. It vanished instantly for another thrust. I shot the coat high over his face, got to one side and the spike appeared again. But this time my hands locked on his wrist and I snapped it back. He threw off the raincoat and thrashed at me with his left forearm, his breath coming very fast. I stayed with the wrist until his fingers opened and the spike with the mottled rattan handle dropped free. Then I kicked it away, let go of his wrist and stood back.

"Grin now, you bastard."

He flung his good hand and I smacked him on the jaw. He went down. He went out.

Nicole stopped running as she saw it. She reached me a moment later, her face flushed. "Jeff, I thought he'd kill you."

He was face down. I turned him over. "Take a look at him," I muttered. "Mean anything to you?"

She looked. "No... nothing. I've never seen him before."

"I'm not too damned sure he's one of Fry's men. I don't think he really wanted to use that spike on me. He must have hoped I'd just scare off. Not cold-blooded enough for one of Fry's water boys. Sure you don't know the guy?"

She was very sure. O.K., I let it go.

I picked up the spike and tossed it as far as I could into the marsh. I left him the rest of the Malacca cane. In case he wanted to go fishing when he woke up.

My taxi was still waiting in front of the hotel, and so was the driver. He was asleep.

I turned to Nicole. "Did you leave anything in the hotel you want to take?"

"Yes. Wait here, Jeff."

She had fixed the big hat on her head and started into the hotel lobby. I stood on the sidewalk for an uneasy moment, and then went after her.

"Hold it, Nicole," I said. "You could be thinking of running out on me?"

She faced me and lifted an eyebrow in amusement. "I suppose I thought of it."

"Well?"

"If you don't trust me you'd better come with me."

I came along. The rummy Dutchman had vanished from the lobby and the only sound was the lazy buzz of flies. We climbed a flight of wooden stairs and turned down a wide hall that reeked of fresh furniture polish.

"Shall we hurry it up?" I said.

"I'll only be a second," she muttered when we reached her door. "Mind waiting out here?"

"I'm coming in."

She gave me an uncomfortable look, hesitating, and then shrugged her shoulders. I followed her through the door.

It was a large room with a plank floor and no carpet. The jalousies had been almost closed against the morning sun, but the walls were nevertheless streaked with light. There was obviously no connecting bath, and I suppose the first thing I noticed was the towel rack over the washstand. It was hung with a pair of hose, a bra and panties, and she headed for them. She felt them and they had dried.

"Do you mind turning your back?" she muttered. "There's not much privacy in here."

If she was really embarrassed she wasn't going to show it, and I was glad for that. But I saw that I had had more brass than sense in forcing my way along. All she had come up here for was to get her underthings, and she had a right to her privacy.

"I'll wait in the hall," I said.

"Just turn around and face the door." It was her cold, businesslike tone again.

I saw her move toward the jalousies and then I faced the door. I felt awkward and maybe a little amused, and I decided she felt that way too.

The brass doorknob caught my eye because it threw off a polished sheen. My first thought was an idle one—the management was Dutch, and old as the hotel was, you had to hand it to the Dutch. They knew how to keep a place clean, even in the tropics.

Then I saw Nicole's reflection in the doorknob. It was a small, convex image in brass. It occurred to me to look away. I tried.

Nicole's voice came to me. "I wish you'd tell me something about yourself. I really know nothing about you at all, Jeff."

My eyes were lured to the doorknob. Nicole's back was toward mine. "As the saying goes," I said absently, "there's not much to tell. I was a depression graduate. I had majored in geology at school but when I got out I couldn't get a job in my line. Ended up on a freighter in the black gang. I jumped ship in Hong Kong and have been knocking around this part of the world ever since. I managed to find time to bone up on oil geology and made some dough at it. And spent it. But I had a good time. No regrets."

In the doorknob, her back looked smooth and evenly tanned and entirely lovely. I kept from staring at the brass reflection, but I couldn't keep from glancing at it. There was something about her both fragile and strong, independent and weak, charming and frightening. As I caught those fragmentary glimpses I knew how much I wanted her, a strong, impulsive craving of the flesh. At the same time I felt cheap for watching, like an adolescent at a keyhole. I turned. She was just buttoning the dress under her chin.

I walked toward her, and she half turned with surprise. I took her shoulders in my hands and kissed her neck.

"I've been watching," I said. "It was impossible not to. You're very lovely, Nicole."

She pulled away. She wasn't amused. Her eyes stared into mine, her expression calm and poised. Then she slapped me.

"Don't get any ideas," she said crisply. She glanced around the room, as though there might be something else she would want to take, but apparently there was nothing else. "We'd better go."

The sting on my cheek passed and left a smile on my face. I felt better for the slap. I had acted boorishly, and she had acted with self-respect. The kid had class.

"Sure," I said. "Let's be on our way. That Englishman isn't going to sleep out on the breakwater forever. Is that all you came for?"

"Yes."

"You travel light."

"Not usually. This time, yes."

I opened the jalousies and sunlight flooded into the room.

"Look, I'm sorry about barging in."

"I'll bet."

"But I'm not sorry for what I saw. I warned you, didn't I? I may fall in love with you." I stepped onto the second-story veranda and checked the street. My taxi was still waiting.

"Don't," she muttered.

"Don't what?"

"Fall in love with me. Don't you think we'd better hurry?"

I was looking down at the movement in the street below, and I felt a sudden prickling at my neck. Near the taxi I saw three Balinese, all haphazardly dressed Western style. I recognized one of them.

"Hold it, baby," I muttered.

He had angular, copperish cheekbones and glossy black hair that must have been soaked in coconut oil. I had seen him in Buleléng with Apollo Fry when they had almost trapped me in the market place.

"Jeff—"

"Relax. It's only a couple of Fry's native boys down here."

I heard the breath escape her lips. We looked at each other, and I saw suddenly how tired and discouraged she was. "I have a feeling my luck is running out, Jeff."

"Don't kid yourself and don't try to kid me." I looked down at the street again. Two of the natives separated from the third and entered the hotel lobby. The odd man began rolling a cigarette and leaned against the fender of the taxi to wait. I turned back to Nicole. "Is there a back stairway?"

She shook her head. "No."

"What a fire trap. Well, we'll get by without one." I crossed the room and locked the hall door. That would stall them for a little while, and we would need to stall them. Then I caught Nicole's hand and took her out onto the veranda, and locked that door after us. I figured the two natives must be halfway up the front stairway by now. "Remind me to buy a gun, will you? I'm getting goddamned tired of running away every time one of Fry's men shows up."

I looked around for an easy way out of this, but there was none. The length of the veranda was separated by rusted iron grilles, like hurdles, providing the balcony of each room with some measure of privacy. The sun beat down out of a clear, hot sky and the white reflection from the walls of the building made your eyes ache. "Come on," I said. "We'll have to go over a couple of these grilles."

Each balcony had its weather-beaten siesta chairs. I pulled off the only pillow on the one beside us and fixed it quickly over the spikes of the grille. Then I cupped my hands and Nicole got the idea. She put one foot in them and I boosted her over and the pillow protected her. She came down on the other side with some loss of dignity, but she was game. I thought I heard a knock at the hall door. I grabbed a couple of bars of the grille, worked my body onto the pillow and dropped down beside Nicole. I tried the door to the adjoining room, but it was locked and I didn't want to make the noise it would take to bust it.

"Not one more?" Nicole muttered dismally.

"One more."

With the pillow over the sharp spike ends, I got her over into the next section and then I came over. I tried the veranda doors, and they opened.

There was someone inside, but I didn't let that stop us. I took Nicole's hand and pulled her after me.

He stood beside the bed with a glass of water in his hand; he was sprinkling the sheets for a slightly cooler siesta. He was a big man in nothing but a pair of oldfashioned BVD's. He didn't flick an eye at our entry. If anything, he seemed quickly delighted to have some company.

"*Tabé.*" He smiled. "*Tabé,* as they say in this blessed island. *Tabé.*"

"Sorry to intrude," I said quickly, walking to the hall door of his room. "We'll only be a moment."

He put down the water glass and sat heavily on the edge of the bed, and for a moment I thought he must be drunk. He was a European with a heavy mustache and a Mediterranean cast to his eyes. "Nonsense," he said. "I'm about to engage in a local custom, the chewing of betel nut, delightfully sprinkled with lime and wrapped in *sirih* leaves. Have you tried it, my young friends? You must stay, and I'll show you how. One must be instructed in these things, and you will find me an expert." He propped pillows behind his back and reached for a small pouch of woven pandanus beside the bed. I tried to ignore him, unlocked his door and moved it open a crack. Nicole stayed close to me.

"Now if I let you stay," the old man began to babble, "you mustn't ask my name. I am one of the nameless these days."

"Sure," I said absently. I glanced through the crack and saw the two native boys stalled two doors down the hall and muttering to each other. They were apparently undecided whether or not to break in.

The old man started himself on a talking jag. "Would you believe it, there was a time when I was the favorite of the croupiers at Nice and Monte Carlo and San Remo? I left the largest tips, you know. You mustn't ask my name—promise me that?" There was a certain agony that rose in his voice, and I couldn't help turning and nodding to relieve his doubts. Then I whispered to Nicole, "They're trying to break down your door."

"What a beautiful green nut this is," the voice beside us exploded with sudden delight. "The betel palm is certainly to be worshiped, you must agree? It makes so many of us so wonderfully happy and it is so cheap, you know. You see, we dab on the lime and then come the *sirih* leaves—here— like this—aren't you watching?"

I took Nicole's hand. The native boys had sprung the lock on the door and were entering the room. I heard the door shut after them. "Come on."

The old man sat upright on the bed. "You mustn't leave me. I won't have it."

We got into the hall and moved quickly past the closed door of Nicole's room to the head of the stairs. Nicole gripped my hand tightly, and I liked the feel of it in mine.

We went down the stairs as quickly and quietly as we could. At the bottom, Nicole gave me a smile. "You're good to have around, Jeff."

"We're not quite out of this yet."

We started across the lobby and I told her to lag behind.

The guy on the fender of the taxi looked up when I came out of the hotel. My face meant nothing to him, which made it easier. I opened the back door of the taxi and he roused from the fender. Then I moved in front of him, pulled him up by his shirt and shoved him into the back seat. He began to yell, so I had to hit him. Nicole didn't need a cue. She came out of the lobby quickly and stepped into the taxi. I told the driver to get out of here and fast. He smelled a big tip, grinned, and went into action.

He made a honking U-turn in the middle of the street. I glanced toward the breakwater and saw that the Englishman had come to and was loping shoreward. In another few moments we were out of town.

I shook down Fry's native, but he didn't have a gun. He carried a knife and I didn't want it. I told the driver to slow down, opened the door and booted the native out. He seemed happy to leave. Then I told the driver to head for Sanur.

"How am I doing?" I smiled.

Nicole didn't answer, but she smiled back. Then she asked, "Sanur?"

"My passport," I said. "I left it in Sanur."

"Regina Williams lives in Sanur."

"I know."

"You've met her?"

"Nice kid. Just completely crazy, that's all."

"Crazy—and dangerous."

I gave her a long glance. "What do you know about her?"

"Did she make a play for you?"

"Does that matter?"

Nicole got out her cigarettes, remembered I was out and offered me one. We lit up, but I began to feel uncomfortable the way she was looking at me. "You seem to have gotten around since I met you yesterday, Jeff."

"Yes, I've gotten around."

"I wish you hadn't."

"Jealous?"

"Worried."

"I think we're going to make out fine."

We kept our voices low against the rattling of the taxi, the yelp of dogs infesting the road and the compulsive honking of the Balinese at the wheel. I looked at my watch. Almost one o'clock. I felt vaguely crowded for time. The passport business could delay me, and there might be trouble at the airport. I'd have to work fast.

"Must I go to Sanur?" Nicole muttered seriously.

"I'm going to need you. But you won't be seen—I'll leave you in the car."

She shrugged unhappily and slipped down in the seat, the hat in her lap. "I'm not used to letting someone else do my thinking for me. It might take a little while to get used to it, Jeff."

"Keep trying. Once we're on the plane I'll resign my command."

"I'll keep trying." She watched me and I felt I was being sized up and I didn't like it. She was playing along with me, because there didn't seem anything else for her to do, but she hadn't surrendered. I was a creature of her own intrigue, and now I had come back to take over. She wasn't going to be easy to take over. Period.

"The stuff you wrote on the card," I said. "Russian, wasn't it?"

"Yes."

"Give me a translation."

The earrings murmured. "No, Jeff."

"Look, baby—"

"Jeff, these people play for keeps. I don't want to sign your death warrant."

I flicked my cigarette out the window. "Noble women give me a royal pain."

"I'm not trying to be noble. You shouldn't be mixed up in this thing. I'm sorry I got you into it. I didn't think—"

"You told me gunrunning," I cut in. "I can't keep fighting in the dark. I've got to know more, and never mind the death warrant business. Fry might be gunning for me right now, although there's a chance he's figured out it would only be a waste of good ammunition. But if I'm going to get a belly full of lead I want to have a head full of facts to go with it. And if I run into trouble in Sanur, I want something to work with. What about Regina Williams? Where the hell does she fit in?"

"Please, Jeff."

"Talk, baby. Talk."

The road followed a wide bay with a muddy, mangrove shore line. Nicole was a long time answering, but she answered. "Regina Williams is buying guns."

"Why?"

"I don't know. But she's buying them. That's what brought Fry to Bali."

"He's selling and she's buying."

"Yes."

"I figure the Scrap Metals Export Company for a blind. But it doesn't fit—your being Fry's partner."

"I know."

"Well?"

She glanced at me with uneasy eyes. "It fits, but not the way it must look to you. Until a couple of months ago I'd never heard of Fry, and I'm sure he didn't know I existed. Must we go into all this?"

"I want to know everything."

She chain-lit another cigarette and exhaled slowly. "I had an uncle in Singapore whose name was Modeste, believe it or not. He was quite a guy, but I guess no one thought so but me. He had had three wives, all Malay women. He was generally drunk and for all I know he used opium. But in his own way, I think he was honest."

"With a name like Modeste Balashov, I guess he had to be."

"Anyway, despite three wives, he had no kids. I was working in a night club in Hong Kong last August when I got word that he was dead and had named me in his will. I inherited a half interest in the Scrap Metals Export Company. He and Fry had organized the firm on a shoestring just after the war. So I went down to Singapore to see what I had inherited."

"I'll bet that made Fry happy."

"He tried hard to buy me out—too hard. I got angry and made up my mind to stick. I was tired of dancing for drunks in little tourist traps, and getting pinched by tinhorn impresarios in my dressing room. I wanted a change."

"I should have guessed you were a dancer," I said. "But I kept thinking of you as some sort of *femme fatale*."

She wasn't amused. "Fry tolerated me, like a bad cold. It didn't take me long to suspect that something was going on behind the name of the company. To begin with, I found out how my uncle had died."

"Murder?"

"I can't make up my mind. They were unloading scrap metal from a ship at the company wharf and he had wandered drunk under one of the cranes as it dropped a load. It must have been horrible. But it could have been an accident."

"Or it could have been set up to look like one."

"I know. I can't believe my uncle was using the company as a blind to sell illegal guns. It wasn't like him. But I think Fry was. I think my uncle may have found out toward the end what was going on behind his back, and Fry killed him."

I nodded. I was willing to believe anything about Fry, as long as it was unfavorable.

"Well— I decided to put on an act," Nicole went on softly. "I made a play for Fry, and it was easy. I think at first I frightened him a little; he's afraid of women. He knows he's fat and unattractive, and instead of chasing women he's chased power and money. I flattered his taste in clothes, I always had a smile for him and convinced him he wasn't fat at all—just husky. It took me a month to bring him to a boil. Then I told him frankly I thought there was something fishy going on in the company, but I didn't care as long as there was money in it. From there on out, we got along fine and he started breaking me in. There was a terrific market for guns in Indo-China, the Malay States, Java. He talked of marriage, and I let him. And when he said there was some business coming up in Bali, I talked him into taking me along."

"How did he get wise to what you were up to?"

She toyed with the hat on her lap. "I'm going to have to pass that up, Jeff. Sorry."

"If it's important, I want to know."

"It's important, but none of your business."

Her eyes flashed up stubbornly; I had obviously touched a sensitive nerve in her story. I shrugged my shoulders and decided to let it go for the time being. "All right, he found out somehow and you decided it was time to take off. You ended up listed as dead with your picture in the paper. Want to tell me about that?"

She took a small breath, and nodded. "I'd rented a car. I was driving near Tabanan on my way north from Den Pasar when I passed a body lying beside the road. A woman. It was very early in the morning and there wasn't any traffic yet. It gave me a terrible shock, seeing her there, and I couldn't make myself stop. I'd heard that the terrorists like to strip the skin from the faces of their victims—especially whites. But after a mile or so, I turned back. She offered a way out for me."

"Sure."

"She was face down. I turned her over. It was hideous."

"Never mind those details."

"The guerrillas had left nothing to identify this woman, not even her clothes. I had hurriedly packed only one suitcase in the hotel, an overnight bag. I got it out of the car and ripped some of my things and scattered them around."

"Switch."

"Yes. Fry knew what clothes I had along. If he thought I had been killed by terrorists I felt I had a chance of getting off the island alive. I abandoned the car on the spot. Eventually I got a bus to Singaradja and checked into a small hotel. I bought a pair of scissors and trimmed my hair very short. I hoped it would change my appearance, but it didn't change it very much."

"Where did the newspaper get a picture of you?"

"Fry. He carried one. I don't know why he let them use it. He wasn't really fooled."

"Maybe he hoped to convince you your trick had worked so you'd drop your guard."

She nodded. We had the windows wide open, but it didn't do much good. The breeze was warm and sticky, and we sat beside each other in the clammy grip of perspiration. The hottest hours of the day had started, and I wished it would rain, but the clouds had gone and left the sun with a clear, merciless sky.

I asked, "Why didn't you head for the airport?"

"I'd checked. There wasn't a flight scheduled until today. But I found out that a freighter was due in Buleléng yesterday, and decided to head for it."

"That would be the *Timor Lady.*"

"Yes." She glanced out the window. We couldn't be far from Den Pasar, and it made her visibly uncomfortable. "I kept out of sight until yesterday noon, and then checked into that hotel overlooking the water front in Buleléng. About the time the freighter came in, Fry showed up."

"Enter Jeff Cape."

"And you. I knew Fry meant to kill me. The idea was a little new to me then, but I've gotten sort of used to it. See—my hands don't even shake any more."

She held them out and forced an uneasy smile.

"You're doing fine, baby."

"I guess you know the rest. I watched you come ashore."

"And got ideas."

"It was a way out. I condensed what I knew about Fry on the back of that card."

"In Russian, so I couldn't read it."

"I didn't think I'd be getting you involved—really involved like this. It seemed worth trying at the time. Did I apologize, Jeff?"

"Sure, but go ahead and apologize again. I like to hear you apologize."

"Sorry."

"What did you figure—if I got that information to American intelligence it wouldn't matter too much if Fry got you and killed you?"

She glanced at me as though I were crazy, and shook her head. "Sorry to disappoint you, Jeff. I'm just not the type who's willing to die for a cause. I wanted to get out of this alive. I still do. All I hoped to do was double the chances of exposing Fry before he does any more damage in this part of the world. I didn't really consider losing my life in the process."

"All right. What about that Chinese—Mr. Chu?"

There was a moment's hesitation, a little catch in her voice when she answered. "Mr. Chu? I don't know him."

"You're lying."

"Am I Jeff?"

I saw that she was going to hold out, and turned away. "All right, let it go. Got another cigarette?"

She had left one hole in her story, and maybe Chu fitted into it. I put my fists in my pockets and stretched my legs. Well, she had talked. For a moment she gave me the illusion that I was learning things, getting an inside look. But there was more. There had to be more. I still felt on the outside of the affair, still trying to look in, and I felt a little cheated. I glanced at Nicole beside me, but her eyes avoided mine as she offered me a cigarette.

For a moment I thought I was getting to know this kid, but now I felt I didn't know her at all, and it made me angry.

It would be easy to hate her, I decided. Or fall in love with her.

Take your pick, Jefferson Cape.

I bent forward and told the driver to stay out of the center of Den Pasar, when we got there, but catch the Sanur road from the side streets. He said it was only a couple of kilometers farther.

"Tuan," he added with a grin. "It is possible we are being followed." He pointed a brown finger toward the rear view mirror.

I turned quickly and looked behind us. We had just passed a lumbering ox-cart piled high with copra, but behind that a black touring car was gaining on us. Fry's car. It was easy to recognize, with its battered fenders. Those damned native boys of his had gotten wise fast.

I turned back to the driver. "All right. Step on it."

He stepped on it until the rambling roofs of Den Pasar came into view far up ahead. Then a faint popping sound reached us. I thought at first those guys must be shooting at us, and the driver pulled his foot off the accelerator. But they weren't gun shots. The explosions went off in rapid strings, and I knew they were firecrackers. The taxi began to coast.

"Get this crate moving again!"

"Look, tuan."

I looked. Up ahead the road was swollen with natives, like a drunken army, swarming and yelling, and coming in our direction. Great wooden cows and bulls and elephant-like animals, brightly painted and heavily ornamented, were carried over the heads of the swarm. Firecrackers pocked the air more loudly now as the wild procession pressed down the road like a human tidal wave, blocking our way.

Nicole caught my arm. "It's a funeral, Jeff."

I glanced quickly behind. Fry's car was gaining. "It may be ours unless we get through it."

The driver pulled along the side of the road, and I yelled at him to try to honk his way through, but he wasn't interested. "What a fine cremation so many *patulangan* will make, tuan. It is the first funeral in many months, and there are many dead saved for the fire of the *balé pabasinian*. See, I count nine already, nine coffins—the animals, tuan. That is where the bodies are."

The wooden animals were swirled above the heads of the mob, and the yelling and laughter mixed with the clash of native instruments and the chatter of firecrackers into a swelling pandemonium. I got out some money and tossed it into the front seat. I caught Nicole's hand and opened our door.

"See how they twirl the animals, tuan, to confuse the dead so they cannot find their way home again." The driver had lost interest in us, and sat transfixed by the pageantry. "Ah, there are the priests. Watch the *baris* dancers. See...."

Nicole held back, and her face was white. "Jeff, I can't. Mobs terrify me. Jeff—"

I pulled her off the seat. She had to come. The half-naked spear carriers, yelling and gesturing against evil spirits they seemed to see, reached us like a crack of lightning bringing a storm. Before I could push the door open wide, the mob engulfed us in a torrent of brown bodies and open mouths. I had gotten one last glance behind and saw Fry's car pulling up about a hundred yards behind in the path of the spear carriers and musicians.

I pressed the door open against the natives swirling about the taxi and pulled Nicole after me. She came, stifling her fright and hardly breathing. Her first hesitation had made me angry, and she knew it. She came with me without resisting.

A string of firecrackers went off almost in our faces and I pulled her to me. When a moment had passed I took a firm grip on her wrist and started edging into the flow of bodies, pushing against it in an attempt to clear a path through the crowd.

The human noises were deafening and the bare feet that thundered about us raised a cloud of dust that wanted to suffocate you under the burning sun. The bright sarongs and naked chests and backs eddied in mock fights around the animal coffins carried along above the procession. The tide surged, and I fought our way into it, threading, pushing and shoving.

Flags and banners on long bamboos flailed the air and we were almost drawn apart. "Stick with it, baby," I yelled, tightening my grip on Nicole's wrist. She couldn't have heard my voice through the din, but she saw my lips move reassuringly. Her nostrils flared with each quick breath and I knew I had to get her out of this.

And then I caught a glimpse of him not far behind: Fry's native trigger boy with the oily hair. He had followed us into the mob. He had a gun in his hand high above his head, but he was being buffeted about and couldn't have taken a pot shot if he had wanted to.

A high priest riding on a bamboo platform bore down on us like a raft on a river of hands. I forced Nicole aside as he passed, sitting imperiously above the mob, strings of shell beads hanging from his ears and neck. We caught his unwilling attention and he watched us with dour eyes, refolding his fingers with their three-inch fingernails. And then he was gone, coming between us and Fry's native.

I tried to move faster and discovered I was yelling as loudly as those around me, only I was swearing. We came into an area of women carrying what I took to be effigies of the dead and for a moment the excitement seemed to ebb and we made our way more quickly. The faces were smiling and the lips were chattering.

Nicole stumbled and I pulled her up against me. We were both breathing heavily.

"Keep a grip on yourself, baby!" I shouted into her ear.

"I'm trying, Jeff."

The tide began to drag us back, and I saw that Fry's boy had managed to cut in more closely. I saw his face and he had begun to grin.

"Come on, baby!"

We pressed forward through the gaiety and disorder. The wooden animals were all behind us now, but tall pagoda-like cremation towers loomed up ahead of us, swaying crazily and sparkling with mirrors and tinsel. Nicole moved with me like an automaton, but she moved and that's what counted. Boys had climbed along the sides of the towers and clung there laughing and yelling to the others below. I pulled aside to let the first go by on the shoulders of a couple of dozen Balinese supporting it with a common yoke of crossed bamboo. We were already on the outskirts of Den Pasar and I saw other Balinese standing on the walls outside their homes watching the procession.

But Fry's native stayed after us and closed in and I knew it was no use. He carried the gun high to keep it free, but no one around was alarmed by the sight of it. Maybe they thought he only meant to fire blanks to add to the fun.

I stopped and spoke into Nicole's ear. "Hang on. I'm going after that guy."

I got her behind me and wrapped her arms around my stomach so that we wouldn't be separated. She gripped me tightly, almost hysterically, and I imagined her hanging on with her eyes shut.

I stopped fighting against the current and let ourselves be carried back. An old man trying to get a sip of wine out of a bamboo tube came in front of me, and beyond him I saw Fry's boy. The old man worked his way out from between us and our bodies were pressed together.

I caught his gun hand before he could lower it, and I saw his fleshy lips curl. We struggled for the gun as the throng carried us with it. I got his wrist bent back, and then the gun exploded into the sky. I wished those around us would scatter to give me room, but if they heard the shot they ignored it, pressing our wet bodies more tightly together. I could feel his breath on my neck, and I could smell the rancid coconut oil in his hair.

He held on. Maybe his two buddies were close behind and he hoped they would catch up. If they were around they weren't catching up in time. He saw that I was getting the gun, twisted himself and tossed it free. It fell into the crowd like a pebble in a torrent.

A shadow kept swaying over us, and I knew we had gotten in the path of a cremation tower. If I stumbled with Nicole on my back I knew the carry natives locked together in the giant bamboo yoke couldn't avoid trampling us. I tried to work to one side, but Fry's boy was going wild, clawing my face and trying to bite me. I shoved his face back but couldn't get elbow room for a poke. Did the Balinese around us think this was only another mock fight, part of the elaborate ritual of the cortege? My insides were torn apart by anger and frustration.

Suddenly I felt Nicole's arms gone from my stomach. A rip tide of movement had caught us as the cremation tower bore down, twisting and dipping in the sun. I saw cold terror on Nicole's face as she was pulled from me, and I reached out for her. But Fry's gunman clawed his fingers over my eyes, trying to dig in, and I couldn't shake him. Nicole was buffeted beyond reach in a flash.

I brought my hand high and sliced it down in a desperate clip to the side of his neck. I gave it everything I had, and it took. His body went lax and his legs went out from under him. I didn't have time to worry about him in the path of the cremation tower. I jostled myself out of the way, off to one side, in the direction Nicole had been carried.

For a moment the tower swayed over me, silks and tinsel dipping down and brushing my head. As it righted itself I thought I heard the yells of the lead men in the yoke. Maybe they had come upon Fry's man at their feet, but the unit of dozens of natives locked together had a relentless flow, and they would be forced to trample him.

I caught sight of Nicole, and tried to put the grisly scene out of my mind. I worked like a madman to get to her, and I got to her.

"Baby, baby!"

There was a hopeless pleading in her eyes when she saw me. Her lips trembled and her face was streaked with dusty perspiration.

A shadow passed and then, like the unraveled ends of a scarf, the procession thinned to natives ceremoniously carrying ropes from the last tower. A few old people who couldn't keep up. Dogs. The funeral had passed us by.

We stood there in each other's arms, the clash and clamor moving down the road.

"Jeff—"

"It's all over. Get a grip on yourself."

"I tried, Jeff. I—"

"Sure you did. You need a drink."

I made her start walking, and stopped worrying about the other two men that had made up Fry's native trio. Maybe they were still trying to fight their way through the mob.

Balinese got down from their compound walls now that the funeral had passed. I looked back once and saw the body in the road. Dogs were already beginning to nose around it.

We found a public fountain up ahead and rinsed our faces.

"Feel better?" I muttered.

She took a breath. "Feeling better."

"That took a lot of courage for you, Nicole. We'll make out."

"It's silly to be afraid, isn't it, Jeff? But I couldn't help it. I tried not to be afraid."

"Forget it."

Fresh water dripped off her chin and the tip of her nose, sparkling in the sun as it fell. "I was in Calcutta during the anti-British riots a few years ago. Since then native mobs—" She shivered at the memory.

"Sure."

She shrugged her shoulders and tried to pass the whole thing off with a smile. "I'll be all right, Jeff. Shall we go?"

I lifted her chin, looking at her, and then I kissed her forehead and her lips. The cold water on our faces ran together. Her arms came up behind my back and I felt her raise herself on her toes. She kissed me hard, and it sent my blood rushing. The sun beat down, drying our faces.

"Oh, Jeff," she whispered. "Darling."

A car honked a few feet from us. When we turned I saw that our taxi had pulled up, and the driver was grinning like a child.

We got in, and I told him to take us someplace where we could get a drink.

"A mighty funeral, yes, tuan? I counted every *patulangan*. What a fire they will make. Seventeen corpses, tuan."

"Eighteen," I muttered, turning for a last glimpse behind.

Chapter Nine

We passed a cemetery, crowded with weeds and bamboo altars, on the outskirts of Sanur. Up ahead, in the town square, a lone banyan tree hovered like a shimmering green cloud over the little shops, the brown walls and thatched roofs of the town. We stopped only long enough to get our directions to Regina Williams' place. Everyone seemed to know it, about two kilometers on the road going north.

I turned to Nicole. "Write out something on the back of a card—anything. Put it in Russian."

She didn't question me. She opened her bag, found her pen and did what I asked. I waved the card and looked at the face.

"You always carry around Fry's business cards?"

She shrugged her shoulder. "There's no law against it."

It didn't seem important. I rolled up the card and stuck it in my shoe. "Give me about fifteen minutes," I said. "Drive anywhere, and come back in fifteen minutes. It shouldn't take me any longer than that. If I don't show, try in another ten minutes. If I *still* don't show, head for the airport. I'll try to meet you there. Park out of danger, and I'll keep an eye out for the cab. But if I get tied up over this damned passport of mine, don't miss that plane. Even if Fry or his boys are hanging around, get aboard. *Find* a way."

She seemed somehow reassured. She nodded. She'd find a way, if it came to that.

The road was banked with palms, tall and still in the afternoon heat. After a moment I could make out the walls and roof of the Williams' place up ahead on the left. I told the driver to stop. I'd walk the rest of the way.

Nicole watched me get out. We might have wished each other luck, but we didn't. I told the driver to turn around and kill time on a side road. I hung around until they were gone. I looked at my watch. It was a little after one.

I walked. Overhead, a hawk was reconnoitering in lazy circles. I cut through the trees and reached the compound wall near the garage. Regina's Buick was sitting out in front of the garage, and a red-freckled gecko was sunning itself on the hood. Mr. Chu's car was gone, and I figured I was in luck.

I climbed over the wall. The lizard reared its head in alarm. *Gecko! Gecko!* I moved around to the front of the house and up the veranda steps. I knocked and waited. The scent of citronella grass hung in the air, but it didn't keep the mosquitoes away. I stood there waiting and slapped one on my neck.

I knocked again. It was siesta time and I knocked hard enough to wake an army. Finally I tried the door. It was open. A tightness developed in my stomach muscles. I wished suddenly that I had a gun, but I didn't and that was that. I walked in.

Regina Williams was at home.

She lay face down on the rattan mat where she had danced for me the night before. Her back was arched, animal-like, one arm outstretched, the fingers clawing. She was still wearing my jacket.

I bent down to her and tried to reject the consciousness of death in the room. I turned her over, and it was like lifting a stone and exposing fiery red ants. Beneath her, the mat was drinking up the blood. She had been shot very accurately in the heart.

It was a moment before I could do anything but fight back a quick surge of nausea. Then an icy fear gripped me. I unbuttoned the jacket and felt the inside pocket for my passport. It was there. The lining of the coat was scarlet and I hesitated to reach into the sodden pocket. I forced my fingers in there and withdrew the passport. The cover and edges were gummy with blood, and I saw that the bullet had cut through it.

I was in trouble, and I knew it. I could be connected to this murder, maybe even charged with it. I glanced quickly at my watch. Nicole would be coming by in less than ten minutes. I had to get rid of the physical evidence that Jefferson Cape had ever called on Regina Williams.

I slipped her arms out of the sleeves of my coat, and balled it up. I hated to leave her half-naked, even though that was the way she went around. But I had to get rid of the coat, and I had to get that blood off my passport. It would be hard enough to avoid curiosity among the customs men with only the bullet hole.

I went into the bathroom and filled the basin with cold water. I immersed my passport, washed it and kept changing the water. It took a couple of minutes before the pink traces were gone. I'd gotten caught in the rain, I'd say. I'd gotten soaked.

I looked around for something to put my coat in. I found some newspapers stacked in the pantry, wrapped up my coat and tied it into a tight bundle. Then I went back into the living room.

Fingerprints.

I went back into the bathroom and wiped off the faucet handles. What else had I touched? The door.

I got that over with and threw the towel in the hamper. I had seen a ceremonial batik hanging on the wall of Regina's bedroom. I got it down and returned to the living room and covered her with it. I looked at my watch.

I'd better get out of here. This was between Regina and her murderer and the police. I wanted on that plane, I wanted to be a couple of thousand miles away before anyone remembered a guy with a hole in his passport who might be involved.

"Gettin' ready to go somewhere, mister?"

I turned. Apollo Fry was standing in the doorway.

Chapter Ten

His neck was white with salve. The *roode hond,* the prickly heat, had spread even to the fleshy pink hand that held the gun.

He stood there like a mountain, blocking the door. He was hatless and coatless and the holster looped over his shoulder was black with sweat. He looked like he'd been working at something. His face was flushed and streaked with perspiration. His shoes were muddy, and he was gasping like a fish out of water. I wondered if he'd been digging a grave for Regina Williams out in the jungle.

"Hello, Fry," I said.

His eyes, with the doll-like blonde lashes, hardly seemed to blink. He took a step forward and shut the door behind him.

"So you came back," he muttered in that sandpaper voice of his. "Well, you came back just in time, mister."

"You look like you've been out digging."

"A grave. We can make it big enough for two."

"Why don't you get off my back, Fry? All I want is to clear out."

His bald head had lost its waxy sheen under close pebbles of sweat, like clear little blisters. Despite his slow voice and the confidence the gun obviously gave him, I sensed he was keyed up and maybe a little scared. "You shouldn't have come back," he muttered.

"She fixed it that way."

He glanced beyond me, to Regina's body. "Her?" There was a contemptuous edge in his voice. "I told her to let you get away. I didn't tell her to fix it so you'd come back. Tough luck, mister."

"She got ideas of her own. Maybe she didn't trust you. She seemed to think when I got back I'd be ripe for plucking. She didn't know I'd already been plucked. Neither did I."

A wispy vanity touched his lips. "I gave you a chance to clear out. You should have taken it, mister."

"I don't follow you, Fry. You had a chance to kill me last night. Why didn't you take it?"

He gestured with the gun toward Regina's body. "Pick her up," he muttered. "I came in to get her, but as long as you're here you can have the pleasure. It won't be a long walk."

"Why didn't you finish me off last night?"

He straightened his shoulders with a rotating movement, as though they ached. Along the sides of his head, the blonde hair was streaked with red and ended in a curliness behind his ears. His nose was sharp and thin, almost pretty, and a size too small for his face. "You didn't know anything. I figured Miss Balashov had only picked up a sucker. You looked like a sucker to me."

"Never mind what I looked like to you. You must have had some doubts to drop me in Regina Williams' lap."

"Sure, I had doubts. I figured she could find out if you knew anything unhealthy. A woman has ways, doesn't she? Especially, *she* had ways."

"And I'd still be on tap if she didn't give me a clean bill of health."

"She called me this morning. She told me you had walked into this thing backwards. I told her to let you go."

I didn't say it, but I thought it. Regina had lied. I hadn't played it innocent and she knew damned well I was onto part of what was going on. She was convinced I had that report of Nicole's, but maybe she had decided to do some quarterbacking of her own. I looked down at her. It hadn't gotten her very far.

"I still seem to be walking backwards," I said. "Apparently, I have a special talent for it. Let's go back to last night. You found that report in the hem of my handkerchief and switched it with a dummy. I stayed fooled for a long time. Regina Williams died fooled."

His grin was a beefy show of vanity. "I told her to look for it, but I didn't tell her where. I figured she'd take you more seriously if she thought you were carrying something that could blow up in our faces."

He seemed eager to explain his own cleverness, and I knew there was more, but a movement outside on the road caught my eye. The taxi. It went by slowly, and the pressure of time crowded in on me. Ten minutes. Nicole would come by for me again in ten minutes. For the last time.

The gritty voice went on: "I figured you'd take your chance and get off the island with that card in your handkerchief. I wanted you to get far, far away before you discovered the switch. For your own good, mister. Too bad you didn't. Let's get her moved."

I kept the bundle tight under my arm. "If I wasn't worth killing last night, why now?"

"You're not very smart, mister."

"That seems to be an established fact by now."

"You know the lady's been murdered, and I know. But I can keep my mouth shut. I can't depend on you to do the same."

"No, I suppose you can't."

"That's right."

"Why did you kill her?"

"Did I say I did?"

"Just cleaning up someone else's dirty work, I suppose."

"That's right. When we get through, you and I, there won't be any murder. None at all. She's missing, just missing. No real investigation on a missing person. By the time someone starts talking murder, I'll be far, far away—like you could have been if you hadn't come back."

"You'll be surprised how far, far away I can get in a short, short time with my mouth shut."

"Too risky. Roll her in the mat. That's got to be buried too."

He moved forward with the gun, and there seemed nothing for me to do but take orders. I wondered about Madé. Where was he? And Regina Williams had said her husband was due back today. This would be a fine time for him to walk in. This would be a fine time for *anyone* to walk in.

I put down my bundle beside the mat and tried not to see Regina's dead eyes. I pulled the ends of the mat over her as Fry moved closer. My pulse was pounding, but I tried to keep my voice steady.

"Find Miss Balashov?" I asked.

"We'll stop her, mister. Don't worry."

"If I were her I'd head for the airport. There's a plane out of there today."

"She won't get aboard. I got a couple of boys down there."

"That's what I figured. You got lots of boys?"

"Lots."

I tightened up on the mat and worked back around to where I'd left my bundled coat. "Is it going to bother you to shoot me in cold blood?"

"Should it? Let's hurry it up." He stood across Regina's body from me, the gun clamped in his hand. I fooled with the mat at a crouch, and he must have known I was beginning to stall, but it didn't seem to annoy him. I got the feeling he would be sorry to kill me only because it was wasted effort. Regina had cleared me; I shouldn't have come back, and he was sorry. He stood over me, morose and calculating, all fat and prickly heat and no emotion.

"I guess she's ready," I muttered.

"We'll go out the back."

I heaved the coat bundle at his face.

The gun exploded wild, and I dove for his wrist. It was thick and greasy with salve, and he twisted loose from my hands. I spun with a fist on its way and cracked it into his chin. It rocked him, but that was all. He clapped both hands in front of him, the gun between. I saw a pointblank shot coming and kicked. His hands flew up and the shot whistled near my head as I dropped. I was fighting crazy, but I was fighting for my life and I knew it. I butted into him and he stumbled back into a glass coffee table. The glass shattered as he crashed into it, and I went with him. I saw that he still had the gun in one hand, held out at arm's length. I didn't try for it. My hand picked up a shaft of broken glass and I brought it in fast over one of his eyes.

"Drop it!" I shouted.

His breath was in my face. He didn't move a muscle. I had a raw edge of glass not more than a quarter of an inch from his eye, and he was looking at it. The air was mixed with cordite and sour perspiration and salve. Blood was beginning to trickle down the glass where my hand gripped it.

I felt his muscles relax under me. There was a small thud as the gun dropped from his fingers.

"All right," I breathed. I didn't budge the glass from his eye, but I moved my body around slowly until I could reach the gun. Once I had it firmly in my hand, I rose, stepped back and turned it on him. "Get up."

"You know a few tricks, mister."

"Get over to the phone." I tossed the piece of glass I held back into the shambles of the coffee table.

"Calling the police?"

"You'll find out. Get going."

He started walking, brushing himself off, but managed somehow not to look beaten. It made me angry; it wasn't a dignity you could admire—he just didn't know any better. Once he got to the phone, I brought the gun hard into his back.

"I'll kill you," I said. "In cold blood. I didn't think I could kill that way, but right now I could. It would be easy."

"You've made your point."

"Call the operator. Get the number of the airport. What's the name of one of your men there?"

He hesitated, but only as long as it took me to jam the nose of the gun into his back a little harder. "Pico."

"Have Pico called to the phone. Tell him Miss Balashov is in Buleléng and to get up there fast with anyone else hanging around the airport."

It seemed to take forever to get the connection through. I kept glancing out the window for the taxi. But Fry was taking orders and that's all that seemed important at the moment. I stood close enough to the receiver at his ear that I could hear the overtones from the other end, and after another delay I knew Pico was there.

Fry spoke softly and to the point. I stared at the back of his neck, peppered with *roode hond*, the shirt collar limp with sweat. As soon as he hung up I brought the gun butt down hard on his naked skull. His feet held up for a crazy moment and I thought he was going to turn. Then he fell.

I got a grip under his arms and dragged him into the nearest bedroom. I got him in a closet and locked the door. Then I went back to the phone and yanked the wires out of the wall. I didn't want Fry coming to and barking out long-distance orders.

I picked up my bundled coat and wiped my fingerprints off the gun. I left it near Regina's body. It was Fry's and if it had killed her I didn't want to carry it around. Anyway, I wasn't going to need a gun any more. In a couple of hours I'd be in Java.

I looked out the window; all clear. I went out the front way and hurried to the road. I saw the taxi joggling up from the south. I ran along the side of the road and the driver made a U-turn, swinging around in front of me.

I opened the back door and jumped in.

The seat was empty. Nicole was gone.

Chapter Eleven

I slammed the door after me and swore. She'd run out. O.K., she'd run out. I wasn't going to spend the rest of my life playing hide and seek with her. Let her go. She could go to hell. There was a plane out of Bali at 1600 and I was going to be on it. I wanted to be far, far away when they started chasing suspects in Regina Williams' murder. Fry must have seen her lying dead in a man's coat, my coat, and I would have trouble explaining away the hole in my passport. If Fry got in a corner, he could make out a case against me. He had walked in and surprised me. We had fought and I had lit out.

I bent forward to the driver. "Did she leave a message?"

"No, tuan. Only to tell you good luck."

"Where did she get out?"

"Sanur. She use telephone there, tuan. When she come out she tol' me to go back for you."

"Did you see where she went?"

"She tol' me to say nothing, tuan."

"Tell me!"

He shrugged his shoulders indifferently. "Another taxi was in the *alun-alun*. It took her away."

I sat back and tried to think. Somehow I had figured she was alone on the island; yet she had put in a phone call to someone. What the hell was she up to? I had the airport cleared; it would have been a cinch for both of us. Damn her anyway. She had lied, she had put on an act. What had she said?—She was going to like having me around. She was lying in her beautiful white teeth. It was an act, and the little earrings made the background music.

Before we hit the main road I told the driver to stop. I got out with the bundle under my arm.

"Wait here. I'll be right back."

I walked into the trees and kept going until I was far in from the road. Then I ripped creepers and dead leaves off the ground and began to dig. I dug with my fingers. I had hardly begun when I heard laughter nearby. I froze. I got up and picked my way toward the sounds. The trees gave way to vines and giant pandanus, and I heard the gurgle of a brook. The laughter was light and playful and feminine. A moment later I could see them. Three Balinese women were standing knee deep in the brook bathing themselves. They splashed each other and giggled, their skin beaded with water that sparkled in the sun. I turned away and crawled back into the trees. For a moment I got a little panicky. I couldn't find the bundle and the hole I'd started to dig. I stopped, catching my breath, and got a grip on myself. I could still hear the laughter through the trees and I could almost imagine they were laughing at me. I started looking again, came to the spot and dug once more.

It came to me as an afterthought—the driver. He could connect me with Regina Williams' place. Well, I'd have to ride out my chances on him. Maybe Fry would kill him, but I wasn't going to kill people to cover up a murder I hadn't committed. But the driver would remember my going into these trees with a bundle and coming back empty-handed. If the police found this bloodstained coat and connected it with me there'd be hell to pay. Maybe I'd be back in the States by then, but I didn't like the idea of leaving this loose end.

I untied the newspapers and removed my coat. I ripped the label off the lining. It was stiff with blood, but you could still read it: *Wing On's, Shanghai.* I'd bought the suit in '47, but Shanghai seemed a lifetime ago. I buried the coat, drawing the leaves and creepers back over the spot. Then I collected more leaves and tied them up in the newspaper, making a bundle about the same shape as before. Halfway back to the taxi I buried the label. Even if the police somehow discovered the coat, they'd never be able to trace it now.

Once the taxi was in sight I swung the bundle by the string and made sure the driver noticed it. I told him I'd gone into the trees on a call of nature and hoped he'd forget the whole thing.

I got rid of him in Den Pasar and changed to another taxi. I had begun to feel fairly confident about cleaning up the loose ends, but I didn't want the driver to have my entire Balinese career at his finger tips. I didn't want him to be able to tell the cops, if he were asked, that I had taken the four o'clock plane to Jogjakarta.

I reached the airport at three-thirty-five. I paid off the cab and looked around, half expecting to see Nicole waiting. She wasn't. I dropped the bundle of leaves in an ash can and walked into the lobby. Beyond the wire fencing a DC-3 was being gassed up, *Garuda Indonesian Airways* set in a blue strip along the fuselage. My plane.

A few tourists were waiting around with their luggage. I headed for the desk.

"Jefferson Cape," I said. "You're holding a reservation."

A young Balinese was behind the desk. He wore a coat and tie and appeared amazingly cool despite the heat. "Yes." He smiled. "I couldn't have held it much longer."

I felt a vague guilt, as though I were running out on Nicole. I had to remind myself that it was she who had run out on me.

He began making out my ticket. "Passport, please."

I handed it across. "I'm hard on passports." I grinned as naturally as I could. "That one's been through hell and high water with me these last two years."

He smiled. It was wet and it had a hole in it. "Yes. Any baggage?"

"No baggage."

He filled in the blanks with a scratchy pen. "Everyone in Bali seems to want space on that plane. You're lucky."

I stood there looking at that pen scratch along, and my blood ran cold. "Look, would you remember a phone call from a woman about two hours ago? English-speaking?"

"Calling from Sanur? Yes, I took it. She wanted to know if you had a reservation."

"What else?"

"If the plane was full."

"What did you tell her?"

"The last space had been reserved about twenty minutes before she called."

"I see."

"Something wrong, Mr. Cape?"

I glanced out at the plane. They had finished gassing and a grease monkey was getting down off the nose. I needed to get on that plane, but so did Nicole. She had called the airport and found there was only space for one of us. She wasn't going to give me a chance to be chivalrous. She had run out. And I had hated her for it.

The pen scratched along, and it seemed to be the only sound in the room. It was going to take me out of Bali, far, far away—beyond the reach of Nicole. I'd never see her again, there wasn't a chance we'd ever meet again. And as I stood there I knew suddenly and surely that I *had* to see her again. I knew I had fallen in love with her.

I brushed his hand and pen off the ticket. "Cancel it," I said firmly. "I'm not going."

Chapter Twelve

To the south, heavy clouds were building up to a thunderhead on the horizon. I stood at the far end of the field, away from the terminal, alone. I wanted to be alone and I wanted to think. I tried to shrug off a feeling of anger and frustration as the plane taxied to the runway. It would have been so easy to get aboard, but I hadn't gone aboard and it was too late to change my mind. The engines burst into a roar. I followed the sleek form as its wheels spun along the runway, and then rose from its brown shadow. In a few moments the plane diminished to a flashing silver in the eastern sky, Vishnu's Garuda bird come to life. In a couple of hours they'd be watching it in Jogjakarta, coming in for a landing.

I turned with a sense of relief. I couldn't have left Nicole behind, and I hadn't. A ship was coming into Benua tomorrow and I was sure she would head for it. So would I.

I cut toward the road. Tomorrow seemed a long way off; I wanted desperately to see Nicole and talk to her and apologize because there had been moments when I hated her. I wanted to look again at those wistful, pale blue eyes, and hear again the little love songs her earrings made when she turned her head.

A bus was coming along the road from the south, and I flagged it. The seats were taken and the aisles crowded. I threaded my way toward the back, and the bus stopped again at the terminal.

Nicole could have gone anywhere tonight; it was futile to attempt to find her. The thing for me to do was lie low until tomorrow. Rent a hotel room and keep out of sight. I'd strike out for Benua in the morning.

A load of passengers squeezed aboard from the terminal. I thought dismally of Fry. It hadn't been smart to lock him in that closet. When he was let out he was sure as hell going to twist things around and try to hang the murder on me. As a fall guy, I had walked in made to order. Damnit—why had Regina had to get herself shot through my passport and in my coat?

Well, I hadn't expected to be around for that. I wished now Fry had gotten Regina buried before I came along. I would have felt a little easier with that murder on ice.

The bus was going to Den Pasar; I'd check into the Bali Hotel. It was big enough so that I could get room service. Once in my room I could stay there. And it was big enough so that—under another name—I might get lost, on the blotter. I figured I still had a couple of hours grace. I had hit

Fry with everything I had and hoped he'd stay unconscious for a week. Still, what if the police did start out looking for me? I hadn't killed her. Why was I letting myself feel guilty?

The door of the bus closed and the engine rumbled. I wished I had a cigarette. I must buy a pack of cigarettes. The bus stopped again almost after it started. I didn't see how anyone else was going to squeeze in, but he did.

I saw the pith helmet first and then the thin, rusty face as he turned. The air in the bus seemed suddenly oppressive beyond the body smells and heat. It was the lanky Englishman I had left unconscious on the breakwater in Benua.

I thought for a moment he had seen me and come aboard; but he turned again, facing forward, and hung on a strap.

We stayed that way, at either end of the crowded aisle, while the bus crawled and stopped from village to village. It must have taken twenty-five minutes to reach Den Pasar. We pulled up at the *alun-alun,* and the Englishman was among the first to step out. He never looked back.

I hung on my strap with a washed-out feeling. My shirt was clinging with sweat and I could feel the perspiration trickle down my legs.

Through one of the dusty windows, I saw him strolling across the square, past deserted tennis courts and out of sight. I got out of the bus and crossed the street. It made me angry that I had let his presence on the bus rattle me. Chances were he had checked the flight, looking for Nicole. Well, he hadn't found her. And he hadn't seen me. To hell with him.

The street was busy with the comings and going of taxis and buses and pony carts. I stood for a moment looking at the low, rambling hotel in front of me. It stood with an air of tropical luxury behind an apron of lawn. Canopied walks stretched out like tentacles from the main building to bungalow annexes.

I started up the long, sweeping driveway. Tinkling native music floated out in little clouds of sound, and I could see Europeans in bright whites on the terrace where a troop of dancers was performing. I couldn't help remembering Regina Williams, dancing to a phonograph record for me. It seemed a lifetime ago—and for her it was.

I entered the lobby from a side door. I stood for a moment, looking around. Idle bellboys in starched uniforms and turbans stood around with a look of expectation, their naked brown feet flattened against the tile floor. The air was cool and faintly sweetened from potted gardenias. I saw no one I knew.

I crossed to the desk. The clerk surveyed me with impassive eyes, wiping the back of his neck with a handkerchief. Both the lobby and the clerk had a firm air of colonialism about them, as though word hadn't yet arrived that the island of Bali was no longer a Dutch possession.

I asked for a single with bath.

"You have baggage, *mijnheer?*"

"I'll pay in advance," I said.

"All right. *Ja,* I'll fix you up."

He seemed to be sizing me up, and I must have looked like a beach-comber. But I spoke English and I was pulling American money out of my wallet and he seemed reassured.

"Hot today," he muttered, turning the register around for me to sign. "We have more rain tonight maybe, eh?"

I didn't feel like discussing the weather. I picked up the pen as he turned to the key rack. I slipped a blotter under the heel of my palm and paused a moment trying to think of a name to sign. I wrote out Charles G. Webster, and put the pen aside.

The clerk counted out my change in rupiahs and rang for a bellboy. *"Jongoes!"*

"Never mind," I said, picking up the key. "I'll find it myself."

"All right, Mr. Webster," the clerk muttered indifferently. "You're in one of the bungalows." He pointed off toward the right.

Even as he pointed a bellboy came in from that direction, from the terrace, and I stiffened. In a bored, accented voice he was calling my name.

"Telephone for Tuan Jeff Cape—telephone for Tuan Jeff Cape—"

The clerk was talking to me. "Something is wrong, Mr. Webster?"

I stood there and the boy started a discouraged swing through the lobby. He looked ready to give Tuan Jeff Cape up. He had apparently been through once before, trying the terrace, and returning for a last try. It didn't make sense—no one could know I was here. I wanted to take that call, I had to know who it was on the other end. The boy gave it up, and cut back toward a bank of phones. I knew the clerk was watching me. I had signed in as Webster, and it kept me from signaling the bellboy. But now I waved an arm to catch his eye and started for the phones. Let the clerk think what he liked. I had to know who was calling me.

"This one, tuan," the *jongoes* said.

I tipped him with the rupiahs in my hand and lifted the receiver. "Hello?"

The line was open, but there was no answer.

"Hello!"

No answer. *"Hello!"* No answer. And then there was a click at the other end. The party had hung up.

I replaced the receiver slowly. I didn't know what to make of it, and I stopped trying. To hell with it. To hell with everything. I was tired and angry and hungry, and they could all go to hell.

When I turned, I saw Mr. Chu standing in the terrace doorway.

He was grinning at me from across the lobby. It didn't make sense to me that he would have placed the call. He must have been sitting out there and heard the bellboy yelling my name. And followed to see if it were answered.

He carried Jong in a cage, and waited there. He had changed into fresh clothes. He gave me an almost imperceptible nod, grinning a little wider.

My first impulse was to run, and I didn't know why. What in hell was happening to me? I had never run from anyone in my life before, and now I wanted to run from everyone. I was getting a fine case of frazzled nerves. If there had been a way I suppose I would have run from that Englishman on the bus. Run. To hell with running. I was tired of running away. I stood there a moment getting good and mad. Then I walked out the nearest door. If Chu wanted me, let him come get me.

I found the bungalow and found my room. I left the door unlocked. The room had a high ceiling and the bed was made up with a Dutch wife and framed in mosquito netting. A screen door led to the veranda. I unlocked it and looked out on a neatly kept lawn and hibiscus in bloom.

Then I went to the phone and ordered a gin and tonic, cigarettes and dinner to be served in an hour. I turned on the overhead fan, sat in a big chair, propped my feet on the table and waited.

I didn't have to wait long.

There was a gentle, almost apologetic knock. I yelled to come in.

The door swung open and Mr. Chu stood there, that affable grin on his face.

"So sorry to bother you, Mr. Cape."

"I told you to come in."

"Yes, quite."

At least, I thought, he doesn't have a gun in his hand. He had the bird cage in tow, and closed the door silently after him. His large brown eyes swept the room in an easy glance, and he seemed pleased. He had changed into sandals and white silk socks and for a moment looked like nothing more than a Chinese merchant on an errand from his shop. I had to remind myself that he had been shooting at me only a few hours before.

"What do you want?" I said.

He set the bird cage near my feet on the table. "Do you mind? Jong hates being caged and lately I have been trying his patience." He lifted the trap and coaxed Jong into the room. Jong made for the four corners.

"Planning to stay long?" I muttered.

"That depends on you, Mr. Cape. I apologize, of course, for having been forced to shoot at you this morning."

"Never mind that."

"We can conduct our business without guns now. It is better, yes?"

There was a knock at the door, and he turned quickly. "Relax," I said. "I ordered a drink."

I paid off the bellboy and carried back my gin and tonic and cigarettes. Jong had stopped fluttering around and clung now to the mosquito netting at the bed.

I sat down again, lit a cigarette and started in on my drink. "Business," I said. "Without guns. What business?"

He tipped his head and the grin began to have meaning. "You carry some information of special value to me."

I felt like telling him he was trailing the field, but when I opened my mouth it was only to take a swallow of gin and tonic. I remembered suddenly the card Nicole had written out for me in the taxi. I had planned to barter it to Regina for my passport, and stuck it in my shoe. I had no idea what she had written except that it was in Russian and of no consequence. I set my drink on the table.

"You think I still have it?"

"It is a possibility."

"Do you know what it is?"

"I have been told a business card with information condensed on the reverse side. Is that correct, Mr. Cape?"

"You're doing fine. What would this information mean to you?"

"I would doubtless find it most valuable."

"Is everyone in this thing out to double-cross Apollo Fry?"

"Mr. Cape, forgive me." The grin blossomed into a leathery smile. "I do not care to be cross-examined."

I dropped my feet off the table. I wanted to get it over with and get him out of here. "All right, let's assume I have this idiotic card. Why should I turn it over to you?"

"I come to do business, Mr. Cape."

"No guns. Money."

He nodded. "You could perhaps get a better price in Singapore. But you are a long way from Singapore and much could happen before you reached a market. I offer you a market here and now."

"What makes you so sure I got into this thing for money?"

"It is illogical that you got into it for anything else."

"Is that what Regina Williams told you?"

"She was not of a mind to confide in me. Shall we set a price?"

"But she did send you through the trees after me this morning."

"It was entirely my own idea, Mr. Cape. When her boy started after you, I followed. I believe we are straying from the issue at hand. You do have the card?"

"Yes."

Jong left the mosquito netting, circled under the fan and settled on my shoulder. If Mr. Chu felt any eagerness, he wasn't showing it. I wanted to shrug the bird off me, but I decided it wouldn't be good business. This Oriental was begging to be conned and I was going to accommodate him.

"What kind of money are you carrying?" I asked.

He knew what I was thinking and nodded. Strictly a cash deal. "A few hundred Indonesian rupiahs. About twelve hundred Straits dollars."

"That's not very much."

He shrugged. "Perhaps too much. We are not sure what is written on the card, are we? We can only guess."

"Do you read Russian?"

"It is not one of my languages, I regret."

"Get out your Straits dollars. You can keep the rupiahs for pin money."

"You will accept such a sum?"

I couldn't tell if he was made suspicious or was merely disappointed at my failure to haggle in the Oriental manner. I had accepted his starting price, even though I was certain he had more money to play with. Well, I didn't want to play.

"That's right," I said evenly. "I'm tired of being chased and shot at and cracked on the head with wrenches. I want out. Show your money and you've bought yourself a little essay in Russian."

He counted the money on the table. Jong seemed to like my shoulder and stuck there even as I bent, pulled off my shoe and extracted the rolled card. It was damp with perspiration, but still in one piece. It must have looked convincing as hell.

He unrolled it, examined Nicole's penmanship and appeared satisfied. I added the money to my wallet and was glad he had come along. At the rate I'd been going through my bankroll I'd be broke in another few days.

Somehow I wanted to ask him if he knew that Regina Williams was dead, because I had a feeling he knew. But to drop the remark would reveal that I knew, and that was information I didn't want to scatter around.

"I shall be leaving the hotel very soon," he said, placing the card carefully in his wallet. "I regret we cannot have tiffin together. I seem to remember extending the invitation."

"I'm curious," I said. "How far were you prepared to go if I hadn't been willing to sell?"

His grin returned. "It would have been quite simple, Mr. Cape." He reached for Jong at my shoulder, taking its body in his palm, and turned the bird's pink legs in the air. I saw a small, steel gaff, fine as a razor, fixed to one of the legs.

A clammy feeling came over me as I thought how many minutes that damned bird had been sitting inches from my bare neck. "Poisoned?"

"Lethally, Mr. Cape." He lifted the trap in the cage and put the serindit away. "I have taught Jong to strike like a fighting cock. At my command, you would be quite dead by now."

Chapter Thirteen

The rain came suddenly, without thunder, like a bathroom shower turned on.

I ate alone in my room, and tried not to think. Every time I started thinking I felt like running. There had been that crazy phone call in the lobby. And Mr. Chu had followed me to my room. This was no place to stay.

And yet, what was I afraid of? Not Fry, and not Mr. Chu. The police? For all I knew I wasn't going to be connected with Regina's death. For all I knew one of Fry's people had let him out of the closet and they had gotten the body buried. The murder might be on ice, the way Fry had wanted it.

I went on eating, but I couldn't stop thinking. The phone call. Someone must have seen me approach the hotel. Hanging up as soon as I answered didn't make sense, but it had to make sense. I considered Fry and Mr. Chu, but eliminated them. The lanky Englishman? Maybe he had spotted me on the bus after all. No, he didn't fit. He couldn't have known my name. That left Nicole.

Nicole—it had to be her. I hoped it was her. That meant she knew where I was. I sat there playing with the idea. If she knew I was here in the hotel she might come. If I pulled out now she'd miss me. There was a chance she might come here. It was a chance I desperately wanted to gamble on. I decided to stick around.

It turned dark as I finished my meal and I switched on the light. The rain fell with a steady hiss beyond the veranda and washed off the eaves in musical streams. The room cooled off at once and I killed the fan. God, would I never get out of the tropics? If I ever got back to the States I was going to light someplace where it never rained.

I got room service to send up another gin and tonic and to clear the dishes out of the place. I sat with the drink for over an hour.

Maybe I had doped it out wrong. That could have been Nicole on the phone, it had to be Nicole, but she might not have any intention of finding me. Or maybe that phony name I had registered under had blocked the way.

I pulled the mosquito netting aside and stretched out on the bed with a cigarette. I felt uncertain and impatient. I really ought to get out of here.

But I stayed. I felt grimy and decided to kill time taking a shower. I would stick around another hour. Then I'd check into some side-street hotel where I wouldn't jump every time a gust of wind rattled the veranda door.

I stood under the shower a long time, and for the first time in hours began feeling like a human being again. I had to remind myself that I was a geologist, that I was the same simple guy who had come ashore only for a drink. Until yesterday, my only nightmares were wells that tapped water or mud, or ten gravity oil, which was just as worthless. I doodled rigs and worried about fault zones and brown sand and whipstock drilling. It all seemed remote now, and not very important.

I was rubbing myself dry when I heard a sound in the next room.

My heart began to pound. That was either Nicole or it was trouble.

I wrapped the towel around myself and paused a moment at the bathroom door, listening. Then I turned the knob and pushed it open.

She was standing with her back to the veranda door. She stood a little stiffly in a blue raincoat, the hood pulled over her hair.

"Hello, Nicole," I said.

She only looked at me, her eyes blue and gently submissive, the lashes wet with rain. It seemed somehow idiotic to be standing here in a towel, and it kept me from crossing to her.

"Hello, Jeff."

I wanted to go in and get some clothes on, but I couldn't make myself leave, not yet. I wished we could both stop feeling a little awkward.

"I was hoping you'd come," I said.

"Were you?"

"I wish you wouldn't stand there as though you expected me to bite you. Come on in."

She pulled back the hood and shook her hair. There was something bewitchingly feminine about her with that black hair cropped short, the little gold temple bells at her ears catching the light. God, I thought, how beautiful she is, and I've got her back.

She moved away from the door. "I didn't want to see you again. I tried to stay away, but—"

"Damnit, don't apologize," I said. "And don't say you didn't want to see me again."

"You should have gone on that plane."

"That was this afternoon. What counts is tonight. Let's not have any more noble ideas."

She picked up the cigarettes from the table. I stood there, watching her light up. She sat on the arm of a chair and turned, facing me.

"Can I deal myself back in?" she muttered.

"You're in."

"I want to stay. Believe me?"

The veranda door rattled with the wind. "Sure, baby. I believe you."

"I'm glad you didn't get on that plane. I would never have seen you again."

"Would that have mattered?"

"Suddenly it mattered very much."

"That's crazy, isn't it?"

"Very crazy, Jeff."

"Why did you hang up on me in the lobby?"

"You knew it was me?"

"It had to be you."

She inhaled deeply, and then watched the smoke drift toward the ceiling. "I was on a bus starting back for Benua. It turned along Pasar Street and as I glanced through the window I saw a man walking up the hotel driveway. I got only a flash. He looked like Jefferson Cape."

"Nice guy. I used to know him well."

"I didn't think it could be him—I was sure he had met that plane. Why didn't he, Jeff?"

"Maybe sometime he'll tell you."

She kept looking at me, and her voice was soft and warm and intimate. "I sat there in a kind of panic. I tried to tell myself it couldn't be you. But a couple of blocks later I stopped the bus and got off. I *had* to know."

I walked to the table, got a cigarette and lit it. She waited, sitting very close, on the arm of the chair. "You had to know," I said.

She glanced away. "I called the hotel. Jefferson Cape came to the phone. I heard his voice, but I couldn't make myself answer. You were free of me, and I kept telling myself I had no right to involve you again."

"So you hung up."

"Yes."

"Damn you."

"It's taken me hours to make up my mind to come here, Jeff." Her eyes came back to me. "Are you angry?"

"I'd have gone nuts if you hadn't come back."

"I couldn't really have stayed away."

"It sounds like you might have fallen in love with the guy."

"Does it?"

"You could do worse."

"I couldn't do better, Jeff."

It was one of those crazy moments. We looked at each other, and suddenly it didn't matter that we had been strangers only twenty-four hours before. We had been in love for hours and a lifetime.

"Come here, baby," I muttered.

She didn't move, waiting on the arm of the chair. I threw down my cigarette, took one of her wrists and brought her to her feet. Her earrings struck faintly, and then her body seemed to flow into my arms.

"Jeff, darling. Jeff."

My lips closed over her words, shutting them off. I kissed her hard, and then our lips softened against each other, apart, wanting each other, and met again. I could feel the muscles along her back ripple faintly under the pressure of her emotions. Her lips searched hungrily for mine, again and again, and it was right. I held a woman in my arms, and her flesh was warm and submissive. I wanted her. I had to have her, now and tomorrow and forever. I felt her hands along my back, keeping me close, and we stood that way a long time.

"I'm in love, Jeff," she whispered. "I can't help it. I love you, darling."

"That's crazy, isn't it?"

"Very crazy. I'd have died if you'd gotten on that plane and left me."

"I couldn't have, baby."

She pulled back a little and she was smiling. "It sounds like you might have fallen in love with the girl, Jeff."

"Does it?"

"Please fall in love with the girl."

"I have. Long ago. I love you, Nicole. I love you desperately."

She tightened against me. "I'm frightened, darling. I don't want to lose you."

"You're not going to, baby. We're sticking together."

"Jeff—"

"Don't say it."

The sudden passion, the quick abandon. They were in her eyes.

"Oh, my darling." She was almost whispering. "We don't have much time."

"No, baby," I breathed, kissing her. My head throbbed, but I tried not to lose control of myself. Not here. Not now.

"Don't you see, they'll come between us. I'll lose you, darling. And I need you so terribly."

"You'll never lose me."

"Jeff—"

"Nicole, baby."

"But I *might* lose you, and at least we can have tonight."

"You don't mean that."

"I...." She stiffened faintly, words unspoken on her lips. She broke out of my arms and turned away. "No, I don't mean that. It sounds so—cheap."

"I love you, Nicole. And it's got to be right. I'll take a raincheck."

"You're a nice guy, Jeff. I don't deserve you."

"All I want you to do is love me. We'll have to get out of here. It's not safe for you. And keep loving me. Promise?"

"Promise."

"I'll go in and get dressed. Chu was here. For all I know he'll be back. This is no place for us."

She hesitated with something on her lips, and then let the words come out. "He checked out of the hotel."

"What?"

"I saw him with his baggage as I came up. He was loading up his car."

"He couldn't be leaving the island, not tonight."

"No."

"You told me you didn't know the guy."

"Did I?"

I remembered her stubborn silence in the taxi when I asked about Chu, and the gap in her story. She had told me she didn't know the guy, but a little while ago she had recognized him on sight. "How did you find out I was in this room? Did Chu tip you off?"

There was a flash of resentment in her eyes. I hadn't meant to make it an accusation and I was amazed at my own sudden suspicion. What the hell, I was in love with her, wasn't I? I must be getting jumpy.

"Sorry, baby," I said.

She turned away. "When I called the desk, they told me there was no Jefferson Cape registered. Then the clerk remembered a Mr. Webster had taken a phone call under that name. He gave me this room number, and I decided to try it."

"That clerk has too good a memory for our good."

"Is Fry still looking for you?"

"He's looking for you, and that's what counts." I picked up my live cigarette from the floor and killed it in the ash tray. The rain was blowing little puddles inside the veranda door. Damn the rain. At least Nicole had had sense enough to buy a raincoat. We would have to find another spot to spend the night. I didn't want Nicole here if Chu came back to tell me I had swindled him. What about the police? I might already be involved in murder. Maybe yes, maybe no, but it wasn't worth the risk to stick around and find out. When tomorrow came I didn't want to be arguing my innocence with the cops; I wanted to be aboard that ship in Benua with Nicole. I wanted to pick up that raincheck.

"We're leaving," I said, starting for the bathroom. "I'll be right out."

She turned. "Jeff?"

"What?"

"I love you, darling. Thanks for saying no."

"It killed me to say no."

"Please hurry."

It came as I stood in the bathroom doorway.

A heavy rustle at the hall door.

Chapter Fourteen

A knock.

I turned to Nicole. "Get out on the veranda."

She nodded quickly and pulled the rain hood over her hair. I met her at the door and took her shoulders in my hands. It seemed suddenly important to kiss her. A moment later I shut the door after her.

The knock came again.

I hesitated, thinking of my clothes in the bathroom. I might be able to throw something on and get out of here. Then a key rattled in the lock, and I thought for a moment it was going to be the maid.

The door swung in. It wasn't the maid.

"*Merdeka, jero.* I will come in, please."

"You're in," I snapped.

Even though the guy was wearing a wet Panama, he had cop written all over him. He was taller than most Balinese I had seen, and lighter skinned, with maybe some Dutch blood in his veins. He was belted in a voluminous black raincoat, and a straw-wrapped *stroodje* burned in his fingers. Whatever was European in him had gone back to native seed. His teeth were filed and stained from betel nut. His face was pock-marked so that the skin had the texture of granite.

"I am Captain Arok of the Den Pasar police," he said, dropping the skeleton key in his raincoat pocket. "You are the one who rented this room?"

"That ought to be obvious. What is this?"

"Then you are Charles Webster. I will see your passport, *jero.*" He moved into the room, glancing around professionally. He looked tired and wet and out of humor. His feet were bare in leather sandals and they left wet tracks.

"Let's get to the point," I said. I knew I'd be sunk if he got a look at my passport; I wasn't going to give him the chance. Captain Arok obviously hadn't come around on a routine check.

His eyes settled on me. "You have a cut on your arm, *jero.*"

"What about it?"

"I am looking for one who wore a bandage on his left arm." The cigarette burned like something forgotten in his fingers as he looked at me. "I am looking for one who calls himself Jefferson Cape."

"I see."

"I am told that you answered a telephone call for Tuan Cape. I asked for your passport, *jero.*"

"Why should Tuan Cape interest the police?"

"There has been a murder on the island."

"Has he been charged?"

Impatience came into Captain Arok's eyes. "You admit you accepted a call for him?"

"I'm not admitting anything."

"*Béh!* Your passport, *jero!*"

My passport had a bullet hole in it, and he wasn't going to see it. "Never mind my passport. I'm Jefferson Cape."

"It was quite obvious. Why did you register as Tuan Webster?"

"That ought to be obvious, too."

"Of course. You hoped to escape."

"No. I could have been on that four o'clock plane if I'd wanted to escape. All I wanted was to be left alone by the police. Sure, I know Regina Williams is dead, but I didn't kill her. What kind of a case do you think you've got against me?"

"Get dressed, *jero*. We will go."

"Not so fast. I asked you a question."

"There will be time for that later."

"There's time for it now."

He snapped his hand to knock the ash off his cigarette. He moved to the bathroom door and looked in. "You have no coat, *jero?*"

"Is it against the law not to have a coat?"

He turned, facing me with controlled anger in his eyes. "*Béh!* The American woman was wearing a coat when she was shot. It has not been found."

"To hell with the coat. You've gotten a statement from Apollo Fry, haven't you? Did you ask him if he killed her?"

He stared at me. "Is it logical that he would kill her and lock himself in a closet? Tuan Fry has made a statement. He came to pay the dead one a call, and found you there preparing to bury her. There was a fight, and you knocked him unconscious."

"It makes sense, doesn't it?"

"It is logical, *jero.*"

"It's backwards, that's all. I suppose you've let him go."

"Get dressed."

"Hold on. You've got Fry's screwed-up story and the circumstantial evidence that I registered under a phony name. Look, I'm sorry as hell Mrs. Williams is dead. But if you think I shot her you're crazy. Did you check ballistics? You must have found Fry's gun there in the living room."

He nodded. "She was killed with a forty-five. His gun was a thirty-two."

Captain Arok's words went whistling through my head. This thing had stopped adding up right. Was Fry there only cleaning up someone else's dirty work? Or had he managed some sort of hocus-pocus with the gun that had killed her?

"Has Fry fitted me out with a motive?"

"The motive can wait, *jero*. Perhaps it was a lover's quarrel."

"There was no motive and there was no lover's quarrel. I didn't kill her."

His eyes smiled faintly and he shook another ash off his cigarette. "I am entitled to my opinion."

"The motive can't wait," I snapped. "Do you know why Fry wants to hang this on me? Because he thinks I must be in Java by now. Did he tell you I was going to the airport?"

"Yes. We checked. Why did you cancel your reservation, *jero?*"

"That's my business. But Fry didn't want you going into the real motives of Mrs. Williams' death. Not for days. Not until he could clean up his affairs here and get out. I was a swell red herring, made to order, and you snapped at it. He's playing you for a sucker."

Captain Arok had wandered back to the bathroom door. My shirt and trousers were hanging on a hook. "We have not recovered the murder gun," he said. "You would be a fool to carry it."

I didn't think of the gun, I thought of the passport in my trousers pocket. I didn't want him poking around. "Relax," I said. "I'll get dressed."

But he had gotten hold of the idea, and as I started toward him he turned with a gun of his own. "One moment, *jero.*"

I looked at the service revolver in his hand, and my muscles stiffened. The bullet hole in my passport would seem to connect me with Regina at the time of her death. Maybe they couldn't hang you for circumstantial evidence, but they could try. I thought of Nicole waiting for me out on the veranda; I wasn't going to let him separate us. I wasn't going to let him arrest me.

He unhooked my clothes and held me back with the gun. A moment later he withdrew my passport. He smiled as he fingered the bullet hole. He took my wallet. Then he threw my trousers and shirt at me. "Get dressed."

He lit a fresh cigarette and waited. I tried desperately to think. I buttoned up my shirt and got into my shoes. Outside, the rain fell with a hoarse whisper and a large puddle had gathered under the veranda door.

He put away his gun; I must have looked thoroughly cowed.

"Just a minute," I said. "Have you established what time she was killed?"

"Does it matter, *jero?*"

"Maybe it does," I said angrily.

He shrugged his shoulders as though he would enjoy any attempt to wriggle out of his circumstantial strait jacket. "From the state of her body it is estimated she died approximately at noon."

My ears began to pound; I had caught hold of something.

"How approximate?"

"An hour either way at most."

"I wasn't in Sanur when she was killed."

"No?"

"I was in Benua."

He glanced at me, and it was obvious he didn't believe me. "You have a witness, *jero?*"

"I have a witness."

The little entertainment was over; his eyes turned angry. If I could prove I hadn't been in Sanur during the murder time, he was going to have to do some fresh legwork. And it was going to be easy to prove.

"I said I have a witness."

He shook the ash off his cigarette. *"Beh!* There is always a witness."

"You've gone off the deep end on a trumped-up story. I walked in on Fry when he was trying to get her buried. Did you let him loose?"

"He came here to the hotel."

"Try him for size."

He straightened impatiently. "You spoke of a witness." Then his eyes brightened, as though he had gotten an intellectual second wind. "Benua is only ten kilometers. You could have made the round trip quickly."

"You're wasting your time. I met a girl shortly before eleven o'clock in Benua. We were together until at least one-thirty. Get out your pencil. She'll make a statement for you. And then you can apologize to me."

"She is here?"

"Out on the veranda."

He gave that a quick interpretation. His grin was the kind you want to knock off. I had taken her to my room, and he had surprised us like some house detective. "All right, *jero,*" he muttered, the gun once again in his fingers. "Let us see this witness of yours. I will of course shoot if you attempt some trick."

"No tricks."

I started for the veranda and he followed close behind. I got the door open and light from the room spilled across the wet porch and against the black, hissing veil of rain. There was a close, voluptuous odor of night-blooming jasmine.

I said, "Come on in, baby."

There was no answer, no movement but the rain coming down hard.

"Where are you, baby?" I hurried onto the veranda and a chill caught up with me. *"Nicole!"*

I spun around in a kind of panic. Nicole was gone.

I stared at Captain Arok. He stood in the doorway, grinning, a nightmarish shape in a black raincoat. The gun rose, aimed at my chest. "Don't make me shoot, Tuan Cape."

I reached out desperately for some answer. I wanted to believe now that Nicole had walked out on me, but I knew she hadn't. She wouldn't. Something had happened out here—something had happened to her.

I glared at the Balinese. "Did Fry come to the hotel with you? When you got a line on my room was he there?"

Captain Arok nodded. He couldn't know what was going through my mind. All he cared about was his murder suspect. Me. I hadn't gotten out of his strait jacket after all. There was no witness.

He motioned me inside with the gun, but I stood there. Fry. He knew he would find Nicole where he found me. He had tumbled to it when I made him call off his hoods from the airport. And I had sent Nicole out here into his arms.

The seconds crowded in on me; I had to get rid of this guy. I had already lost too much time trying to convince him that I was innocent while Fry moved in on Nicole. I wanted to turn and run. The gun held me there. He'd be pulling the trigger before I reached the edge of the veranda.

"All right," I breathed. "Let's go."

I hoped he'd put the gun away once I was back in the light of the room, but he didn't. He was going to hold onto it. He seemed convinced I had gone out on the veranda only as a trick, and lost my nerve.

We crossed the room. When he reached the hall door he opened it. I started through, and lost my sense of caution. He switched off the light. I spun, blocked off the gun and hit him. I smashed a fist into his jaw. Desperately. Hard.

"*Adoh!*"

His breath caught and his body hurtled backward.

I slammed the door. I ran like hell.

I reached the end of the hall before the first shot came. It echoed in the bungalow like a cannon. I plunged into the darkness of the lawn, into the rain. I ran toward the street, but it was a long way off.

Rain thrashed over me, changing my clothes to heavy rags, and I kept running. I stopped halfway to the street and felt swallowed by the blackness.

I saw Captain Arok under the lighted walkway to the main building. He stood there, gun raised, his eyes searching for some direction worth following.

I glanced at the distorted lights of the main building, at the canopy over the entrance, at the driveway. A pair of headlights came on. A touring car started from under the billowing canopy along the driveway to the street.

I saw a battered fender. *It was Apollo Fry's car!*

Captain Arok was watching the car as it moved slowly down the lighted driveway. I took off toward it with my heart in my throat. It was no race, and I knew it. But I kept running, and let Captain Arok take his pot shots if he wanted to. The rain fought me back and my shoes sank in the flooded lawn. The car was picking up speed rapidly.

It glided past as I got to the edge of the driveway. My feet came onto wet gravel and I raced toward the street, trailing the car as it slowed to make the sharp turn.

The brake light flashed on and I was close enough that the glow turned me red. Almost at once Captain Arok saw his chance, and the air cracked behind me. The car began the swing into the street and the brake light went out. I hooked my fingers onto the spare tire. I pulled myself off the ground as the car shifted into second.

I remembered a luggage rack between the tire and back of the car, and started climbing around. A hand came out of nowhere, cold and wet, closing tightly on my wrist. I went stiff.

The voice was almost at my ear.

"Let me give you a hand, commissioner. There's always room for one more."

Chapter Fifteen

The sedan had turned left on the main drag and picked up speed quickly. The street was dark and deserted and the lights were out in the shops. My feet found the luggage rack, and I swung around behind the tire.

He let go of my wrist. "That's it, commissioner."

The rain swept over us. I could barely make him out, a large spidery shape with legs curled up behind the tire. The lanky Englishman. "You get around," I muttered.

"Some bloke shooting at you, was he?"

I turned up my shirt collar and buttoned it, as though that would do any good. "Never mind that—is the girl in the car?"

"Think I'd be tagging along otherwise? What's your interest in the young lady, commissioner? I can't figure you out, for a fact."

We passed some vagrant light at the edge of town and I saw him, that thin, rusty face and the dripping pith helmet tugged square on his head. "Who the hell are you?" I snapped.

"Lionel Tibby's the name. Singapore."

"Who hired you?"

"I'm not likely to be telling you that, am I? A bit confidential, you know."

"You're not working for Fry. I can figure that out for myself."

"That's right, commissioner."

"Any idea where he's taking her?"

"I expect we'll find out if we don't drown first. Come now, what's your game?"

"Do you have a gun?"

"I have, but don't get any ideas. I should've made use of it on you this afternoon, that's a fact. Thought sure I could send you packing with my trick Malacca. My mistake."

We had left town behind us and I thought we were heading for Sanur, but we began to climb almost at once and I knew the sedan had turned off in another direction. I had a feeling it might be a long trip. I shifted and tried to get a little more comfortable. It was no use.

"What do you want with Nicole Balashov?" I seemed to be yelling against the wind, but I didn't think they could hear us in the car. The rain tore the words off my lips.

"The girl's alive then, is she, commissioner?"

"Haven't you learned that much?"

"Oh, I've had a bloody time of it, what with you getting in my way just as I was about to stroll up to her. A chap has to make sure of his facts. The paper said she was dead. You're positive the lady is Nicole Balashov?"

"I'm not positive of anything."

"I haven't had a real look at her, worse luck, and I'm not enjoying this ride one bit."

There was something disarming about him, but something phony, too, like a man playing a part. I warned myself not to take his affability at face value. But I was glad he had a gun. We were going to need it.

"Why are you interested in Nicole Balashov?" I said again.

"It's a sticky business, commissioner, and as I remarked, a bit on the confidential side. No hard feelings. You stuck on the girl?"

"That's my business."

"So it is. Just thought I'd ask. No hard feelings."

The sedan raced through the black villages, rousing only the dogs to eddies of barking. I learned to anticipate the swerves and turns and braced myself. My legs were stiff and my joints already ached. I was cold; rain peppered my face and collected in the folds of my trousers.

I turned my head toward his ear. "What are you going to do when this damned car stops?"

"Remains to be seen, commissioner."

"Why are you in this, Tibby?"

"I say, call me Lionel, if you will. Never did much go for the name Tibby, but it runs in the family, worse luck."

"How did you happen to take this ride?"

"A bit of luck, finally. Was just going back to the hotel when I saw them, his arm tight on hers, mind you. So I jumped on and here I am."

"She told me Fry is going to kill her."

"Oh, that's quite likely."

"Well?"

"You can depend on me to do my bit, commissioner. Though I would like to make certain it's Nicole Balashov herself before I put myself out any."

"Fry wouldn't have trailed her all over the island if she weren't."

"I've been thinking that—still, a chap likes to be sure of his facts all the way round. Can't be too careful of the facts in a business like this." He leaned his head a little closer to mine. "Friend to friend—what's a nice one like you doing mixed up in this? The minute I first laid eyes on you, I saw you weren't the type."

"Don't worry about it," I snapped.

"She wouldn't be hard to fall in love with, would she?"

I clamped my jaws.

"You're a bloody fool, if I may say so," he went on. "Let your friend Lionel Tibby give you some advice that's not half bad. Get clear of this business.

Someone's going to get hurt, and I wouldn't want it to be you. The girl's poison for a chap like you, and that's the truth. Get clear, commissioner, that's my advice."

"Go to hell."

"Didn't think you'd listen. No hard feelings."

The car was grinding up a mountain road and we fell into silence. It occurred to me that Lionel Tibby trusted me even less than I did him. Did he expect me to take his warning, say thanks and hop off?

The rain struck with a thrashing force that made me went to duck, but there was nothing to do but sit there and take it. I felt as though we had come halfway across the island, and I wondered how much longer my muscles would keep wedged in place without cramping. Then I thought of Apollo Fry sitting only a few inches from me in the comfort of the car and I managed to hate him for it. And I thought of Nicole, and knew I'd hold on.

We kept climbing and the air turned colder. Within another ten minutes my teeth were chattering.

"I can't take much more of this, I can't," Tibby said suddenly. "I haven't been this cold since I left London. That's the bloody tropics for you."

"We're slowing down."

The brake light turned the road behind us red. We seemed to be stopping for no reason at all. There was no village here, only open highway. I thought quickly of Tibby's gun and wondered if I ought to trust him.

"Mum's the word, commissioner."

The car came to a full stop, the motor idling, and the brake light went out. I unwound my legs and crawled down. My knees didn't want to support me and I held onto the tire for several painful moments. The fronds of the palm trees snapped in the wind. I finally moved out of range of the taillight. I could sense Tibby beside me nursing his legs. I didn't know why we had stopped here in the middle of nowhere, but if the car took off again I wasn't sure I'd be able to climb back on.

Tibby touched my arm. "Look—to the right, commissioner."

I wiped my eyes and saw a sudden pair of headlights leap out of the jungle. Then the sedan's lights flashed out an answer of recognition, and all went dark again.

"I'd say the big boy'll be changing cars," Tibby muttered,

I caught his arm and tightened. "Give me your gun."

"I'll handle it, commissioner. Don't go making a bloody fool of yourself."

"I said—"

"Truth is, lad, I don't have a gun."

"*What?*"

"It's back in the hotel, worse luck. Only wanted to keep your spirits up. All we can do is watch what goes on here."

I let loose of him as the back door of the sedan opened. The dome light came on and I heard Apollo Fry's heavy voice. He sounded happy. "Good, good. There's someone to meet us."

I saw a black umbrella poke through the door. It was snapped open and then the car springs creaked as Fry unloaded his bulk to the ground. He had a flashlight and I dove for the palm trees at the edge of the road. Tibby had the same idea.

Fry turned the beam into the jungle and after a moment picked out three men moving toward us through the trees. I didn't like what I saw: natives in army fatigues, and they carried burp guns in the crooks of their arms. This wasn't any army maneuver. We were in the mountains and these boys were guerrillas. Fry had a rendezvous with terrorists.

I stood watching, the blood pounding in my head. If this was a nightmare, I wanted to wake up. Now. It was time, before I got myself killed.

"Easy, lad," Tibby whispered in my ear. "There's more to this than meets the eye. I'll thank you not to do anything rash. We'll have our chance."

I shook him off. The three guerrillas reached the side of the car and Fry, under a cascade from the umbrella, played the flashlight in their faces. They were young and ragged and unsmiling. Their voices were loud against the rain.

The one who spoke had an insolent face. *"Tabé, tabé—*you are many hours late."

Fry said: "I only just got your leader's message."

"He does not like to be kept waiting."

"It was unavoidable, I tell you. Is that as close as you can bring your car?"

"Are we so crazy as to connect our road to the highway, fat one? Too bad if your shoes get muddy walking a few steps."

"All right—never mind."

"Who is the girl? We were not told you would bring a girl."

"See she doesn't escape," Fry barked.

The outlaw spat in the rain. "There's not room for all in the jeep."

"One of you can walk." Fry turned and spoke into the car. "Not much farther for you. Get out."

I heard Nicole's voice. "You always win, don't you, Apollo?"

"Always."

I began to see a line of action for me. It was all I could do to make myself stand there. I watched as she got out of the car in her pale blue raincoat, the hood thrown up over her hair. Fry turned the flashlight into her face. Her eyes avoided the glare, but her expression was stubborn and resolute.

"Why don't you kill me and get it over with?"

"Afraid to face him?"

I lost their voices as Tibby leaned close to my ear. "It's the driver I want to deal with, commissioner," he muttered. "If you're smart you'll jump back on the luggage rack when the car pulls out. I hope to be driving."

"I'm staying."

There was no time to argue it out; he moved away quickly. The five of them grouped themselves, Fry alone under the protection of his umbrella. He held them there long enough to get his cigar going again, and then they started single file through the trees.

I heard the sudden grinding of gears, and turned. The sedan took off like a jack rabbit. Within seconds, the taillight dissolved in the rain, and I wondered if Tibby had had a gun after all. The driver obviously hadn't given him any trouble.

Fry kept his flashlight at Nicole's back as one of the guerrillas led the way. I began to follow. Once we entered tall jungle the pelting rain vanished; it was like walking under a leaky awning. Nearby, I heard the sudden chittering of monkeys alarmed by the activity below. I pulled aside wispy ferns, like giant spider webs, and tried to keep up. I came onto the heavy stink of durian; a tree must have dropped its ripe fruit during the heat of the day. Then I saw the jeep, and held back. It stood waiting on a narrow road cut through the trees.

One of those natives was going to be left behind to walk. I'd get him—and his burp gun.

They spoke in low voices and I couldn't catch the words. But I saw Nicole being forced into the front seat. Fry hoisted himself in the back, directly behind her. Then he gave his flashlight to the guerrilla being left behind. The motor turned over and the headlights snapped on. The jeep pulled away slowly through the mud.

I didn't want to let it get very far.

I stepped into the road. The native started to walk after the jeep, probing along with the flashlight.

I leaped forward and hooked my arm around his neck. I yanked back and pulled him off his feet. The flashlight flew upward and he yelled. I carried him to the mud.

And I heard another voice.

An extra pair of hands clamped onto my shoulders. Another terrorist had come out of nowhere. He got my arm locked behind me, and then they were both on top of me and my face was in the mud.

They rolled me face up, and a bare foot slapped down under my chin, like a hand strangling me. I spat mud. One of them got the flashlight and turned the beam into my face. Then the nose of a gun touched my teeth, and I could smell the wet oil.

They looked down at me and laughed. I damned them and damned myself. I should have guessed a fourth native had been waiting in the jeep—the driver. *Two* men had been left to walk back to camp.

The two of them discussed me quickly in Malay. They tried to decide whether or not to kill me on the spot. I felt the rain wash the mud from my face, and then I heard one of them sneer in English.

"A white man."

Chapter Sixteen

"On your feet, white man."

The barrels of two guns shifted around me as though I were an untouchable. A hand began to paw over me. "I have no gun," I snapped.

"No money, either?"

"No money."

"*Bey!* It doesn't even pay to kill you." He translated this into Malay for the benefit of his partner. They both laughed.

"If you're going to shoot," I snapped, "never mind the ceremony."

"You are impatient to die? Explain what you are doing here."

"I'll do my explaining to your chief."

"You came in the car with the others?"

"Not exactly."

"Maybe the Anak Agung will like to hear your explanation. All right, walk. We will take a short cut."

They poked me forward with the noses of their guns. The flashlight guided me, and we walked. There were the wet, flapping sounds of the jungle all around us. They kept up a speculative conversation behind me in Malay, and they took turns keeping a gun in my back. My feet were numb and every muscle in my body rebelled, but I kept moving.

I thought hopelessly of Nicole. I wasn't going to be much good to her now. I remembered Tibby's words: *Don't go makin' a bloody fool of yourself.* The guy had the gift of prophecy. I wondered briefly what he was up to. But it didn't seem to matter. The gun prodded me along the road.

The road passed down through a ravine and at the bottom my feet moved through shallow running water—a dry stream, probably, just beginning to fill up from the monsoon. We left the road there and moved upstream. The jeep, I figured, had been lucky to get across.

I lost track of the minutes; it seemed as though I was stumbling through water for miles. I stopped trying to think. I let the guns poke me along and wanted to be somewhere else, anywhere else.

We left the river bed and cut through close jungle. The beam of the flashlight danced ahead of me along a footpath. I tried to shield my face from the dripping vines and fronds that slapped me as the guerrillas pushed me forward. We began to climb sharply and my knees didn't want to work. I kept stumbling, but hard jabs of the guns brought me up. I don't think they'd have let me lie down and die if I'd been ready to give up. I was beyond anger. I moved along like an automaton that needed oiling.

Finally the ground leveled out and the men behind me resumed their chatter. We were approaching camp and I straightened my back. I tried to get a grip on myself. I had to keep my head now.

We broke into a clearing and I saw light.

Dogs came out of nowhere and barked at my feet. Above their yelping I caught the sounds of music through the rain. I thought I must be hearing things.

We reached a wall and the two natives shouted into the darkness ahead. The dogs got brave enough to nip at my ankles, but I was too tired to kick them off. Other Malay voices came toward us and another flashlight snapped on in front of me. I was given a shove through an opening in the wall. My back was bruised from jabs of the gun, and I got another jab that made me want to turn and swing. I kicked at the dogs instead.

We were in a courtyard gone to bamboo, like weeds, and I saw a palatial stone house beyond, its windows boldly lighted. The music reverberated through the rain, a rolling complex of drums and cymbals and husky flutes. Jungle had leaped the courtyard walls and the house stood like something captive in a tangle of crawling leaf and bamboo. I was pushed to the wide veranda. A houseboy came to the door.

After a moment's discussion, I was led inside. The music stopped abruptly. About a dozen Balinese men were seated with their instruments along one side of a bamboo mat laid over a dirty marble floor. A wide-eyed boy in a spangled headdress and brocades was poised on the mat, his knees under him, his arms outstretched in some sort of ritualistic dance.

Every pair of brown eyes in the room turned on me. The native faces seemed out of place in this house. It must once have been the mountain retreat of some wealthy European, and probably abandoned during the war. I glanced around quickly, but Apollo Fry and Nicole were nowhere in sight. I didn't have time to wonder about it. I saw a familiar face and a familiar grin.

He was seated on the far side of the native *gamelan*, a stocky Chinese with a shaved head and a leathery, wrinkled skin—and a serindit asleep on his shoulder.

Mr. Chu and Jong.

Mr. Chu nodded. He grinned wider.

Looking me over sullenly from a rattan chair beside the veranda windows sat the man who was obviously chief of this mountain camp.

He was a grim-faced young Balinese, probably not yet thirty, and oversized for his race. His eyes were dark and brooding as he listened to the pair of guerrillas who had brought me in. There was only one thing I could read from his bronze face. Whoever I was, I wasn't welcome.

They made a long story of it, and I waited. The Balinese ate rice with his fingers out of a pisang leaf. A Javanese batik came high around his waist. The ornate handle of a silver kris rose from behind one naked shoulder, stuck in a cloth wrapped just below his chest. He wore a turban knotted in front and jauntily pleated.

As he ate, I watched the black coral bracelet on his wrist. I remembered the bracelet Regina Williams had worn. Black coral.

Finally he dismissed the two men, finished the rice and wiped off his fingers with the pisang leaf. He looked up at me. "I speak English," he said. "It is your language, yes?"

"Yes."

"I was educated in Holland," he added with a touch of brashness. "I speak four languages." He seemed anxious to let me know he wasn't a run-of-the-mill native. As he spoke, there was something both insolent and aristocratic in the way he held his shoulders, in his glance and tone of voice. "Lately I have had excellent tutoring in English. But that is beside the point, yes? Who are you?"

I answered mechanically, but I thought again of Regina Williams. *This was where she fitted in.* And it suddenly made sense. Nicole had told me she was buying guns from Fry, lots of guns. They had to be for this would-be Balinese strong-man. He probably appealed to her as a type. She wouldn't have been able to resist an adventurous love affair with an outlaw.

"You are a tourist?" He smiled sarcastically.

"I told you, I'm an oil geologist. I just finished a two year contract in Java."

"*Choba!*" He grinned. "They have many bandits in Java. I would not feel safe in Java."

He seemed to expect me to smile at this comment, but I let it pass. "I could use a drink," I said.

"What was your business near the main road at this hour?"

I glanced at Mr. Chu, who sat like a well-behaved spectator, saying nothing. I faced the Balinese again. "I hooked a ride. It ended there."

"Perhaps you came with Tuan Fry?"

"Look, I'm sorry to break up your concert. I didn't ask to be brought here."

"But you must feel privileged. The army searches all Bali for me, but you find me. Many would consider it a great honor to see me in the flesh. They tell me I have gained quite a reputation in the cities."

"The army couldn't be looking very hard."

"On the contrary. But it is not difficult to hide oneself in two thousand square miles of an island. Why did you come?"

I glanced at Mr. Chu. "Maybe he can tell you."

The Balinese lifted a black eyebrow. He seemed suddenly off guard. "You are a friend of the General?"

The *General?* I stared at the Chinese, and he sensed my own astonishment. The General nodded. "Were you deceived, Mr. Cape?" he remarked. "So—it is not the little Mr. Chu. It is General Chu, of the People's Liberation Army. Yes, that is much different, eh?"

"Much," I said. I kept staring at him, a Red Army man, and tried to adjust my thinking to it. What the hell were the Reds getting behind these bands of left-over soldiers from the Indonesian war? They weren't missing a trick, not when there was a chance to stir up trouble.

I turned to the Balinese; there was no point in attempting to fake about my position, not with Chu here to put him straight if I tried. "All right," I said. "I came with Fry. Where is he?"

"Perhaps you can tell us. We wait."

I shook my head. I shouldn't have beaten the jeep to camp, not on foot, but I did. Maybe the damned thing ran out of gas. I was anxious to see Nicole, but afraid for her to walk in.

"I'm tired and wet and cold," I said. "Do I have to stand here all night?"

"Perhaps."

"What are you going to do with me?"

"We will wait for Tuan Fry. Perhaps he will have some ideas."

Sure, I thought, he'll have ideas. I knew I'd better work fast. "He'll advise you to kill me," I said. "Do you generally take his advice?"

The members of the *gamelan* watched without understanding, like an audience at a puppet show in a foreign tongue. The Balinese didn't appear to like my question. His voice turned surly.

"I am one who makes his own decisions," he said. "Do you not know who I am?"

"You're running a terrorist outfit, that much is obvious. I guess there are plenty of guys like you making a living at it in Bali."

"A poor living," he said, with a touch of pique. "But we are gathering our forces. Soon there will be only one 'outfit'—under my command. I am disappointed that my notoriety has not reached your ears. I am the Anak Agung of Tjandana."

"Fine."

"In your tongue, I am a prince. I prefer to be addressed as Radja."

"I'll keep it in mind."

He glanced toward the Chinese. "The General would like to call me Comrade." It was a cool look, and I gathered that the relationship between them was not warm. He turned back to me. "Obviously, my hereditary title is no longer recognized by the new government of these islands. I made the political mistake of siding with the Dutch in our late war. So instead of a prince, you have the honor of standing before an outlaw."

"That's what I figured."

"In due time Bali will recognize me. I hope you are not wasting sympathy on me."

"I've been wasting it all on myself. I told you, Fry will want me killed."

"If necessary, it can easily be arranged."

"It's not necessary. I'm offering to pay you a heavy ransom for my life." I was going off the deep end, but all I wanted was time—and to stay alive. It would take him days to discover I couldn't write a check for a dime.

The Radja's eyes studied me. He gestured to the houseboy, who brought him a cigarette and lit it. "Why does Tuan Fry want you dead?"

I watched his eyes closely. "There's an American woman in Sanur. She was murdered today. Her name is Regina Williams. Maybe you knew her." He didn't blink. "Yes. I received word." He didn't blink, but his voice lowered and his expression hardened. I had guessed right. She meant something to him, and maybe now she meant revenge.

"I didn't kill her," I said slowly. "But Fry has the Den Pasar police convinced I did. A dead man can't defend himself. Fry will want me dead. He doesn't want that murder properly investigated. You ought to be able to figure out why."

The Radja didn't move for a long time. Smoke curled from the cigarette in his long, brown fingers. He wasn't jumping at the bait. "I will think about it," he said. The financial bait had a more compelling scent. "How much money can you produce for ransom?"

I knew I'd better be convincing, and thought carefully before speaking. Enough to tempt him, but not so much as to raise his suspicions. "I have almost two hundred thousand rupiahs in the Java and Escompto Bank in Jakarta," I said evenly.

A smile touched his lips. He liked the sound of it. "How quickly can this sum be delivered to me?"

"Get me a pen and paper. I'll request the money be transferred to any bank you choose on the island. One of your men can go with me to pick it up. Say, three days."

I glanced at General Chu. He had long ago resumed his role of spectator, slightly amused by the performance.

"When the two hundred thousand rupiahs are in my hands," the Radja said, "you will go free. I will have your letter posted tonight."

I felt a temporary sense of relief. I had bought myself time. Fry would have trouble throwing his weight around when it would cost the Radja two hundred thousand rupiahs. He muttered to the houseboy, who reappeared a moment later with a ball-point pen, paper and envelope. There was no place to write but on the floor. I got down and started the letter. The orchestra waited without a sound, the Radja waited, General Chu waited. I couldn't have felt more conspicuous in a spotlight. I wrote a fast note.

There was still Nicole to worry about, but at least I had won the first inning. What the hell was keeping that jeep?

When I finished the letter, the houseboy picked it up and carried it to the Radja. He read it over twice, glanced at me thoughtfully, and sealed it. Then he arranged for it to be dispatched to the post office in Den Pasar.

I was in.

"Consider yourself my guest," he said with imperious charity. "You must join us for the rest of our entertainment. My *gamelan* is the finest on the island, but unfortunately these men cannot make a public appearance. So they play for me at night when there is no danger of visitors in the jungle. You will find their music soothing, yes?"

He gestured to the orchestra and the jangling notes resumed. I would have liked to go to bed, but I wanted to be here when Fry and Nicole walked in—if they walked in. No chair was offered me, so I settled myself on the floor and rested my back against the wall. The boy dancer faced the Radja and picked up where he had left off. His movements were graceful and exotic, mostly arms and zigzagging head. Before I realized it, the houseboy was beside me with a tray. It contained a decanter and glass and pack of English cigarettes. I said thanks and poured a drink. It tasted like warm poison. It was palm beer.

I lit a cigarette and tried to relax. The little cymbals and gongs fluttered like a metallic beat of wings, and the boy danced. I watched the Radja. He had taken out a small mirror and sat pulling hairs from his face with two silver coins.

I poured a second glass of beer and let it set fire to my stomach.

Chapter Seventeen

General Chu fell asleep sitting in the chair, and I envied him. The music rang through my ears like a delirium and I wished it would stop. The beer had given me a headache. I smoked cigarettes and sat there slapping mosquitoes on my neck. I wished the night would end.

I watched the Radja. He had long ago finished plucking his face, and I recognized the signs of impatience. Where was Fry? Suddenly he rose and sliced his hand through the air. The *gamelan* went silent. He had had enough.

The abrupt silence brought General Chu awake with a start. The natives picked up their instruments and moved silently out of the room.

We were left alone, and the Radja glanced irritably at General Chu. "We will wait a little longer," he said.

General Chu put the serindit in his traveling cage beside the chair and got to his stocky legs. "It is almost midnight," he said. "The American will not come. Perhaps he does not mean to do business with you. I go to bed."

"He'll be here," the Radja snapped. "Return to your chair."

The Radja began moving about, the kris at his back flashing as he turned. General Chu set the cage back on the floor and settled himself philosophically in the chair again.

I forced myself to stay awake. I kept a cigarette going and worried about Nicole. I tried not to jump to conclusions. If Fry had stopped to kill her out in the jungle, it wouldn't have taken this long. And I was reassured by his remark as she stepped out of the car—*"Afraid to face him?"*

He was bringing her here to face either the Radja or General Chu. I asked myself why? I couldn't find an answer.

Then the dogs in the courtyard set up a frenzy of barking, and the Radja's jaws gripped. "He is here."

I braced myself. There were heavy footsteps on the veranda and suddenly Apollo Fry stood in the doorway, his legs muddy to the knees and his face livid. He didn't wait to catch his breath; he was in a rage and his eyes didn't pause long enough to notice me.

"The Balashov woman," he blurted out. "I was bringing her here—she escaped us in the jeep. If you want any guns get some men out in the jungle to find her. I tell you, she'll ruin me."

His words pounded through my head. *Nicole had managed to ditch him.* Sure, I thought quickly, she can take care of herself. That's what she told me once. I might as well start believing it.

The Radja stood before him in a fit of disgust. "You fool!"

Fry shook off the judgment. "I tell you, get some men out there. She can't have gotten far. We did our best looking for her."

The Radja cut him off. "All right, we will find her for you. Where did it happen?"

"Coming up the hill on that sharp turn."

Fry moved aside and let the Balinese through to the veranda. It was my turn to grin, and I wanted to grin, but I couldn't. Maybe Nicole would beat her way to Benua after all. That left me here to twiddle my two hundred thousand rupiah thumbs.

I heard the Radja shouting commands in Malay and Balinese and sensed general movement in the courtyard. Fry stepped dismally into the room, his anger giving way to humiliation. His eyes lit on General Chu, who had remained contentedly in the chair.

"So your clever partner continues to evade you." General Chu smiled. "She is a desperate woman—but so very adroit, eh?"

"He'll find her," Fry muttered, straightening his shoulders confidently. "His men know this jungle like the back of their hand." He looked away from the Chinese and saw me for the first time. It jarred him. He squinted as though I couldn't be real.

"You're tracking mud," I said.

He found his glasses and shoved them on. It was me, all right. "What the hell are you doing here, mister?"

"Trying to keep alive," I said. "And I'm doing fine so far."

He took a step closer to me. "I thought they arrested you."

"That should be obvious. I escaped."

"We'll see about you, mister."

"Take it easy," I said. "Your Balinese friend likes my company. He wants to keep me healthy for a while."

"He's a punk," Fry muttered, turning with disgust. "We'll see about you."

"You're repeating yourself."

The Radja came in from the veranda, lit a cigarette impatiently and eyed Fry with obvious contempt. "So you wanted to bring the girl here. *Choba!* I loan you my best men to keep her from leaving the island, and when you have her, she escapes."

Fry took off his hat and wiped his forehead. "It could happen to anyone," he protested. "She rode with the driver. I had a gun on her all the time. She was crazy to try."

"Not so crazy," the Radja cut in. "You waste my time and my men over this girl. I am tired of these delays. I am interested only to get some guns."

Fry was anxious to acquit himself. "She can't have gotten far, but if she gets to the authorities with what she knows you won't get any guns."

"How did it happen?"

"We were climbing slowly, the mud was bad. There was that turn, and she leaped. I wouldn't have believed it could happen so fast."

"You must have been asleep with the gun."

"We got out and did our best to find her. In the rain and trees she disappeared. But your men will find her. You'll get your guns."

The silver kris gleamed as the Radja turned his back to Fry. The Balinese had a flair for effect. "Thank you for your confidence," he said.

I glanced at General Chu. He was still a quiet observer, only now a comedy was unfolding before him and he watched with silent contempt.

Fry unbuttoned his raincoat and attempted a firmer manner. He nodded his head toward me and caught the Radja's eye. "What about this guy? Maybe you don't know he's wanted for murder. The police are looking for him."

The Balinese smiled faintly. "*Choba!* Then he is all the more welcome here."

Fry returned the smile, fat and unctuous. "He murdered Regina Williams."

The Balinese glanced at me, but spoke to Fry in a sullen voice. "If he is the guilty one, I will make him suffer in a special way."

"Take my word for it. Turn him over to the police."

"The man worries you, salesman."

Fry began to lose his patience. "Be smart, understand? Give the police time to start snooping in your girl friend's background, and they're going to come up with you and me, and that won't be good, will it?"

"So now it is the police who worry you. They do not worry me."

"No?"

"I am considering that you may have performed this murder."

Fry bristled; he wasn't having any of that. "Listen to me, wise guy. Don't you suppose I know she paid your bills? I can't sell you guns if you don't have the money, can I? No, I didn't kill your bank account. I don't give a damn who killed her. It was a bad break she had to get herself murdered now. What's important is to keep the police from nosing around. I don't want them in my hair—is that clear?" He tossed me an angry glance. "And I'm tired of combing *him* out of my hair. He knows too damned much. We can make him look like a suicide. Throw him to the police and they'll be satisfied. They'll close the case."

The Radja pulled at the band of black coral at his wrist. "You have it all figured out, fat one."

"I stay in business by figuring things out."

"I stay in business with guns. In three days I will have money for a shipment. We will discuss the details in the morning. You are tired. The boy will show you to a room."

Fry's nostrils flared. "What about Cape?"

"I will figure what to do with him without the advice of the traveling salesman."

"Don't be a fool!"

"If we do not find this woman partner of yours, it is clear your usefulness will be at an end. Perhaps it will be amusing to deliver you to the police. I promise, tuan, to make it look like suicide."

Fry stood there bristling and then stormed out of the room. The Balinese watched his exit with a smile on his face. "*Choba!*" he said.

I was provided with a room on the second floor with a guard outside the door. The houseboy lit a coconut-oil lamp and left. I looked at my bed. It was a native-style affair with pallets laid over bamboo instead of springs. The mosquito netting hung in shreds. I was too tired to give a damn. I stripped off my wet clothes, hung them around the room and killed the lamp. I stretched out. If the Radja's men didn't bring Nicole back by morning, I'd pull out. I'd have to find a way.

Chapter Eighteen

I awoke. I found myself on my elbows blinking in the heavy blackness of the room. For a moment I didn't know what had frightened me out of my sleep. Then I heard it—the close beat of wings.

I lay back slowly. Judas, I thought angrily, it's getting so I'm afraid of the dark. A bat. I listened, tracing the sound as it circled the mosquito netting. Then, suddenly, it stopped.

I was wide awake, listening, wishing it would find the window and get out. I reached beside the bed to the floor, where I had left my cigarettes and matches. I struck a match and looked around. The light flickered, throwing crazy shadows around the walls. A moment later I saw it, a few inches from my hand, clinging to a tatter of mosquito netting, not black wings but speckled blue.

Jong!

The match went out and I sat there unable to move. The little serindit with a poisoned gaff on its leg. Chu's killer. Jong. I broke out in a quick sweat. There was a flutter, and I heard the bird make another circuit of the bed. In a moment he would find his way into the cage of netting. I risked a match and almost at once saw him fly through a rip and inside.

I shook out the match and rolled quickly onto the floor. I struck another match. Jong was fluttering around inside the netting. I watched with a mixture of horror and fascination, a harmless bird trained to kill, and I tried to figure a way to kill him. Then, as if by accident, he glided through the netting and was loose in the room with me again.

The match went out and I lit another. He swept by me and I ducked. I gripped my trousers in one hand and began flailing at him. In the blackness I felt the scrape of a wing at my ankle. I was afraid to move, even though he must be frightened now. I had to have light. I got a match in my fingers even as I flicked the trousers around me, and managed to strike it. I saw Jong blunder back into the netting.

I dropped the trousers and yanked down the scaffolding around the bed. The torn netting fell over the pallets like a crushed tent, and I hoped Jong was trapped. I went for the door, and pulled it open. The native boy roused himself. At the same moment I saw Mr. Chu coming along the hall.

He wore a pongee kimono, and carried Jong's empty cage in one hand. The guard got quickly to his feet in a fluster of embarrassment at having been asleep, and blocked my way. General Chu approached with his meaningless grin.

"I am looking for Jong," he volunteered. If he were surprised to see me still alive, he didn't show it. "He escaped his cage. You have seen him, perhaps?"

"Don't let's kid ourselves," I muttered, my jaws tight. "Go in and get him. Next time he comes flying around me, I'll break his neck."

"Ah, you are annoyed, Mr. Cape. I apologize for Jong."

He entered the room and I lit the coconut-oil lamp. I watched as the Oriental pulled aside the rags of netting and freed the serindit. He picked the bird up familiarly, but without emotion, examining him as you would a delicate toy that might have gotten out of order. Then he placed him back in the cage.

"All right," I said. "Now get out."

"Poor Jong has had a fright," he remarked. "You are to be flattered that he has come to like you so much as to find his way to your room."

"Maybe he got in through the keyhole. Look; I don't like generals and I especially don't like Red generals. I'm telling you to get off my back. Next time you try to kill me you'd better not miss. I'm liable to get mad and beat hell out of you."

The little wrinkles took hold in that leathery, Chinese face, and he nodded. "I will explain to Jong."

"Go on. Beat it."

I lit a cigarette after he was gone and sat on the edge of the bed thinking. It could have been a nice, simple death. A flick of that blade. Silent. The Radja would have blamed it on Fry. The Radja would have seen me as a two hundred thousand rupiah corpse. A lost investment.

I sat there and everything suddenly made sense.

I looked out the window. Dawn was beginning to shoot across the sky. I realized for the first time it had stopped raining.

Fry came to breakfast with a gun in his hand. His face was tight, his eyes bagged and bloodshot. He had apparently had a bad night. "All right," he said patiently. "Now we'll do things my way."

The Radja was eating a mangosteen. He glanced contemptuously at the gun. "I would advise you to put the gun away, fat one."

"Did you find the girl?"

The Radja returned to the mangosteen. "No."

I sat there stirring a cup of coffee. General Chu had gone out on the veranda to give Jong some morning sun. So Nicole had made it, I thought. All I had to do was get out of here.

Fry didn't put the gun away. His little eyes snapped, and he meant business. "If you think I have to grovel to sell guns, you're crazy. I've put over big deals, you understand, *big* deals. In Java and Malaya and Indo-China.

You're a small-time operator in my book. I did you a favor coming here."

"You are amusing, fat one, with a gun in your hand."

"If you want guns—good American guns—you'll start taking orders from me. First, get some more men out around the island. The Balashov woman probably headed straight for one of the ports again." He lifted his chin to point at me. "He goes to the police. And I'm not waiting three days for my money."

If the Radja had a temper, he wasn't ready to show it. "You wish me to sell out to the gentleman from Peiping. That is interesting."

"I do a cash business. He'll provide you with the cash. Maybe you can throw your weight around among these natives of yours, but don't try it on me. If you want guns, you'll do business my way."

"I see."

The gentleman from Peiping chose that moment to return from the veranda. He glanced at Fry's gun and sized up the situation quickly. He seemed to approve. He settled himself in a chair without comment and set Jong's cage on the floor. He seemed like an old actor awaiting his cue with the greatest of patience.

"Well?" Fry muttered.

The Radja pushed aside the crusty rind of the mangosteen. He wasn't intimidated by Fry's gun, but it was clear something Fry said had gotten through to him. "I ask you to wait a mere three days for your money. I will have ample cash."

"In three days I expect to be back in Singapore. Either we clean this up fast or you can go looking for someone else to sell you guns."

The Radja got up. "I do not wish to tie myself to Peiping."

"That's your worry."

"Do not point your gun at me."

"Make up your mind."

Something on the floor caught the Radja's eye. I saw it as he bent down to pick it up.

A gold earring. Shaped like a temple bell.

Chapter Nineteen

I didn't make a move.

Nicole was somewhere in the house. I felt suddenly crushed and wildly desperate. The Radja's men had found her and I wanted to go to her.

But I made myself sit there. The Radja was playing his own game by keeping Nicole out of sight. He preferred to keep Fry waiting and sweating. But I saw the handwriting on the wall. Nicole was back, and that put Fry in business again. The Radja wanted guns, and he must know he was holding a weak position. His cavalier behavior of the night before could only have been raw vanity. He obviously disliked Fry and hated tying himself to General Chu, but he was in the middle and knew it. He glanced at me, his plucked eyebrows sharp and expressive. It was a cooling glance. The two hundred thousand rupiahs I represented wasn't going to do him any good at that. I was expendable. Only one thing kept him out of the palm of Fry's hand. A native's pride and a prince's ego.

Fry sensed that he had made progress and stopped brandishing the gun. His voice turned unctuous and conspiratorial. "Listen to me, son. You'll be able to build yourself a real little army. You'll be boss on this island in no time."

"I am prepared to be patient."

"Time and money and guns. Good guns, mind you, American guns. You've got a fine future, if you use your head."

"It's a sucker's deal," I said sharply.

Fry snapped the gun toward me in a fit of annoyance. "You, mister, we're going to see about you."

"I didn't figure you for a Commy. I thought you were just a common, garden variety rat."

"I'm not a Red, mister."

"Just a rat, eh?"

"Listen—"

"Make it look like suicide, Fry."

He was working up a head of anger, but I didn't think he'd pull the trigger and make it murder. "You tempt me. Don't worry, we'll fix you up real nice. *Real* nice."

"Go to hell." I turned quickly to the Radja. "Don't let Fry sell you a bill of goods, payable in Peiping. You won't be your own boss. You'll be taking orders."

The Balinese cut me off with a sweep of his hand. He didn't want any advice from the bleachers. He knew he was all dressed up with no place to go unless he got guns. He wanted his private army, and I saw that he would deal with Fry *and* the Reds to get it if there was no other way.

He faced Fry. "When will I get my guns?"

"A week. Stop the Balashov woman, or there may not be any guns. I told you to get some men out."

"She is here."

"What?"

A smile of contempt came onto the Radja's face. "Did you think my men would not find her?" He indicated with a gesture of his head that she was upstairs. "I will go and bring her to you."

"Now you're talking!"

The Radja started off, the kris riding high and ominously on his back. I crossed the room after him. I wanted to see Nicole alone, if only for a moment.

"You! Stop where you are!" Fry's voice came out in a commanding burst, but I ignored it. He was ahead of the game and I didn't think he'd shoot. He didn't. I left him there, stewing in his own frustration.

"I want to see her first, Radja," I said.

He gave me an amused, sidelong glance. "You think you can escape with her?"

"I only want to see her. No tricks." I kept up with him, and he didn't turn me back.

But he didn't lead me upstairs. I followed him toward the back of the house and out the back door.

"I thought you said you had her upstairs," I said.

"She can wait a moment. I have something to show you first. It will make an impression on you and discourage you from attempting escape. I wouldn't like you to try."

"No kidding?"

He smiled. "No kidding."

He led me across the muddy, overgrown courtyard to a clearing near the back wall. A small, square area had been fenced on three sides with bamboo. As we approached I thought I heard a faint, human moaning inside the fence.

When I stood beside him at the open end of the layout my blood turned to ice water. A native boy was prone on the ground, his wrists and ankles tied to stakes.

"You recognize him?" the Radja muttered.

"The boy you had stand guard outside my room."

"He fell asleep."

"You know?"

"Discipline is necessary—even among outlaws. This one will not fall asleep again when I mean for him to stay awake."

The boy lay there naked, his eyes barely open; his brown face deeply cut with lines of pain I couldn't understand. "He's had enough," I muttered. "Why don't you let him up?"

"It will be a few hours before he really feels the pain. There is only fear on his face now. He knows what's coming."

"What?"

"In this climate bamboo grows almost an inch an hour. A young shoot has been entered into his body. We will let it grow until sundown."

"Good God!"

"You are shocked by this Malay torture?"

"It's inhuman. For God's sake, cut him off those stakes. He'll go mad."

"There is plenty of bamboo growing here. Don't make me select a young shoot for you."

The boy's face was heavily beaded with sweat, and his eyes slid toward us with a silent pleading in them. I bent down to him and began untying one of his wrists. The Radja stood behind me, and he started to laugh.

But he didn't interfere. In his eyes I must have been making a fool of myself. I had shown compassion for someone he chose to think of as less than human.

Once I had freed him, the boy turned over on his stomach, disengaging himself from the torturing shoot, and began to sob. The Radja started back across the courtyard, and after a moment I caught up with him.

We re-entered the house in silence. He had made his point, and there was nothing more to discuss. I was on good behavior. He could handle bad behavior if I made it necessary. Think twice.

There wasn't going to be a chance to make a break for the jungle with Nicole and get free. I'd have to find another way.

When we reached the second floor, my skin went prickly. I saw a guard standing outside one of the rooms with a burp gun at rest in the crook of his arm. Nicole would be in there.

The Radja didn't bother to knock. He walked in. He didn't walk far.

Nicole's voice.

"Get out!"

It met him like a slap in the face, and it stopped him. On some impulse, the guard tried to block my way. I grabbed him and shoved him across the hall.

"Don't stare at me—get out. *Get out!*"

"You must come downstairs," the Radja said. "Do us the courtesy to hurry."

Her tone was crisp and enraged. "Will you—"

I was in the doorway, and she saw me. And I saw her. She was beside the far windows under a blaze of sunlight. She was bathing. She was sitting in a few inches of water, her knees drawn up, in a galvanized iron tub. She had washed her hair and was rubbing it dry. Her dress lay across the bed.

She stared at me. The anger left her face; amazement and then disbelief came into her eyes. She seemed to forget the Radja was in the room. "Jeff...." The crispness vanished.

I turned on the Radja. "She told you to get out. She meant it. So do I. Get out."

He hesitated, and then turned with an indifferent shrug of his shoulders. "Yes." He began to grin, like a boy discovering an unexpected fact of life. "I will wait in the hall."

"We'll be right out."

"She is very beautiful. *Choba!* It is a pity."

I shut the door on him and turned. Sunlight flooded across Nicole's shoulders and made her black hair glisten. She tried to cover herself with her hands, but there was no embarrassment in her eyes. It was too late for that. She wanted me here, and I wanted to be here. "Hello, baby," I said.

"Jeff."

"What have they done to you?"

"Jeff, darling."

I walked slowly across the floor, and it creaked. "If he touched you—"

"No. I'm all right, darling."

I reached sunlight and she rose out of the tub into my arms. Her breath caught as our lips met, and her body clung to mine, as though she would drown if she didn't hang on. The strains and doubts and anxieties dissolved in an overpowering relief at having found each other, at being together again. My lips couldn't get enough of her, and my arms tightened.

"Jeff, darling."

The sun was strong and warm against us, and for long moments nothing mattered but that we were in each other's arms. "Baby—"

"Don't let me go, Jeff. I need you so terribly."

"We'll get out of this somehow."

"I thought I'd never see you again."

"Yes."

"How—?"

"Never mind how I got here. We're going to get out. Trust me, baby."

"I tried to get away. My luck has run out."

"Don't say that."

"It's no use, Jeff."

"Listen to me."

"I love you so very much, darling."

"Nicole—"

Our voices stopped under a turmoil of embraces and kisses. My hands moved along her wet back and her fingers dug into mine. And then I broke away.

"Get dressed."

"Yes." She had drawn the mosquito netting from the bed to dry her hair, as there was no towel, and now I ripped down yards of it.

"We're going to have to gamble. I think we'll make it if I can keep my head. Are you game?"

She stepped out of the tub and I threw the netting around her body. "I'm game, Jeff."

She dried herself quickly, and I stood looking out of the window. The jungle stretched to the horizon, a living tangle of green things. It depressed me. I wanted out. If we ever got out of this I never wanted to see jungle again. I hated the heat and the sweat and the insects. If we ever got out....

Nicole had the dress over her head when I turned. She pulled it down deftly, straightening the seams as if it mattered. Well, we might as well get it over with.

"Come on."

"Love me, darling?"

I caught her hand and pulled her to me and our lips touched softly, and then desperately and with finality.

"I love you, baby. More than anything on this earth."

"Then it doesn't matter what happens, darling."

We picked up the Radja in the hall, and the guard followed with the burp gun in his arm. This is it, I thought uncomfortably. And someone's going to get hurt.

Nicole carried the blue raincoat, and we walked. It seemed miles. And then we were downstairs, and the living room lay expectantly before us.

Nicole's hand tightened in mine when she saw Fry. We stopped. There was a moment in which no one moved. And then Fry strode toward us, his eyes gleaming with a sense of victory.

"So we meet again, my girl!"

He tore her out of my grip, and I don't think at that moment he knew I existed. My arm drew back and I froze in order to keep from throwing a fist into him. I made myself hold back. I wasn't ready to cash in my chips, and that would do it. I had a card to play, and I'd better play it right.

Fry pulled her before General Chu. "Have a look at her, Chu. Is she the one?"

I held back. It was the Chinese Nicole hadn't wanted to face. This was the hole in her story. And it was going to be filled in. The moment frightened me; it was something Nicole hadn't wanted me to know, and I was suddenly afraid of it. I'd feel like a chump if she were a Red. A chump and a sucker.

General Chu grinned at her, the way he had been grinning at me. "So we meet again. It has been many years, eh? Our countries are no longer allies. So now we meet again as enemies."

Nicole faced him stubbornly. She said nothing.

Fry was impatient. "You're sure she's the same girl?"

General Chu nodded. "A different name. The hair short. But the same girl. From the picture in the paper, I could only suspect. Now that I see her, there is no question."

Fry straightened his shoulders. "That settles it," he said bitterly. "She's taken me for a ride."

"But cleverly," the Chinese remarked with obvious appreciation. "Always cleverly. In Shanghai, during the war, she posed as White Russian, but that was only to fool the Japanese. A talented woman. We worked well together in those days. Her name is certainly not Balashov. But she is most certainly an agent of American Intelligence."

I felt a catch in my throat. I knew now why she had tried to run out on Fry. With General Chu in the deal, the first time they met he would recognize her for what she was.

Fry pulled her wrist back and stared at her with sweet rage in his eyes. "Balashov's niece, eh? And I fell for it. I inherited a partner—a goddamned phony planted by the government." He twisted on her wrist, hurting her. "Maybe they'll pin a medal on you. Too bad you'll be dead."

I wanted to kill him, but I stepped back. The native who came in with us still balanced the burp gun in the crook of his arm. He probably didn't understand the English, but the scene held him in a kind of childish fascination, a cigarette dead in his lips. There was a live cigarette in my fingers, and I caught his eye with it. He took a couple of steps toward me to pick up a light.

I knocked the gun out of his arm.

"*Adoh!*"

The gun clattered to the floor. We both went for it, but I got it and swung the stock up under his chin. The cigarette in his lips went flying. His head snapped as though I had broken his neck.

I swung the nose of the gun into the room.

"Hold it!" I yelled. "I'll kill anyone who moves!"

Fry turned his head and stiffened. He was still carrying a gun in one hand, but he saw that I'd press the trigger before he could raise his arm to aim.

"Take your hand off her, Fry!" I snapped.

He let go and Nicole moved away, like an old hand at this sort of thing. She got behind me. The Radja stood flatfooted, either amazed or bewildered, I couldn't tell which. Then he began to smile.

"Mr. Cape, it happens I have few guns and almost no ammunition. The gun you carry is empty."

The room was deathly still, except for General Chu. He reached for the bird cage beside the chair.

"You heard me, General!" I said. He straightened with a sheepish grin. The Radja could be faking, and we all knew it. Even he seemed suddenly uncertain about the gun in my hands. There was always the chance the native boy had dropped a few shells into the gun. Empty guns had a way of shooting people. I looked at Fry. "Turn around," I said.

Maybe he thought I was going to try the gun out on him. His lips sagged. "Take it easy now."

"Let me see your back!"

He eyed the burp gun and turned. I made it fast. I crossed to Fry and jammed the nose into his flesh. "Maybe this gun of mine is empty," I said. "You figure it out, Fry. I can try it out in a split second and you'll know for sure. Hand back your automatic or I'll squeeze hell out of this trigger."

I watched the sweat in the folds of skin at the back of his neck. His prickly heat had gotten worse. I figured he was no hero and no gambler when his life was at stake, but he was going to have to gamble now. He hardly seemed to breathe.

"I'll count to one," I said.

He handed the automatic back.

I got a good grip on it, stepped back and pointed the burp gun toward the ceiling. I pressed the trigger.

It was empty.

Fry turned and I threw him the burp gun. "Tough luck," I said. I got back with Nicole and stared at the Radja. I knew there was little chance of getting out of camp, even with an automatic in my hand. I'd need the Radja. And maybe I'd get him.

I spoke to Fry. "I'm going to do you a favor," I said. "Maybe I'll never get out of this thing alive, but I want you to know. Your friend Chu has your card in his pocket. He bought it from me for twelve hundred Straits dollars. It's got writing on the back. Nicole here goes around writing interesting things on cards. All about you, Fry. How you operate. Facts. Chances are the Reds will keep you in line and your prices down with a little blackmail. Think about it, Fry. Chu leaves here alive and your secrets are out."

Fry stared at me. He didn't seem to know whether to believe me or not. I didn't care. The Radja believed me, and saw what could be a crack in the plan for his gun supplies. Fry might not want to play ball with Chu after all. He might want to kill him.

I faced the Balinese. "You said you wanted to get the guy who murdered Regina Williams. Is your word any good?"

The Radja's jaws were set. He didn't answer.

I waved the automatic toward the gentleman from Peiping. "There's her killer, the guy you want to do business with."

The Radja seemed to marshal his self-respect, but I wasn't sure his impulse for revenge would rise above his ambition. "You speak without proof."

General Chu stood quietly. He showed no alarm in his expression.

"Take my word for it," I snapped. "He killed her and he tried to kill me, and it fits. Correct me, General, if I stray from the facts. It's really a big operation, isn't it? You boys are jockeying for position in Indonesia. It's made to order, a new country with plenty of growing pains and lousy with unorganized terrorists. The brain trust in Peiping learned the Radja here wanted to buy guns and sent out the General to buy them for him and tie him up in Red tape. The General gets here and finds the Radja already has someone lined up to pay his bills—an American girl named Regina Williams with more money in the bank than she knows what to do with. The idea of playing around with a dashing Balinese nobleman, especially an outlaw, appeals to her."

"She loved me," he snapped defiantly.

"Sure, sure," I said. Regina Williams probably didn't know what it was to be in love, but that was beside the point. "It probably gave her a giddy feeling of power to finance a vest-pocket rebellion on a vest-pocket island. Hell, maybe she thought you'd make her queen."

"She was a queen," he said broodingly.

"Anyway, she offered to pay and Fry came to sell and General Chu saw he was going to be left out in the cold. He had to remove Regina Williams and her non-political bank account. I think she suspected what he was up to. There was a moment yesterday when I thought she was going to shoot him dead on the ricefields. Maybe she tried. Maybe she was just a lousy aim."

I glanced at the Chinese. He kept that goddamned grin on his face. He wasn't worried. He had sized up the Balinese and knew I was wasting my time.

I turned back to the Radja. "I'll hand it to you for this; you really didn't want to do business with Peiping. You jumped at the chance of paying your own way with a little ransom money."

"*Tiada rotan, akar pun berguna,*" he muttered with a brief smile. "If there is no rattan, a creeper serves."

"All right, the General comes to camp all ready to set you up with a Red exchequer and he finds this creeper on hand. Me. Worth two hundred thousand rupiahs. He tried to cut that out from under you, but he missed. Look at him, Radja. He's laughing up his sleeve at you. He's got you all doped out, hasn't he? He knows you're going to let him get away with it. He figures you for a chump with guns on the brain."

The Radja shot a troubled, moody glance at General Chu, and it was easy to see he was struggling with his Balinese conscience. Maybe Regina Williams had really meant something to him, but she was in the past now and General Chu could guarantee his future. Nothing would bring Regina Williams back to life, and a fit of vengeance could cost him everything. Still, I knew his pride had been brought to a simmer. I would have to bring it to a boil.

"Regina Williams loved you," I said. "And she was murdered for it. Fry didn't give a damn about her when she was alive, but he hated her when she was dead. He tried to throw her in a hole in the ground in order to save his own skin. He didn't give a damn who killed her. All he cared about was keeping the police from stumbling onto his business here. But they're going to stumble onto it. He won't have any guns for you in a week or a month or a year. Wise up, and tell the bum to clear out. American Intelligence is onto him. Even Regina Williams spotted him for a bumbler. I think if she had lived she would have told you to buy your guns from someone else. Am I wasting my time?"

The Radja fingered the coral at his wrist and watched Fry bristle with contained anger. "The fat one puffs up like a frog in the *sawahs.*"

"You're boss around here," I said. "These guys pushed Regina Williams around. They're trying to push you around. Good God, even a coolie would tell them where to get off."

"It is so." The Balinese nodded, his legs spread under the sarong. His hand flicked back and drew the kris from his shoulder. The blade shone like a silver snake. "My word is good."

If he was going to make a little speech, that was as far as he got. There was a clatter on the veranda and barking in the courtyard. We all turned. The door flew open and one of the Radja's men began yelling at him in Balinese. It was clear something had happened.

The translation came quickly. The Radja's nostrils flared as he spoke. "The army is in the jungle. We are being surrounded."

Fry burst into profanity. In the moment's distraction General Chu had picked up the bird cage and snapped a gun into his hand. A .45. I saw too late that it had been concealed under the cage. He tossed the cage wildly and ran toward Nicole. I fired and missed and was afraid to shoot again. He dug the gun into her back and gave me a quick command.

"Drop your weapon."

The Radja turned, the kris stupidly in his hand. The noise of the explosion cleared and there was only the squawking of Jong as he circled the room in fright. He had gotten free of the cage.

I dropped the gun.

Fry was there almost before it hit the floor. He turned it on the Radja. "Get us out of here."

General Chu cut him off in a flat voice. "I will give the orders." For the first time he took on military bearing. He stepped away from Nicole and faced the Radja. He had been immobilized by the confusion, but the sight of General Chu facing him with a gun in his hand brought a show of courage.

"So you take over command," the Balinese muttered. "All right, we will watch you fight an army without ammunition."

General Chu bared his teeth and fired point blank.

Twice.

The room froze. Only Jong was in motion, gone suddenly wild.

Terror held the Radja's eyes open. Two red lines came onto his chest. He took a halting step forward with the kris. His lips fluttered with pain, but he couldn't get out a word. He made a crazy motion with the sword, but it wouldn't reach the Chinese; astonishment was rigid on his face. His black eyebrows arched. He was dead before he collapsed on the floor.

Maybe Fry thought he might be next, because he looked at General Chu and didn't know what to do with the gun in his hand—shoot or wait and see.

"We will remain," the Chinese informed him. "The army will come. They will find we have been held prisoner by these bandits. To the army we will say we overpowered him as they approached."

Fry took to the idea, and smiled. He stared at Nicole. "All right, *all right,* now we're getting somewhere."

Jong sliced low near Nicole's head and I grabbed her arm to pull her down. General Chu turned to us. "These two will not be able to correct our story if they are dead. They will be found against a wall in the courtyard. It must appear the work of the Radja."

The rumble of confusion outside the house died away; the Radja's men were taking to the jungle without command.

Fry went to the window and looked out. "We'd better hurry," he said.

General Chu turned his familiar grin on Nicole. "So this is the way it ends for you—the traditional death for spies. Against a wall."

Fry left the window and saw General Chu's back. He stopped, the gun hanging in his hand. I watched and knew what was going through his head. It would be so easy at this moment to kill the Chinese. Maybe I had been right—maybe General Chu *was* going to attempt some sort of black-mail.

Jong whisked through the room like something gone berserk with fright. He swooped blindly as Fry stood there.

"Fry—*duck!*" I yelled.

He reacted instinctively to the warning. He dropped down and General Chu spun around. Jong came in over Fry's back and stopped himself with a flutter of wings in General Chu's face. Then he sank in and beat his wings orgiastically, clinging there.

"*Ai-e-e!*"

The Chinese dropped his gun and pawed frantically at the bird.

I dove for the gun. Fry saw my movement behind General Chu and squeezed his trigger before he could aim. I tilted the gun off the floor, between General Chu's spraddled legs, and shot. I got Fry in the face.

I jammed the gun in General Chu's back. He turned, twisting his two fists. Jong. We heard the neck break. Blood tricked from a small cut on General Chu's leathery neck.

He walked away from me and picked up the bird cage. He threw Jong's broken body inside, as if it mattered. Then he looked at me, grinning. I had become the spectator. "I will sit down to die," he mumbled. "The poison works quickly."

Nicole crossed to me and buried her head in my chest.

"I say, commissioner, this place looks like a blooming abattoir."

I looked at Lionel Tibby as he stood in the door. Behind him, the court-yard was scattered with native soldiers in khaki poking through the bam-boo. Tibby came in with an officer behind him.

"I thought you'd scared off," I said. "Who the hell are you, Tibby?"

"Sorry to leave you stranded on the highway, commissioner. I figured that driver could lead the army boys to this place, and I don't play a lone hand when I can avoid it. We sweated the boy until he decided to cooper-ate fully, as it were. There's quite a roundup going on in the jungle, I can tell you. Hello, Miss. You all right?"

Nicole nodded and took my arm. "Let's get out of here, Jeff."

Tibby kicked the pith helmet back on his head. "A blooming abattoir, if I ever saw one."

"Who are you working for, Tibby?" I snapped.

His sunburned face broke into a smile. "Uncle Sam, if you want the truth, and me as English as the Queen herself, God bless her." He looked at Nicole. "Central Intelligence, Miss, the same as you. They had me chase down that story about you in the papers. We figured Fry had caught onto you, right and proper, and you might need a bit of assistance. If I may say

so, I've had a time catching up for a talk with you." He nodded toward me.
"Was doing fine there in Benua until this chap comes along with his big
fist. Will someone tell me how he got into this?"

"Let's go find a bar," I said. "I need a drink."

We went out on the veranda. We would have to walk to the main road,
and it was going to be a long walk. The shaggy jungle beyond the walls
was a mixed green, steaming under the midmorning heat.

We were crossing the courtyard when Nicole discovered she was missing an earring.

"It's in there," I said, nodding toward the house.

Nicole turned away with a shudder. "Never mind it, then, Jeff."

We started walking again. I felt as though I were starting from scratch,
meeting her for the first time. "Funny," I said. "I don't really know your
name. I fell in love with a kid named Balashov."

"I've used so many names, Jeff, I'm not sure I remember my real one.
Does it matter?"

"Have you ever used Cape?"

"No."

"You might try it."

"Might."

"Look, I'm damned if I'm going to marry a spy. You'll have to do something about that."

"Yes."

We stopped. It was long overdue. I kissed her under the burning sun.

"All right," I said, and we began walking again. "What the hell are you—
White Russian or American?"

"Both, Jeff. My father was an American, but I grew up in China."

"You never had an uncle named Modeste Balashov in Singapore?"

She shook her head. "He had no relatives we could find out about. When
he died, there was no will. We made up a will for him, naming me bene-
ficiary and forging his name to it. Dates set back, filed—all legal. It fooled
Fry, and that's all we really cared about."

"And that put you on the inside of the Scrap Metals Export Company."

"Defunct, as of today. I finally found out what we suspected; he was
smuggling guns out of the States in loads of scrap iron. He stockpiled them
in a godown in Johore."

"Is that the information you wrote out for me in Buleléng?"

"That and a little more. The address of the godown. The name of a ship
due in Singapore next week with a load of guns."

"There's a ship due in Benua today. We might as well catch it."

"I'll have to write out a report for Tibby."

"And resign."

"And resign."

Later, Captain Arok of the Den Pasar police handed me my passport, my wallet and a flowery apology. General Chu's .45 had not only killed Regina Williams, it had killed her houseboy, Madé, as well. The police discovered his body in the grove of palms behind her house.

Tibby went down to Benua with us and saw us off at one o'clock the next morning. The freighter *Ricardo de Alba* was bound for Panama. The captain couldn't speak English, so he married us in Spanish a couple of hours out at sea.

Then we went to our cabin. It was going to be a long way to Balboa—and I was glad.

THE END

Malay Woman

By A. S. Fleischman

Chapter One

It was hot. It was hot and fatigue was beginning to catch up with me. An early squall had wet down the rambling Singapore skyline and now the twin hangars of Kallang Airport steamed under the blazing midmorning sun. I paid off the taxi, got hold of my scuffed pigskin bag, and started toward the waiting room. My eyelids smarted and my legs were beginning to ache. I hadn't had any sleep—how many hours had it been?

A Chinese box wallah, loaded down with crude Malay jadam work, saw me coming and got on my back at the entrance doors.

"Best make, master, real Malay silver, proper price, ah, yah...."

"*Ming-jih! Ming-jih!*" I muttered, brushing past him into the shade of the waiting room.

I stopped at the ticket counter and nodded to the Britisher on the other side. "When's the next flight off the field?"

"To where?"

"I'm not particular."

"We've a plane for Melbourne at eleven-five, but—"

"Is there an empty seat?"

"Quite, but—"

"I'll take it."

I got squared away on the ticket, checked my bag through customs, and got my passport stamped. I glanced at my watch. Twenty minutes to wait. Then I could take it easy. All I needed was for my luck to hold out another twenty minutes. The big thing was to put a lot of sea miles between Inspector Kris in Sumatra and Jock Hamilton, me. Fast.

Twenty minutes. There was time to call Gabb, I thought. I'd feel like a bastard running out without letting him know and telling him good-by. I stepped on my cigarette and headed into a phone booth. Even if the call were somehow traced, I'd be out of reach before it could be followed up. I lifted the receiver and made myself relax. Stop worrying, kid. The Singapore police don't know you're in town; they couldn't know you crossed over from Sumatra last night. Put in the call.

I got the long-distance operator before I could change my mind, and lit another cigarette.

"Person to person," I said. "Gabriel Wing, Silver Jubilee Rubber Estate. Kuala Tang, Selangor. I'll hold on."

I opened the door a crack for air and glanced out at the crowded waiting room. After a moment a voice broke in over the loud-speakers, announcing the morning flight to Melbourne. From Melbourne, I decided, I'd grab a freighter for the States. Or Mexico. Or Panama. Or anywhere it was headed. What did it matter? In a fistful of minutes I'd be walking out on most of the years of my life. All I had to show for it was a couple of hundred Straits dollars and a jagged scar near my left thumb put there with a tapping knife when a Malay ran amuck in the lines. Well, I'd get used to living without the sulphurous smell of raw rubber in my nostrils and the caterwauling of Tamil and Malay and Chinese in my ears. I'd get used to living without Eden, my wife.

"Can't you hurry it up, operator?"

My wife. It was a bitter taste on my lips. How many guys had there been? How many smiling bastards had made a sap out of me? It couldn't have begun and ended with the young Javanese headman on the Number Three *kaboon* in Sumatra. I remembered Eden's shopping trips to Singapore. What a laugh! Every few weeks. Sure, laugh like hell. For three years she had been a thousand Greek goddesses turned into one long-legged American blonde. But Monday morning the marble had cracked and I saw that she had been rotten, a beautiful counterfeit. But I hadn't shot her. I was sure I hadn't shot her. I was sure. And now I really didn't give a damn who killed her and I wasn't going to get morbid about it. I was going to get clear of the mess, and forget it. But I wondered if I'd ever really be able to believe in another woman again.

"Wing here!"

It was Gabb's clipped, robust voice, and it put a smile on my face. I could see him at the rattan table three hundred miles up the west coast of Malaya, his polished half boots spread on the polished Ipoh marble floor. He was a giant, curly-haired Eurasian, half black Irish and half Singapore Chinese, and the only guy in the East I really gave a damn about. I was going to miss him. He'd ask about Eden, but I'd pass it off somehow. I'd need money to keep going once I reached Australia; he'd wire it, no questions asked.

"Hello, Gabb," I said.

There was a pause. No one called him that any more and I thought he'd catch on fast.

"Singapore? What is this, a wrong number?"

"Wake up, Gabb," I muttered. I hated to mention my name over the phone, but there wasn't time to fool around. "It's Jock Hamilton."

"Who?"

"Jock—"

"There's a bloody mistake." His voice was cold. "I don't know any such party."

"What the hell," I snapped. "Are you drunk this time of day?"

"See here—"

"Listen to me, Gabb." Sweat was trickling down my wrist. There was no time to argue. "I've got to make it fast, so listen closely. I'm through in Sumatra. I've left the plantation. I'm taking a plane out of here in a few minutes and I'm calling to tell—"

"I couldn't be less interested," he cut in. "Check the operator. She's given you the wrong number."

There was a click in the earpiece, like the sound of a cricket.

"Gabb—"

I could feel the heat of my breath bounce back from the mouthpiece. A chill cut through me. This was crazy. I'd know Gabb's voice anywhere; there had been no mistake. He'd introduced me to Eden, and I wondered if somehow the news had reached Silver Jubilee. I hung up slowly, my mind spinning. My world had begun coming apart at the seams about thirty hours ago, and this seemed the final kick in the face. Gabb didn't know me.

I wiped the sweat off my chin. No, I told myself, even if the news had reached him somehow, Gabb wouldn't cut me off. He had never liked her and he told me I was crazy to expect a beautiful woman to take to the isolation of plantation life. You can't teach a frog to live under a coconut shell. Gabb and his goddamned Eastern proverbs. Well, maybe he'd been right. I got out of the booth. I had needed to talk to Gabb, but I could forget that too.

An Indian woman in heavy jewelry and a purple sari went into the booth. I stood for a moment in the salt breeze that swept through the waiting room and it made me aware of the dampness of my suit. I watched the Melbourne passengers gather at the field door. A couple of minutes. I crossed to the newsstand and bought a copy of the Straits Times to read on the plane. I felt angry and confused. Gabb must have had a reason, but I didn't think it was Eden. What was going on up at Silver Jubilee?

When I looked at my watch I realized the line was being held up at the door. My restlessness sharpened. And then it came, a sudden announcement over the loud-speakers.

"Attention, please. British Imperial Airways Flight Two-seven-four to Melbourne, Australia, is delayed one-half hour. Attention, please...."

I watched the other passengers drift away from the door, but for a moment I stood there frozen. My call to Gabb— No. Hell, no. That didn't make sense. A thousand routine reasons could have caused the delay, not Jock Hamilton. Sweat it out. Inspector Kris is still looking for you in Sumatra. Relax.

I took a bench away from the others and opened my paper. I glanced quickly at the heads, but there was no story about the Sumatra murder. I skimmed through the pages a second time.

Nothing. O.K., Inspector Kris was sitting on it. It had cost him face when

I'd got away and he wouldn't advertise it in the papers unless he had to. My eyes lit on a story date-lined Selangor. More than eighty young trees had been slashed on the Jade Tiger estate in a new outbreak of Red terrorism. Jade Tiger... I remembered. It lay just across the river from Silver Jubilee. I wondered if Gabb were having bandit trouble again. Even so, that wouldn't explain his cutting me over the phone.

I tried to read the sports page, but I couldn't keep my mind on it. The waiting room was beginning to get crowded. I got through fifteen or twenty minutes somehow. I smoked my last cigarette, folded up the newspaper, and went back to the newsstand. I got a pack of Capstans.

And I saw them walk in.

The police.

I turned my back slowly and it took me a couple of seconds to get hold of myself. The police. Two Malay constables and a Britisher in whites.

They headed through the crowd toward the passport control desk. I tried to tell myself they couldn't have come in looking for me, but I was kidding myself and I knew it. I risked another glance across the room. The Englishman was checking the list of passengers.

Don't get rattled, I thought. They couldn't know you on sight. Don't try to figure it out. Pay for your cigarettes and walk away. There's still time. It'll take them minutes checking around the place for you.

I glanced toward the far doors leading out to the airport driveway. It was going to be a hell of a walk. I paid for the cigarettes and left the counter without waiting for change. Walk. You've got a chance. Take it easy.

I walked. There was the heavy sweet smell of hair oil as I brushed past a Malay porter. I got halfway across the floor and my name burst out of a thousand loud-speakers.

"Mr. Jock Hamilton—telephone."

I felt as if a spotlight had been flashed on me and my blood went cold. I was scared and I knew it. I shouldered past a knot of tourists and kept my eyes on the glass doors. Only a little way farther. Who the hell wanted me on the phone? Had I mentioned where I was to Gabb? A trick, maybe. Did the inspector in whites think he could lure me out of the crowd with a phony call?

The doors were open for the breeze.

I got through them.

My eyes squinted in the unshaded sun and I kept walking. It was a moment before I recognized the police car parked in front, and then I saw the Malay in khaki watching me. I kept going, but he took a step toward me and I knew I was going to be stopped. For an instant my mind froze.

He had broad, cinnamon cheeks and a British accent. "Orders, tuan," he said, touching his cap. "I must see your identity card."

He seemed uncertain of himself. Maybe he'd been told to watch for an American, but I'd lost the obvious tags years ago. I was wearing a pair of English Veldtschoen, my linen suit was cut by a Chinese tailor, and the ends of my heavy eyebrows were bleached by the tropical sun. There was a chance, I thought, that I could bluff my way past this guy.

"What's the trouble?" I asked.

"Routine, tuan."

His eyes settled on the deep scar at the base of my thumb. It meant something to him, and I knew then that the Singapore police had a description of me. He was a little guy and I was born big, but I knew I was going to have to hit him. He took a step backward and reached for his whistle. I swung. I hit him harder than I wanted to, and I was sorry.

He went clattering back into the fender of the police car and I ran. The driveway was lined with taxis and one of the drivers began blasting his horn.

I cut across a patch of lawn and ran along the white siding of one of the hangars. Other taxi drivers picked up the signal and their horns turned the driveway into a bedlam. I began to feel like a two-bit criminal, and it hurt.

Across the highway I could see the rooftops of the Happy World amusement park and headed toward it. I was sure I had knocked out the Malay, but the taxi horns would bring the others out of the waiting room.

There was nothing to do but take my chances. I wouldn't stand a chance if Inspector Kris got hold of me.

I reached the trees along Mountbatten Road and cut into the traffic lanes. I heard a police whistle begin to shrill above the clamor of taxi horns behind me.

I dodged traffic and got yelled at in half a dozen accents. I reached the far side, leaped down the steps, and entered the amusement grounds.

The noon sun was blast-furnace hot and the wide lanes were almost deserted. I was wet. I could smell fresh pineapple and roasting goat meat and my stomach turned. I got out of the main lane, but there was no shade and I kept going in the sun. Siamese *romvong* music blared out over the grounds from one of the small dance halls.

If I could get to the other side, to Geylang Road, I might be able to flag down a taxi there.

I could hear police whistles, and nearby some Dutch soldiers were clanging away at clay tigers in a shooting gallery. The cops must be trying to stop traffic and get across the highway. I was doing fine.

I walked fast. It would be crazy to run. I hurried around a bank of sideshows just beginning to open up for the day. And then I could see the backside of the wooden entrance arch on Geylang.

I walked out, and luck was waiting for me. A taxi was just pulling out of

the shallow drive and I whistled and ran for it. I got hold of the back door handle and the driver braked. He must just have let off a fare; I got in.

"Back to town," I said. "Make it fast."

The taxi was a prewar Citroen that sounded like a truck. It had everything but speed. I kept watching behind until we crossed the swampy Kallang River. There was no one following. We reached the intersection at Lavender Street, where a turbaned Sikh constable raised his white gloves to interrupt the flow of Kallang traffic. We stopped and waited and I tried to relax. Trishaws and pedestrians crossed in front of us. At noon Lavender Street looked like almost any other Singapore street; the square black-and-white opium signs had long ago been taken down, but the Chandu shops were still there, and so were the brothels and dance halls and streetwalkers. My old man had introduced me to Lavender Street, but that was a long time ago.

The Sikh turned and waved us on. I settled back against the cracked leather seat and tried to light a cigarette, but my lighter wouldn't spark. I gave it up angrily and got a light from the driver.

"The Raffles, tuan?"

"Just keep driving."

I tried to think. That had been close. Something had gone wrong, but I couldn't figure out where. The phone call—had Gabb been trying to reach me at the airport? Where did I go now? To Gabb? Why not? Never mind the way he'd acted when I'd called. I'd be safe at Silver Jubilee if I could get there. It was remote. The highway didn't reach it. There would be only the mail boat at Kuala Tang to sweat out and the river traffic from Kuala Lampur.

I liked the idea. I unfolded my newspaper, turned to the financial page, and checked over the schedules of the Straits Steamship Company. If the Reds were fired up again, Gabb could use me. In his last letters he'd written that he'd been buying land and enlarging the estate, and maybe I could oversee one of his new *kaboons*. I wanted to stop running and go on living. What would I have done in the States? The only thing I knew was rubber. It had been a crazy idea to run out on myself.

I saw that the S.S. Perak was sailing at three-thirty on a west-coast run. That meant, I figured, it would get me to Kuala Tang sometime tomorrow morning. If I could get aboard.

I bent forward and told the driver to head for the docks along Keppel Road. We passed the banks and European business houses behind their heavy stone facades and crossed the hot steel of Elgin Bridge. The Singapore River below warmed itself in the sun and hardly seemed to move. I glanced along the brown colony of sampans clustered like wooden shoes at the far bank. It was a reassuring sight. I wasn't going to leave this steaming, smelly corner of the world. It was the nearest thing to home I had, and I liked it. I'd stick. Inspector Kris would never trace me to Silver Jubilee, and in six months or a year he'd forget me.

I paid off the taxi a few blocks from the harbor and walked the hot pavement. If the police had been watching the airport for me, they'd be watching the docks. I couldn't risk buying passage and showing my passport. I didn't want Inspector Kris following me up the coast of Malaya.

I heard a drone in the sky and saw the silver flash of a plane banking above the Victoria clock tower. The British Imperial Airways flight to Melbourne. I was glad to see it go without me. All I'd lost was my bag—my shaving gear, some underwear, a couple of shirts. There hadn't been time to take much, the way I'd pulled out of Sumatra. At least I had a suit on my back and a couple of hundred Straits dollars in my pocket.

I spotted a turbaned Sikh standing his beat at the intersection, his brass buttons flashing gold in the sun. I made up my mind not to flush every time I saw a cop, and kept in the open. I was damned if I would start thinking and reacting like a criminal.

I reached the docks and a moment later I saw the blinding white bows and single stack of the S.S. Perak. Not far off, on the burnished surface of the water, sampan coolies were dragging up edible seaweed.

The burning concrete pressed through the soles of my shoes and I moved under the shade of a godown balcony and looked over the ship. It looked old, but austere and intimidating, like a seagoing dowager. The cargo hatch was open, and I could see dim lights inside the ship, but the dock gang had knocked off during the noon-hour heat. Boxes of tinned butter and Australian canned milk were piled up beside the ramp, waiting to be loaded aboard.

My eyes moved up the side of the ship and I saw two Malay seamen fixing a shade tarp across the bow stanchions on the main deck. The gangway and companionway were unattended. I looked at my watch. It was almost three hours before sailing time; the passengers hadn't begun to arrive, and the police, I figured, wouldn't show up until later.

I didn't like the idea of holing up in the heat below deck. White men don't stow away on these coast runs, I told myself. Never mind the open cargo hatch. Walk aboard as if you had shore business up there. It's direct, and it'll work. Get going, kid.

I stepped on the butt of my cigarette and had to beat down a sort of stage fright. I didn't like it. I was a big, easygoing guy; I hadn't liked hitting that cop at the airport and I didn't like turning myself into a stowaway. I had never run away from anything in my life before and it cut me to be running now. I had begun to dislike myself the moment I made up my mind to leave Sumatra. Well, it was done. There was nothing to do but keep going.

I glanced again at the gangway, creaking gently in the sun, and looked along the dock. It wouldn't stay deserted long. In the shade of the next godown I saw a dozen coolies on their haunches around some coins, gambling against which one the next fly will land on. They didn't know I existed.

I straightened my shoulders and walked back into the sun. I crossed the hot concrete to the gangway and started up. Maybe I'd taken half the length when a sunburned ship's officer appeared at the top. He started down in a rush.

I kept going. We met and he touched his black visor. "Pardon me, old chap."

We passed each other and I took a breath. He had something on his mind, but it wasn't me. I was glad I had no suitcase to bother with; I didn't look like a passenger.

I reached the deck landing and kept walking. I could hear a clatter of dishes from the galley and there was a smell of curry in the air. I went up the nearest ladder, and Singapore's steep tile rooftops spread out before me. If I were lucky I'd pick a cabin that would sail empty, and I figured my best chances were in first class.

I turned into the passageway. Clear. Louvered doors stood open from the cabins. I could hear dance music coming from the radio shack and it made me aware that life was going on around me even if I couldn't see it. A steward appeared at the other end of the passageway and I kept moving. I crossed to the port side, saw no one, and walked into an after cabin. It was done.

I glanced around quickly. I'd have to leave the door open as it was. The cabin was paneled in mahogany and smelled of furniture polish. The bulkhead fan was off and the room was stuffy. Through the closed porthole I could see the tin smelting chimney on Pulau Brani island. It was done, but I couldn't just stand there. The bathroom was out, but there was the wardrobe closet. I opened one of the two doors and decided it would do. Later, if someone checked into the cabin, I could leave when it was clear, maybe at dinnertime. I walked in, closed the door, and settled against the bulkhead to wait.

The closet was hot and airless, and within half an hour I was sitting in my own sweat. I tried to doze off to kill time, but my nerves wouldn't ease up. I was too tired to sleep. Memories plunged in on me. I remembered a thousand Edens—Eden sitting with Gabb at the bar of the Raffles Hotel the first time I saw her. Eden yelling herself wild at the race track at Bukit Timah. Eden in a tight print dress. Eden under a *jarang* sun hat on the plantation in Sumatra. The love and the sudden fights and the illusion of being in love. Eden dead, and I couldn't remember. Eden bloody in that green dinner dress she'd just brought back from Robinson's in Singapore. The slick-haired Javanese who admitted he was her lover. Inspector Kris. The crazy shock, the wildness, and the daze. And then the running away. Not from Inspector Kris; from Eden. I had stopped caring. You can't teach a frog to live under a coconut shell. I was sorry if I had killed her. All I remembered was waking up Monday morning with a bad head when I knew I hadn't been drunk the night before. A taste in my mouth. And I saw Eden on the rattan rug, the green dress, and the blood. She'd been dead for hours.

I must have dozed off. I became conscious of new sounds around me—passengers coming aboard. My senses sharpened. The plates I sat on had grown warm; the ship was getting up steam. It must have taken another hour. I don't know how I got through the minutes, but finally I heard the thick blast of the whistle. My hopes soared. The cabin was going unoccupied. It was a break. Once we got under way I could get out of here for a while. I'd find the bar and get a drink. I'd be just another passenger.

I felt the ship's throbbing as if it were my own pulse amplified. The engines were turning over. I heard a shout of voices from the dockside and realized the lines had finally been cast off.

At almost the same time I heard the scrape of a suitcase beside me, and my hopes died. The fan was snapped on. I had company. I might be stuck in this damned closet for hours.

Voices came very clearly into the closet.

"Shut the door, Hoven." English.

A gruff Dutch voice answered. "What about the gun? You got it aboard, *ja?*"

Chapter Two

I could hear the whir of the fan. I didn't want to listen to the conversation, but the two men were within a few feet of me. They were none of my business, they were just a pair of voices, but I didn't like the sound of them. They spoke in low tones and I heard every word.

"Piffle dust." It was the Englishman, and he sounded buoyant and amused. "We won't need a gun for this."

"I like better a gun," the Dutchman objected. "I like better to do things my own way."

"You're an elemental creature, Hoven, but I like you. And I suggest you keep your voice down."

"Never mind—"

"Sit down. Did she come aboard?"

"If you didn't almost miss the boat, you would have seen her," Hoven said. "*Ja*, she came. Better you missed the boat. I can do the job alone, by myself."

"You wouldn't be thinking of the money, Hoven, would you? You ought to be grateful I'm willing to cut you in. But of course you're not. You're elemental. I wonder why I look after you."

"Never mind what I am, Edgett. I attend to business. Not like you, living the high life with empty pockets. Maybe you cut me out again, *ja?*"

The Englishman laughed. "Piffle dust, Hoven."

"Come, we get down to business." Hoven was obviously a man without a sense of humor. I wondered what the hell I'd walked into. I wanted to shift my position but I didn't move. I heard the click of a cigarette lighter.

Edgett said, "Plenty of time. Which came first, Hoven? This filthy weather or the gin pahit? I'm going to the bar."

"Never mind gin pahits." Hoven's voice stiffened. "We talk now before you get drunk."

"I'm wilted."

"We talk now. You stay away from the bar, *ja?* Because I say so."

Hoven must be a big bruiser, I thought. Edgett sounded intimidated.

"Piffle dust."

"You don't leave the cabin."

"You're a bore, Hoven, but I like you."

I could hear the defiant chugging of tugs maneuvering the ship into the stream.

Hoven said, "So—you reached the buyer, *ja?* That's why you were late, maybe."

"I was late, my excellent bourgeois friend, because I'm never on time."

"Ach!"

"As a matter of fact, I couldn't reach the Nabob. But there's no question about it. We do the job and he'll pay. He always has. You're tight as a drum. Calm yourself."

"I should never have trusted my gun to you. Without a gun it is not so easy. With a pillow around the gun there is little noise."

"Leave it to me. I have talents."

"*Ja*, with women you have talents."

"Exactly."

Hoven sighed. "She is pretty, this Allison woman. I wish maybe she wasn't so pretty."

"Did you locate her stateroom?"

"She is on the other side of the ship. Cabin Eight."

"You're efficient, Hoven. A true Dutchman. In another year you'll have saved enough to go back to the old country."

"*Ja*, I save, but I can never go back." He sighed, then said, "Why a man should want this woman dead I don't understand. You have seen her? She is young."

"Ours not to reason why, Hoven. Ours to collect a princely five thousand dollars."

"It is not so much when we split."

"You forget, Hoven, in this business we compete with coolie labor. It's a good enough price in this part of the world."

"She's English, the girl?"

"Australian. Runs an upcountry plantation all by herself. Her husband was killed last year by the bloody Reds."

"It's no life for a woman, all by herself."

"Stubborn as the weather, this one. She was in Singapore trying to hire an estate manager, and it gave me a lively week scaring off any takers."

"You have worked often for this buyer, Edgett?"

"When the Nabob needs things done in Singapore, it's Will Edgett he calls. You ought to appreciate the contact I've made for you."

Hoven didn't answer. The smell of cigarette smoke drifted through the closet louvers and I wished desperately I could light up. I was starved for a smoke. The ship began to creak slowly and I knew we were under our own steam. I wished I could get up and get out. I'd already heard too damned much. If one of them decided to hang up a jacket and opened the wrong closet door— I tried not to think about it. Edgett sounded the nearest to me, and I thought he must be in the chair under the fan.

He said, "It'll be easily done. See here, I'm not a bad-looking chap, and there's nothing like a sea trip to start an idle romance. I shall have Kay

Allison swept off her feet before we see the coast of Johore, Hoven."

"This one looks to me like she don't get swept off her feet."

"Piffle dust. They're all alike. A cocktail. The wind on deck and the sun setting behind the jungle. I'll charm her, Hoven. I'll bring delight to her last hours aboard ship."

"You're a machine, Edgett. You aren't human. Never mind you charm her."

"And in the dark hours on deck you will find us suitably cozy and alone in long chairs. Are you listening, Hoven?"

"*Ja*, I listen."

"Suddenly from behind her chair those fine strong hands of yours reach out for her lovely, lovely neck. I promise she won't utter a sound. My hand will be over her mouth. Then—a quick burial at sea. I shall conduct services."

I rubbed the heavy sweat off my face. For all his rakish talk, this guy was a cheap, cold-blooded killer. I couldn't let it get started; I'd have to stop them. Somehow I'd have to queer it, but queer it without getting caught up in the mess. I was a stowaway. I was walking a tightrope.

"*Ja*," Hoven muttered. "I suppose it will work."

"Of course it will work. The ship is due in Malacca Town at two in the morning. We walk off. *Fini*. It may be weeks before she washes up among the mangroves. The fish will have pecked away at that tanned flesh and devoured all evidence of foul play."

Hoven was impressed. "You have brains, Edgett, but still I don't like you."

"Piffle dust."

"*Ja*, piffle dust."

The ship's bell rang out. Four o'clock. There was nothing to do but sit tight until they left. Edgett was hard up for a drink. He worked on Hoven. He'd stay out of the ship's bar, unless, of course, there was the opportunity to buy Kay Allison a cocktail. The sooner he was able to start the machinery of their shipboard romance, the better.

Hoven relented. "One gin pahit, maybe."

"I shall get you boisterously drunk in Malacca Town."

"In Malacca Town we will see. I take a nap now. But it is too hot to sleep."

I worked my knees slowly. We were left alone and I knew I was going to be stuck in this foul closet for hours more. My skin felt raw and bruised and my bones ached. I heard the springs creak as Hoven stretched out on the bunk. Then I heard a newspaper crackle.

It must have taken him an hour to read that newspaper. I heard every page turn. I thought, If only he'd fall asleep, I could grab the chance of getting out of the cabin. But Hoven didn't sleep. He smoked. He went to the bathroom, leaving the door open. He picked up the newspaper again. The ship's bell chimed the long, miserable hours. I thought I'd go nuts if I had to stick in the closet another hour.

Hoven was in the bathroom when Edgett returned. I could hear a mumble as they talked briefly while Hoven washed up and the dinner gong sounded in the passageway. They stayed in the cabin about another fifteen minutes.

Then I heard the door close after them. I was alone.

I waited about a minute. Then I opened the closet door and the shifting light in the cabin made my eyes squint. I started moving. A thin breeze funneled in from the porthole and I stood for a moment gulping air, my skin dripping sweat. I went into the bathroom and put my face under the faucet and drank. I let my hair soak up cold water. I don't know how long I was in there. I felt dizzy and a little sick. But my head finally began to clear and I tried to clean up. I knew my suit looked a mess, like yesterday's laundry, and wondered if I'd be crazy to show myself on deck. Or in the bar. Well, I could get something tailored in Kuala Tang. I'd start feeling human again when I reached Silver Jubilee. Right now I needed a couple of stiff drinks and I had to figure out what to do.

I straightened my tie and peered at myself in the mirror. My face had taken on a gaunt, furrowed look and my eyes looked black and sightless. I needed a haircut. Eden used to cut my hair and it was rough over the ears. I was beginning to look like a beachcomber, I thought. I turned away from my reflection and heard a key scrape in the outer door.

I froze. I glanced quickly around the small bathroom. There was no place to go but the shower stall. I stepped away from the mirror and flattened myself against the far wall and wished there had been time to draw the shower curtain.

I caught a flash of a man in the mirror, a thin face with wavy hair. It couldn't be Hoven, I thought, so it must be Edgett. He began to whistle absently. I heard a suitcase snap open. A moment later I knew he had a gun in his hand. I heard the soft click as he sprang the magazine, apparently to check it, and then the thrust as he snapped it back in position. Silence. I didn't breathe. What the hell was he doing now? If he stepped into the bathroom I'd jump him. I tried to trace any sound of him and I thought he must be at the bunks. Then I heard the rustle of cellophane, as if he were opening a fresh pack of cigarettes. He must have told Hoven he'd forgotten his cigarettes, I decided. But he'd come back for the gun.

He stopped whistling.

"You're a fool, Hoven," he mumbled. "That's why I like you. Piffle dust."

He walked out.

My muscles eased up. I'd been a jerk to let myself get trapped in here. Well, I'd been lucky, but I couldn't go on pressing my luck. I walked back into the cabin. Double cross, I thought. Hoven was going to get the short end of a double cross. The Englishman had recruited him for the fall guy, but that was Hoven's worry. I didn't kid myself—Edgett was tricky and dangerous and I'd better not let myself get in too deep. But I *had* to take the risk of queering Kay Allison's murder.

Cabin Eight.

I'd better talk to her. If she were warned, and had any brains, she could look out for herself. Once I tipped her off, I could wipe my hands of the whole rotten mess. Then I could start nosing around for a safe place to ride out the voyage.

I opened the door a crack and looked along the passageway. A Chinese amah with two white children was coming and I shut the door. A moment later I was in the passageway.

I crossed to the starboard side and made up my mind to forget I was a stowaway. I'd be taken for a passenger; maybe a bit seedy, but no one was going to bother me.

I followed the numbers and found Kay Allison's cabin astern. I wondered if this were crazy. I could write an anonymous note. But would she believe a note? The thing would sound like an absurdity. She'd think it were written by a lunatic.

I stared at the polished brass number on the door. Get it over with, I thought. If she's not going to believe you, you'd better find *that* out.

I knocked.

There was no answer. I felt conspicuous standing in the open corridor, and I hit the wood harder. But it was no use; she wasn't in. She'd probably gone down to dinner.

It was a loose end, and I wanted to tie it up. I was annoyed at the delay. I tried the knob; the door wasn't locked. I had an impulse to walk in and wait her out. Then I changed my mind, left the door, and started forward.

I needed a drink.

Chapter Three

"A sundowner, tuan?"

The bartender had two gold teeth in front and they glinted with his smile. I took him for an Achinese Malay, taller than the home-grown variety and more heavily bearded. The saloon was almost empty; the only other passenger at the bar was a white-faced Englishman in new ducks. He looked young and green and straight from the London fog.

"A sundowner," I said.

A newspaper lay at the corner of the bar and I kept glancing at it. Stop worrying, I told myself. You checked the paper at the airport. There was nothing about you. Don't jump out of your skin every time you see a newspaper.

The Englishman looked my way with a timid smile. I ignored him; I was in no state of mind to get into conversation with a brand-new colonial. I watched the twilight fade into purple through the saloon windows and wished the Malay would hurry with my drink. An early bridge game was getting started on the port side. The ship begun to pitch slowly.

My drink came.

I said, "What time do we get to Kuala Tang?"

"Should be nine-thirty of the morning, tuan."

I picked up the chill glass and wet my throat. The drink was worth waiting for.

"*Sénang, tuan?*"

I nodded. "*Sénang.*"

He moved away and I put my cigarettes on the bar. I got one between my lips and tried my lighter again. I wondered why I had taken it with me from Sumatra. It had been a gift from Eden on my birthday and it seemed crazy to be reminded of her every time I lit a cigarette. But it had an old mechanism that I'd always liked, a couple of wings you twisted to release the spring, and it was covered with golden hamadryad skin. She'd picked it up on a trip to Palembang.

"I say, let me give you a light." It was the young Britisher. He slipped off his stool and came closer with a pocket tin of Australian wax matches. He struck a light and I turned for it.

"Thanks."

"Going far?"

"Far," I said. I took a drag on the cigarette and held down the smoke, enjoying it. That had been too long to go without a cigarette. I wished the guy would go back to his stool.

"What does *sénang* mean? I'm frightfully new out here, you see. I've been brought out on a mining job in Kinta."

"*Sénang* means anything you want it to mean," I said. "Peace, happiness, plenty of money in your pocket, a good wife, a good drink—*sénang.*"

"Tell me, the snakes are bad out here, aren't they? I'm a bit worried about that."

"You may never see one."

"I shouldn't want to let the others see that I'm frightened."

"Everything's going to be *sénang,*" I said.

"What? Oh, yes, I certainly hope so. I shall be here two years."

I tried to get back to my own thoughts. I was sorry Kay Allison hadn't been in her cabin. I wondered what the hell had built her up into a target for a pair of professional killers. She was worth five thousand dollars dead to someone—the buyer, the Nabob. I couldn't help admiring a woman trying to run a plantation by herself, but she must be doing a lousy job, I thought. No woman could handle the natives. And Edgett had picked up some extra chips putting pressure on any overseer she'd tried to hire. Well, that was none of my business. I kept glancing at the newspaper.

"Do you know if there are any bandits around Kinta—the bloody Reds, I mean?"

"No, I don't know," I said.

"Can I buy you a drink?"

"I'm doing fine on this one." I caught the bartender's eye and nodded toward the newspaper. He brought it over and I flipped it open.

It was the Straits Times, but the front page was different and I became quickly apprehensive. It might be a later edition than the one I'd picked up at Kallang.

"Tell me, does one *ever* become accustomed to the heat out here?"

I skimmed the front page quickly.

It was there. I saw it just below the fold on the right-hand side.

SUMATRA MURDER
SUSPECT EVADES
S'PORE POLICE

I folded the paper over and looked at the Englishman. "Good luck," I said.

"Thanks, old man. Everything's going to be *sénang.*"

I left money on the bar and walked out with the newspaper in my hand.

I read the article on deck. A breeze sweeping off the bow rustled the paper in my hands and I held tight. I read quickly. Dangerous and probably armed, it said. That was crazy. It gave a rundown of the break from Kallang Airport and the search that had followed in the maze of Happy

World. A cordon had been quickly thrown around the amusement park, but the American had slipped through "with criminal cunning." Singapore officials, co-operating with Sumatra, had immediately spread a net over the entire island. A quick arrest was assured. Inspector Ian Dykes, of the Central Police Station, was quoted as saying, "The bounder doesn't stand a chance of squeaking through."

There was no picture. I was relieved, even though I knew there couldn't have been one. I had burned every snapshot in the house before I left the plantation. But there was a description, and it had me cold. Over six feet, rawboned, age about thirty. Slate-blue eyes, cropped brown hair, deep scar on left hand near thumb. Approach with caution.

Exasperation kept me from reading to the end. They had written me up like a hardened criminal.

The air was freshening with the coming of night. I went down the ladder to the main deck and walked. I wondered if the Malay bartender had read the paper. I hadn't made any effort to keep my scarred hand out of sight. What about that damned little Britisher? The sky was purple and the ship's lights were beginning to trace themselves on the sea. I walked to the rail, twisted up the newspaper, and gave it the deep six.

At least I knew where I stood. There would be other copies of the Times aboard. I'd have to be careful. Still, it was a break for me that the cops felt so sure I couldn't get out of Singapore; there would be no sense of alert outside the colony.

I lit a fresh cigarette from the stub. All I could do now was wait. Wait for Kay Allison to get back to her cabin. There were Edgett and Hoven to worry about now.

I leaned on the rail and watched the distant shoreline, vanishing in the dark smear of the horizon. I could feel its presence, jungle-clad and ominous. I had never got used to the jungle at night.

I don't know how long I stood there. When I moved away from the rail, stars spread over the black sky like scattered rice. I'd try Cabin Eight again.

I tried. She hadn't come back. I stood in the passageway and my impatience turned to anger. How long did Kay Allison need for dinner? I was damned if I was going to kill time wandering around the ship. I'd wait for her in the cabin. I wouldn't have to worry about myself in there.

The stateroom was dark. I shut the door after me, and it happened—fast. I heard a sudden rustle, my muscles grabbed, and then something hard jarred my head. I felt my hands slap the deck and noises spiraled in my ears. I remember trying desperately to get up, to reach out. I remember the shudder of rage and a shoe kicking into my stomach—and then the flash of pain dimmed and there was only a whirling suspended blackness and Eden appeared laughing. Eden turned insanely green, her face, her lips green, her hands, the shining skin of her body, bright jungle green....

I heard the slow creaking of wood. There was the near fragrance of mimosa about me and a hot pounding in my head. My eyes opened, and I saw a tanned foot in a narrow thong sandal. I stared at it, but for a moment it carried no meaning. A hand touched my shoulder and I tried to shake it off.

"You needn't—" A woman's voice, low and throaty.

The sandals moved away and the room held a crazy silence, like time stretched into slow motion. I shook my head. The light was on and it glinted off the brass fittings. I could feel the breeze of the fan. I pushed myself off the deck and I saw her.

She stood against the mahogany door.

"Shall I get the ship's doctor?" she asked.

"No."

"You're hurt."

"Forget it."

"But—"

"I said forget it."

I got off my hands and tried to find my balance. I could feel her eyes on me, cold, watching, sizing me up.

"Who are you?" she said.

"I'm not staying long enough to get acquainted."

"Rough as bags, aren't you?"

"Sure." I straightened and took a good look at her. She stood on long, tanned legs and her feet were bare in the leather sandals. She seemed younger than I had expected, and it came as a mild shock. This had to be Kay Allison, but she couldn't be more than twenty-five, I thought. Her nose and cheekbones had a thin scattering of freckles, and except for lipstick she wore no make-up. The sun had put small wrinkles at the ends of her eyes. She wore her reddish-blonde hair cut short for the heat and the dress was a sleeveless linen affair, smoke-gray, tight at the waist with a belt of large silver coins.

"You needn't stare at me," she said quickly. "I think you'd better—"

She was stacked. I noticed the low, square-cut neckline of her dress without really wanting to. There was something honest and genuine about her that made an automatic appeal to me, and I felt a vague resentment. They all looked honest and genuine at first, like Eden.

"Kay Allison?" I said.

"Yes."

"Sit down. I've got to talk to you."

"I think you might tell me what you were doing in my stateroom."

"It's going to sound crazy," I said.

"Yes, I'm sure it will."

I rubbed my lips and then found the rawness above my right ear. A gun butt? A gun butt—Edgett. It had to be Edgett. Edgett and the Dutchman, and this was the woman they'd been commissioned to kill.

"I think I walked into a trap laid for you," I said. "If you're not going to sit down, I will."

"You said you weren't staying that long."

"Relax, baby."

She came away from the door, but she didn't relax. She got a tin of Players out of her straw bag and lit one. I sat on the lower bunk and tried to rub the ache out of my eyes. I wondered when I'd ever felt so tired. "Does the name Edgett mean anything to you?" I asked.

She took a deep drag on her cigarette. She didn't answer.

"Will Edgett," I said.

"We met this afternoon," she said in that low, soft voice of hers. "I don't see how that could possibly interest you."

"It does. He made a pass at you, didn't he?"

"You might call it that."

"He plans to kill you."

If the idea startled her, she didn't show it. She turned from the porthole and the coins at her waist flashed. "But that's absurd."

She was a cool article, and it made me a little sore. "You asked what I was doing here. I'm trying to tell you."

"Why should he want to kill me? It's—"

"There's a quick five thousand dollars in it for him," I said.

"What do you mean?" Her eyes, jade green and alert, steadied on me. She couldn't have been impressed with what she saw.

"Edgett and a Dutchman named Hoven came aboard to kill you," I said. "Because they've been hired. Someone is putting up that much dough to get rid of a planter's widow named Kay Allison. You."

"Me."

"You think I'm making this up, don't you?"

"Aren't you? No one cares that much about me, dead or alive."

"You're wrong. The buyer, the Nabob. That's what they call him. I was in a position to overhear them planning it. Never mind how, just start believing me."

She looked away. She wasn't buying it. She seemed to resent me for suggesting the crazy idea. "Thanks for warning me. I can take care of myself."

"Damnit," I said, "listen to me. Edgett expects to lure you on deck tonight. You'll be strangled and pitched overboard and they'll collect some chips for their troubles. That was the plan, but after what happened to me in here

I'm not too sure of it now."

"If you think I can be frightened—"

"No, I doubt if anything really frightens you, baby."

"Certainly not Edgett."

"Fine. All I came in here for was to tip you off."

"You needn't have bothered."

"I'm beginning to be sorry I did."

"Look." Her shoulders gave a little. Maybe she was beginning to play with the idea, I thought, that I might not be out of my mind. Her eyes softened, but they kept trying to make sense out of me, the rumpled white suit, the scuffed shoes, the big, sun-darkened hands. I glanced down at the scar and my thoughts jolted. I covered it. She must have noticed it. I wondered if she'd seen the paper and how closely she'd read it. "Look," she said, and her voice carried a sort of contempt. "I don't go for terribly sure men with a flare for women. Edgett didn't get to first base with me this afternoon."

"Maybe that explains it," I said. The scar meant nothing to her, I thought. She wouldn't be talking to me this way.

"You keep *not* making sense."

"Believe me, I'm trying," I said. "Does this make sense? Edgett struck out with you this afternoon. He has a gun. He decided to wait in your cabin for you. I knocked at the door, something you wouldn't do, and it alerted him. He wasn't going to risk being found in your cabin when I opened the door. I just got it shut behind me and he worked fast. That's why you found me stretched out in here."

The impact of murder was beginning to take hold of her, I thought, but she wasn't going to lose her self-possession. "You're serious about this, aren't you?"

"I've got a headache that's very real, baby." I stuck a cigarette between my lips and remembered my lighter wouldn't work. "I could use a light."

She came toward me slowly and fired a man's lighter. Her husband's, I thought. When I saw that her hand was shaking a little, it startled me. This kid was human after all.

I sucked in on the cigarette and she turned away, her sandals whispering faintly. I watched the smooth lines of her back, the way her hips worked. I began to like what I saw. I couldn't help thinking how unlike Eden she was. Kay Allison was pretty, but Eden had been beautiful. Beautiful and rotten. Eden would have covered her freckles, Eden wouldn't have cut her hair for the weather. Eden was something sculptured out of perfumes and cosmetics and imported dresses. This kid wore her clothes with an air of indifference and she didn't give a damn about the freckles. I found myself wanting to like her, and then I thought to hell with it. They were all the same. You like them, you trust them, you believe in them, and they foul the nest. They don't have to be beautiful for that. Even this kid....

She said, "You're a planter, aren't you?"

It took me off guard and my eyes flashed up at her. Had she read the goddamned paper? "What makes you ask that?"

"I'm interested."

"Forget me."

"There are things about you—"

"Like what?"

"Your hair looks as if it had been cut by a native boy."

"Wrong."

"There are a lot of little things. Planter?"

"Tourist," I said. Wild guess, I thought. Hell, who wasn't a planter out here?

"Look, if Edgett can't get to you any other way, he might try a pot shot through the window while you're asleep in your bunk. I'd close it and cover it with something and be damned careful about answering the door."

She glanced at the open window, framing a patch of night sky, and rubbed her arms as if she felt suddenly cold. For all her easy self-possession and pride, Kay Allison was scared, I thought. And I was sorry. But there was nothing more I could do for her.

"I'll get going," I said.

"Am I supposed to lock myself in this cabin?"

"That's up to you."

Anger began to catch up with her and her eyes widened. "Is there any reason why the captain—"

"There is," I cut in. "Edgett and Hoven haven't committed any crime yet."

"But if you told him what you've been telling me—"

"I'm not interested in meeting the captain. That's final."

"I don't understand."

"I told you," I said. "Forget me. Forget what I look like, forget you ever saw me. I stuck my neck out coming here, and I don't expect you to understand that, but don't drag me into trouble you don't know anything about."

"You needn't raise your voice."

"I'm sorry."

"But even if I get through the night, there's tomorrow and the next day."

"I haven't thought it through that far. All I know is you're in danger tonight."

Her manner stiffened. "All right. Thanks for warning me. I'm sorry about your headache. I can look out for myself. Good-by."

I felt it was a bad note to walk out on, but I couldn't think of anything more to say. I turned the knob. "Good luck, baby."

But even as I walked out I knew it was no good. I'd been crazy to let myself get personally involved. She had no intention of sticking to her cabin; I could feel it. It would be an act of intimidation and she wasn't going to let herself be pushed that far.

"I say—hello."

It was the green Britisher I'd met in the bar. I shut the door behind me and nodded.

"See here, we're neighbors. I'm just across the hall. Come in for a drink. I bought a bottle of Meukow brandy in Singapore. Let's have a go at it."

"Save it for snake bite," I said, and walked away. I should have had brains enough to check the passageway before I left the cabin. Now I'd been seen coming out of Kay Allison's cabin.

"Well—*sénang*, old man."

I walked out on deck and tried to shrug off my discomfort at seeing the guy. What if Edgett pulled off his murder? Kay Allison shot in her cabin. The little Britisher in his brand-new ducks would remember me for sure coming out of the cabin. I was easy to describe. If the ship were given a search, I'd be turned up—a stowaway. A stowaway already wanted for murder.

I wouldn't stand a chance.

I walked forward, past empty deck chairs, and knew deep down I wasn't out of this mess yet. I'd better not trust Kay Allison to look out for herself. I couldn't afford to.

I'd better figure out something fast.

Chapter Four

The salt air had picked up a chill and I threw up the collar of my coat. My frame ached the way it does after an attack of fever and I knew I was going to fold up pretty soon. I hadn't eaten since morning, but I didn't care about that. A place to sleep. Put Edgett and Hoven on ice and start nosing around for a place to sleep.

Waves broke from the bow and foamy claps of sound. I saw the lights of the saloon windows and thought: A drink would pull me through. A drink would cut the fuzz in my head. But even as I walked toward the lights, I knew I wasn't going to go in. Not unless the place was empty.

It wasn't. I stood there peering in the window. I saw the bar and about three passengers drinking and the Malay setting out a plate of katchung seeds. There were others in the saloon, laughing, playing cards, reading the papers. I'd be a sap to walk in there.

I shrugged and turned away. Low clouds were riding in over the ship and the stars were sputtering and disappearing. It was going to rain, I thought. Great. That was all I needed. I might be a stowaway, but I was damned if I was going to sleep on deck in the rain.

I walked back toward the stern. I tried to run things through my mind again. I hoped I was only kidding myself, but I knew I wasn't. If Kay Allison were found dead in her cabin, the little Englishman would remember me and I'd be turned up. Well, Kay Allison had begun to take my warning seriously, but that was as far as it went. She was a little scared, but mostly, I thought, she was angry. Beneath the resolute coolness, it seemed to me, Kay Allison had a temper. She might do anything.

Hell, she might even go to the captain. I should have anticipated that and done it all in a note. But I'd been right—she would have shrugged off a note.

Within a few minutes I found myself back at the saloon windows. Spindrift flecked across my face like cold sparks. If I kept the scar on my hand out of sight, in my pocket.... No. All I needed was one smart bastard to get wise. Just one.

I saw a stiff-backed woman writing a letter at one of the desks along the far windows and the idea of the note hit me, but with a difference.

I saw the way out. I'd need paper and a pen. It would be easy. The idea took hold of me. If only Kay Allison had brains enough to stick to her cabin until I could tie things up for her. And myself.

I entered the saloon from one of the inside doors and turned my coat collar. My hands were cold. I fell into a corner writing desk and could hear card players behind me. I found a stick pen and a few sheets of the ship's stationery. I addressed an envelope to Edgett and Hoven, and hesitated, wondering how to start. Then I wrote:

Gentlemen:
You silly bastards couldn't conspire to change your pants and get away with it. If the Nabob (or the buyer, as you call him, Hoven) didn't have a sense of humor he'd have put coolie labor on the Kay Allison murder. And it wouldn't cost $5,000.
Forget it. If anything happens to Kay Allison you'll both get a quick trial. On the other hand, you may not get a trial at all. You might wash up among the mangroves along the coast.
Edgett, better tell Hoven you brought his gun aboard after all. He likes better a gun. As you said, he's an elemental creature. But I don't think he's going to like you for planning a double cross. I have a couple of theories on how you might have brought it off, but you won't be doing anything. You'll just be sitting tight until Malacca Town.
Piffle dust.
I'll be watching to see that you both walk off the ship at 2 A.M. It's not a bad hour to get drunk.
Watching.

That was enough. I thought for a moment and then signed it *Pawang*—witch doctor.

I sealed it in the envelope. They'd know they'd been overheard and it would startle hell out of them. I began to grin. They'd still be wondering in Malacca Town how it could have happened. They'd be crazy to touch her.

The important thing was to get the note to them before they acted. I wondered if either of them had come into the bar.

I rose from the desk and risked a glance. I didn't see Edgett, and I didn't know what Hoven looked like.

I saw Kay Allison. At the bar.

I wiped my lips. The bartender was setting a pink drink in front of her. She knew I was here, I thought; she must have seen me when she walked in. She crossed her tanned legs and the coins at her waist glinted like mirrors. There was a stubborn tilt to her chin, as if she were asking for trouble and knew it.

It came as I stood there. Edgett.

He paused in the far doorway, a cigarette between his red lips, a starched handkerchief foppishly stuck in his breast pocket. He had his eye on the bar and started across the saloon. He didn't look my way.

I couldn't make myself leave. Edgett took the empty bar stool next to Kay Allison. I slipped the envelope in my pocket. That would have to wait. Something was going to happen, and right away. With a gun in his pocket he might softly attempt to force her out on deck. I wondered if Hoven were waiting out there. Kay Allison fired her lighter and drew in on her cigarette. The damned little fool.

Edgett snapped his fingers for the Malay, ordered a drink, and checked the back of his hair with his long fingers. Near me a newspaper rustled, and I knew I was crazy to stand around this way.

He turned. He began talking to Kay Allison. I watched the thin, grinning movement of his lips and wanted to cross over and break it up before it got started.

And then it came—but not the way I'd expected.

Kay Allison slipped one long leg off the stool and her hand flew. She slapped him hard. The clap came as a rifle shot in the quiet saloon, suspending all movement.

Edgett took it. He sat there like so much stone. It must have astonished him and he was obviously trying to keep a grip on his composure. His face was white. You could tell he really wanted to break her neck. He had a touch with women—they didn't slap him, not Will Edgett. Kay Allison had humiliated him in front of more than a dozen passengers; he'd make her pay. But he couldn't try anything rough. Not here.

His drink came. He knocked it over with the back of his hand, threw a bill on the bar, and strode out, stiff-backed and even smiling a little.

It was over.

A murmur spread through the saloon. One of the card players began riffling the deck and someone laughed.

I couldn't take my eyes off Kay Allison. She picked up her pink glass and relit her cigarette, and if there was a nerve in her body it didn't show. She looked beautiful sitting there, a tanned figure in a smoke-gray dress. Her short, copperish hair gleamed. She was right, I thought. She could take care of herself. I felt like buying her a drink.

As I watched she began to turn, glancing across the saloon.

Our eyes met.

She knew I'd been watching. Had she put on this little show for my benefit? She made it a long glance, with a faint smile on her lips. Sure, she could take care of herself. See?

I made a gesture toward the deck. I'd better put her straight fast.

I watched her pick up her tin of cigarettes and lighter. Then I left.

I was waiting on deck when she came out. She carried her drink and the faint fragrance of mimosa came with her.

"Did I do all right?" she said.

"You're an elemental creature," I said, "but I like you."

"If you want to know the truth, I'm scared." The wind rustled her hair. "Let's walk."

"You're going to your cabin."

"I loathe my cabin. Anyway, I had to do something. You think I'm a fool, don't you?"

"I think you've got what it takes. Come on."

"It was really funny. He turned to me and said it looked like we were in for a bit of a squall and that's when I slapped him. You should have seen his face. He thinks he's rough as bags, but that stopped him."

"I saw his face. Don't be too sure."

"With all those people watching—he wouldn't dare touch me now."

I took her arm and made her start walking with me. "There's Edgett."

"You're making me spill my drink."

I stopped and took the glass out of her fingers. It was a pink gin, but it would do. I swallowed it down and heaved the glass overboard.

"I'm old enough to drink, you know," she said.

"But too old to spank."

"Don't be angry with me."

"Look, Mrs. Allison—"

"Kay."

"Mrs. Allison. Do me a favor. Lay low for just a little while. I finally used my head, and I think we can stop worrying about this thing. Will you please do what I say?"

"Oh, now *you're* getting rough."

The rain started. It came in big, splattering drops and I hurried her toward a companionway. She was keyed up from what she considered a victory over Edgett, but it would pass, and I was sorry. I got a kick out of being with her and sharing her victory.

She unlocked her cabin door. I said, "You're catching on.

"I don't even know your name."

"Does it matter?"

"There's something strange about you. I'm intrigued."

"Forget me."

"You keep saying that."

"I keep meaning it."

She had hung a sharkskin jacket over the window. I felt silly doing it, but I checked the bathroom and the closet. No one.

"I guess you'll live," I said.

"Don't go yet."

"I'll be back. And I'll explain."

"Don't go."

The jazzed-up feeling was wearing thin; I could see the change in her eyes. She'd slapped Edgett, she'd got it out of her system, but she hadn't really solved anything. "Look. I thought about seeing the captain, but I didn't. I began to worry about you. I suppose that was crazy when my life is at stake, but there was something about you—"

"This can wait."

"I don't want it to wait. You've got to see the captain with me and have these men arrested."

"No."

"But *why?*"

I could hear the rain blowing along the deck and the sound depressed me. "It wouldn't do any good," I said. "Edgett could talk his way out of it."

"That's not why."

"I suppose it isn't."

"Then I'll go myself."

"I told you I've got the situation licked. These two jokers will leave the ship at Malacca. I promise you that."

"But don't you see, I've got to find out who hired them. There's tomorrow to worry about."

"I'm sorry, baby. I can't help you there."

"You're maddening!" Her eyes flared. "I'm not going to let myself be killed. Even if these two leave the ship—"

"Look," I said patiently. Why not tell her and get it over with? I was shot. I couldn't keep going round and round on it. She wouldn't give me away, and it would be so much easier. "Look, I can't see the captain with you, and if you involve me I'm sunk. I don't belong on this ship. I'm a stowaway."

Her eyebrows tilted. There was an awkward silence, and then her voice softened. "A stowaway!"

"I was hiding in the closet of their stateroom. That's how I happened to hear them talk about the Nabob and the five thousand dollars and Kay Allison."

She turned away, as if she were suddenly embarrassed. "I must seem terribly ungrateful. I'm sorry. I didn't mean to get hysterical."

"You didn't."

"Haven't you the fare? Are you broke?"

"I have money."

"But I can loan you—"

"I said I have money."

She bounced the lighter in her palm. "I've never met a stowaway before."

"I've never been one before."

She smiled in that open, capricious way of hers. "Want to tell me more?"

"No."

"Where does a stowaway sleep?"

"I'll let you know in the morning."

She moved away on her sandaled feet and turned, studying me as if she were seeing me for the first time. "There's an empty bunk in here."

"Look, don't worry about me."

"I'd feel safer with someone here. Really."

She wasn't kidding anyone, but I liked her for trying. At the same time she managed to make it clear; she was offering an empty bunk and that was all.

"Well?" she said.

I knew I looked like a big, sweaty bum, but that didn't seem to bother her. I was tired and rumpled and God, it would feel good to take a shower. And to sleep between sheets.

"Sure," I said. "Hell, yes."

Chapter Five

When I got back from Edgett's cabin, Kay Allison was in the shower. I stripped off my coat and threw it across the upper bunk. Either Hoven or Edgett had been in. I had seen the light through the door louvers and I had heard someone rustling around inside. I had shot the note under the door. It must be getting a reading right now, I thought.

I played around with my cigarette lighter for a couple of minutes and finally realized that the spark wheel was worn out. I tossed it on the bunk irritably, found the heavy tin lighter Kay used, and got a cigarette going. I emptied the ash tray and saw it in the wastebasket.

A discarded newspaper.

I blinked wearily. I listened to the hiss of the shower. What the hell, she couldn't have read the story. She wouldn't fool around with me if she knew. A stowaway, yes, but not a guy wanted for murder.

I got out the paper and shook off the ashes and cigarette butts. I'd go crazy trying to destroy every copy of the Times around. The shower trailed off and I opened the paper quickly. I looked at the front page and stopped frowning. It was the early edition. I tossed it back into the wastebasket. There was nothing about me in the early edition. I began to relax.

Kay Allison came out of the bathroom and I turned.

She looked different. Her hair was wet and toweled and darker. She had wrapped herself in a man-sized pongee kimono—her husband's, I thought—and it made her seem smaller and more fragile. She wore fluffy yellow mules and she trailed the fresh scent of soap and powder as she crossed past me to the dressing table. Her eyes avoided me, and I felt like an intruder.

"Is it done?" she muttered softly.

"Done."

"Then I suppose there's nothing to do but wait."

"I suppose," I said. They must have got together on the note by now, I thought. They ought to be going nuts trying to figure out where they had fouled themselves. I liked the idea. "O.K. if I wait in the shower?"

She sat at the dressing table, the pongee sleeves hanging from her tanned elbows, and went on toweling her hair. But she didn't answer. I shrugged and walked into the bathroom.

I stripped and turned the water on hot and pelting. I stood under it for a couple of minutes just letting the spray hit my skin and take some of the ache out of my bones. The ship was rolling enough to make me spread my feet. I soaped and washed off and let my mind stall. I didn't want to think about anything. I wanted to stand there forever.

When I turned off the water the room was steaming, but for the first time since I'd left Sumatra I felt fresh and clean and alive, and it was good. It was the way you felt after you made the round of the lines and came in out of the sun for a shower and breakfast. Well, tomorrow I'd be at Silver Jubilee and maybe I could forget. Tomorrow Kay Allison would have passed out of my life, and that was just as well. She was pretty, and as reckless as the laughing *punai*, and I liked her for it. She had freckles and a shiny nose and she didn't dazzle me the way Eden did, and I liked her because she didn't dazzle me.

I frowned. I didn't want to be reminded of Eden and I didn't want to think about Kay Allison. I wanted *sénang* for just a few hours.

I came out of the bathroom barefooted with my trouser cuffs rolled around my ankles. I wished I'd had a change of clothes. I'd tightened my belt another notch and it made me aware that I had lost some weight during the past couple of days. Well, I wasn't hungry. Maybe tomorrow I could eat.

I put my shoes on the floor of the closet and hung up my shirt, blotchy with sweat. It would be dry by morning. I turned and ran a hand through my wet hair. Kay Allison was still at the dressing table. She was brushing her rusty-blonde hair with absent motions.

Our eyes met in the mirror and for a moment I saw a flash of resentment. She looked worried and unsure of herself. And then it hit me. She was a little scared of the situation she'd waltzed herself into. She was a little scared of me, and it made me angry.

"Say the word and I'll get out," I snapped.

Her shoulders gave a little. "No, don't go."

The squall rushed along the deck and the ship's bell clanged through the storm. About five hours to wait for Malacca Town, and then I could stop listening to the bells. Kay put down the hairbrush and looked at me in the mirror. "You don't have to tell me your name," she said.

"It's Jack." That was close enough.

"You lied to me, didn't you, Jack?"

"I probably did. About what?"

"You said you weren't a planter."

"Does it make any difference?"

"Yes."

"Then I'm a planter."

She turned from the mirror and faced me. "I was admiring your lighter. It has acid stains on it. Acetic acid makes stains like that. But I was only guessing, except that you don't look like a tourist."

"The hell it has," I said. She had the lighter on the dressing table and I picked it up. There *were* stains on it. You use acetic acid to coagulate latex in the big vats, and it had shaped up her guess. But it was crazy, because I'd never noticed the stains before and I didn't remember ever dropping the lighter around the factory room. Maybe I was so used to handling the damned thing I had stopped really seeing it. But as I looked at it now I wondered if it was my lighter at all. And that was crazy, because it had to be. It was one of the few things I'd taken with me from the plantation in Sumatra and I'd never seen another like it.

"Was it supposed to be a secret?" she said.

"What?"

"Your being a planter."

"No," I said. She knew I was a stowaway, she knew I was a planter, and tomorrow I'd be gone. What difference did it make?

"I've never met a Yank planter," she said.

"There are a few punks like me."

"How did—"

"How does it happen to anyone?" I really didn't want to talk about it and wished she'd give it up. "You need money and money grows on trees out here. That's my life story."

She studied me for a moment and those jade eyes of hers took on a questioning smile. "No."

"Go to hell." Politely.

"You're not so hard to size up."

"Why bother?"

"You've got big hands and broad shoulders and you need a frontier to move around in, don't you?"

I picked up her tin lighter and lit a cigarette. "Maybe that's part of it." But there was more. There was the need to put down roots somewhere. Ever since I was a kid I'd been drifting with my old man from one entrepôt to another on the China coast. He was an itinerant hedge lawyer, a big guy like me. But he drank too much and he hated too much because it cut him the way the white man was turning the East into a gigantic bargain basement. He'd fought for the coolies and Malays in the white man's courts and generally he'd lost and generally he wasn't paid even the few coppers he charged. He'd died in the Malay quarter of Singapore with the smell of cheap arrack on his lips, and they didn't even give him an obit in the papers. I was old enough to see that he'd been a misfit in the courts; he was too big and rough-cut to be taken seriously in the world of fine print and crisp linen suits. He was a legal buffoon. He'd lived and fought and built nothing. Even his half-naked clients distrusted him and made their private jokes. Well, I loved the guy. I made up my mind to build something with my hands. And finally there was Sumatra and I had cleared the jungle and planted more than a thousand acres in rubber. Oh, it was fine. And then there was Eden.

Kay Allison had something on her mind and I realized she was warming up to it. "I was in Singapore trying to hire an overseer," she said.

"I know."

"Something frightened them off."

"The Piffle Dust Kid."

"What?"

"Edgett. I overheard that too. He'd been hired to put pressure on any takers you might have had."

"But why?"

"You must know the answer to that. I don't."

"But I have no idea."

"Someone has put a price on your head," I said. "You must have *some* idea who's behind all this."

"That's what's so maddening. I don't."

I watched her face and wondered if she were only pretending. You don't make enemies without knowing it. She had an enemy, and it looked to me as if he wanted not only to kill her, but to louse up her plantation as well. Without an overseer it would go to pot.

"Think about it," I said. "You must have crossed someone and crossed him so it hurt."

"That's absurd."

"I wouldn't know."

"Wait! There was a Chinese working for me that I had to sack. He was headman of some contract workers, but he was always drinking and leaving bottles around and the mosquitoes would breed in them. I suppose he really hated me, but that was months ago. I haven't seen him since."

"That's a start."

"The only other person I could imagine wanting to hurt me is a retired planter I know in Singapore. He wanted to marry me and was crushed when I turned him down. But I'm sure he—"

"What's his name?"

"Tom Bayfield."

"Tom Bayfield the Nabob. Maybe it fits."

"He *does* have a rather violent temper. But it's unthinkable he'd do anything like this."

"Sure," I said. "Sure."

"Jack?"

"I'm going to turn in."

"The overseer's job—it's yours if you want it."

It stopped me. So that was why she'd been trying so hard to size me up. "Just like that?"

"Just like that."

I put out my cigarette and our eyes met again. "You don't know anything about me," I said. "There are planters and there are foul-ups."

"I'm willing to take the chance."

"You're crazy."

"I could get along with you, I'm sure of it. And I wouldn't interfere on the estate work."

"What happened to your last overseer?"

She didn't hesitate and I could tell she was going to be honest about it. "He broke his contract and walked off the plantation. He got the idea somehow that he was being poisoned. The one before that—"

"I think I get the idea."

"I'm not pretending the job's got bells on it." Absently her fingers checked the neckline of the kimono. For all her airy poise, there was, I thought, a certain innocence about her. "Things have gone to pot and there's plenty of hard work to be done. I'll keep running things if I have to. But I'm not fooling myself, Jack. I need a man on the estate and—"

"I'll do."

"Don't put it that way."

"Is that why you offered me the spare bunk, to con me into a job?"

"I'm not trying to con you into anything."

"Well, I'm not looking for a job," I said.

"But—"

"Let's forget it."

"You needn't lose your temper."

I turned away. It would have been so easy to say yes, I thought, and it angered me that I had been tempted. She was offering the kind of job that appealed to me, but there was more. There was Kay Allison, and she was no longer just a name. She was flesh and blood, a long-legged kid someone wanted to kill, and I liked her. I had no business feeling anything. Sure, I was sharply conscious of the clean scent of a woman in the cabin with me and my eyes had strayed along the lace shadows beneath the pongee kimono. And maybe for a moment I'd thought it would be nice to go on seeing her, and that was crazy. I'd had it. I'd had it for a lifetime to come.

She turned back to the mirror and picked up the brush again. "I didn't really expect you to take the job. Has Edgett frightened you off like the others?"

"What the hell?"

"I'm getting used to it."

I held my fire and let it pass. My eyelids had lead in them and I couldn't have gone even one round on the damned thing. She must know Edgett had nothing to do with it, but maybe it helped to think so. What difference did it make what she thought? Tomorrow I'd be at Silver Jubilee. I had my own headaches and she had hers and I couldn't see that two headaches were better than one.

I don't remember when she turned in. I stretched out in my trousers on the upper bunk and fell asleep with the light in my eyes and the creaking of woodwork in my ears. The ship's bells kept rousing me, and then it was dark in the cabin, and after a couple of hours I knew I wouldn't stop hearing the goddamned bells until we left Malacca Town and the Nabob's hired hands behind. At one-thirty I got too restless to sleep any longer and climbed down from the bunk. I got my cigarettes in the dark, but couldn't find her lighter and had to give it up. I sat heavily in the chair and then I began to sense that something was wrong. The cabin was strangely quiet. The rain had passed. The ship had come into smoother waters and not even the paneling whispered. There was something missing. It was too silent.

Was I alone? The idea startled me. I couldn't hear the sounds of Kay's breathing, and a sort of panic came over me. Had Edgett and Hoven—

I stumbled out of the chair toward the lower bunk and reached out. There was empty air where her body should have been. My hands stopped on the flat sheets.

Kay Allison was gone.

Chapter Six

I tucked in my shirt on the way out of the cabin.

The passageway was deserted. I got to Edgett's door and tried it. Unlocked. I shoved it open; the cabin was a dark, silent box. I hit the light switch.

The cabin was empty.

The *Pawang* note hadn't stopped them. They'd got to her, they'd lured her out of the cabin, and I'd slept through it. My eyes burned and my stomach throbbed cold and hollow.

I loped along the wet decks. Edgett and Hoven couldn't have left the ship; they must be waiting somewhere to go ashore. I saw beads of light along the coast. Malacca Town. We were coming in.

I saw no one. Life had vanished from the ship as if I were walking a derelict. My shadow moved ahead of me in the moonlight and against the bulkhead the long chairs stood like gaunt skeletons.

The saloon windows were black. I passed toward the ladder for the main deck and a weak flare of light glanced off the windows, as if someone had lit a cigarette. I stopped. There was someone in the saloon.

The wooden door was tight from the weather. I got it open and walked in. The big room was dark except for the silvered rectangle of light that came in with me from the door. At first I saw no one. The air held a cachet of stale cigar smoke and the empty furniture stretched through an infinity of darkness.

"I'm over here."

There was the red dot of a cigarette at the bar.

The voice was Kay Allison's.

It was crazy. She was alive. I came to my senses, but I couldn't unwind. I stood there. I had made a fool of myself, and my anger changed colors like a scarf passing through a magician's fist. She was alive, great, but I had lost my head. She should never have left the cabin, and I stood there hating her for it.

I picked my way through the furniture to the bar. I was damned if I would let her know I had gone stumbling around the ship like a goddamned madman.

"*Tabé, Tuan Besar,*" she muttered. There was something surly in her voice.

"*Tabé.*" I sat next to her at the dark, empty bar and put a cigarette between my lips. "The *Tuan Besar* needs a light."

"Yes, Big Master."

"Maybe you like to drink alone in deserted bars," I said. "Maybe you're funny that way."

"If you came after a drink," she said with the air of a bar fly, "the service is frightful."

"I came after you."

"How touching."

"What's eating you, baby?"

"See? I ordered three drinks ahead when they closed down. Wasn't that bright of me? Can the two of us get drunk on three drinks?"

She got around to lighting my cigarette and the flame reflected sharply in the bar mirror. I saw the three glasses in a neat triangle in front of her. Pink gins. Two empty.

"Maybe you wish you could get drunk on pink gins," I said. "But you can't."

Her bantering tone sharpened and it was no longer banter. "Maybe that's none of your business."

"Maybe I was a sap to come looking for you."

"Maybe you were."

"Maybe you couldn't sleep when there was a stowaway in your cabin."

"Maybe I didn't want to."

"All right," I said. "We'll get drunk on three gins."

"Don't do anything rash, Big Master."

"That," I said, "is where I came in."

Her hand came through the darkness and stopped me.

"No—don't go, Jack."

"Find yourself another pincushion."

"I've been sitting here trying to get drunk and trying to loathe you. I couldn't do either."

"The ship's slowing down."

"Do you know how long it took you to go to sleep in my cabin?"

"I'm glad you're so worried about the Nabob. He only wants to kill you."

"In the tropics a woman is old at twenty-seven, isn't she?"

"Sure," I said. "Ancient."

"Does it astonish you that I have been attractive to men?"

"No," I said. "It doesn't astonish me."

I finally caught on and it should have been funny, but it wasn't. She had had just enough alcohol to dissolve her jaunty self-possession, and I saw she was only a woman with a woman's crazy way of thinking. At first she had worried that I would try to crawl into her bunk, and when I hadn't it had been a kind of slap in the face. It was at least equal to her fear of Edgett and Hoven, a purely female equation.

"You might have been courteous enough to make a pass at me," she said.

There was a clink of glass and I realized she had begun to work on the last gin.

"What would you have done?"

"I would have slapped you. Hard."

"Shall I tell you you're very, very pretty and I didn't want to be slapped? Hard?"

"The ship," she said, "is slowing down."

"Shall I tell you I took you for about age twenty-two? Shall I tell you that a woman trying to run a rubber plantation means something special to me, because I know what you're up against, and it killed me to turn down your job?"

"God stone the crows, if you start feeling sorry for me I'll scream."

"Let me finish," I said briskly. "You sized me up wrong, baby. Better get that straight. You took me for a big, hard-working stiff down on his luck, but it's only an optical illusion. I'm a fraud. I did you a favor when I turned you down. The best thing I can do is get out of your life fast."

"How very noble!"

There was more, but I didn't say it. There was the Nabob and I wished I could stick around long enough to run interference and I felt like a coward because I couldn't. I wasn't just any guy. I was wanted for murder. I had no right to bring that into her life. Somehow, sometime, she'd find out. She had enough trouble on her plantation without me.

"We're coming in," I said shortly. "I'm going on deck."

She was strangely silent once we left the saloon. The few scattered lights of Malacca Town where clear and large and we could even make out the old clock tower and the jetty.

"Pretty, isn't it?" she said.

"Pretty as hell."

The air smelled freshly of the tropics and the sea. The ship anchored and a shore launch pulled away from the jetty and nosed toward us. I could hear stirrings of life below on the main deck and I began to feel like a gambler who had thrown the dice and was waiting for the numbers to come up.

"Edgett and Hoven must be down there waiting," I said. "Once they go ashore we can stop worrying for tonight."

"I stopped worrying," Kay Allison said, "when I met you."

"Piffle dust."

"I mean that, *Tuan Besar.*"

We stood at the rail and watched the charcoal shadow of the launch approach. Under the night sky Malacca Town slept in a forest of rickety piles along the sea. There was enough moon to brown the sail of the fishing boats in the river and the whole scene was impossibly peaceful. But I wasn't really watching it. I was sharply conscious of the scent of mimosa, Kay's perfume, as she stood beside me. I wished I could get rid of the chip I had put on my shoulder. I really wanted to be friends, if just for tonight. The launch came to the gangway spotlight, and new passengers came aboard the S.S. Perak. We waited and we watched; there no longer seemed anything to say. Mail sacks, newspapers, and luggage were thrown aboard the launch, and then the handful of passengers bound for Malacca Town started down the gangway from the main deck.

They appeared. Edgett and a hulk of a man with rounded, brooding shoulders. Hoven.

Kay's hands gripped the rail and her casual attitude vanished as the tense little scene unfolded below us.

"Jack, it worked!"

I felt no sense of victory I just watched. Edgett went first, his face cold and set under the gangway lights. He was a dangerous man and I found myself hoping he wouldn't turn up in Kay's life again. Hoven, with a black oil-silk raincoat over one arm, carried the suitcase they had brought aboard. They glanced neither right nor left, but rigidly toward the launch below, like a pair of actors who had fumbled their lines and were anxious to make a quick but unruffled exit. In less than a minute they sank from sight under the launch canopy. Finally the bell clanged and the engine growled. The launch pushed off and started back for Malacca Town.

"Exit Edgett and Hoven," I said.

We were left alone. There was nothing to worry about until morning, but I didn't feel like thinking about tomorrow. Kay turned and our eyes met. It was different. For a moment the lights of Malacca Town vanished. We both wanted each other and we knew it as we stared into each other's eyes. But the moment passed and she dropped her cigarette over the side.

"I just made a pass at you," I said.

"And I just slapped you."

Chapter Seven

I picked up my clothes and tried not to wake her. Dawn was breaking across the open window and a cool, soft breeze flowed into the cabin. It seemed somehow necessary to leave without saying good-by. I didn't want her to know when I had left the ship. After leaving Malacca Town we had made stops at Port Dickson and Port Swettenham; if she ever found out about me, she couldn't pinpoint me in Malaya.

I put on my coat and stood for a moment in the center of the cabin and tried to think. Did I have everything? From the lower bunk Kay's breathing was soft and intimate and trusting. I hadn't touched her; I hadn't even tried. She lay on her side now, her back toward me, and my eyes followed the smooth rise of her hip under the sheet. I would never see her again, and I was sorry.

I turned away bitterly. Forget her. I rubbed my face and it was rough. I had to have a shave. I had to figure a way off the ship. We'd reach Kuala Tang in about three hours, but I couldn't wander around the ship with a beard. I was seedy enough without that. I'd *look* like a stowaway.

I found the men's room and cleaned up. Three hours to kill. I looked at myself in the mirror and I looked like hell. My eyes had taken on something sharp and wary and unnatural. They seemed to have become smaller and darker in my slack face. I ran my fingers through my whiskers and thought of the green Englishman going out to the tin mines. He'd have a razor.

I finished up at the basin and remembered they'd put newspapers ashore at Malacca Town. I couldn't risk having the same thing happen in Kuala Tang. Chances were good, I thought, that the S.S. Perak was carrying the late edition, the one with the story about me. Once I got ashore I'd have to do something about it. I didn't want the news about me fluttering all over Kuala Tang.

I went back along the passageway toward the Englishman's cabin, across from Kay's. He'd probably be still asleep. I knocked lightly.

I knocked again, harder.

Finally I heard his piping voice. "I say, I say—hold on."

The Englishman opened the door, and his face was pink and fuzzy with sleep. He stood barefooted in striped pajamas. It took him a moment to get me in focus and then his eyes brightened.

"I say, you fellows get up early out here. I'll have to get the hang of that, eh?"

"You'll get the hang of it," I said. "Look, I just discovered I've forgotten to pack my razor. Any chance of borrowing your gear?"

"Of course. Do come in."

I shut the door behind me and he went toward his suitcase. He came up with a Rolls razor in a leather pouch, a brush with an ivory handle, and shaving cream.

"Use my lavatory if you like," he said. "We can chat."

"Thanks."

"Tell me, did you see her?"

I picked up the gear and walked into the bathroom. "Who?"

"The girl I met in the saloon last night. I only just got to bed a few hours ago."

"Sounds like you had a real night."

"Oh, nothing like that. But it *was* rather exciting. I've promised to write her, of course. I wish you'd seen her! Marvelous black hair. She's part Portuguese."

I ran water into the basin and began lathering my face. "Swell."

"I hadn't expected to meet anyone Portuguese out here. Remarkable place, isn't it? Full of the unexpected. I suppose I'll get used to that."

"Swell."

"Of course, she's a bit older than I am, but we got along nicely. There is something about being aboard ship, isn't there?"

"Swell." I stropped the razor and wondered what the hell he was talking about.

"Comes from a very old family in Malacca Town. You see, that's where the Portuguese comes into her family. Did you know the Portuguese settled Malacca Town?"

"I seem to have heard it somewhere."

"But then the Dutch came, and so she's part Dutch."

"It figures."

"I daresay. Exciting type, she was. Oh, I shall like it out here. You don't meet women like that in Blackpool."

"I daresay," I said.

"Of course, there was a bit of embarrassment at the end. You see, she had a hatbox sort of thing and I insisted on carrying it to the gangway when the shore boat came alongside. A police official got out and boarded us."

The razor froze on my neck. "What did you say?"

"Police official—detective, I suppose. First thing he did was check the men on the main deck ready to go ashore on the little boat. You see, I still had the hatbox, or whatever it was, in my hand, and he thought I was going ashore. I protested of course—it was quite ridiculous—but you know the police mind."

"Yes," I said. I tried to go on shaving.

"Had an electric torch, he did, and asked me to show my hands, Well, once he saw my hands it made things all right somehow. Remarkable, don't you think? What do you suppose he was up to?"

He kept running on, but I stopped listening. A cop had come aboard from Malacca Town. They had traced me. How? The taxi driver? I should never have had him take me so close to the wharves. But the cops couldn't be sure I had got aboard the S.S. Perak. They must have made some sort of check on the ship as soon as we pulled away from Malacca Town. They might decide to search the cabins now that it was morning. Hadn't this barefooted Britisher wondered about the scar on my hand? I'd better get out before he got a brainstorm.

"It seems a bit amusing now," he was saying. "But you see, when he flashed the light on my hands there was *lipstick* smudged on one of my fingers. It was really quite humiliating."

I rinsed the lather off my face and cleaned up his gear. I checked him in the mirror. He was lying in his bunk, his knees crossed, and he was stretching his pink toes. I cinched up my tie and got back into my coat. I put a cigarette between my lips. I'd hang around just long enough to get a light.

"Everything *sénang*," he said when I came through the bathroom door.

"If I had a light, everything would be *sénang*."

"Here—do take the box."

"Thanks."

"Jolly fine day, it looks like."

"Sure," I said. "Jolly fine."

Forward, I saw a crew washing down the forecastle deck. Where could I hole up? In another half hour first breakfast would rouse the passengers and the ship would come to life. Kay's troubles had gone ashore at Malacca Town, but mine had come aboard. The police. I turned and went aft and knew I had to get squared away fast.

I glanced out at the distant shoreline, a green thickening of the morning horizon. Swim? Sure, and sink. The shape I was in, I probably couldn't swim a mud puddle.

I peered down at the after well deck. There was a mounted crane with orange metal housing, and I considered that. But if a search of the ship were made, I'd be trapped. I was damned if I was going to let myself be trapped. We were so close to Kuala Tang I could almost smell it. Three hours. All I had to do was last another three hours.

I glanced back at the white lifeboats suspended from davits outward along the deck. There *was* a way, and suddenly I saw it. I took a hungry drag on my cigarette, stepped on it, and walked aft.

I was on the starboard side and that wouldn't work. The starboard side would face Kuala Tang when we pulled in, and the sightseers would be on that side of the ship. I'd look funny as hell coming out of a lifeboat in all that company.

I made it snappy to the port side, and luck ran out on me. There was someone on deck—a stocky colonial type in knee-length khaki shorts. He stood at the rail watching a white tern that was pacing the ship. A god-damned bird-watcher.

I had to get rid of him.

I slowed my stride, and he turned with a hearty grin.

"Frigate bird," he announced.

Have it your way, I thought. But get lost. "There's a flock of green *punais* or the starboard side."

"Not really! Pigeons this far from shore?"

"They're nesting in some floating mangrove."

"You don't say! I must see that!"

"Better hurry."

He moved off briskly, with the air of a dedicated man. I watched him vanish along the deck and checked in the other direction. There was a breeze and you could feel the coming heat of the morning lurking behind it. I was alone.

I stepped out between two lifeboats and undid the tarp at the bow of one of them. The sea was calm and so silent that the small noises I made seemed loud enough to wake the ship.

I got hold of the gunwale and worked myself under the tarp and into the dark grayness of the boat.

There'd be a rope inside. I found it. I moved along the outboard side of the hull, secured one end of the rope to an oarlock, and made some heavy knots along the line. I loosened the tarp amidship on the outboard side, free enough so I could slip out quickly if I had to. Then I stretched out along the ribs of the boat. If the search came, I'd be ready.

I heard the breakfast chimes come and go. I heard bits of conversation, carried along like scraps of paper in the wind. The ends of the tarp made slapping noises and time dragged. I thought of a cigarette, but the smoke might catch someone's attention. I thought of Kay Allison. The Nabob. I thought of breakfast—and suddenly I was gripped with hunger.

Voices. Close. I came quickly alert. Footsteps had stopped outside the lifeboat.

"Is all this foolishness absolutely necessary?"

"I assure you, Captain, it's not foolishness."

"See here I haven't had a stowaway aboard my ship in over a year. The passengers are already beginning to wonder what's going on. I don't like it, I tell you."

"I shall have to question them if we don't turn the bounder up. We've a hunch he got aboard your ship."

"Rot."

I felt a tapping of knuckles against the wooden hull. "Tell me, Captain, do stowaways ever really hide out in lifeboats?"

"Utter fiction."

"So I suspect. Still, I should like a look."

They moved off and I figured they were starting with the end boat. I worked fast and quietly. I let the knotted line out over the seaward side of the boat, about three feet of it, enough to hang onto. Then I worked myself through the loosened tarp and outside the boat.

I held on like a monkey on a stick. I kept at a crouch, making myself as small as possible, hoping the lifeboat would shield me from the men on deck.

I watched the water glide beneath me. I could see shifting fragments of my own reflection down there, like something seen in a broken mirror. It looked like a hell of a way down, and I raised my eyes.

They came. I could hear them. I could hear the rustle of canvas as one end of the tarp must have been pulled back. A leafy shadow passed over me, and I could almost feel it. The white tern crossing over the ship.

I took a firm grip above the knot with one hand and held the tarp edge in place above my head. How closely would they check the boat? A glance? They'd be looking for a man and a glance would tell them the lifeboat was empty.

I hung on.

"Quite empty, Captain."

"It's utter fiction, you know."

"Shall we have a look at the lifeboats on the starboard side?"

"The whole thing's preposterous."

"As long as it's preposterous, I should like to be thoroughly preposterous."

"We shall be stopping in half an hour. Will you want to go through that Scotland Yard stuff at the gangway again?"

"I'm afraid so."

Their voices drifted away on the breeze. I was staring at the sweat rolling down my wrist.

I hoisted myself back into the lifeboat and stretched out across the bottom. My muscles were shaking. I let them shake.

Chapter Eight

The ship's whistle blasted over the water and echoed from the hills. Kuala Tang. We were coming in, but I couldn't swim ashore in a linen suit. The heat of the day had started. I could see the sun in pinpricks through the tarp, and the lifeboat was airless and hot. I was rolling in sweat.

I got out of my coat and stripped down to my trousers. I pulled off my shoes and socks. I got my pocket knife and cut the legs off my trousers at the thighs. They'd pass for hand-me-down shorts. I got my wallet, passport, and odds and ends together. I buttoned the stuff in my two back pockets. There was no longer any point in holding onto the cigarette lighter Eden had given me. It didn't work and to hell with it. I'd toss it overboard.

The ship's whistle blared again.

I remembered my other trips to Kuala Tang. I remembered the native boys diving for coppers when the boat anchored off the mouth of the river. The sun had long ago turned me as brown as a Malay. In the water I might pass. A bunch of screaming Malays and I'd pass.

Except for my hair. I cut a large square out of my shirt and tied it around my head. It would do for a *udeng*. It would have to do.

I could already hear the thump of the screws churning in reverse. We were stopping.

I felt around for something heavy. There was a small anchor and I cut it loose from its line. I gathered together my clothes and shoes and tied them to the anchor. It was important, I thought, to leave no sign that I had ever been around. I pulled in the rope I'd left dangling over the side, undid the knots, and recoiled it.

I was ready. I would have to gamble that the port decks were deserted. But hell, a town had come up to starboard and everyone would be looking it over.

I lifted the tarp and dropped the anchor over the side. The splash sounded like an explosion to me. I waited. No voices along deck. Nothing.

I wriggled out. The white brightness of the morning hurt my eyes and I squinted. I held onto the gunwale for a moment, took a breath, and let myself go.

The still water raced up for me. My feet shattered the surface, and the sea closed around me. I sank like a plummet and thrashed to stop myself. A shock of coolness swept over me and I floundered in a sort of violent slow motion. I rose along the monstrous white belly of the ship, almost luminous in the clear, deep water. I broke through the surface and gulped for air.

I shook my hair and peered up to the rail, but I saw no one watching from deck. I began to swim aft and finally reached the shelter of the stern. The screw blades gleamed ominously just below the water's surface. I got hold of the rudder shaft and stopped. There it was, not more than five hundred yards away—Kuala Tang. I stared at it. Houses with blue and white and terra-cotta walls dozed in the sun. Along the river mouth a leafless jungle of stilts held aloft the Malay quarter, with rickety ladders going down to the sampans and fishing proas below. I could see the austere brick building on the hill overlooking the Straits—the Planter's Club, flying the Union Jack. Kuala Tang looked even smaller than I'd remembered it. A morning mist still lingered from the wild green hills behind town, and in the distance a range of mountains stood with an indigo profile against the sky.

Bumboats had met the S.S. Perak and the penny divers were there too, frolicking with a rubber ball and waiting for the coins to start coming.

I touched off with my feet and swam deep underwater, coming up behind a sampan loaded high with a dozen tropical fruits. I started off again and a coin struck the water near me. I went down and met a thrashing swirl of brown arms and legs. I swam off to the right and came up behind the others. A young Malay broke surface and exhibited the coin between his chalky white teeth.

I kept low in the water, treading, and looked at the gleam of the sun on my wet, bronzed arms. I would pass from up there. I'd be more conspicuous streaking for shore; I might catch that cop's eye. Coins were in the air. No Malay would run out on that.

Why not wait it out here in the water? Wait until the S.S. Perak left me behind. Stick with the divers until the goddamned ship took off. Why not?

It seemed the least risky, and I made up my mind.

"Me! Tuan! Throw me!"

The coins slacked off and the Malays started bouncing the rubber ball off the side of the ship. A piece of silver flicked my head; I turned and went down. What the Malays thought about my being among them I didn't give a damn; but suddenly I hated every passenger at the rail. The great white man's sport—throwing pennies to watch some poor bastards fight underwater for them.

I let the coin go and took my time coming up. The more time I spent underwater, the safer I'd be. When I broke surface I saw the shore launch ride in along the gangway. I risked a glance along the rail and wondered if I'd see Kay Allison anywhere up there. I didn't, and I was just as glad. She was a moment in my life, and it was finished.

I glanced back to the gangway and saw a couple of seamen going down with mail sacks and newspapers. There was a loose end I had to tie up. Once I reached shore I'd have to figure some way of killing yesterday's paper. I couldn't let that description of me get loose in Kuala Tang.

Finally a couple of passengers started down for the launch. There came a flurry of coins and I dove. My wind was giving out and I decided to ease off. I had to last. When I came up for air I saw another passenger stepping down the gangway.

A woman.

Her white dress caught the morning sun. She wore a wide-brimmed hat. She moved down the steps, tall and composed, and she might have been any planter's wife coming home after a shopping trip to Singapore. But it wasn't any planter's wife.

It was Kay Allison.

"Tuan! Tuan! I catch! *Tengok!* Me! Tuan!"

I tried to shut the yells out of my ears. Had she recognized me down here? No—she wouldn't be crazy enough to leave the ship because of a guy she called Jack. There had to be a better reason. She *belonged* in Kuala Tang. Her plantation must be somewhere around here.

She was home.

I kept my face all but submerged and watched her board the launch. She sat under the canopy, across from the other two passengers, her back toward me. She didn't know I existed.

I don't know what kept the launch, but it hugged the gangway for at least another ten minutes. Finally the little bell clanged and the little engine roared. A few sampans in the way scattered and the boat started back for shore.

I stuck behind the divers and wished to hell the S.S. Perak would get on its way. Kay Allison in Kuala Tang. I was sorry. Still, the rubber estates spread for miles over the hills and I might never see her. It would be better that way.

I lost track of time. Hunger pains caught hold of me and I began to worry about a cramp. The ship's blast finally came. There was a final tracery of coins and the S.S. Perak began to move. The screws thumped. The divers and sampans turned for shore.

I spit water. I had made it. That cop from Malacca Town could go on inspecting the ship all the way to Panang.

A Malay rested in the water and faced me with a grin.

"Tuan works hard for a penny."

I grinned back at him and tried to pass it off as a white man's lark. "*Seronok sunggoh.*"

"*Gila betul!*" He laughed and swam away.

Sure, I thought, I was certainly crazy. He caught hold of a sampan going in and I followed his example. I got a boat of my own and let it tow me toward shore.

I kept my eyes on the jetty. The launch was tied up alongside, and I wondered if there was any chance the newspapers hadn't yet been taken into town.

The sampan headed toward the native quarter and I dropped off about fifty yards from the jetty and began to swim for it. It turned into a long, agonizing haul. When I reached the ladder I didn't have muscles enough to go up; I just held onto a rung trying to get back some wind. I could see the launch on the other side of the piles, lazing in the sun.

I figured the newspapers might be stacked on the jetty and finally dragged myself part way up the ladder. The newspapers were nowhere in sight, and my hope of intercepting them faded.

I saw a Malay in a greasy yachting cap and I took him for the coxswain. He was on his haunches, gossiping with some other natives, just forward of the launch. I decided to have a look inside the boat.

I dropped down the ladder and swam between the tarred piles. I reached the launch and pulled myself over the side and looked in.

The newspapers were there, stacked on the bottom with the sacks of mail.

I hoisted myself over. There were three bundles of papers under the canopy and I tried to work fast. I checked the dates. Three days' worth of the Times. I picked up yesterday's stack and then I froze. I heard footsteps above on the jetty.

I dropped quickly behind the mail sacks. The boat rocked and I knew the coxswain had jumped aboard. There was laughter on the jetty. If he came aft I'd hit him and then get that bundle of newspapers over the side.

But he didn't come aft. I heard a forward panel slide and after a moment the boat rocked again as he left it. I didn't stop to figure out what he'd come for.

I lifted the bundle of papers over the side and lowered it quietly into the water. Then I let go. I watched it sink, flashing dully, to the bottom. A lot of planters were going to miss a day's news, and I was sorry.

I lowered myself into the water and worked my way ashore through the piles. I didn't feel like walking in as if the jetty were a red carpet.

I spread-eagled on a patch of beach at the edge of town and let the sun dry me. I had sent a native boy to buy me something to eat with a wet Straits dollar and he came back with fruit cradled in his sarong—a ripe durian that smelled like hell, a cluster of sausage-like bananas, some mangos, and a couple of ruby-skinned mangosteens. He had probably picked up everything in his back yard, but I liked his broad-faced smile and decided to let him keep the dollar.

"*Apa namo?*" I asked.

"Abdul, tuan."

He unsheathed his parang and cut into the thick, spiky hide of the durian. The fruit let out its sturdy fumes, but I had long ago learned to wade through the odor to the custard-like pulp, and I was damned hungry. He handed me the opened fruit and I told him he could take off.

He moved away reluctantly, as if the whole thing were a morning adventure that he hated to give up. He walked down the beach about thirty yards and sat in the sand, watching me eat.

I ignored him and ate. Flies came in on the durian like bees streaking for home and I had to give it up. I tossed it as far as I could, ate a couple of bananas, and peeled a mangosteen.

The sun baked my muscles and I felt my strength come back. I had made it to Kuala Tang and my spirits began to buck up. Gabb was eight kilometers away. The murder in Sumatra was a wide stretch of blue water away, a country away, a world away. I was safe.

I had to get some clothing. I couldn't walk around in a ragged pair of shorts.

I went to work on a mango, but it came from a bad strain and tasted faintly of turpentine. I heaved it into the water and filled up on bananas and mangosteens. Then I washed my face and hands in the tide and started for the outskirts of town.

I found some open-air stalls and picked up a pair of canvas shoes and went into a Chinese dry-goods store and got fitted out with white ducks and a loud, shortsleeved sport shirt.

"Latest style from Singapore, master."

I paid up and left the store feeling as dressed up as a window dummy. I remembered a tailor shop near the Planter's Club and walked up the hill. I got measured for a linen suit. It would be ready in twenty-four hours.

I was almost out of money, but it no longer mattered. I ought to be at Silver Jubilee before noon.

I decided against telephoning ahead and having Gabb send the car for me. After the mess that had followed my call from Singapore I didn't want to get anywhere near a phone.

I found Kuala Tang's only taxi shimmering in the sun opposite the government resthouse. The driver was nowhere around and I pressed the horn button, but the horn didn't work. I stood around, and finally he showed up, barefooted, fat as Buddha in a checked sarong, and just as happy-looking.

"Do you know the road to Silver Jubilee?" I asked.

"Yes, tuan. You wish to go to Silver Jubilee?"

"That's the general idea."

"But my car is lacking armor."

"Get in and let's go."

"There are bandits on the roads," he protested, pointing in the general direction of Silver Jubilee. "Since the trouble started again my taxi stays in town. I cannot take you, tuan. The Communists do not like me. See, I am too fat, and they believe one as fat as Majid must be rich. If I were rich, tuan, I would order armor for my taxi—isn't that so?"

He was trying to say, I thought, that he wouldn't take a white man along the plantation roads with the Reds acting up. He didn't want to have to collect his fare from a corpse.

"If I may suggest, tuan," he replied anxiously, "perhaps Tuan Wing will send one of his cars for you. They have armor as thick as the *penyu*. I wish I had such a car."

"I'll walk," I growled.

"I would not advise it, tuan. If I may suggest—only an hour ago I saw Tuan Wing's wife walking into the Planter's Club bar. Perhaps she is yet in town and would give you safe journey back."

"Wing's *wife?*"

"Yes, tuan."

I stared into his brown marble eyes. Gabb married? That was crazy; he hadn't written me a word about it. Or had he merely picked up a jungle wife—a Malay, a Tamil, anything around?

"What does she look like?"

"Ah, pretty, tuan. There is no other in Kuala Tang like her. The *Tuan Besar* brought her from Singapore perhaps six months ago. It is said she is originally from Indo-China."

"She is French?"

"I know only the gossip." There was something close to a leer on his face, but I let it pass. "If you wish, I will help you find her," he went on. "But already she may have returned to the *kaboon.*"

"Sounds like I can spot her by myself," I said. "Thanks."

"*Tida apa.*"

It took me less than ten minutes to cover the few streets of the European quarter. Why the hell hadn't Gabb written me that he'd got married? I wondered how welcome I'd be around Silver Jubilee if Gabb had a wife around. I might mean trouble with the police, and he might not go for it. The taxi driver hadn't told me all the gossip about her. He had kept the rest of it behind that leer. I began to feel uneasy.

I couldn't find her. I ended up along the river and decided it was crazy to be within a few miles of Silver Jubilee and not be able to get there. I was damned if I was going to leg it in this sun. I went back to Majid and his unarmored taxi. I threatened to beat hell out of him in two languages. I paid in advance and he finally agreed to drive me halfway to Silver Jubilee. That was the best I could do.

We followed the river, crossed a wooden bridge, and within a few minutes entered the jungle. The road was narrow and the wall of palms and banyans and wild rubber trees seemed to cut off the air and reduced the sun to freckles of light. The taxi was sweltering and I began to soak through my new clothes. High in the foliage there was the cry of monkeys as they raced through the leaves. I had a fresh pack of cigarettes and I lit up. To hell with Gabb's wife.

Majid began to accelerate. There was an armored sedan stalled in the road ahead of us, and I saw it.

I leaned forward. "What the hell are you doing?"

"It's a trick, tuan!"

"Slow down!" I shouted. "They need help."

"Tuan—"

"Stop the car!"

He braked and as we drew closer I saw a Malay working under the hood. The jungle Reds couldn't move with an armored car, and I didn't think it was a trap. The sedan looked like a Mercury dipped in steel with slits where the windows had been. We pulled up behind it and I got out. The Malay came out from under the hood. He welcomed me with his eyes.

"Maybe I can help," I said.

There was a legend painted on the sedan door: Jade Tiger Plantation. I was glad we had stopped. It lay across the river from Gabb's estate, and maybe I could get a lift all the way in. Jade Tiger. I remembered the piece I had read in the Singapore paper, the guerrilla trouble, the slashed rubber trees.

"I think the fuel line, tuan."

If this was a Red trick, there was going to be a slaughter. Majid and me. I walked forward and then the door opened behind me. I spun. A woman stepped onto the road.

"*Tabé,* Big Master."

It was Kay Allison.

Chapter Nine

There was no surprise on her face. She took in my ducks and canvas shoes but her green eyes made no comment. She looked impossibly cool under the big hat, cool and pretty and composed. The white dress made a sharp contrast against her tan; she had the air of someone on her way to a cocktail party at which she expected to be bored. Nearby an argus pheasant sent its *ku-au, ku-au* shivering through the leaves.

"So you're Jade Tiger," I said.

"You can read," she said. "I keep learning things about you."

"Maybe I can fix your fuel line."

"I'm sure you can do anything."

This was no place to talk; I left her standing there. The Malay had balanced a gun beside him on the fender, and I took over under the hood. It was about ten minutes before we had the engine running again. I wiped my hands and went back to Majid and told him he could go back to town.

Kay was waiting in the back seat and I stuck my head in the door. "I could use a lift."

"Get in."

I got in. The air-conditioning had stopped working when the car stalled and the heavily armored car was an oven. I shut the door and we started to move. She lit a cigarette with her big tin lighter.

"Did you follow me ashore?" she asked through a breath of smoke.

"No," I said. "I didn't follow you."

"This road doesn't go very far."

"It goes far enough."

"Really?"

"Silver Jubilee."

Her eyes flashed my way. After a moment the jungle began to break apart and we passed an occasional atap hut and stray native rubber trees with vericose trunks. "I see," she muttered.

Her reaction, like a chill, left me puzzled. "What does that mean?" I asked.

"It means we'll be neighbors."

I lit a cigarette and knew she was faking. But she had made a quick recovery and she was smiling again. I glanced through the window slit at the blocks of harsh sun that fell across the road. The jungle was gone; we were in the rubber. We were on the edge of some rolling estate and I could see an army of half-naked tappers laboring in the orderly green forest.

"Shall I make an absurd confession?" Kay said. "I was hoping you'd followed me ashore and had decided to oversee Jade Tiger. I was glad to see you."

"You gave a start when I mentioned Silver Jubilee."

"Did I?" A crescent-horned buffalo had wandered onto the road and the driver honked around him. "I suppose I was thinking of Monique."

"Is that Gabb's wife?"

"Haven't you met her?"

"Until an hour ago I didn't know she existed."

"She exists. You'll find that out."

"I can't wait. I take it you don't get along."

"Gabriel and I always have," she said grimly. "Oh, I can't really blame her. She's had things rough, and now that she's the *mem* of a large estate I suppose she worries she'll wake up someday and find herself back in the streets. It must give her nightmares."

"Tell me more."

"There's not much more. Monique's terribly jealous. She won't let Gabriel set foot on Jade Tiger and I'm no longer welcome at Silver Jubilee. Do you suppose she hired those two men to kill me? It hadn't occurred to me before."

"You're not serious."

"The Nabob—she'd like to be called that, even if it is meant for a man. Monique the Nabob. Has a rather nice sound, don't you think?"

"Why should she be jealous of you?"

"Shall I make up a reason or tell you the silly truth?"

"I'll take the silly truth."

"She's made herself believe Gabriel and I were more than mere neighbors before he brought her to Silver Jubilee. I admire him, Jack, and he's amusing and a lot of fun, but that's as far as it goes. I'm sure they have big scenes over me. Poor Gabriel!"

"Where the hell did he find her?"

"The silly truth again?"

"The silly truth."

"On Lavender Street in Singapore."

I winced. You could find anything on Singapore's boulevard of sin, none of it very pretty. "That doesn't necessarily mean—"

"We'll be charitable and say she was a dancer in one of the cafés. She *does* dance."

I wondered how much of this to mark off as one woman's cattiness toward another. I knew Gabb, and this didn't sound like anyone he would marry.

"I'll give her your regards," I said.

"Duck when you do."

A small stream with a filigree of jungle debris floating on the surface cut a weaving boundary between the two estates. I remembered that it served as a gutter, carrying the plantation refuse out to the Straits of Malacca, and provided Silver Jubilee with its resident population of mosquitoes. I saw the log bridge ahead and told the driver to stop.

"I'll walk the rest of the way," I said. "Thanks for the ride."

"Staying long, Jack?"

"That depends."

"On Monique?"

"Let go of it, baby. I'm not interested."

"I feel very cruel at the moment."

"Are you going to do anything about the attempt on your life?"

"I have already."

"What?"

"I sent a wire to friends in Singapore."

"Sounds brilliant."

"Asking them to hire a private detective to investigate Edgett and Hoven. I also made up my mind not to brood about them, although I *do* feel as if I'd almost been run over by an automobile."

"What about the ex-planter who wanted to marry you?"

"Tom Bayfield? I can't make myself believe he has anything to do with it."

"I hope your detective gets on the ball."

"Meanwhile I'll wear a gun and shoot at trespassers."

"Does that include me?"

"I don't know. Cross over, and if I don't drop you, keep coming."

We left it at that, and the sedan, looking Martian in its preposterous steel jacket, took off in a cloud of red laterite dust.

Once the car was gone, the burning midday silence closed around me. I paused for a moment on the bridge and looked upriver to Silver Jubilee's native kamponga private village of bamboo long houses, sided and roofed with atap. I could see a thousand washings poked into the air on bamboo poles, like flags waiting for a breeze. My glance passed to the beginning of the rubber, regal old trees with leaning naked trunks as striped as barber poles from tapping wounds. The trees were in fruit and there was an occasional crack high in the air, like a gunshot, as a pod burst in the sun and scattered its seeds.

Welcome, I thought. Welcome with a twenty-one-gun salute.

I began to walk, keeping to the road until I found a spot in the barbed-wire fencing that I could get through. The way would be shorter through the trees and I'd be out of the direct sun.

I thought of a lot of things as I kicked along, my canvas shoes soaking in the dust. I thought of the crazy way I'd met Kay on the ship, and then I wondered about those acid stains she'd first noticed on my cigarette lighter. At first it had puzzled me, but it had seemed too trivial to care about. Now I was bothered. If it wasn't the same lighter Eden had given me, where the hell had I picked it up?

I passed under the green leafy dowagers of the plantation, trees that must have been nearing forty years and pushing retirement. I could hear latex drip into the tin cups, like a forest of leaky faucets. It was a long walk, but I took my time and enjoyed the familiar sights and smells. An occasional late-blooming tree put out its sweet, exotic scent and I felt back in my element. This was where I belonged and my pulse beat a little faster.

Finally I could see Gabb's house. It stood on a hilltop overlooking the entire plantation, a peaked house with a wide veranda and long windows open for any stray breeze. With the sun overhead, the shades had been drawn up.

My shirt was sticking to my back when I reached the veranda. There was a faint tinkle from decorated glass wind bells hung at the corners. I knocked. I could hear no sounds from within the house, but after a moment the door opened and a houseboy I didn't recognize stared out at me with sullen, speckled eyes.

"Is the master home?" I asked.

"No, tuan."

"Tell the *mem* there is a caller."

"The *mem* is not here, tuan."

There was an air of insolence about him and it brought out the surly part of my nature. "Do you know how to fix a stengah?"

He nodded. "Yes, tuan."

"I'll wait inside," I said. "With a stengah."

He began to protest, but I pushed past him. The marble floor, quarried in Ipoh and brought down the coast in lighters, gave the living room an atmosphere of pleasant coolness, and two electric punkahs swirled from the high ceiling. It was familiar, and yet everything was different. The fine old teak furniture was gone; the room now looked Western and commonplace, like something copied from a page of a glossy American magazine. There was even a chaise longue, but at least it was upholstered in batik.

The houseboy moved off grudgingly and I lit a cigarette. I walked from window to window looking at the rubber foliage stretching in every direction, like vistas of green clouds. I got through part of the cigarette and the houseboy came with my drink on an ornate *jadam* tray. At least *that* was the same, I thought, picking up the glass.

"When do you expect the master back?" I asked.

"He left no message."

"Is he somewhere on the estate?"

He nodded faintly. "The bandits came last night to the Number Three *kaboon*. There were many trees killed. He is there."

I frowned and took a swallow of the drink. Terrorist trouble again. I was glad I had come. Gabb ought to be able to use me. I could earn my keep.

Chapter Ten

An armored Chrysler came flashing up the road and turned into the shade of the garage. A moment later I saw a figure in knee-length drill shorts and a Port Dickson hat stride with rattling steps past the veranda windows. I heard Gabb burst into the room behind me.

"Mahmoud!"

The houseboy appeared even before the echo returned from the corners of the room.

"Mahmoud, I'm hollow! Get—"

And then Gabb must have noticed me leaning back in my chair, feet on the window sill, a glass and cigarette in my fingers. I turned and got up grinning.

"Jock!" Gabb exploded. "You son of a thousand prodigal Scots, what are you doing here?"

"Drinking your whisky."

"We'll get drunk as county Cork!" He followed his booming voice across the room and we pummeled each other like a pair of kids. "Had your shower? Tiffin? You look like hell, but it's good to see you. Mahmoud! None of your bloody curry for tiffin! I want a feast on the table in half an hour. Jock, did you bring fresh clothes? No? I've got two dozen suits—pick what you want. I thought you were on your way to the States!"

"It was too far to walk."

"Come along!"

"Mahmoud said you had bandits last night."

"Twenty-eight trees slashed. It could have been worse. Thirty-five-year-olds."

I followed him through the house and we went on talking in the shower pavilion. It was always a little hard to keep Gabb in focus; I had set off the exuberant Irishman in him and only if you looked closely would you recognize the Chinese outcroppings in his white face. His eyes were set with only a shadow of the Orient, but enough to give his handsome features a faintly exotic cast. Only the cheekbones really betrayed him, but he was always in motion, as if to keep you from looking too closely, and he never allowed his face to brown in the sun.

Yet I knew he took a fierce pride in his Chinese blood and never set foot in the Planter's Club for fear some pukka sahib might get under his Eurasian skin. He liked to talk about his father, an herb doctor who had won a Queen's Scholarship and returned to Singapore to practice medicine

Western style. I had never heard him mention his mother, except that she had been Irish. I had always suspected he despised her, but at the same time she had given him his white skin, his towering build, and his blue eyes. Gabb had been graduated from the King Edward VII College of Medicine, but with the degree in his pocket he'd got himself a common clerk's job on a rubber plantation in Pahang, where I'd originally met him. He'd never practiced. He considered his medical degree a great Irish joke.

"You must meet Monique!" he burst out while I was soaping myself. "You'll see why I waited so long to get myself *a poombalie,* Jock!"

"Why didn't you write that you'd got married?"

"But I did!"

"Like hell. Why the big secret?"

"What?"

"Not a word out of you."

"I wrote." His voice was brisk and sure. Then he laughed. "Maybe you don't read your mail."

I was startled. "Sure," I said, trying to think it through. "Maybe that's it." Maybe I hadn't read my mail. Had Eden destroyed some of his letters? But that didn't make sense. There was no reason to do that.

"Jock, it's good to have you with me!" He was off again, like an old drinking partner. "You know I'm sorry I had to cut you when you phoned from Singapore. It killed me to do that."

"It damned near killed me."

"My line's been tapped."

"What?"

"Tapped. I knew we were being overheard. I figured you didn't want that."

I was toweling myself and it stopped me. He must know about the trouble in Sumatra, I thought quickly. He must know about Eden. But in his own way he was telling me I didn't have to talk about it if I didn't want to. We could let the subject drop, but he had to warn me about the phone.

I decided not to let the subject drop. "Tell me more."

"A police sergeant from Kuala Lampur paid us a visit Tuesday." He burst into a laugh. "It seems the police figured you might head for Silver Jubilee."

"Crazy," I said.

"Absurd. I told him that."

"What did he tell you?"

"A bloody fable about you and Eden."

"It was true, Gabb."

His voice dropped. "She's dead, eh?"

"Yes."

"I'm sorry, Jock."

"Don't be sorry, Gabb. She was rotten."

He shrugged. "They're all rotten—some more than others. But I know you like a brother, Jock. You didn't murder Eden. Even if you say so, I won't believe it."

"I'm just not sure."

"What, man?"

"It's mixed up. I keep telling myself I didn't do it, because I don't think murder is in me—drunk or not. But the truth is, I'm not positive."

"Of course you didn't do it!"

"Listen, Gabb. We had a drink after dinner. Eden was wearing shorts around the house, I remember that. She was nervous, but you know how high-strung she got at times. It was nothing. We didn't have a fight."

"She wasn't made for plantation life. Not Eden."

"You warned me a long time ago."

He shrugged it off with a smile. "Will a hill crumble at the bark of a dog? You had to find it out for yourself."

"Let's skip the wisdom of the East. There are about thirteen hours I can't find in my head. I don't sleep late, but the next morning I did—I still can't figure it. When I finally woke up I saw Eden in a green dinner dress. And she was dead. Maybe I got drunk and maybe we had a fight and maybe I killed her. We used to have some awful rows. I might have really lost my head. But I don't remember getting drunk and I can't figure out why she got all dressed up."

"The important thing, my friend, is to make up your mind what you're going to do."

"I have. I'm going to forget it."

"That I don't believe!"

"Why not? In six months or so it'll blow over. I'm not going to fight it. She wasn't worth the trouble. She's dead, that can't be helped now, and I really don't give a damn."

His eyes narrowed, but there was still something left of the smile on his lips. "May this old friend be permitted another bit of wisdom? The Malays like to say that the mouse deer may forget the snare, Jock, but the snare doesn't forget the mouse deer. You must clear yourself, Jock. It's the only way for an honest man to live with himself."

"And say I find out I *did* kill her. What does an honest man do then?"

"Then," he said, laughing, "it's time to run."

I got into white shorts and a clean shirt that Mahmoud had left in the shower pavilion for me, and put my feet in wooden *t'rompoks*.

"It's not worth the gamble," I said. "There's an inspector down there with ideas of his own. His name is Aziz ben-Kris, and this is his first important murder, and he isn't going to let it get away. His off-the-cuff reconstruction of the crime almost convinced me."

"Bah!"

"Eden was sleeping around, including my head *mandor.* I got jealous. I shot her. I suppose it does make sense."

"See—it doesn't even convince me. Jock, someone murdered your wife. Perhaps even the *mandor,* eh? Maybe, yes, she was rotten. But you must *catch* this murderer."

"I'm just not that much interested."

"You're a fool. Do you think it's safe for you here?"

Our eyes met. "As safe as anywhere," I said.

"No," he muttered grimly. "The police found a letter I had written to you."

"That's impossible. I burned up everything that might start the police pestering my friends."

"This letter you didn't burn. In it I told you the estate was getting too big for me to handle and I wished you'd give up your few acres in Sumatra and join me. From this letter the police arrived at the opinion you might show up at Silver Jubilee, eh?"

I stared at him, and it made a kind of sense. If Eden had held out one of Gabb's letters, that might be the letter the police had found and I had missed burning. But why would Eden give a damn about any of Gabb's letters? It bothered me.

"So," Gabb went on, "they came from Kuala Lampur to talk to me and they tapped the wire in case you attempted to get in touch with me."

"Which I did."

"It made trouble?"

"Quite a bit."

"You can stop worrying about the phone." He laughed. "It is now out of order. I had my clearing gang fix that, eh? When the company finds the trouble it will look like a wawa chewed the insulation. Perhaps it will take them another day to find it. But you see, the police were right. You came to Silver Jubilee. It's not safe for you here."

"Does that mean you don't want me here?"

His hands shot up in exasperation. "I tell you only what I think, Jock. I expect you to make up your own mind." His temper cooled. "Meanwhile, my house is yours."

"Let's eat."

"A feast! Perhaps Monique is home now to join us. You must see her— an angel, Jock! Ah, my life has become sweet. See how she has changed the house? It's a show place now, eh? This morning she went to visit at the Straits View Plantation. You remember Mrs. McWortor. No? And as Scotch as yourself! Down with fever again and Monique is helping to care for her."

"Monique—" I stopped myself, and the wooden pattens on my feet made clacking sounds along the floor. Why tell him I thought Monique had gone to the Planter's Club bar this morning? Hell, maybe I was jumping to conclusions. Maybe Mrs. McWortor needed a drink.

"Monique," I said, "is a pretty name."

Gabb put my passport in his bedroom safe. For the benefit of Monique, the houseboys, and anyone else in Kuala Tang, my name was to be Jack Gordon. We took the name off a gin bottle. As long as I was determined to stay, Gabb was determined to make Silver Jubilee as safe as possible for me.

Monique didn't show up for lunch.

If Gabb was piqued, he kept it hidden behind a rapid flow of reminiscence. Between the roast squab and the sambals of rice and dried prawns, the bottle of imported sherry and Gabb's rushing voice, I had little time to sort out my thoughts. The business of the letter or letters worried me. I didn't know Gabb was married because those letters didn't get to me. I had burned all my mail, but the police turned up at least one of Gabb's letters. Had Eden hidden it from me? Was that how I missed it? What the hell was she up to?

But most of all I wondered if I really ought to stay at Silver Jubilee. I had already brought Gabb some bad headaches. His phone had been tapped and he'd put it out of order to protect me. The police had come from K.L., and they might come again. Maybe I'd better clear out. But for today I knew I wasn't going anywhere. It felt too damned good to stop running. I thought of Kay.

"Your neighbor across the river gave me a lift in from Kuala Tang," I said.

"What neighbor?"

"Kay Allison."

He was refilling my glass, and the topaz flow of sherry vanished. "You met her in Kuala Tang?"

"I came up from Singapore on the boat with her."

"Did she tell you anything about me?"

"Everything."

His voice had an unfamiliar doubt in it. "Like what, Jock?"

"The name," I said, "is Jack."

He finished filling my glass and chuckled. "I'll try to remember. What did she say?"

"That she was only a platonic friend of yours, despite the gossip."

"Ah, that is Monique for you! One look at the Australian and she figures things out, eh? It's too bad. Kay needs help since her husband was killed, but me—ah, Monique is too jealous even to let me set foot on Jade Tiger. She is having bandit trouble too over there."

"I saw it in the paper."

"A year ago we thought we had them cleared out of the jungle, but now they are back again, like the fever."

"Someone tried to kill Kay aboard ship."

"It will never end, until— What?"

"A couple of hired killers."

"You're joking!"

"I'm not joking."

"But who—"

"She doesn't know."

Gabb had stopped eating. The news alarmed him and a harsh frown settled on his pale face. "This is a new trick! Are the Reds out to get us personally—not just the trees?"

"That might be it."

"Did she bring back a new overseer? Ah, that's what she must have! Two bloody fists to run the *kaboon* and deal quickly with trouble."

I told him the rest of it, Edgett and Hoven and the reason she hadn't been able to bring back an overseer. He listened carefully, without interrupting, like a doctor being told symptoms that might suggest a cure.

"I must do something to help her," he said when I had finished. "She is alone out here and it has worried me for a year. It's ridiculous for a woman to run a rubber *kaboon*."

"I keep asking myself why she doesn't sell and get out," I said.

"Why?" He was off again. "Why do any of us stick, Jack? It's bad enough with the terrorists, but rubber has fallen three and three-quarter cents just this week. A few planters have pulled out, but the stubborn ones stick. We are fools! You remember the herd of elephants that trampled my saplings the last time you were at Silver Jubilee?"

"They still giving you trouble?"

"Still. We are like the elephants. We remain, like idiots. See, we have cut back the jungle to plant rubber, driving the herd back and back, yes? But will they go away? A few, perhaps. The timid ones. But this land they liked, and they keep returning to break our fences and damage our trees. We want the land too, and not even the Reds will drive me away."

"That answers that," I said. "Kay is anything but timid."

Gabb emptied his glass in thirsty gulps. "With her there is more," he said, recklessly slapping down the glass. "There is crazy pride. Her family in Sydney is rich. Any day you can see them in the society pages down there. They warned her she was a fool to live here on the edge of the jungle. They were against the marriage. You never met Eric? A fine man, he was, and a good planter. She loved him, but two months after he brought her home to Jade Tiger he was dead. No, Kay will never go back. She must prove to her family she was right. And she has come to love the land now that her husband is dead. She is a rare one, Jack. Rare."

I nodded.

"Come," Gabb said, getting up from the table. "It's too hot to discuss these things. We'll have a siesta, eh? And later you will meet Monique."

Later, I thought, I'd go over to Jade Tiger. I felt an overwhelming need to talk to Kay. I was sorry the phone was out of order. If trouble cropped up she wouldn't be able to reach me. I felt as if I ought to check on her every half hour, and then I shrugged off my fears with a private grin. I was forgetting. Kay was pretty damned good at looking out for herself.

"That's what I need," I said. "Sleep."

Chapter Eleven

I awoke slowly and something was wrong. I opened my eyes and the room was dark. That was crazy. What had happened to the sun? And then a sharp awareness came over me. There was someone in the room.

I snapped on the bed lamp. The mosquito netting seemed to enclose me in a box of weak yellow light. And then I saw the figure standing close outside the netting, peering in at me. A warm breeze was flowing through the shades, billowing the netting so that the figure seemed to waver, like a reflection seen in the water.

Mahmoud.

"The *mem* wishes to know if you are awake," he said.

I rubbed the sweat off my face. "Have you ever heard of knocking?"

"She waits on the veranda for you."

"What time is it?"

"Almost nine, tuan."

"Clear out," I said. "Tell the *mem* I'll be there in a few minutes."

The houseboy left and I sat on the edge of the bed with a cigarette. Mahmoud gave me the creeps. I'd tanked up on sleep and now my head felt fuzzy. My skin was sticky with perspiration. I picked up my clothes, took a short shower, and finally showed up on the veranda. Gabb was nowhere in sight.

But Monique was there.

She was waiting in a long chair with a drink in her hand and her shoulders bare and glistening in the heat. Insects were singing all over the place. She turned a moody smile on me as I came up.

"You're Gabb's wife," I said. "Hello."

Her eyes were large and dark and they covered me in a weblike glance. The smile brightened a little. "Sit down, M'sieu Jack. I have been waiting to meet you."

"What happened to the sun?"

"I made it go away so you could sleep."

She wore something strapless made out of Javanese batik, full of scarlet and black and full of Monique. Large gold rings caught the light at her ears. Her hair was night black, combed to one side with a certain careful abandon.

I sat down. She stared at me with unabashed frankness and I began to feel uncomfortable. She was quite beautiful and quite young, but that wasn't what bothered me. There was something aggressively lonely and unhappy about her, and she wore it like a chip on her shoulder.

"You slept through dinner," she said. "Gabriel refused to wake you. I will have Mahmoud bring you some food."

"I'd rather have a drink," I said. "Where's Gabb?"

She tipped her head in a sort of bored gesture. "He sets out guards because the bandits may come again tonight. You are old friends, yes?"

"Yes."

"I'm glad you are here. It becomes lonely."

"I suppose it does."

"We have no visitors except the bandits. You will stay long?"

Everyone seemed to be feeling me out on that. "I don't know," I said.

"But you must stay!" she said with sudden brightness.

I looked at her. She really meant it and I grinned to myself. "You're talking me into it."

"You are from Singapore, M'sieu Jack?"

"Not exactly."

Mahmoud appeared with a tray of drinks, as if he were a mind reader, and I began to wonder about Kay. I damned the telephone. Maybe I'd take a run over when Gabb got back with his car.

When I turned my head, Monique was still staring at me. I got a quick impression that startled me. I was something new at the plantation, a stranger, and it was as if her emotions had been waiting, leechlike, for something to pass. I'd better watch my step.

"I was a dancer," she said. "Did Gabriel tell you about me, M'sieu Jack?"

"You must dance for me sometime," I said absently. I crossed my ankles and glanced out over the rolling night mass of trees stretching like a ground fog to the Straits.

"I'm very good," Monique said simply, as if there was no room for argument. "I have—what you call it?—imagination, yes? But Gabriel doesn't like to watch me dance. He doesn't understand—you know?"

She was running him down, and I didn't like to hear it. Gabb must have been mad to bring a dancer to live with him at Silver Jubilee. I wished he'd hurry back.

"I have performed many places," Monique said with a touch of naive arrogance. "I started in Saigon. You have been to Saigon?"

"Yes."

"I was born there. My mother too was a dancer. It must be in the blood, to be a good dancer."

"You must dance for me sometime," I said, before I realized I was repeating myself. I kept listening for the sound of Gabb's Chrysler on the road. It would soon be too late to go to Jade Tiger, and suddenly I wanted very much to see Kay. Monique was unloading her life story, as if it were the only thing she had of her own on this sprawling estate, and I wasn't really very much interested.

"My mother was killed when they threw a bomb into a café where I was dancing," she said softly. "The Viet Minh. Such murderers! Like here. They are all the same, the Reds. *Cochons!* They kill without reason. I was only sixteen when it happened."

"I'm sorry."

"Then I find out all about the world. It is hard for a girl of sixteen, eh?" I could do without the self-pity. I just nodded.

She faced me sharply. "You have heard the gossip about me?"

"No," I said.

"You will. None of it is true."

"I'll remember that."

"They despise me in Kuala Tang. The women. Because I was a dancer, not like them, mere housewives, eh? But I'm boring you, M'sieu Jack."

"Not at all," I said. I thought I heard the distant whine of tires. I put out my cigarette and walked to the railing.

"It is a beautiful plantation, even at night, yes?" she said with a flash of pride. It was hers. Not bad for a girl who had found out about the world at sixteen, eh?

"Quite beautiful."

She was the *mem* of a big estate, and she should have been happy, but she was a dancer, and an artiste needed an audience and applause and adoration. She was caught, and I found myself beginning to feel sorry for her.

Headlights vanished and reappeared like a will-o'-the-wisp through the trees. That would be Gabb. I could feel Monique's eyes measuring my shoulders.

"Come, sit down," she said. "In a moment I must share you with Gabriel."

The car grated up the hill and swung along the driveway. In the searchlights that lit up the grounds as an antibandit precaution, I saw at once it wasn't Gabb. The sedan braked below us and a Malay flew out of the door. It was Kay's Mercury, and my vague fears turned into a quick sweat.

The Malay stopped midway up the steps when he saw me on the veranda.

"The *mem* says you come quick! There is bad trouble!"

Monique hardly let him finish before she was on her feet. "Tell *mem*," she said icily, "her troubles do not interest us at Silver Jubilee. Tell—"

"Let's go," I said to the Malay.

"M'sieu Jack—"

I shot a glance her way. Monique's face was flushed with rage. She was suddenly unreal. There were cruelty and jealousy and danger in her eyes. I wondered how I had thought her beautiful a moment ago.

Chapter Twelve

It was a wild ride and my thoughts raced ahead of us. The Malay bore down on the accelerator with his naked foot and I didn't slow him up by asking questions. He assured me Kay was alive and that's all I gave a damn about. I wondered bitterly if the Nabob had got in another try. At the same time, my pride quickened. Something had happened at Jade Tiger and she'd sent for me.

We wound up through the groves of Jade Tiger and after another moment I could see the house in the searchlights. Maybe there was another terrorist raid on the rubber, the goddamned Reds. I left the car almost before it stopped and raced up the steps to the veranda. The door opened and I saw Kay in a quick silhouette against the bright living room.

"Kay—you're all right?"

I held her tightly in the doorway. Her body was tense, but I could feel a tide of relief go through her.

"I'm all right. I tried to phone."

"It's out."

"Jack, it's terrible! I—"

"Come on, get a grip on yourself." I led her into the living room and really saw her for the first time. She wore a short housecoat and her legs were in silk pajamas. She had obviously already gone to bed. Now she wore a gun belt and the holster had a gun in it. She was keyed up and I realized I'd never seen her that way before. Even on the ship her fright had never quite crystallized. It had never appeared in her green eyes. Now it was there.

"What happened?"

She put a cigarette between her lips; I took the lighter out of her fingers and lit it for her.

"I tried to phone the constabulary in Kuala Tang. They were asleep—it was maddening. And when I tried to call you at Silver Jubilee—"

"I know."

"I'm terribly relieved you're here."

"The Reds again?"

"I don't know." She exhaled smoke in a harsh pause. "When I got home this afternoon one of my field conductors reported that Ahmad was missing from the estate."

"Ahmad?"

"The *mandor* of the Malay workers. He grew up on this estate, Jack. He could handle any job from timber clearing to tapping, and he did it with a marvelous smile. I could trust him and I did. Ahmad was the closest thing to an overseer I had."

"Sure, a good *mandor* is hard to find."

"It wasn't like him to leave the *kaboon* while I was away. He's been gone two days."

"Hell, maybe he's found a girl on one of the other plantations."

"I was hoping it would be as simple as that."

A houseboy came into the room with a pot of tea and some native sweet-meats. He wore a smile too, and I thought suddenly of Mahmoud and his faintly contemptuous, speckled eyes.

"You must drink, *mem*," he said softly. "It is not good for *mem* to smoke so much. Bad for the nerves. Tea is better."

"Take it back, Dollah," Kay said, without, somehow, sounding unkind. "I couldn't."

"I leave, you drink, yes?"

Dollah left, his smile firm and boyishly commanding. She would drink, yes. I poured out a cup and made her take it. She finally sat down.

"Then Ahmad didn't go off to some *poombalie* on another plantation," I said.

"Dollah found him, Jack. I have some mango trees growing behind the hospital house and Dollah decided I wanted some fresh fruit before I went to bed. He went out to pick a few mangos and he found Ahmad. There was a knife in his back. He must have been trying to crawl to the hospital. Jack, he's *dead!*"

"Is he still out there in the trees?"

She nodded. "Jack, what's happening here? I can feel it. There's some-thing—something horrible and secret."

"Dollah!" I called. I turned back to Kay. "Don't try to call the police again."

"What?"

Would I never get off this tightrope? I didn't want cops getting that close to me. They might not find Ahmad's killer, but they'd sure as hell find me. I think I realized at that moment that I was a damn fool for hanging around Kuala Tang. I ought to clear out. If only I could manage a couple of days to get back on my feet before I began running again. The thought of running had a sharper cutting edge than before. I would be running away from Kay and I wasn't sure I could do it. Without an overseer and with her *mandor* dead, she had to have help. She needed two big fists on her plan-tation—Gabb had said that—and I had two goddamn big fists.

"Promise me, baby." I almost shouted it. "Don't call the police."

Her green eyes steadied on me. "Jack, sometimes you frighten me."

"I know these small-town cops," I snapped. "A murder comes along and they turn into hot-weather *Fuhrers.* Who else knows about Ahmad?"

"My Number Two boy."

"The driver?"

"Yes."

"Can he keep his mouth shut?"

"If I ask him."

"Tell him. If anyone asks, Ahmad hasn't returned."

"What are you going to do, Jack?"

"I don't know. But I don't want the cops—not yet."

She put out her cigarette. Maybe I frightened her a little, but she trusted me. "All right, Jack."

"And keep that gun on your hip."

Dollah appeared from the kitchen and I told him to get a flashlight. I followed him through the house to the back door and it came to me in a rush that murder had begun to cling to me like so many leeches. Eden and the attempt on Kay's life, and now her *mandor.* For more than thirty years I had never been closer to murder than the newspapers, but suddenly everything I touched seemed bloody. It was goddamned strange.

The night was heavy-sweet with jasmine as we crossed the garden toward the work buildings. In the searchlights I could make out the squat shapes that would be the factory, the nursery, the godown, and the hospital. We left the illuminated area and Dollah began to use the flashlight. Once we reached the brow of the hill I could see a few night fires dying out along the river. The native lines. A pheasant flushed at the sound of our footsteps, ripping the silence with its *ku-au, ku-au.*

I followed Dollah through the foliage and in another moment he spread some leafy mango branches and the flashlight stopped weaving.

It glinted off the kris handle that rose like a marker out of Ahmad's young back. A monitor lizard as long as my arm scurried out of the light. A praying mantis was startled from the white-streaked body and vanished in a green flutter. I bent down and saw streams of white ants ignoring the flesh and feeding at Ahmad's sandals, his belt, his cheap watch band. The mantis had been lured by the ants, the lizard by the mantis. Death was always a nightmare in the jungle.

I looked up at Dollah. "We'll have to bury him. Can you get a shovel?"

"Yes, tuan."

He let me have the flashlight and hurried off to the nursery shed. I looked along the stiff form of a man who'd once been able to smile. I could still get the sweet scent of the pomade that plastered down his thick black hair. But the smell of quickly rotting death was beginning to envelop even that. He couldn't have been dead too long, I figured. A few hours in the tropics makes a hell of a difference, and I wondered how many tortured hours he'd been creeping toward the hospital. Perhaps a day of starts and blackouts. He'd probably been knifed far from here.

I barely breathed, hating to take in the odor of death, and fought to keep from retching. I stared at the kris handle. There was no chance for finger-prints, and that, I thought, made it a goddamned good murder tool. It was carved as a stylized bird with a long beak and there wasn't enough uncut surface to leave any hope of prints. The carving was rough; the kris looked cheap and commonplace. But once Ahmad was buried there'd be nothing else to go on, and I set about withdrawing it.

It came more easily than it should have. When I looked at the blade in the beam of the flashlight I saw why. My mind started spinning. Most kris-es have wavy, snakelike blades. This was as straight as a kitchen knife.

I wiped the blood off on some leaves and looked again at the handle. The bird's head plus the straight blade made it not so common, at least in the state of Selangor. This kris came from some other part of Malaya. I had come across a thousand different knives before and I tried to force recog-nition out of my memory. But the thousand krises blurred. I couldn't iden-tify it.

Dollah came back with the shovel and we picked a small clearing under a casuarina tree. It took only half an hour to get the job done in the soft, rust-colored soil.

I managed to get the kris cleaned up before I brought it into the house. Kay had herself pretty well under control and I showed her the murder weapon.

Her eyes avoided it.

"I want you to look at it," I said. "You've been around these things. Have you ever seen a kris like this?"

"Jack, knives are as common as sarongs."

"But even sarongs are different, depending on where the batik is made."

She made herself look at it. "I think that's supposed to be a kingfisher's head," she muttered.

"What about the blade?"

"I've seen straight ones before."

"You don't know where it might have come from?"

"No. What difference does it make? If the Reds killed Ahmad, it won't do any good to trace the knife."

"I don't think it was the Reds. They don't leave a man in his clothes, and especially they don't leave a wrist watch. I'm hoping Ahmad's death has no connection with the Nabob and the attempt on your life, but I can't shake the feeling that the connection is there. Look, baby—"

"I want to call the police. I *must!*"

"Damnit, give me a couple of days. Two days. Someone is trying hard to keep your *kaboon* from operating and I'd like to find out why. But don't put the police on my back."

"You're afraid of them, aren't you?"

"Two goddamned days and maybe I'll be ready for them. Will you do that for me?"

"It was the same on the ship, wasn't it?"

"I'm sorry."

"Why do I go on believing in you? I don't even know your last name."

"It's Gordon."

She shrugged, and I knew she didn't believe the lie.

I said, "Are you afraid of staying alone, Kay?"

"I'm not alone. There's my Number One boy and my Number Two boy. No, I'm not afraid."

"Well, maybe I am," I said. I called Dollah back from the kitchen and told him to roll a couple of field conductors out of their beds. They could spend the night on the front and rear verandas. I'd feel better.

"Kay baby, you've got to think why someone wants to kill you. There's got to be a reason, and it must be staring you in the face. Ahmad may have found out something while you were gone and that might be why he was killed, so he couldn't talk. Until something better comes along, I'd like to think that's the connection."

"Would Monique want to kill me and bankrupt the estate?"

"I'll ask her."

"She's quite cunning. It would be like her to go about it very darkly."

"Keep thinking," I said. "Go back over the last few years of your life. That Chinese you fired because he left empty bottles around. Bayfield. There's got to be something behind you that's making all the trouble."

"Are you going now?"

"It's late and you must be dog-tired. Put the kris somewhere. I'm not going to tell Gabb about this. He'd only get excited and rush over and Monique would take off his skin."

She rose from the webbed rattan chair and gave me a hard smile. "If you know where I can hire a good overseer, let me know."

"I'll let you know."

"Good night, *Tuan Besar.*"

I checked the verandas and the Sikhs were there with their curled beards, their chesty bodies, and their rifles.

Kay would be safe.

Chapter Thirteen

I don't know what time it was when I got back to Silver Jubilee. Despite the searchlights, the house seemed heavily asleep. There was only a nightjar awake to greet me on the veranda, with a tocking in its throat, like a cheap alarm clock running down. Time—that was all I wanted. A couple of days. Time enough to find out what the hell was going on and make sure Kay would be safe when I pulled out. I had a crazy kris to go on, and that was a start.

Mahmoud had been left waiting up for me. He let me in.

"The *Tuan Besar* has gone to bed?" I asked.

"There is early work to be done," Mahmoud said, as if to acquaint me with the facts of estate life. "The *Tuan Besar* sleeps now."

"Wake me at five-thirty," I said. "Tell the *Tuan Besar* I want to make the morning rounds with him."

"Yes, tuan."

It puzzled me that Gabb hadn't waited up to find out what the trouble had been at Kay's. Then I realized Monique may never have told him there was any trouble at all. "M'sieu Jack? He is at Jade Tiger." Period. End of report.

I went out to the pavilion, took a long shower, and got back into my clothes. Then I walked to my room, smoked a last cigarette as I undressed again, and went to bed. Finding a murder at Jade Tiger had keyed me up and I had a hell of a time relaxing. In the darkness and quiet of the room a sort of despair came over me. If only I could say yes to the overseer job.... But I'd only be kidding myself. If I had any brains I'd clear out of Kuala Tang fast. The kris in Ahmad's back kept reminding me of Inspector Kris in Sumatra, and I'd come to upcountry Malaya to forget.

Fine chance. What chance did I have of getting to the bottom of the trouble at Jade Tiger in a couple of days? I ought really to pull out and let Kay call in the police. What the hell, had I fallen in love with her? At first I had thought she was only pretty with the shadow of freckles across her nose, but suddenly I thought the freckles were beautiful and her green eyes and reddish-blonde hair had taken on a special quality. It was going to hurt to walk away from her.

I threw an arm over the Dutch wife and made myself go to sleep.

I'd been through this before, hadn't I? There was someone in my room. I could sense it, someone standing near the bed. I wasn't sure I'd even been asleep, but I must have been, and I roused swearing. I snapped on the light.

It was Monique.

She stood beyond the netting and her voice was soft and throaty. "You are awake, M'sieu Jack?"

"I am now," I said.

"I have been waiting for you to come back."

She wore a shy smile, but she looked weird as hell. The brooding loneliness was gone from her wide, brown eyes. Even through the netting and in the weak light, her skin glistened, and I realized she had rubbed it with coconut oil like a Tamil woman. She wore a filmy lavender sari, and she was barefooted, and there were brass bells fastened at her ankles and small cymbals on her fingers.

"You wanted to see me dance." She smiled, and there was a flush of intrigue in her smile. "I dance."

"It's a hot night," I said. "This can wait."

"You worry about Gabriel?"

"Maybe you'd better go back to bed."

"He sleeps like a bear," she said firmly. "And I touch the cymbals very light, yes? *Oui,* like this."

The cymbals struck and shimmered softly in the room.

I managed to keep my voice low. "Get out."

She laughed softly. She entwined her arms, like two glistening snakes, and the finger cymbals beat faintly again, and again, and then she began to dance.

I stared through the netting and wanted to feel sorry for her, but I couldn't any more. She was getting a charge out of the danger of being in my bedroom. The ankle bells and finger cymbals murmured a soft, exotic beat, and my anger soared. O.K., she was lonely and unhappy on the plantation, and suddenly I had come along to break the boredom. It must have hurt when I had run off to Kay earlier in the evening, and now she was making a quick and desperate play for me. I watched the excitement grow on her pretty face; she was in her element now. She was dancing and she had an audience, but the sight of her and the smell of her was beginning to disgust me. I pulled aside the mosquito netting and stood on my bare feet.

"I'll tell you again," I said through the brass jangle. "Clear out."

She began to hum as she danced, coming closer, a malevolent blackness in her eyes. She stopped in front of me and entwined her oily arms around my neck and beat the cymbals in my ears.

"You want me to go, *mon ami?*" Her laughter was taunting and sensuous, and she pressed her glistening body against me, warm and moving and animal-like. "You want me to go, eh?"

The cymbals crashed in my ears like something mad. The heavy smell of coconut oil was making me sick.

"*Get out!*"

"Make love to me, M'sieu Jack."

I got hold of her wrists and twisted her arms off my neck. I stared into her eyes, hating her. She spread her cymbaled fingers like the jaws of a snake and for a moment there was only the muted rattle of the bells at her ankles. Then the brass snapped at her fingers and fire leaped into her eyes.

"Is it Kay you—"

"Shut up and get out."

"*Salaud!* Monique is not lovely, eh? Monique—"

I picked her up under the shoulders and knees and carried her across the floor. She beat at my face and the ankle bells jangled. I dumped her on her feet in the hall.

"Good night, baby."

"I will make you pay, *M'sieu Crapule!*"

"Go to hell."

I put the door between us and locked it. I stood there a moment, and I was shaking a little. This was the girl Gabb had married. The girl from Lavender Street. Lonely and mixed up and starved for excitement.

I lit a cigarette and sat on the edge of the bed and wondered if I ought to spend another night at Silver Jubilee. She'd try again. I knew her type and I knew she wouldn't leave me alone. I didn't want to sleep with Gabb's wife. The poor dumb bastard, he must be blind. She was Eden in coconut oil.

It took me a hell of a time to fall back to sleep.

Chapter Fourteen

There was only a web of light in the eastern sky when we left the bungalow. Gabb wore riding breeches and puttees and his Port Dickson hat. I remembered he was generally silent and morose for the first dark hour of the morning and we did little more than trade nods. Hell, I didn't feel like talking myself. You don't tell your best friend his wife tried to crawl into bed with you.

I followed him to the Chrysler in the garage and I saw Monique's car, an armored Ford with white-wall tires. We drove to the native lines along the river. The cook fires were already going, and in the predawn they created twisting shadows in the kampong. The Malays were always harder to get out of bed than the Tamils and the Chinese, and we started at the Malay longhouses.

The *mandor*, an old man with a straight, muscular back, met us and followed us through the buildings. There were no windows, only a door at either end, and the air was foul from the exhaust of sleeping men. We went along the passageway between the rooms, looking in at the sleeping benches. Mosquito netting hung from the rafters, like giant spider webs. Gabb carried a changiwood cane and used it to wake the late sleepers. They reacted to it as to a tap from a magic wand, and they all awoke with the same words on their lips—*sahya sakit*. Sick.

After feeling their pulses and looking at their tongues, Gabb would send them on their way. He found five Malays running a temperature and one tapper he thought might have blackwater fever and made arrangements with the *mandor* to send them to the plantation hospital.

When we reached the Tamil lines the women were already cleaning the floors with fresh dung. I followed along silently, sorry I'd come. The kampong was old and ramshackle and out of the imperial past.

By the time we reached the Chinese workers, the trees had picked up the dawn and heavy dew began to drip from the leaves. Gabb's mood brightened and he joked with the *kapela*, the headman of the Chinese contract workers. For those few minutes he was a Chinese, and I stood there feeling strangely a world apart from him.

I guessed Kay was out in the lines across the river. A hell of a job for a woman. Why hadn't I gone over and got the day's work started for her? It was bad enough without an overseer, but even her *mandor* wasn't on tap any more. Ahmad was dead and she needed him. Well, what good would it do if I pitched in for only a couple of days? Unless she got an overseer who could stick, Jade Tiger was sure to flounder.

The human machinery of the plantation spread out from the lines, the timber clearing gang, the lalang diggers, the pest- and disease-control workers, the army of tappers. By the time the sun had detached itself from the fringed horizon, the native lines were as deserted as a ghost town. We stopped to smoke a cigarette.

"You were up late last night." Gabb grinned. "Good company, my Australian neighbor, eh?"

He broke into a laugh and I changed the subject. "You could turn your lines over to a museum," I said. "I don't understand how you keep your workers."

"New houses cost money, my friend."

"Times have changed, even out here."

"That's your bloody Singapore blarney. I've seen the slum clearance with the fine white walls and the electric lights—and in two years it'll look worse than this. Give them an atap roof and a couple of yards of mosquito netting and they're happy."

"Not any more, Gabb."

"Don't be a fool!"

"I'll bet fifty per cent of your workers are Reds."

"What!"

"That's what makes a Red out here—an atap roof and a couple of yards of mosquito netting. You're going to have to face it, Gabb."

He passed it off with a laugh. "Next thing you'll be telling me to give them breakfast in bed."

"I'm not trying to tell you anything."

"Come along, Jack!"

Well, Silver Jubilee was his business. I came along.

It was a big estate and we buzzed around in the armored car checking the work in progress. It had doubled in size since the last time I'd seen it, the year before Eden and I had got married. Gabb had recently bought up a new piece of land, a small run-down *kaboon* nestled up against the jungle, and the once cleared acres were shoulder-deep in lalang grass.

"I'll have it back in shape in a month," Gabb said, tugging at the brim of his hat. "If the bloody terrorists give me half a chance."

"Any trouble last night?"

"Nothing that's been reported yet. We might get the army planes to blast them out of the jungle."

"There's a lot of jungle back there to blast."

He whipped his cane through the grass. "A Chinese owned this *kaboon*. The Reds scared him out. Unless we get the terrorists out of the jungle, I'm not going to have any neighbors!"

Where we couldn't drive, we walked. The sky was a fresh blue and the sun was clear and sharp. We walked through the deep shade of the rubber, some of the trees at least ninety feet high. You'd catch a spot of color among the trunks, the bright sarong of a tapper as he bent to recut yesterday's wounds and fix the cup for the latex. Gabb kept a brisk pace on foot, and I remembered my own mornings among my own trees in Sumatra. I felt thoroughly alive and for a little while I felt goddamned happy. It gave me a lift to watch an experienced tapper at his *kanack,* his assignment of trees, caring for them like pet cows. I was in my element. I was glad I had come along.

In another hour it began to get hot.

"Gabb," I said, "when's the last time you saw a straight-bladed kris?"

"A week ago. There's a tree getting the bloody pinks."

He left me standing and found the nearest tapper, pointed out the diseased tree, and gave him hell for failing to get the P. and D. gang on it.

A week ago. Maybe this wasn't going to be hopeless. Gabb returned and we began walking again.

"Where, a week ago?"

He turned and laughed. "You want to start carrying a knife, do you? I can let you have a gun if you're that worried."

"Where did you see it?"

"The kris?"

"A straight-bladed kris."

He stopped to wipe the sweat off his forehead and fixed the straw hat at a sharper angle. "There was an Indian on an oxcart through here selling stuff to the natives. You know, batik and Zam-Zam and what not. He had a couple of krises and I remember there was a straight blade. Junk. I'd have bought it myself if it were any good."

"Junk?"

"The handle was gone. He'd fixed up a piece of bamboo for the handle. Junk."

I killed my cigarette. That was that. I tried again. "Ever hear of a kris handle carved like a kingfisher's head?"

"I have."

"With a straight blade?"

He turned his head and gave me a curious frown. "There's something on your mind, Jack. Did someone try to throw a kris in your back?"

"Not yet. I got to thinking about a straight blade with a kingfisher handle, but I can't place it and it's been bothering me."

"I've seen a dozen of them and so have you. *Kris pekaka*—kingfisher kris. They carry them around Patani. Come along, Jack."

Patani—the east coast. That gave me something to go on. You can generally spot an east-coast Malay as easily as any other stranger to the Malacca coast. His features lack the fine cut of the Malacca Malay. The east-coaster is generally flat-nosed and he carries around a little more jowl.

Well, maybe I had something and maybe I didn't.

We walked back to the road and piled into the car. It must have been almost nine o'clock. Gabb headed back toward the house for a shower and breakfast.

"Do you know of any Patani Malays around here?" I asked.

"You want to buy a kingfisher kris, Jack?"

"Yes," I lied.

"Ask Kay. I remember there's a family from Patani in her lines. Hungry?"

"Starved."

"You broke your arm, you know."

"What are you talking about?"

"I've got to take you to the hospital."

"Maybe you'd better start over. I don't follow you."

He laughed and gave me a wise look. "Maybe you were too busy to listen to the radio last night. You were on it, old friend of mine."

"Radio Malaya?"

"The news. We're going to cover up that scar on your thumb. I'm thinking I'd better put your entire arm in a cast, just to make it look good. It might be too obvious if I merely taped your hand, eh? Ha! If you had your way there'd be radios in the lines. One look at your thumb and all the natives would have recognized you!"

Chapter Fifteen

I shaved and ate my breakfast with one hand. I resented the plaster cast the moment it began to dry. It was hot and heavy even in the batik sling, and it slowed up my movements. But at least I could stop worrying about the scar on my thumb. That was the goddamn giveaway. The scar. Once I left Kuala Tang it would be a lot safer traveling in the cast, and I figured I'd better get used to it. But Gabb had put enough quick-setting plaster on my arm to balast a fishing proa.

I didn't want to think about where I would go or when. A couple of days one way or the other couldn't matter and I wanted that much time to follow up the kingfisher kris.

Monique came to breakfast in a tight print dress and a dozen wire bracelets on her wrists. Her dark eyes were wide and cheerful and you'd never guess I'd thrown her out of my bedroom last night.

"M'sieu Jack—your arm!"

"It's nothing." I grimaced. "Just a scratch."

"*Mon Dieu,* I don't understand!"

Gabb cut in with his big voice and laid it on thick. "M'sieu Jack has bone trouble. He should have been wearing a cast for months. Ah, the doctors in Singapore—what do they know? Me, I will fix him up." He thumped his chest with his palms. "Did I never tell you I am a doctor?"

"You joke."

"It's a joke, but it's also true."

"M'sieu Jack—"

"Eat your breakfast, Monique, eh?" There was a faint warning in Gabb's voice, and she picked it up. The subject lingered for a moment and finally disappeared.

"When will the telephone be fixed?" Monique complained. "We might all be murdered in our beds by the guerrillas and there'd be no way to call for help."

"Today maybe they will repair it." Gabb passed me a look as if to say, Don't worry, my friend. Once they find the spot and repair it, another monkey will chew another spot and it will be out of order again. See, I take good care of my guest.

"I hope it stays fixed," I answered firmly. It would make keeping in touch with Kay a hell of a lot easier. "It's rotten for you to be without a phone."

Gabb shrugged with a grin. "That is the trouble with these modern toys, eh? You come to depend on them and they let you down. Like women, eh,

Jack?"

I glanced up sharply, wondering how he meant me to take it. Monique cut in.

"You slept well last night, M'sieu Jack?"

"I slept fine," I said, stirring my coffee. Had Gabb noticed something? Despite Monique's airy cheerfulness, it seemed to me she was jockeying for position. She would get back at me. I'd spurned her and she'd make me pay for it. I began to feel crowded.

Suddenly I wished to hell I'd never set foot on Silver Jubilee.

"I'm glad you slept well, M'sieu Jack."

Gabb began talking about rubber prices and Monique allowed herself to be cut off. I thought about Kay. She had been too upset last night to listen to her radio. What would she think if she found out I was wanted for murder? She already had a strong sense of awareness. She knew something was wrong. She knew damned well I was running away from something, and Radio Malaya would fill her in if they were still broadcasting items about me. I'd better get over there and put her radio out of order.

"Gabriel," Monique protested, uncapping her lipstick, "M'sieu Jack has no interest in rubber prices. Don't make such boring talk."

Gabb looked at me as if to say, She's right. We're talking like planters. It's small things like this that can give you away. We must be careful, eh?

Mahmoud moved in with a platter of fresh fruit and I lit a cigarette. Suddenly Monique put her hand on my plaster cast.

"It is so white, M'sieu Jack." She frowned. "One moment! We will write our names, yes? When I was a girl and broke my wrist, all my friends wrote their names. I was very proud of my cast, I had so many friends."

I tried to withdraw my arm, but she held tight and began writing with the lipstick. Gabb burst out laughing.

"She is still a schoolgirl, my wife, eh?"

"I—"

"It is a pretty name, Monique," he said, enjoying my discomfort. "Wear it proudly, my friend!"

It was finished within seconds, and the crimson letters stood out large and searing against the white plaster.

"Now it's your turn, Gabriel," Monique said brightly.

"Me? I'm not a schoolboy." He got up from the table, his laughter booming in the room. "Now I must check accounts. This afternoon I'm going to K.L. by river and you must take care of my Monique. I have business that can't wait and I apologize. But I will be back tomorrow."

I looked up at him and his news paralyzed me. I didn't want to be left alone with Monique. Was he such a fool that he trusted her? A hell of a schoolgirl she was! But he trusted me. I was his best friend, wasn't I? Suddenly I wondered if he had his own reason for putting a cast on my arm. It would be hard to make a play for his wife when I was carrying around a ton of plaster. Was that why he'd laid it on like crazy?

There were a few last moments of conversation, but I lost them. What sort of trap had I walked into? If I smeared off Monique's name it would amount to a slap in the face, and Gabb would take offense. I had an impulse to get a hammer and break the goddamned cast to bits, but I just sat there. I'd let him put all that plaster on my arm, and if it wasn't there when he got back he'd know what to think. You can't make love very well with a cast on your arm. He'd held back the information that he was going to K.L. Now I couldn't get rid of the cast without arousing his suspicions.

I stared down at the bright red lettering on the cast. "Monique." As if she owned me. What would Kay think if I walked in with that on my arm? Monique had been way ahead of me. Did she think this crazy business would keep me away from Jade Tiger?

"I'm going for a walk," I said angrily.

It took me a long time to leg it to Jade Tiger, and by the time I got there the sling was wet around my neck and my arm was numb. I kept glancing down at the humiliating lipstick marks. I'd make Kay understand. Maybe we could make a joke out of it.

I found her in the factory behind the house. The tappers were filing in with their buckets of latex, like milk, and she supervising the weighing and testing and making entries in the log. She looked up smiling. Her gun, in its holster, lay on the accounts table.

"*Tabé,* Big Master."

Nearby, latex was coagulating in big aluminum vats; the room was hot from the fires and smelled of sulphur. She was dripping sweat, but somehow she looked completely beautiful to me. "You look busy," I said. "Can I help?"

She saw my arm in the sling. "Jack, what happened to you?"

I couldn't face it here, and I tugged the batik over so that it pretty much covered the lipstick. "Nothing serious," I said. "I broke my leg."

"Jack—"

"Please, baby. It's only a joke. It's coming off tomorrow."

"I don't understand."

"Don't try." I was holding up the routine. "Get back to work."

"I'll be finished in another hour."

There was nothing I could do; she had the routine down cold. I watched the tappers carefully as they came in off their *kanacks,* hoping to spot an east coast face. But I found myself watching Kay instead. It was almost one-thirty when the last of the tappers checked in for the day. Tapping is strictly a morning activity, as the real heat of the day slows down the flow of sap.

Finally she lit a cigarette and turned to me. "Tiffin?"

"I'm not hungry."

"Then come watch me eat." She picked up her gun and we started out of the factory.

"That kris comes from around Patani," I said when we were alone. "Gabb recognized it by description. He says that you have some people from there working for you."

"Gabriel has a good memory."

"I watched your tappers come in. I didn't see anyone who looked east coast to me."

She was quick to resent the suggestion that one of her own men might have killed Ahmad. "They're not tappers. I'm sure you're wrong about them. They're brothers and very good workers."

"I'd like to talk to them," I said.

"Now?"

"Now."

"They're on fence patrol. We ought to be able to drive quite close."

She told Dollah to hold tiffin and then got the Mercury out of the garage. I got in beside her and managed to keep the brand on my arm out of sight. I kept asking myself why the hell I didn't just wipe it off, and then I'd go over the whole thing again in my mind and I'd come up with the same frustrated feeling. I'd be tampering with Gabb's emotions, and I knew better.

We left the car on the road and walked about a quarter of a mile through scented trees to the edge of the estate. The heat was thick and heavy.

"Shall I tell you again?" Kay muttered.

"Go ahead."

"You're making a mistake. The Tulloh boys couldn't have done it. They're happy here. They wouldn't make trouble."

"I didn't say they killed Ahmad."

"But that's what you're thinking."

"All I care about is finding out who's got it in for you."

Half a dozen Malays were repairing the fence and they stopped with little grins as we approached.

"*Tabé, mem.*"

I spotted the Tulloh brothers easily, stocky men with sweat rolling down their hairless chests. Their expressions were shy and sensitive, as if they felt like outsiders in Selangor. I found myself liking them on sight.

"Elephants broke through here last night, *mem*," one of them explained in a soft voice, pointing out the broken fencing. "Now we fix good."

I could see trampled saplings in the area, rubber five years along that would take five years to replace. Kay only shrugged, as if she was used to the elephant damage and the terrorist slashings. They had become part of the daily routine of her life. But I wondered how much longer she could hold out.

"Tuan Gordon will ask you a few questions," Kay said, a little stiffly. She was embarrassed, and I was sorry.

But I had a feeling I was striking out even before I got started. Kay knew her men and intuitively she knew that neither of the Tulloh boys would make trouble for her. Both were carrying common parangs. I glanced at the sweat-darkened sheaths and my hopes began to fade. A native boy who owned an ornamented kris would wear it any day over a parang, but the sheaths I saw looked as if they'd been soaking up sweat for years.

I said, "How long have you been away from Patani?"

The brother who appeared older did the talking. "We have never been in Patani, tuan."

"Were you born there?"

"No, tuan. In Port Swettenham."

"Have you ever seen a *kris pekaka?*"

"Yes, tuan."

"Where?"

"Our father brought one from Patani."

"Where is your father?"

"In the *tokong*, tuan." In the family shrine.

"Where's his kris?"

"It hangs still in the *pajak lelap.*" The pawnshop. "Someday we will redeem it."

Kay gave me a slightly victorious glance, but at least she'd begun to smile again. I went doggedly ahead. Ahmad's murder was one key to the Nabob and the trouble at Jade Tiger—it had to be.

"Do you know anyone else from Patani living around Kuala Tang?" I asked.

"There is Inche, tuan."

"Inche?"

"He has a small *kaboon* near the river. Perhaps five kilometers along the road. Inche grows getah on land of his own."

I turned to Kay. "Do you know the place?"

She nodded. "It's quite easy to find."

"Let's find it."

"Not till I've had tiffin." Her mood had brightened. "Dollah will be furious."

We walked back to the car and I slumped in the seat trying to sort out my thoughts. It was almost too hot to think. If Inche turned into a dead end, what then?

The cast on my arm had begun to chafe; I'd done a lot of sweating and moving around. Gabb must have known damn well that after a few hours in this heat the cast would become a torture. Had he been figuring on that to keep me away from Monique? I'd been crazy to let Gabb do this to me.

The car pulled in under the shade of the garage. I stared at the lipstick and decided to get it over with as we started up the veranda steps.

I pulled back the sling. "I've been branded." I frowned. "Pretty, isn't it?"

Kay's green glance passed over the giant, vivid letters. Her expression didn't alter. "I'll have Dollah set an extra plate for you." She turned sharply. "You must be hungry by now."

"I want to explain," I said.

"It's self-explanatory. Would you like a stengah first?"

I caught her wrist and pulled her around to face me at the top of the steps.

"Thanks for being sore." I grinned.

"What?"

"It tells me you give a damn."

"Let go of me."

"Suddenly, I want you to care."

"I couldn't care less."

"Cut it out, Kay."

"You're hurting my arm."

I pulled her to me. She wasn't like the others, like Eden and Monique; she wasn't that beautiful. She was only pretty, with sun wrinkles at the edges of her eyes and freckles across her nose. She was only pretty, and it made a difference. She was something apart, a woman I'd begun to believe in when I thought my emotions were all washed up. "Maybe I'd better tell you," I said. "I'm in love with you."

"How very dull." Her eyes were fiery. "Are you quite finished?"

"Not quite." Anger caught up with me. I forced her chin up and kissed her lips. She stood cold and unyielding and a moment later she slapped me.

"Monique is a pretty name," she said. "But I don't like it staring at me while I'm being kissed."

The houseboy came to the door. "Tiffin is waiting, *mem.*"

"Dollah," I said, "get me a hammer."

I pounded on the cast behind the house. I kept hitting Monique's name and finally it disintegrated, like a nightmare breaking up. The cast shattered and hung on my arm in chunks of plaster and gauze. I pulled off the stuff and felt a surge of release. To hell with what Gabb thought. He must have left for Kuala Lampur by now, I realized, and when he got back he could think what he liked. Plaster had taken hair with it, and my skin burned. I looked at the scar on my thumb, like an old enemy returned. Well, I'd manage. I cleaned up my arm as best I could.

The radio was a soft voice in the room when I walked back into the bungalow. An Englishman was giving the news, and the gears of my mind caught. Kay had taken a quick shower and changed into fresh clothes. She was fixing flowers on the table. I listened for a moment, picking up the drift of the news. Radio Malaya was explaining the latest fall in rubber prices. I crossed the room and snapped it off before the news spread to general topics. Like Jock Hamilton.

Kay turned.

"Do you mind turning the radio back on? Rubber's gone down another half cent."

"Tomorrow it'll go back up," I said. Damnit, why hadn't I put the radio out of order earlier? I thought bitterly. I should have done it while Kay was logging in the tappers. "I've got to talk to you."

She returned to the flowers. "You love me. I think you covered the subject."

This brisk cynicism was something new and I didn't like it. "I haven't even begun," I said.

"Dollah," she said, as he came back with a water carafe, "please turn the radio on."

"Don't go near it," I snapped.

He gave me a nod and a grin and started for the radio. He took orders from her, not from me. I cut across his path, pulled the radio around, and grabbed all the wires within reach.

Kay bristled, but her voice came out cold. "You needn't have done that."

"I said I wanted to talk to you."

"I think you'd better go."

"I'm taking the job."

"What?"

"I'm the new overseer on Jade Tiger."

There was a taut silence, long enough for her expression to change. "Jack—"

"Do I stay or not?"

Her lips parted and then something soft, almost moist, came into her eyes. "You said—"

"I said I loved you."

"Kiss me again, Jack. Stay. Please stay, darling."

We met in the center of the floor, and it was different.

Her lips were soft and yielding and it took a long time.

Dollah stood by grinning.

Chapter Sixteen

I wasn't going back to Silver Jubilee.

I drove Kay's Mercury along the river road toward Inche's place, and I brought the kingfisher kris with me. Later I'd go into town and pick up the linen suit I'd been measured for yesterday.

Yesterday? It seemed a month ago. Sumatra was a year ago. Like everyone else, I'd struggled against "Malaya memory" ever since I'd settled in the East; it had always seemed somehow important not to let my sense of time be crushed under the heavy monotony of the heat and the rains. It was a merry-go-round that never stopped, the days and nights always the same length, the seasons a rumor, until your memory became a sort of endless checkerboard. But suddenly I wanted to give in to it.

I wanted the past to flicker and blur and fade. I wasn't sure I remembered what Eden looked like any more. I didn't want to remember. All I gave a damn about was Kay.

She loved me, didn't she?

She'd whispered it in my ear.

I looked out through the windshield slit at the orderly rubber sweeping by. What if she found out about the murder in Sumatra? Would Inspector Kris forget? Like hell he would. The police mind didn't fall into Malaya memory. I'd bring only trouble to Jade Tiger.

I drove a little faster and the parade ground of trees gave way to lalang and clumps of jungle festooned with vines and orchids and aerial roots. It had been crazy to let myself fall in love. Maybe I'd been a fool, but I just didn't give a damn any more. It was no good trying to talk myself out of Kay. I loved her. Goddamn it, I loved her.

I saw the answer. I couldn't go around lugging the baggage of my past. *I had to find out if I had killed Eden.*

Sure. Sure, it was the only way. I had to start caring who'd killed her and take the chance that it wasn't Jock Hamilton. I had to be innocent. I had always felt that in my bones. I wasn't a killer. It had to be someone else!

Clear myself. That was the answer. Clear myself, or never come back.

The road was narrow and the jungle thickened. Branches lashed the armor as I sped along. I'd go back to Sumatra. I'd hang around long enough to make sure Kay was safe, dope out what the hell was going on, and then I'd return to Sumatra. There'd be no future for me at Jade Tiger unless I could purge my past. Why had I been kidding myself? There was no other way. I'd go back my own way. The important thing was to keep from getting arrested and go back my own way. I'd find out what had happened during those blank hours in my mind when Eden was murdered. And then I'd get Inspector Kris off my back. I hadn't killed her. I had to believe that.

But I wasn't going anywhere until I found out who was trying to foul up Jade Tiger and kill Kay Allison. Maybe this road would take me where I wanted to go. Inche.

I left the car on the road and walked toward the house. It was set in a clearing hacked out of the jungle across the fence from Silver Jubilee. It was a postage-stamp *kaboon* of not more than two dozen rubber trees. The house stood on stilts with a hog penned in beneath. There was a rusted tin roof and family pictures hung on the front wall behind the veranda. Amber sheets of latex that had been coagulated and rolled hung on the veranda railing to dry.

I put out my cigarette and climbed up the short ladder. The door stood open and I saw a Malay woman of about forty sitting inside with a *roco* smoking from her lips. She was working a rolling pin over a mass of dirty coagulum, forming it into the sheets I had seen drying on the veranda. Her eyes looked morose and tired, and her face was worn. She seemed disinterested in my approach.

"I'm looking for Inche," I said.

No answer.

"Are you Inche's wife?"

There was only the squeak of the rolling pin as she spread the coagulum across the table. Dried "amber blankets" were stacked in a corner, and putrification was heavy in the room. It was a homemade rubber factory, like thousands of others scattered across Malaya, turning out a low-quality product for the lowest price.

"Where do you sell your getah?" I asked.

"Inche is not home."

"Where is he?"

"He will not come back."

"Where did he go?"

"He will not come back."

Her eyes were dull, but full of suspicion, and I knew I was far from welcome. The room odors seemed to reach out and cling to my clothes. Inche wouldn't be back. What did that mean? Had he taken off into the jungle? What did *that* mean? If the kris was his, maybe he had come to realize it could be traced and had run away.

"I've got to talk to him," I said.

She didn't answer.

I carried the kingfisher kris in a cloth, and I unwrapped it. "Is this your husband's?"

Her eyes gave it a brief, unwilling glance. She pressed down harder on the rolling pin. She wasn't going to talk. She didn't have to. It was Inche's kris. Inche, who had a few trees of his own, milking them each day like cows.

"If I turn this over to the police," I said, "they'll find Inche. And they'll hang him."

"No, tuan. They will not hang him."

"You know how to get in touch with your husband," I snapped. "Tell him I'll be at Jade Tiger tonight. Tell him to come and see me. Perhaps I will help him."

Who had ordered Ahmad's death? The Nabob? I had to find that out, and Inche could tell me.

The rolling pin squeaked. "Inche goes nowhere."

"Tell him."

"He is dead. I buried him by the river an hour ago."

I cut off toward town. I began to feel tired and uncertain of myself. The only lead I had was buried by the river. I had been able to get no more than that out of the Malay woman. Inche was dead. How or exactly when he had died I could only guess. But it no longer really mattered. Inche was a lost cause.

I crossed the bridge into Kuala Tang and could see the Planter's Club on the hill. The late-afternoon heat had settled over town like a pulsing headache. Nothing seemed to move but me. I shot past a Peking cart loaded with sugar cane and turned up toward the tailor shop.

I parked and reminded myself that Radio Malaya might still be broadcasting my description. It would take only a few minutes to pick up my suit, and I had enough money left to buy a decent pair of shoes. I could remember to keep my scarred hand out of sight that long.

The Chinese, dressed Western style, had my suit ready.

"Guaranteed fit." He beamed. "You see."

There was only a low lacquered screen to change behind, but I stripped. The shop was small, and with its glass windows, I felt as if I were changing clothes in a fish bowl. A couple of women with the air of planters' wives passed, glanced in, and moved regally on. With a decent suit on my back I could stop feeling like a poor relation in hand-me-downs. I could send Gabb back the clothes I had borrowed.

"You like?"

"I like," I said, standing in front of the mirror. "Are they wearing canvas shoes with linen this year?"

"I fix."

He went into the back of the shop and returned a few moments later with his arms loaded with shoes. I tried on the various pairs, but they were all too small.

"You wait. I get right size."

Maybe he had a relative in the shoe business. This time he left the shop and I picked out a handmade shirt and a black tie from his racks. He returned from the street within five minutes and he had a pair of perforated white oxfords. Even though I didn't like them, they were a fit and I said O.K.

I was sweaty and wanted a shower before I wore my new suit, so I went back behind the screen and got out of the cool linen suit and told him to wrap it up.

As I glanced through the window Will Edgett passed.

For a moment I was too startled to react. I must have been seeing things. It was a mistake. Edgett and Hoven were in Malacca Town. But even after the window was clear, the image of what I had seen sharpened in my mind. It *had* been Edgett! The guy who had been hired to kill Kay was in town.

I was half naked behind the screen. I reached for my trousers and buttoned up on the way out. The Chinese got in my way and I shoved him into a showcase.

"Tuan, tuan—"

When my feet hit the hot pavement I realized I was still in my socks. I stood outside the tailor shop and looked along the street in the direction Edgett had been going.

It was deserted.

I had to get my hands on him. I'd find out what was going on—I'd beat it out of him. I didn't have to worry about being found as a stowaway now.

The pavement roasted my feet. I'd be memorable running around town this way. I hurried back into the shop and into my shoes.

The Chinese obviously thought I'd gone suddenly berserk, and he kept his distance.

"I'll be back," I shouted. "Have my stuff ready."

Edgett must have turned into one of the shops along the street, I thought. He shouldn't be hard to find.

But he was. I strode along the street glancing in all the shops, and finally reached the bottom of the hill. It began to exasperate me. He had been so goddamned close I could almost have reached out and collared him.

I spent almost an hour. I covered every square foot of town. I checked the register at the government resthouse. It seemed impossible. He'd vanished. Was it only my imagination playing tricks?

That was crazy. I'd seen him. Flesh and blood. Will Edgett.

I walked into the Planter's Club and asked around. Then suddenly it hit me. He might already have started for Jade Tiger!

I went out again and hurried to the car. Edgett must want that five thousand dollars like mad to try pulling off the killing on her own estate.

The Chinese was there when I reached the car. Berserk or not, I owed him some money. I tossed him damned near all I had and threw my new suit and shoes in the car. Then I got going.

Chapter Seventeen

There was a man in rumpled whites lying at the edge of the road.
Edgett?

I had my foot to the floor and spotted him about 150 yards ahead. The
jungle filtered a still greenish gloom along the road, and through the slit
of the windshield the man seemed little more than a smear of white paint
against the red dust.

My first impulse was to shoot past him. But as I came closer my foot
dropped off the pedal. Edgett might have been crazy enough to try walking to Jade Tiger. If it wasn't Edgett, it was sure as hell some planter lying
there. He might still be alive. I couldn't leave him there.

I touched the brake and I could see him more clearly. His tan shoes had
a high shine even in the jungle light. He lay on his stomach and a Panama was tilted on his head. I stopped just behind him, but I didn't get out
of the car.

If that was Edgett out there, he'd shrunk at least a foot.

It could be the terrorists out to pick up an armored car if they could get it.

I glanced around the interior of the car. I hadn't brought a gun, and none
had been left in the sedan. For a moment I considered forgetting the guy
in the road and getting to hell out.

But it might *not* be a trap. That guy out there might need help.

I glanced through the side slits. I saw nothing but the lined green face of
the jungle on either side. I made up my mind not to leave the car. But I'd
find out fast if the white man in the road was unconscious, dead, or only
faking.

I put the sedan in low and steered close alongside. I stopped when I
thought he must be just outside the far door and let the motor idle. I got
the kingfisher kris in my hand. I opened the door a couple of inches, ready
to slam it at the first sign of trouble. I hated the time I was losing, but I
couldn't just abandon the guy.

The jungle was strangely still. What did *that* mean? I wondered. Had the
monkeys and pheasants been frightened off? I looked down at the leg of
the man in the road. It seemed goddamned cruel, but I stuck the tip of the
kris through the door opening toward his leg. If he were a live decoy he'd
let me know.

The sharp point reached the linen of his trousers and I shoved. The dead
man came to life with the howl of a skewered animal.

I slammed the door and through the side slit I got a flash of the man I'd taken for a planter. He was a native garbed in whites. He was on his feet and yelling, and then there were a thousand voices from the jungle. A couple of bullets rang off the armor and I felt as if I were sitting in a shooting gallery. I threw my foot on the clutch, but even before I could get back in gear a native jumped on the hood and blotted out my vision through the slit. I could hear the clatter of others piling on the car; the shooting had stopped. The car was being mobbed.

I let out the clutch, trusted to instinct, and got up speed. I flash-braked, and the slit cleared as the native clattered to the fender. I started again and this time I could see. I don't know how many guerrillas I was carrying. If they thought they could get a gun through a slit and shoot me, I didn't give them the chance. I swerved all over the road. I got up to about thirty miles an hour and flash-braked again. There was a wild clatter and a wake of pained yells and curses. A moment later the shooting started again, and I knew I was free of riders. The armor rang like a bell, but all I worried about was losing a tire. I didn't make a very good target; I zigzagged from one side of the jungle to the other and finally the road curved and put me out of sight. The shooting died away.

It was over.

I lit a cigarette and called myself every kind of sap in the book.

Jade Tiger had its name on the side of the sedan. I had a sudden feeling that the ambush had been meant for Kay Allison.

Dark clouds were rising from the south and in less than an hour it was going to rain. I drove into the garage and leaped out of the sedan. I had shot almost an hour in town looking for Edgett when he might already have come out here. Daylight was fading, but the heat held on, close and muggy.

I went up the veranda steps and I could hear Kay's voice. She was on the telephone. My muscles eased; Edgett hadn't come. I'd been a fool for letting my fears get out of control. He'd plan something reasonably clever; something with an escape hatch. He must know he could walk into Jade Tiger to earn his five thousand dollars, but he wouldn't be alive to walk off. I wondered if he'd ditched Hoven in Malacca Town.

Kay rang off as I came in the door.

"Telegram from Singapore," she said, a sort of bitter amusement in her eyes.

"I thought you were wearing your gun."

"It gets very warm wearing a gun."

"I want you to take it even when you go for a shower."

"Yes, Big Master. Did I tell you? I just got a telegram from Singapore, darling."

Calm down, I told myself. You've had a scare. It's over now. "Congratulations," I said.

"My private detective has traced Edgett and Hoven."

I put out my cigarette. "Go on."

"He says the two of them left Singapore two days ago aboard the S.S. Perak."

"The guy's brilliant."

"He wants to know if he should continue working on the matter."

It was a grim joke. We didn't laugh.

She said, "Shall I pay him for his startling intelligence?"

"Better give him the sack."

"I just did. By telegram."

"Sit down and listen. Edgett's in Kuala Tang. I saw him an hour ago, and I thought he'd come out here."

"Jack—"

"I saw him and I lost him. Now will you get your gun and put it on? Because I love you?"

"Hoven?"

"I don't know. Maybe. Or maybe my letter broke up their partnership. All I saw was Edgett."

"He wouldn't dare come out here."

"It depends on how hungry he is for the Nabob's fee. You can count on one thing, he didn't come to Kuala Tang for the climate."

"Did you talk to Inche?"

"No. He's dead."

She turned. The thing was building up, like the clouds on the horizon. Two natives dead and now Edgett had shown up. "What about the kris?"

"It was his, all right. It looks to me as if I was on the right track. Inche knew something. Someone got worried, and shut him up for good."

She faced me. "Someone?"

"Either the Nabob or a reasonable facsimile. We'll get the answers from Edgett. I'm glad he's around. Frightened?"

"No." She hesitated. "Yes—I suppose a little."

I stationed a Sikh with a rifle at the bottom of the Jade Tiger road. I left a description of Edgett and instructions to bring him in under guard if he was found nosing around. The last thing I wanted was for Edgett to get killed as a trespasser. I wanted to talk to him.

The Sikh, after a knowing glance at the sky, had brought his rain cape with him, and I supposed I might only be wasting his time. Once the rain hit, only a fool would be out in it, and I had stopped thinking of Edgett as a fool.

I went back to the bungalow, showered, and got into my new clothes. The gloom had lifted a little around the house. Kay had a sundowner waiting on the veranda and I flopped in a long chair.

"You look terribly handsome." She smiled. "Very pukka sahib."

We talked and I worked on my drink. I told her about the ambush and apologized for getting some of the dust knocked off her car. We watched the Sumatra roll in, lashing the rubber trees a mile away. It crept closer with its howling voice and wet fingers. And finally it reached the bungalow, but we stayed out on the protected veranda and Dollah refilled our glasses.

A Sumatra. A dozen hours ago this same rain might have been lashing my own trees and my own house across the Straits of Malacca.

"What are you thinking, darling?"

"Someday soon," I said, frowning, "I'm going to have to leave. But I'll be back."

"I love you, Jack. Can't you tell me?"

"No, baby. I can't tell you."

She reached across the long chairs and kissed my cheek. "Then I won't ask you again."

"And when I get back," I said, "we'll do things to Jade Tiger. We'll make it the best goddamn plantation in Malaya."

"It once was."

"How many trees have the terrorists ruined?"

"Altogether?"

"Altogether."

"More than three thousand."

That figured to between seventeen and eighteen total acres put out of production. It meant about six thousand pounds of crude rubber a year lost.

"Have you replanted?" I asked.

She shrugged and played with her glass. "What good does it do? When we had Red trouble a year ago, they hacked any trees they could reach. But this latest outbreak is different. They go after the saplings."

"That doesn't make sense."

"I'm sorry, but that's what they're doing. They even broke into the nursery once and destroyed the seedlings. Occasionally they'll slash a few aging trees."

"Then your best trees are still in production."

"Fortunately, they've been left alone."

I picked up my drink and stared out at the blackening sky. I'd never heard of terrorists caring about which trees they slashed. It had been the same at Silver Jubilee. I remembered now that Gabb had said the last raid cost him a number of saplings.

Kay said, "Shall we go in?"

"Not yet."

"I've fixed up a bedroom in the bungalow for you."

"Don't you have overseer's quarters?"

"I don't mind your living in the house."

"It may start a lot of talk."

"Are you worried about my reputation?"

"I suppose I am."

"I'm not, darling."

She smiled, and a little later we went in to dinner.

"It's for you, Jack."

Kay held out the phone, and her green eyes went cold. I wasn't expecting any calls, and for a moment I only stared at her. Monique? By this time the line to Silver Jubilee must be back in order. But I didn't think Monique would call me—not here.

The Sumatra had settled into a night sheet of rain outside the windows. We had finished dinner and were having cigarettes. I left the table and took the phone out of her hand.

"Hello?"

"This is Mahmoud, tuan." There was alarm in his voice. "*Mem* says you must come at once."

"What's wrong?"

"Come at once."

"Tell me what's happened!"

"Bandits are at work on the *kaboon*."

"Put *mem* on the phone."

"*Mem* cannot come. She has been hurt."

I glanced across the room to Kay, who had picked up her cigarette and seemed to be trying not to listen. I glanced at the black downpour framed by the windows. "All right," I said bitterly. "Tell *mem* I'll be over right away."

I hung up and faced Kay. "There's bandit trouble at Silver Jubilee. Apparently they've been shooting things up around the house. Monique's been hurt."

"I'm sorry to hear that," Kay said stiffly. "I've always been fond of her."

"Cut it out, baby! Look—Silver Jubilee's the last place I want to go tonight. But I've got to help out. Gabb's in K.L. and she's over there alone."

Her eyes softened a little. "Of course, darling. I don't mean to say things like that. I just do, from time to time."

"Do you mind if—"

"No. Take the car."

"Tell Dollah to go down and alert your lines. The bandits might decide to move across the river."

"I doubt it."

"What do you mean?"

"Even the Reds know enough to keep in out of the rain."

It made me a little angry. "These boys are eccentric," I snapped. "They only slash saplings."

"You're keeping Monique waiting.

"If she's trying to pull something, I'll break her neck."

"I'd rather you didn't." She reached up and kissed me. "I don't want you to get that close to her, darling."

"The phone's working now at Silver Jubilee," I said. "If you need me, call. But I may be back pretty damned quick."

"Do come back quick."

She watched me go, giving me a small unhappy smile. I hung around Jade Tiger long enough to get a turbaned field conductor on the veranda, taking up his gun post as he had the night before. I didn't think I'd have to worry about Kay's safety, and that was something.

I followed under the shelter of the eaves and reached the garage without getting wet. I backed out and started for Silver Jubilee.

Chapter Eighteen

Monique was lying in black pongee coolie slacks on the chaise longue. It was obvious from the ash tray that she had been chain-smoking for hours. She was reading a scrapbook of press clippings. Monique and where she danced, I thought angrily.

The houseboy retired in silence once he let me in, and I came quickly to my senses. There were no bandits. Kay had been right. There was only Monique.

"*Bonsoir*, M'sieu Jack," she said throatily, without looking up from the clippings. Despite the calm arrogance of her manner, she was nervous. I could see it.

I stood on the marble floor and tried to clamp down my temper. She was a kid. She was beautiful lying there, unhappy and suddenly jealous—and poison.

"I missed you today, M'sieu Jack."

"Fine."

"I have been lonely."

"Have you?"

"Very lonely, M'sieu Jack." She turned a page. She went on reading. "The Australian girl—"

"Never mind the Australian girl—"

"You are angry, M'sieu Jack? What a pity."

"You needn't have invented the bandits."

"Would you have come otherwise?"

"No," I said. "I wouldn't have come."

"So I invented the bandits. Sit down."

"I'm not staying long enough to sit down."

She lifted one shoulder. "But of course you *are* staying, M'sieu Jack."

"You've got something on your mind."

"*Oui*, I have something."

"Well?"

She turned another page. Smoke curled past her face. She pretended to read again.

I turned sharply and walked back to the door. She was Gabb's wife, and I was sorry, but she could go to hell. I had been tricked into coming and I felt like a fool. The important thing was not to lose my temper. The important thing was to leave before I cut loose on her. The knob turned, but the door only rattled in the jamb. Mahmoud had locked it and taken the key.

Monique pretended not to notice.

I said, "You're full of tricks tonight, aren't you?"

She turned another page of clippings.

I crossed to the chaise longue, took the goddamned book out of her hands, and flung it to the floor.

"Well?"

Her large, moody eyes covered me with that same weblike glance she had used the first time we had met. She wore a sheer brocaded blouse with a mandarin collar that gave her neck long, fragile lines. Her nervousness was disappearing.

"Monique," she muttered, watching me, "always gets what she wants."

"What do you want?"

She smiled, but it was only window dressing. She shrugged. Tonight she was the girl from Lavender Street, and it wasn't very pretty. "You."

"I'm glad you spelled it out," I said coldly. "Maybe I didn't make myself clear last night. I'm not interested in Monique. You've wasted your time. It won't work. Is that spelling it out clearly enough?" I picked up the scrapbook and put it back in her hands. "I hope I didn't lose your place."

"Still you worry about Gabriel?" She pulled up her knees. "See? I don't worry about him when he is far away."

"I'll bet you don't."

"I used to be angry when he'd leave me and go to Singapore. But I learned to amuse myself. Often he would go to Singapore."

I glowered at her. "Are you trying to say something?"

She shrugged, and there was a certain derision in her dark eyes. I thought of Eden's shopping trips to Singapore, and the cigarette lighter with the funny acid stains that nagged my mind, making me wonder if the lighter was the same one Eden had given me, but it all seemed beside the point. I watched a girlish pout form on Monique's lips, and I felt silly standing there letting her watch me burn.

"Come, sit down, beautiful fool," she said wryly. "I will fix you a drink myself."

"Never mind."

"M'sieu Jack," she purred, "am I not lovely tonight? You find me irresistible, yes?"

"I'm trying to resist breaking your neck. Mahmoud!"

"Is the Aussy girl as pretty as I?"

I tried again. "Mahmoud!"

"He will not come, mon ami. Only when I call. You wish to go?"

"You catch on fast."

"But you will not go."

"Watch me."

"Do you forget?" Her tone sharpened. "Monique always gets what she wants."

"Listen," I said. "Listen. Get it straight. I find you easy to resist and goddamned tiresome. Now get your hooks out of my life. I'm not interested. Go to hell. Good night."

Was she deaf? "A stengah, M'sieu Jack?" She smiled. "I'm an expert at fixing a stengah."

To hell with Mahmoud; I didn't trust myself to stick around any longer. I crossed to a window, picked up a chair, and slammed it into the glass. It was a crazy impulse, but I was damned if I would go around trying all the doors, and I wanted out. The glass burst, but when the chatter of falling pieces died away, Monique was back with her shrewish, purring laugh.

"The Aussy girl waits for you, eh, M'sieu Jack? You have no time for Monique?"

I was too mad to think straight. I went on with the chair, ramming the spires of glass around the sill. I could smell the rain now, and it smelled warm and fresh. I tossed back the chair. It seemed a ridiculous exit, but I didn't feel ridiculous. I knew damned well Monique's dark eyes were on me, watching, smiling. I got one long leg out of the window when her voice stopped me.

"Your stengah is ready—*Jock Hamilton!*"

I froze.

Beyond the veranda, the rain rode in on a moaning wind. For a moment time stalled on me. Then I turned. I saw her standing at the bar with my stengah in her hand. Her eyes were surly and swirling with contempt.

She knew who I was. What else did she know? Did she know the police were looking for me? Of course. That was her trump card. She could turn me in, and she would. Why kid myself?

"The name," I said, "is familiar."

"You think I was fooled?" She jerked her head angrily. "*Salaud!* I have known since the moment you came. *Oui,* I know about you. Perhaps now you want your drink, eh?"

I left the window and walked slowly across the cold marble floor. "Have you called the police?"

"Not yet."

"What are you waiting for?"

The smile was back. "Come, M'sieu Jack. Have your drink. It isn't necessary to talk of these things. Now we understand each other, eh?"

"It's very necessary. I didn't kill my wife."

"That doesn't interest me."

"How did you know about me?"

"When the police came to question Gabriel, I heard. He didn't know I was listening, but Gabriel thinks I'm a child. That is funny, *n'est-ce pas?*"

"I'll laugh later."

"When you came suddenly to Silver Jubilee, I knew it must be the man the police ask about. And last night on the radio—your thumb, yes?"

"The giveaway."

"But of course! Ah, you look so worried, M'sieu Jack. Do you think I would give you away to the police?"

"I think you would."

"But Monique wants to protect you!"

"Let's stop playing games," I said harshly. "I drink your stengah and sit on your chaise longue and you keep your mouth shut. That's what you're thinking, isn't it?"

"Is it such a bad time for love when it rains?"

"I have no intention of being blackmailed into bed with you."

"It is such an ugly word, M'sieu Jack. And Monique is so beautiful. I—"

"Sure, you always get what you want."

I stopped in the center of the room and my thoughts ran wild. Plantation life bored her and I was to be tonight's entertainment. I couldn't bear the sight of her, but I stared at her. She could be dangerous as hell, but I wasn't going to be parlayed into bed with her. I thought of Kay waiting for me at Jade Tiger. Edgett was loose in Kuala Tang and I wanted to be with Kay. I couldn't let Monique put the cops on my back. I had to find Edgett and find out who was behind the trouble at Jade Tiger.

I needed a day. One more goddamned day.

But I wasn't buying it with Monique's little blackmail.

"I'm walking out of here," I said.

"You wouldn't be such a fool."

"Maybe it hasn't occurred to you," I said. "I really despise you. I didn't mean to keep it a secret."

"To me it's only important that I like your shoulders. *Oui,* you are strong, like steel, eh? I would like that. Gabriel is big, but he is soft—like cotton."

"He loves you," I snapped.

"He loves his acres of getah, not Monique! He stands on the veranda and almost as far as the eye can see he sees his trees growing. That's what he loves. Me, I am only an amusement."

"I don't find you amusing."

"I promise you, I can be very amusing."

"I don't think you're going to call the police."

"It would be a pity, eh?"

"Has it occurred to you that I might kill you to keep your lovely mouth shut?"

"Mahmoud will protect me."

"Who will protect Mahmoud?"

"M'sieu Jack, you talk like an idiot. You say you are innocent. Would you kill me, and become truly a murderer? I am not afraid. No, *mon ami.*" She walked slowly toward me, the glass in her hand, a sultry smile on her lips. "The ice melts."

"To hell with the ice."

Anger flared in her eyes again. "I have only to reach for the phone. It works now!"

I strode across the floor and yanked the phone out by its roots. The drink came flying through the air and left a wet stain on my shoulder. I stared at her, and it was all I could do to keep from knocking her to the floor.

"*Saleté!*" Monique exploded. "You think that does any good? Go back to Jade Tiger! She is very fine, eh? What is Monique? A dancer from Lavender Street. The Australian wouldn't even ride a trishaw along Lavender Street, eh? I know about her airs and her fine family. *Oui, I* know. Freckles, she has!" She put her hands on her hips and laughed. "Freckles like pockmarks! You think she is beautiful? Go back to her, *murderer!* But maybe *now* she won't want you."

"What are you trying to say?"

"I sent a note, *M'sieu Crapule.* I told her what you are!"

"What!"

"*Oui!* Now she knows you are a murderer. At this moment she reads my letter. Go back to this fine one, eh? See if now she will take you in her arms!"

Her voice was ratchet-like in my head. I glared at her, wanting to kill her as she stood there. Kay knew. For a moment I couldn't think. I was stunned; I was stopped.

"Well?" Monique grinned suddenly. "What are you waiting for?"

I found my voice. "Shut up."

I had to clear myself. When I went back to Jade Tiger I'd have a clean bill of health. There was no other way. But how far would I get if I walked out of here and Monique sent word to the police. I'd never get out of Kuala Tang.

I was boxed in.

"Now we will be friends, eh? While it rains?"

I must have looked funny, just standing there. My fine resolutions turned to water.

"I go to bed now, M'sieu Jack."

I just looked at her.

"Good night, M'sieu Jack." As if nothing had happened.

Her rage had flickered and gone out like a candle, leaving only a wisp of smoke. She smiled airily and turned with a small absent shake of her dark hair, and walked toward the hall. She was going to bed. She knew how to get what she wanted.

And she wanted me.

Well, what difference did it make? I couldn't go back to Kay, not tonight. She already knew there was something in my background I'd been hiding. Now she knew the answer, and to hell with it. Monique had beaten me.

The Ipoh marble was cold under my feet. I glanced at the broken window, but there was no escape now.

Well, I thought, is pride so hard to put aside? It wouldn't be the end of the world if I gave in to her blackmail, and tomorrow it would be forgotten.

I crossed the room to the bar and poured myself a drink. Gabb's wife. My best friend. No, it wouldn't be forgotten. He'd know. It would tear him apart.

I finished the drink on my feet. I listened to the heavy roar of the rain. I don't know how long I stood there before I realized Mahmoud had come into the room.

"Well, what do you want?" I shouted.

"The *mem*—"

"Never mind the *mem*."

"Follow me."

"I'll find her myself."

"As you wish, tuan."

I poured another drink and it brought some feeling back to my stomach. That goddamned houseboy of hers gave me the creeps. This whole house gave me the creeps. I was sorry I'd ever set foot on Silver Jubilee.

I emptied the glass and wondered what it would be like to touch a woman I hated. The thought of her lips, of her arms, of her breath hot in my ears was chilling. I found myself wiping my lips.

I put down the glass and tried to keep Kay from rising to my mind. I shrugged grimly. For the first time in my life I felt unmanned.

I went looking for Monique.

The door was open and the room was dim. She hadn't turned on the light; she had set a pair of coconut-oil lamps flickering beside the bed. The flames sent shadows licking across the room, until the room looked like a cheap upcountry brothel. Monique lay behind the mosquito netting, parted like curtains, with a Lavender Street smile on her face.

"*Tabé,* tuan," she said.

"*Tabé,*" I said.

She was a woman. She was any woman.

I took off my coat.

Chapter Nineteen

Monique. I knew now why Gabb had married her.

The coconut oil had long ago burned out, but it left a rancid odor in the room. Monique lay sleeping on the other side of the batik-covered Dutch wife. The rhythm of breathing depressed me. I sat up and reached through the netting to the cigarettes and lighter on the bed table. The Sumatra had passed on. The house was still, except for the dripping of the eaves.

I stuck a cigarette between my lips and for a moment it almost seemed funny. Well, she'd boxed me in and what was I supposed to do—cry in my beer? Mahmoud, bring me a beer. Were you at the keyhole, you son-of-a-bitch?

I bobbed the cigarette grimly and lit it. Gabb had married a French postcard, but that was his affair. What time would he get back? He'd know. He'd size up the situation in a glance. He had an Irish temper and a Chinese gift of noise. He'd want to break me in two.

He'd warned me. He'd put a cast on my arm.

I peered at my cigarette in the darkness. It had a different taste. American? I had been smoking Capstans for years; it was an acquired taste, and I'd acquired it. These must be Monique's cigarettes. I still had the lighter in my hand; it had the familiar feel of my lighter. My mind began to clear. I remembered. I had dropped my lighter overboard because it had stopped working.

But this felt like my lighter.

I fired it, and looked at it under the flame. What the hell—it *was* my lighter. There was the gold hamadryad skin. There were the goddamned little wings you twisted to release the spring.

I looked for the acid stains Kay had noticed on the ship, the stains that had made her wonder if I might be a planter after all.

There were no acid stains.

I came fully awake. This didn't make sense. My lighter was somewhere at the bottom of the harbor. Duplicates?

It had to be. I calmed down. Eden hadn't given me the only snakeskin lighter ever made. Well, so what? Monique had one too.

I put it back on the table and said to hell with it. I wondered what time it was. There was that chill in the air that comes before dawn, and I got out of bed. I picked up my clothes and walked out to the shower pavilion. The shower had a feeble spray, but I stayed under it a long time. Why wait for Gabb to get back? I asked myself. Walk out. Why let the poor bastard get wise? When he saw the cast missing from my arm, his suspicions would start working.

Go where? Over to Jade Tiger?

I'd stick around and face it. I'd get Monique off my back.

I dressed and walked through the sleeping house to the front veranda. The long chairs were furry with dew, but I didn't give a damn. I stretched out and listened to the faint *ku-au, ku-au* of a pheasant off in the rubber. Dawn began to break up the night sky, and I watched sunlight dart through the treetops. In a little while Jade Tiger became a bright forest across the river.

I must have fallen asleep in the long chair.

There was a raucous laugh in my ear and a big hand shoved my shoulder. "Is this the kind of welcome I get? Wake up, you lazy son of a hedge lawyer!"

Gabb was back.

He stood over me, casting a giant's shadow with his back to the rubber and the sun. "You're back early," I said.

"There's work to be done! I'm not on vacation like a man named after a gin bottle!"

He was back early. What the hell, I thought, did he expect to catch me in bed with his wife?

I was stiff from the chair. I sat forward and rubbed my neck. "What time is it?"

"Past nine. Hungry? Give me time to shower and we'll have breakfast on the veranda. Where's Monique?"

I looked up and saw his eyes pass along my arm. The cast was gone, but there was no chink in his grin. "I suppose," I said, "she's in bed."

"She ought to be lashed, eh? What can you do with these city wives?"

"Monique is *not* in bed." She came through the door in white shorts, a scrap of batik for a bra, and wooden *t'rompoks* on her feet. They clattered slowly on the veranda as she went to Gabriel and let herself be kissed.

"Any bandits last night?" he asked. "You were safe?"

"A few bandits, Gabriel. But I was safe."

I grimaced as I got a cigarette going. She was even inventing bandits for him.

"Soon it will be over," Gabb said, with a wave of his hands. "Today the army sends a few planes over the jungle to bomb them out, like last time. It will be something to watch, eh?"

Monique didn't share his enthusiasm. "Take your shower. Mahmoud has breakfast almost ready."

He tousled her hair and loped off into the house.

Didn't he suspect? Did he think I'd spent the whole night in a long chair?

Monique slipped into the chair beside me and bent to take a light from my cigarette. "You slept peacefully, M'sieu Jack?"

"Why don't you clear out of his life?" I said. "You hate it here."

"You expect me to walk out on the richest planter in Selangor?"

"When he finds out what you are, he'll kill you."

"What am I, *mon ami?*"

"A goddamned animal."

"Be kind to animals, M'sieu Jack."

She laid her head back and crossed her legs. It was impossible to insult her; I should have had more brains than to try. She had made me come crawling to her and she loved it. She was playing a dangerous game, and she loved that too. This was the morning after, and she was luxuriating in her victory.

"You know what I think, M'sieu Jack? You are afraid, perhaps, Gabriel will kill you."

"I wouldn't blame him for trying."

"You think he doesn't suspect?" She laughed softly. "Always he suspects, *mon ami*. Now he is in the house asking Mahmoud. Mahmoud will swear you slept in your proper bedroom. I told you I would protect you, M'sieu Jack."

"Does he always believe Mahmoud?"

"You will see."

"I hope to hell he doesn't!"

"Don't talk like a fool."

Mahmoud began setting breakfast dishes on the veranda, his speckled eyes avoiding us. I sat with my cigarette and felt like a cheap conspirator. My stomach was empty, but I didn't feel hungry. Suddenly I knew that if I hung around I was going to put Gabb straight. I wasn't going to sit through breakfast, eat his goddamned food, and pretend nothing had happened. I'd better leave before I tore up what little happiness he'd built up with Monique. I'd get going and see if I could turn Edgett up.

"Tell Gabb I went to Kuala Tang on business."

She laughed, or maybe it was a sneer. "You are afraid to face him, yes?"

"I'm afraid if I have to look at him again I'll open up. I'm funny that way."

"Perhaps you don't go to Kuala Tang. Perhaps you go to Jade Tiger, eh?"

"Why don't you get off my back?"

"You think I care? Go. You become tiresome."

I got to my feet, but hesitated a moment. "There's one thing I'd like to know. Where did you get that cobra skin cigarette lighter?"

"That? It isn't mine."

"No?"

"It belongs to Gabriel."

"Where did he get it?"

"Ask him."

"It's not that important."

"You will be back for tiffin, M'sieu Jack?"

"It's goddamned unlikely."

I walked along the veranda, hurried down the steps, and cut out toward the garage and Kay's sedan. It seemed strange to be finally walking away from Monique. Just like that. A few hours ago it had seemed impossible. She must be laughing at me, I thought. She knew I wasn't going to Jade Tiger. She'd fixed up my welcome there.

A *chickak* lizard scurried across the path toward the house. I walked a little faster. I damn near began to run, as if I might not make it before Monique put another big hook into me. She had me scared; I admitted it. But when I heard a voice break out over the veranda, it wasn't Monique's.

"Jock, my old friend—stand where you are!"

I had reached the edge of the garage and I turned. Gabb was standing at the end of the veranda and the sun sparked off the nickled barrel of a revolver.

"Come, my old friend! We'll have a bit of breakfast together!"

There was a grin on his face, fury in his voice. He knew. The gun was aimed directly at me. Mahmoud had got his signals crossed.

I started walking back.

"A man's no good without breakfast in his stomach, Jock!" The gun followed me. "I wouldn't shoot an old friend when he was starving, would I?"

"You can cut the low comedy, Gabb."

"Cheat me of your company at breakfast, Jock? Where are your bloody manners, lad?"

I started up the steps and the revolver was waiting for me. Mahmoud was setting out fried eggs as if nothing were happening a few feet away. So he'd got tired of covering up for Monique, I thought. What the hell, maybe he was in love with her. Maybe he just couldn't take it any more.

"That's it, old friend." Gabb gestured with the gun. "Over there, next to the young beauty from Lavender Street. We'll all sit and have a hearty breakfast."

"You can put away the gun," I said. "Stop making a fool of yourself."

"A fool, am I? How right you are, old friend!"

"Cut it out."

"Did the cast get in your way, lad? You must tell me at what delicious moment you broke it off. Midnight? Two in the morning? Or was it early afternoon?"

I saw that the gun was covering Monique as well. She'd obviously been ordered to the table, and she held a fork clutched in her hand. "Mahmoud lied to you!" she spat.

"I'm sure he has, my dear. But not this morning."

"He's a pig!"

The gun exploded and shattered a windowpane behind Monique's head. Her pendant earring shook.

"Did I miss you, my angel? Do forgive me." Gabb's insane grin turned back to me. "The eggs are getting cold, old friend. Shall we sit down?"

"You're not actually going through with this farce," I snapped.

"But I have a taste for farce. It's the Irish in me." He waved his gun toward the empty chair beside Monique. "Do you mind sitting next to my wife? A bit of a schoolgirl, but I daresay she doesn't bore you."

"Gabb—" I started.

"Sit down!"

I gave it up and took the chair. I looked at three eggs steaming on the plate before me. They smelled of hot grease, and my stomach contracted.

"That's better," Gabb muttered, grinning once more. If only he'd stop laughing and smiling and grinning, I thought. He sat across the table from us and laid the gun beside his plate on the crisp linen tablecloth.

"Now, then, my angel," he said to Monique. "You can say grace. Thank the Lord for your daily bread."

"Gabriel—"

"In French. It always sounds better in French, don't you agree, Jock?"

"I don't think any of us are hungry," I said. "Let's get it over with."

"I'm quite hungry! One must take adultery with a grain of salt. Monique, my angel," he said, shifting his attention, "do pass the salt and get on with the prayer."

Monique was staring at her lap. "I have forgotten my prayers."

"How inconvenient. Let me prod your memory, eh?" He picked up the gun and suddenly Monique's lips began to move. *"Notre Seigneur qui—"*

"Louder, my dear!"

"Notre Seigneur qui est au ciel...." Her voice trembled. Her arrogance was gone. She looked scared.

Gabb stared at her as the words ran over her lips, and I watched him. It came as a shock that there was really no hate in his eyes. He was *enjoying* this. I saw suddenly that he was having a whale of a time. He was being cruel and righteous and he was loving every goddamned minute of it. He didn't really care that his wife had spent the night with another man. All he wanted was to catch her at it. He must have been building up to this for months, armoring his fierce pride.

Monique finished and Gabb salted his food. "Well done, my dear. Now

eat your eggs. Shall I tell you about my trip? We made excellent time on
the river both ways. Jock, have you seen my cabin cruiser? A bloody fine
job she is."

"For God's sake, Gabb."

"Monique, my angel, you're not eating."

"I cannot eat."

"But of course you can." He shoved her plate closer with the tip of his
gun. "You love eggs. Never got enough of them as a child, did you?"

"They make me sick!"

"Really? Then you must have a second helping. Mahmoud!"

"Please, Gabriel—"

"Now you will eat!"

Monique gingerly broke a yoke with her fork, and Gabb burst into a roar.
He laid down the gun and his glance turned to me.

"Rubber's up a half cent," he said, as if it were the greatest news in the
world. "I heard it in K.L. Those eggs too well done for you, Jock? No
appetite this morning, eh? Come, come, food out here mustn't go to
waste."

"Get it over with," I said. "What are you going to do?"

"But you're not eating."

"No," I said. "I'm not eating."

"Does my hospitality bore you? You sample my whisky, you sample my
wife—and now you want to go."

"I'm wondering if you really give a damn."

"My whisky is very dear to me."

"Come off it."

He began to frown. "Am I not human, old friend? What is it the natives
say?"

"Let's leave the goddamned natives out of it."

"I remember. 'A cheating wife is an elephant with two mahouts!' It
makes a ridiculous picture, eh?" He wiped the egg from his lips and picked
up the gun again.

"But it's not true!" Monique protested. "Please—"

His glance silenced her. His extravagant mood had turned into something cold and deadly. "Imagine two mahouts on one elephant!" He was
talking to me. "I *will not* be laughed at! No, my friend, I will do the laughing. Mahmoud!"

"Gabriel—"

"*Mahmoud!*"

The servant came onto the veranda, his eyes seeing no one but Gabb.

"Yes, tuan."

"Mahmoud, you will take my car and go to town." Gabb threw the keys at him. "You will tell the constable I'm holding Jock Hamilton at Silver Jubilee."

"I understand, tuan."

"Go quickly and bring him back."

My pulse began to hammer. So that was it. He'd get his revenge, nice and legal. I looked at the revolver in his hand. It would take a long reach and I knew how fast and straight Gabb could shoot.

Mahmoud left the table and started for the garage. Gabb faced me again with a bitter grin on his lips.

"You think I would shatter my life, like you, because of an elephant with two mahouts?" He turned to Monique and there was contempt in his eyes. "Ah, the elephant eats. Jock, have you ever shot an elephant?"

"Gabriel," Monique whispered, and I saw that her fright was becoming terror, "you make—"

"Let me explain it, Jock." He was becoming expansive again. "It is the greatest sport—but it is an art. It is not for the timid."

"I know how to shoot an elephant," I muttered. It seemed a ridiculous thing to say. I'd better try for the gun the second he laid it down again.

"The wind is important. You must never let the beast get your scent in the wind, eh?" He lit a match. "In Selangor the wind shifts every few minutes. You check with matches. See it?"

Smoke trailed from the match across the table toward Monique. She stared at the gun and her nostrils flared with every breath.

"Ah, already the wind has given me away. The beast is warned."

"Gabriel!" Monique cried out. "Listen to me. It is true what Mahmoud told you. *Oui*, it is true. I would have told you myself. I fought this creature of a friend of yours. This pig! How I fought him! *Oui*, with my teeth and my fingernails, but he has muscles like steel. I—see, I tried to run out the window, to escape this filthy—"

I turned sharply. Her voice was rising to a scream and I felt like strangling her. But what difference did it make what Gabb thought now? He hadn't hesitated to turn me in.

"Of course, my angel." He gestured with the gun. "Come here."

"You believe me, my husband."

"How could such an innocent face lie? Stand beside your husband. How lovely she is made, eh, Jock?"

Monique left her chair for the other side of the table. She was trying to smile. "*Oui, mon ami*. I wanted to tell you. See, the window is broken. I fought like a tigress!"

Gabb got to his feet and kept the gun in his hand. "I was explaining how to shoot an elephant, isn't that so?"

"Gabriel!"

He ignored her. "The frontal shot is worthless, Jock." He touched the point of the gun to her forehead. "The Malaya elephant takes it like a bee sting."

I found my hands gripping the edge of the table. Was he going to kill her in front of my eyes? What would he tell the police—that I had shot her? I was already wanted for murder. They'd find it goddamned easy to believe.

"Gabriel, my lover!" The sweat gleamed on Monique's face and her eyes were full of wild appeal. "Believe me! I had no power against—"

"It is the ear shot you must try for, Jock, my friend." He grabbed her hair and pulled back her head. He laughed and traced the nose of the revolver over her skin. "See, just in front of the hole of the ear, there is the spot you must try for."

I heaved the table over and dove across it for his arm. Dishes and silverware clattered to the floor, and I saw Gabb shove Monique away. He exploded in a laugh and the gun whipped my face, cutting with the sight. He sliced down with the edge of his other hand and clipped the back of my neck. I hit the floor dazed, with the sound of Gabb's laughter in my ears.

"What a hero you look, old friend, lying there with the broken dishes, eh? Did you consider my wife worth risking your neck for?"

I shook my head and my hand came away from my face smeared with blood. It had been hopeless trying to get at him from such a crazy position.

"Let her go," I said. "She's not worth this."

"Did you think I would shoot her? But I was only explaining about elephants, my friend." He righted the table and pulled me to a chair. "Monique, my angel, why didn't you run? Too frightened to run, eh?"

"Let me go, Gabriel. Oui, it is as he said." She was completely cowed and her voice was in tatters. "I'm not worth it. I—"

"Agreed. I tired of you months ago. You are worth only laughter."

"Oui, laugh. I'm only good to laugh at. Now I can go, eh?"

"When you came you had nothing, remember? Yes, you will go—also with nothing."

He strode across the floor and ripped the batik from her. Within seconds he had pulled every stitch of clothing off her.

"That's the way I found you!" he shouted. "Now go. Go back to Lavender Street!"

"Gabriel!"

"You have no money? Perhaps in Kuala Tang you can earn your fare back to Singapore."

"But you cannot let—"

"Out of my sight! Let them laugh at you along the road. They will see how I have thrown you out of my house."

I heard the clack of her *t'rompoks* on the veranda. I saw her bare back as she went down the steps into the sun. She kept her shoulders straight. Her terror had gone. There could be only fury in her eyes now, I thought. She had survived—on Gabb's terms—and it must have been galling. But she had survived and some of her pride survived too. The sun turned her skin golden and she walked as if she knew she made a beautiful sight. Gabb stood watching her.

"She goes off into the trees to walk. Perhaps one of my tappers will get her a sarong."

Maybe he still cared a little. But he laughed.

I nursed my face and Gabb strode back and forth along the veranda, grinning and enjoying the feel of the gun in his hand. He was buoyant and I could almost forget he was marking time until the police came. What would he do if I tried to make a run for it?

I knew the answer to that. He'd shoot like hell.

"I have made something of my estate, eh? Do you know I'm one of the biggest landowners in Selangor? Look at my trees. Beautiful, eh?"

The sun was broiling and you could hear an occasional pod explode. What had Monique said? "He stands on the veranda and almost as far as the eye can see he sees his trees growing." I was looking out at the lush trees across the river. Jade Tiger. *Almost.* My thoughts jarred; the pieces were beginning to fall in place.

Monique's bag had spilled out on the floor. I turned and picked up the snakeskin cigarette lighter. "Is this yours?"

His revolver flashed in the sun. "There's a car coming."

I could hear it on the road below, but for a moment I didn't give a damn. "The lighter," I said.

"You're interested in such novelties? Yes, it's mine."

"Where did you get it?"

"Unique, eh?"

"Where did you get hold of it?"

He hesitated, glancing at me with an off-center grin, and shrugged. "In Singapore."

"Eden bought me one just like it," I said. "In Palembang."

"I've never been in Palembang."

"That's not what I was thinking."

"What do I care what you think? Stand where you are!"

The police were already on the estate and winding closer. I eyed Gabb's revolver and glanced down to the road; it was now or never. But when I caught sight of the car, I saw that it wasn't the police.

"You're getting company," I said. "In a taxi."

He saw it too. "All right, stand there. I'd be delighted if you tried to break away. It would give me a good excuse to shoot you down."

"Go to hell."

The taxi swung in front of the house and I recognized the overweight Malay at the wheel. Majid. The back door swung open and a lanky guy in a wilted linen suit got out of the cab.

"I say," he beamed, spotting Gabb on the veranda, "your phone's been dead and I've had a bloody time of it getting a ride out here. This insane taxi driver insists you've got an army of blasted terrorists around. I've been trying since yesterday to get him to bring me out."

It was Will Edgett.

Chapter Twenty

"You fool!" Gabb exploded. "What are you trying to do, coming here?"

"What?" Edgett started up the veranda steps. "Well, I thought I'd better report exactly what— You see, there was this note on the ship, and—"

"You bloody idiot!"

Edgett saw me and vague recognition struck. "Hello. Haven't we met before?"

I didn't hang around long enough for him to place me; Gabb must know Edgett put an official seal on my interlocking suspicions. If Gabb had any brains he'd try to silence me before the police showed up.

Gabb had brains. And suddenly I had become dangerous to him.

The window I had broken the night before stood only a few feet away. I turned and leaped through it.

I must have been out of sight almost before Gabb realized what was happening. I raced through the house and reached the back door before I heard his voice booming through the hall. I pushed through the door and leaped the back veranda rail to the gravel footpath. The garage was to my right. I crouched and ran.

"Jock!"

His voice was in the open. It burst through the trees like thunder. I got to the end of the house and he spotted me. And Edgett's memory finally clicked. "That's the chap was on the boat!"

"He's your bloody *pawang*, you idiot!"

I sprinted for the protection of the garage and a shot rocked the still morning. A stone flew apart on the path in front of me and Gabb was bellowing warnings to Edgett.

I got around the garage wall and had the ignition key in my hand when I reached Kay's sedan. Footsteps pounded on the veranda. I piled into the car and got the door locked. I turned the key and pressed the starter. The engine wouldn't catch.

I kept working on it, and then there was the pounding of footsteps in the garage. I got a flash of Gabb as I glanced through the window slit. His high cheekbones were mirrors of sweat. He pressed the gun tip to the slot, but the engine caught and I let out the clutch in gear. The car jerked and stalled as he fired.

His shot went wild, but the explosion burst my eardrums. The car started and I backed out blindly, spinning the wheel. The armor rang with another hit. I got into low gear and shot forward past the house. I saw

Majid's unarmored taxi ahead of me on the road. He'd probably taken off at the first sound of firing.

Gabb emptied his revolver in a blind fury; slugs peppered the car, but he was wasting ammunition and time. I overtook Majid fast and rocketed down the winding road. Monique's Ford was still behind in the garage and I thought Gabb must have come to his senses. He'd probably hurried into the house to get some cartridges and find the ignition key. Monique sure as hell hadn't taken it with her.

I could get a gun at Jade Tiger. Gabb would guess I'd head there. I hated to lead him there, but I saw no choice. And I had to talk to Kay. I had things to tell her. Maybe she wouldn't want to see me, but she'd have to listen.

I reached the bottom of the hill and turned off toward the river. Where were the police? I got to the bridge. When I entered the Jade Tiger road I saw the field conductor still standing his post. He waved and I stopped short. I backed up and opened the door to talk to him. I knew damned well if he tried to stop Gabb from coming onto the plantation Gabb would blow him apart.

"Knock off," I said. "Go get some sleep."

He grinned in his black beard and nodded.

I slammed the door and tooled up the road to the bungalow. Dollah was sweeping the veranda and he stopped to peer at me. I pulled the car around back, left the motor running, and started for the house. If Gabb made it faster than I hoped and the breaks went against me, I'd need those extra seconds. I wanted to lead him away from Jade Tiger as soon as he showed.

I strode through the kitchen. "Kay!"

The house was quiet as hell. I entered the living room and I saw her. She was standing at the window with her back toward me. She didn't move.

"Kay—"

There was someone else in the room.

There was a man seated in a rattan chair. A little man in a soiled suit. There was a *stroodje* curling smoke from the brown fingers of one hand and a police pistol in the other.

It was Inspector Aziz ben-Kris, from Sumatra.

Chapter Twenty-one

"You will raise your arms, please."

His teeth were yellow and his glossy hair was long over his ears. He wore a black fiber fez and he wore it at a rakish angle.

I glared at him, startled for an instant, and then too weary to give a damn. He'd caught up with me, but we were still a long way from Sumatra. He held an inspector's rank but he had the rulebook mind of a constable, and I'd met it head on before. When the Dutch were kicked out of Sumatra and the other islands of Indonesia, vacancies were left and Aziz ben-Kris found himself with an office of his own and a brass title on the door. He grinned at me slightly, as if he were polishing up the title in his mind.

"What brought you?" I muttered. "Last night's rainstorm?"

He acknowledged his victory with a smile. He could afford to smile now. "The mouse deer may forget the snare," he said, "but the snare never forgets the mouse deer."

"I've heard that before."

"You will raise your arms."

"I don't have a gun."

"But I do. Up, please."

I thought quickly of the car with the motor running out back, but I couldn't leave. I couldn't even try. Not yet. I ignored Inspector Kris's gun and strode toward Kay. She was wearing that belt of old silver coins, and as she stood at the window they gleamed.

"Look, Kay, hate me if you want to," I said uneasily. "You know about me and I didn't want you to know—but I guess it really doesn't matter any more."

She turned and her green eyes were moist and tired. She smiled stubbornly, a private smile just for me, and suddenly her eyes were lovely. "I don't hate you, Jack. I couldn't."

"The name is Jock," I said bitterly. "Jock Hamilton. The little man with the gun says I killed my wife."

"Must I believe the little man with the gun?"

Inspector Kris was getting impatient. "I have extradition papers," he said from behind us. "Now we will go."

"Listen to me, Kay," I said. "I know who's been making all the trouble at Jade Tiger and I know why. He's on his way over and you'd better have your boys break out some guns. I don't want you to get hurt."

"Jock—"

"Gabb is the Nabob."

Her eyes widened, but I didn't let her disbelief get into words.

"Get going," I snapped. "Break out some guns!"

But she only stood there. "What about you?"

"The little man standing behind me has a funny mind." I glanced out along the veranda, but Dollah had finished up with the broom and taken off somewhere. "Inspector Kris thinks murder is always a family affair— he read it in a book somewhere. Nothing short of a confession is going to change his mind."

"Darling—"

"Sure, he's going to have a hell of a time getting me out of here when Gabb shows up. He doesn't know that yet. Maybe I'd better tell him. *Will you get some boys and some guns!*"

I turned and Inspector Kris nodded with his yellow grin. "It will not be so hard." He produced a pair of handcuffs.

"That's not what I mean," I said. "Kay, hurry!"

"I heard your talk of guns," Inspector Kris said. "I'm sorry, but the young lady will remain in the room until we go. I'm not so easily tricked."

"Listen," I shouted. "You're a cop. There's a man coming over here who hired a couple of professional killers to work on the *mem*. That's a crime, isn't it?"

"If true. But I have no authority in Malaya. I'm a visitor. I have only extradition papers."

"Don't listen to him, Kay!"

She lifted her chin slightly and that familiar self-assured look came into her eyes. "I intend to protect myself, Inspector."

"I must ask you, please—"

"You'll have to shoot me to keep me from walking out of this room."

Kay began to walk. Inspector Kris saw the situation slipping out of his hands, but he couldn't shoot.

"I warn you," he complained, "I shoot my prisoner at the first sign of trickery."

She kept walking. He couldn't stop her and he knew it. He let her go, bit his lip, and did the only thing he could think of. He told me to hold out my hands.

"It would save my country money, tuan, if you tried for my gun. It would also be simpler to return you in a coffin to Sumatra."

I eyed his gun and thought of the car idling out back, but I held out my wrist. He might be a rotten detective, but even a blind man could hit me at less than a yard.

"I'll take your warning," I said.

He slapped one cuff on my wrist. It grated and locked. "How the hell did you trace me here?"

"It was very easy. I received a telegram."

"*What?*"

"It informed us you were hiding at Silver Jubilee. I immediately crossed the Straits by police launch. It is waiting for us at the jetty in Kuala Tang."

"Who sent the telegram?"

"Please, your other wrist."

"*Who sent it?*"

"There was no signature. Anonymous. It is often that way."

"Where did it come from? I've got to know!"

"Kuala Lampur."

I held my one hand free of the cuff. Kuala Lampur! It jarred me. *Gabb had turned me in!* Not just an hour ago. Yesterday! And it had nothing to do with Monique. I stared down at the Inspector and quickly decided to save the island of Sumatra some dough.

"Your other wrist, tuan!"

I froze with my arm wide. I could hear the hum of a car speeding up the road. At the same instant I saw Kay across the room. She had taken off her shoes and she stood in the doorway with a double-barreled Jeffery Special in her hands. My God—if she pulled the trigger she'd blow us both apart. It was an elephant gun!

Stall, I thought quickly. I matched up my wrists. Keep him talking. "You win," I said. "I still don't understand why you were waiting for me at Jade Tiger."

Kay didn't make a sound.

"I regret the imposition. The *mem* has been most kind." He cracked the other cuff on my wrist and his confidence flowered. "There is only the one police car in Kuala Tang and it broke down in the storm last night not far from here. I walked in the rain and saw lights here. The Indian at the bottom of the road conducted me to the house and the *mem* was kind enough to allow me to stay. This morning I waited for the car to be fixed and take me to Silver Jubilee, but you saved me the trouble. Perhaps that will be my friends now."

"I don't think so," I said.

He grinned and looked out the window and Kay stopped a few feet behind him.

"Drop your gun, Inspector!"

He spun, but the sight of the elephant gun paralyzed his trigger finger. It was almost funny to watch. His jaw fell, his eyes bugged with shock, and he dropped the gun.

I stooped and got it off the floor and turned it on him.

"Unlock these damned things. Make it fast!"

"The keys are in Sumatra, tuan."

"Never mind the stall!"

I peered through the window and saw an armored car flashing up through the trees. Kay stepped closer and prodded him with the rifle.

"Unlock him, Inspector!"

She was cool as hell.

Inspector Kris went through his pockets, fumbled the keys and dropped them. He was stalling. He believed that was the police car from Kuala Tang. All he had to do was keep me in cuffs a minute more.

I lost my temper. I raised my gun in my hand as he bent for the keys, and I struck him with the butt.

He folded with an airy sigh.

Kay swept the keys off the floor and unlocked the handcuffs. "That's Monique's car coming."

"I know. Did you get your boys alerted for trouble?"

"There wasn't time."

I turned desperately toward the window. "Maybe I can scare him off with your elephant gun." I bent and got hold of Inspector Kris and dragged him out of the living room and into the nearest bedroom.

"Take his revolver," I snapped. "Stay with him, and when he comes to, keep him off my back."

"I don't want to sit this out, darling. I can fight too."

"*Hurry up!*"

She gave me a grim look. "All right."

I closed the bedroom door on them and picked up the rifle. At least she wouldn't catch a stray bullet in there.

I got to the front windows as Monique's Ford pulled up in the drive, its white-wall tires rouged with laterite mud. There were only two shells in the gun, but I let go with one of them. The explosion rocked the house and filled my nostrils with cordite. It struck armor and must have split the eardrums of the two of them inside. Or had Gabb ditched Edgett as worthless, and come alone?

The Ford moved and turned at the corner of the house and crept back again, as if reconnoitering. Gabb wasn't going to be scared off. The car kept on the move in front of the house, like a nervous crab on the beach. A shot burst from the armor slit and shattered a window near me. I stayed low, following the car with the rifle sights. Gabb let go with another shot. He'd spotted me at the window.

I moved to a new position. My hands began to sweat on the metal of the gun. The Ford kept cruising. What was Gabb waiting for? I'd been a damned fool for not getting set with a box of cartridges. I wondered if I dared yell out to Kay. Better not take the chance that Inspector Kris was coming to.

Well, all I needed was one shot, and I'd save it. Gabb would get tired of roaming and breaking house windows. If he misunderstood my silence, he might figure he'd got in a lucky shot and come out from behind the armor. I'd be ready.

He had nothing to worry about if he killed me. He was doing the police a favor, wasn't he?

He got tired of shooting and a long silence settled over the morning. The Ford kept roving in front of the bungalow, turning at the corner and passing back again. What the hell was he waiting for? Did he think he could starve me out?

I crouched at the window and all the little things that hadn't made sense during the last couple of days began to make very real sense. There were the months of trouble Kay had been having on Jade Tiger, the overseers who had been frightened off, the slashed trees—-only the very young and the very old—and Ahmad with the kingfisher's kris in his back. It all made sense, and I knew it added up to a hell of a lot more than just Jade Tiger.

"Don't move!"

The voice came from inside the house, behind me.

"Don't turn or I'll shoot you in the face!"

I froze. It was Gabb's voice.

"Did you think that was me in the car?" I heard his steps come closer. "It's Edgett. Me, I got out of the car in the trees and walked in the back door. What an idiot you are, old friend!"

"You're full of surprises."

"Fire the rifle in the sky until it's empty."

I fired it.

"Now you can turn around."

He was still using the nickel-plated revolver and it looked more deadly than before. "An elephant gun, eh?" He burst into a roar and took a step toward me. A victorious grin pinched his eyes, and unmasked the Oriental in him. "Were you hoping for the ear shot?"

"I should have lit matches," I said, getting off my knees. "I should have tested the wind for smell."

"Where are the others?"

"I cleared the place," I said. "I figured you'd show up."

He squared his sweat-blotched shoulders, grinning, luxuriating in the moment, and took another step. "Such a pity you came to Silver Jubilee! Now you know something about me, and one old friend dislikes shooting another old friend."

"We can drop the old-friend crap. You've hated my guts for years." After the first smack of disillusion, I knew now what made Gabb tick, and the pieces matched up to beat hell. I'd been going around in a stupid haze because I thought Gabb was my best friend. It wasn't even good for a laugh any more.

"Turn around," he said. "Walk slowly onto the veranda. If you walk too fast my friend Edgett may think you're running away and shoot. Slowly, eh? We will go in the Ford and pick out a nice spot for you."

I glanced from the revolver to Gabb's beaming face and decided not to argue. I had misjudged him in the past, but I wasn't misjudging him now. I saw him finally for what he was—a brutal, ambitious Eurasian with hardened instincts of self-preservation and a flair for cruelty. He'd survive. I had to die. He'd pull the trigger now if he had to, but it would cheat him of an extravagance. He would enjoy watching me sweat.

"Slowly," I agreed, turning.

I glanced out through the screen door. The Ford, its steel armor splattered with red mud, had stopped opposite the veranda steps. I began to walk, but my mind raced. Gabb swung around behind me, not close enough to matter, his boots creaking in slow motion. When I reached the door I stopped and kicked it open. Flies scattered off the screen.

All right, I thought. Let Edgett line up his sights. There was going to be some shooting and I hoped Kay, if she'd been able to hear from the bedroom, had brains enough to stay put.

"Not *quite* so slowly," Gabb sneered. "Now—in the car."

"You'll never get away with this."

"No? But you're wrong. They may even give me a medal. Capturing a public menace—a murderer. Shot trying to escape. Even the police will believe that."

"Go to hell, old friend."

I leaped through the doorway, hit the veranda flat—and the crossfire flashed over my back. There was the quick bark of Gabb's revolver close behind me, but Edgett let go wildly and his first slug must have staggered Gabb, standing directly in the range of fire. A silence cut in. I whirled and pitched into Gabb as he drew his gun hand away from his shoulder. He'd been hit, all right.

We went down together inside the doorway and rolled across the living-room floor.

I worked on his broad wrist to loosen the revolver, but his fingers froze around it. If Gabb had been jarred by the shock of catching a slug, he came quickly back to life. Before I realized it his free hand had found the handcuffs and he began flailing my face. He swore and writhed under me and began to grin.

"Keep grinning, you crazy bastard," I heard myself yell. *"You killed Eden!"* His eyebrows creased and for a moment I thought he was going to laugh in my face. "What do I care what you think?" he grunted, and the jangling handcuffs sliced into my ear.

I swung a foot to nail down the gun, and bounced my knuckles off his chin. His shoulder had tracked blood across the living-room floor, but he was a god-damned buffalo and he wasn't going to weaken. I ground his hand under my foot and smashed another right into his face and saw fresh blood etch into the creases of his grin.

"You killed Eden and you put up the money to murder Kay!"

He wasn't interested and he wasn't very much worried. Edgett was right outside, wasn't he? Edgett ought to be on his way into the house.

But Edgett didn't show and Gabb made a mistake. He twisted sharply and too heavily. His fingers jerked under my foot, got rolled open and smashed.

In another second I had the gun.

The muzzle must have looked big and black and about to erupt. Gabb froze there on the floor.

I waited on one knee and caught my breath.

"You stinking half-breed," I said, and he winced at the word. "You sent the wire to Sumatra turning me in. You wanted to make sure the case got closed—with me taking the rap."

"For your own good—to clear yourself."

"Sure," I sneered. "Sure."

I tore the handcuffs from his fingers and got around him so I could watch the doorway for Edgett. Sweat and blood were smeared across Gabb's face, masking his expression.

"Put away the gun, eh, Jock? I'm rich. I can—"

"You didn't get that cigarette lighter in Singapore. Eden bought it in Palembang. She gave me one for my birthday and sent you the other as a gift. Admit it!"

There was cunning in his eyes, but fear too. "No. I can help you escape. I have cash in the house. All you want."

"Look at me," I said. "I'm laughing."

"Jock—"

"Admit it!"

"Yes... Eden gave me the lighter."

"Was she in love with you?"

"Let me get up. We will talk."

"Move anything but your mouth and I'll blast your rotten brains. Was Eden in love with you?"

His lips tightened. I grabbed his wet hair and jammed the gun in his left ear. He stiffened. His lips began to flutter.

He talked.

His voice came out high-pitched; the words tumbled out in a flow of rage and desperation. "You want the truth! I was in love with Eden! For years! Even before you married her!"

"Louder. Yell it out!"

His blue eyes strained toward the left side of his face and the gun fixed in his ear. "My Chinese blood—she didn't like that. Not to marry. But to meet me in Singapore—that was different."

"Her shopping trips," I said sourly. "Spare me the details."

"I built up my estate from nothing. Fast. To dazzle her, eh? How rich I could make her, and how happy! But there was my blood. When I married Monique she became jealous. She kept those letters from you, and the police found them."

"And beat me to Silver Jubilee."

"How they must have hurt, my letters! It was *me* your Eden loved. *Me! Me!*"

"You," I said. "You were in Sumatra the night she was murdered. You were in my house. When you left you picked up my cigarette lighter by mistake. And I carried around yours, with acid stains on it, wondering how the hell they got there. You were in my house that night, and you murdered her! Yell it out!"

"She begged me not to come to your house at all. She was afraid I would tell you about her trips to Singapore to meet me. I came to tell you."

"So I'd throw her out and maybe you could pick up the pieces."

"But she drugged you before I came. You were already asleep when I reached your house."

Sweat was rolling off my finger onto the trigger of the revolver. I don't know what kept me from squeezing it. I remembered the taste in my mouth the morning I'd found Eden dead. So that was it; she'd drugged the sundowner I'd had on the veranda. If she'd left my drink alone she might still be alive.

"We loved each other!" he said fiercely. Did he think it tortured me to hear it? "I would have taken her back with me to Silver Jubilee."

"Just the three of you."

"Monique I would have thrown out. One tires of a *poombalie*. Today I tired of her. Monique I could always send back to Lavender Street. Like today."

"But it didn't work."

"Eden had a temper."

"I know."

"She said she would never come to live with me. She was vile. She called me a half-breed, and I lost my temper—"

I shoved hard on the gun and must have touched his eardrum. "Scream it out!"

"*Yes, I killed her!* Now you know, but the police will never believe you!"

All I could hope was that Inspector Kris in the next room was conscious and listening.

"Eden was only the beginning, wasn't she?" I growled. "Your ambitions caught fire and there was Jade Tiger sitting right under your nose. You had to have it! So you could stand on your veranda and own everything in sight."

Sweat pooled around his eyes; he was a fraction of an inch away from death and he knew it. "Jock, listen—"

"You tried to intimidate Kay by scaring off her overseers, but she would-n't budge."

"I can make you rich." There was something close to a sob in his voice.

"Monique invented the bandits last night. But you've been inventing them for a long time!" Contempt and fury built up in me and I barked it out. "A handful of your own natives could slash a lot of trees! Only the saplings and the old rubber!"

"You would be a fool to shoot me."

"It made sense. You didn't want to put the plantation completely out of production—you expected to get your smelly hands on it! Your home-made Reds did just enough slashing to make it convincing. And you con-vinced everyone the bandits were back! Is that the way you picked up the other *kaboons* you've added to your estate?"

"Take away the gun, eh, Jock?" He was trying to smile, to play the old-friends game, but a tremble broke through on his lips. "We—"

"A frightened planter will sell cheap, won't he?"

"Jock!" It burst off his lips like a plea for help.

"*Answer me!*"

"Yes!"

"But you made sure a few of your own trees got slashed along with the others. Just to keep anyone from getting ideas."

"Yes."

"Louder!"

"*Yes!*"

"But Kay wouldn't scare off like the others. And most of all you wanted Jade Tiger. So you hired a couple of Singapore idiots to keep the blood off your hands."

"It was a mistake."

"With Kay out of the way, her family in Australia would be glad to find a cash buyer even at a cheap price, and you'd be there with the cash. When the Reds move in, even rubber land is hard to sell."

"What will you—"

"Why Ahmad? Did he get wise to your Silver Jubilee Reds?"

"He discovered Inche slashing trees."

"And Inche knifed him to keep him from exposing your real-estate schemes. Is that right?"

"Yes."

"Keep talking."

"I can't."

"Maybe I can fill it in. When I asked you yesterday about the kingfisher kris, you got worried that Inche might talk if he got arrested. So you hurried over to his little *kaboon* and made sure he wouldn't."

"No. He's camping in the jungle. I told his wife—"

"To hell with Inche."

I heard a noise behind me. It was Kay and it was Inspector Kris. His face was solemn and officious.

"I believe," he said, "Tuan Wing is now my prisoner."

Kay was beaming. "He heard, darling. Both of us. We heard it all!"

I knew from his voice that Inspector Kris had got his gun back from Kay. "All right," I said. "He's your prisoner."

I let go of Gabb's hair and unplugged his ear. Kay ran toward me and she was almost crying.

Gabb pulled himself up by a chair and shook his head. Suddenly his hands tightened on the chair and he hurled it into Inspector Kris's face. In another instant he was streaking for the back door.

I squeezed the trigger twice and missed twice. I tore loose from Kay and ran like hell.

He made it to Kay's Mercury. Hell, I'd even left the motor running for him. The tires screamed and I was left standing on the back veranda.

I hurried back into the house. Inspector Kris was sitting on the floor, stunned and bleeding. The chair had come hurtling into his face. I picked up the elephant gun.

"Get me some shells for this thing! Kay, quick!"

"The Inspector—"

"He'll live. Hurry!"

I heard the Mercury careen around the house and take off down the road. I went to the window and checked on the Ford out front. A moment later I saw the door open and Edgett stepped cautiously from behind the armor.

It was easy to figure. He'd been sitting tight, hoping for the best, but now that the Mercury had sped away he obviously thought I had taken off in it and Gabb must be lying in the house with a couple of slugs in him. Kay brought me a dusty box of shells. I loaded up and emptied the remaining cartridges into my pocket.

Then I waited.

Edgett's footsteps were light on the veranda. He stopped to listen, heard nothing, and opened the screen door.

He saw the elephant gun in my hands, but he didn't have any more sense than to try to shoot it out.

I blew out his guts, if he had any.

I stepped over him and hurried onto the veranda, but Gabb was already out of range.

Kay was beside me. "I'm going with you!"

"Kris needs help."

"I'll drive. You can't use that rifle and drive too. Dollah will come out of hiding and help Inspector Kris."

"All right, let's go."

Edgett hadn't killed the engine and we got under way fast. Gabb had reached the bottom of the Jade Tiger road and we caught glints of the armor as he crossed the bridge toward Silver Jubilee.

"Step on it," I said.

She stepped on it, but we didn't gain. Gabb was driving hell out of the Mercury. He didn't head for the Silver Jubilee bungalow, but followed the branch road along the river. And suddenly there was a rumble in the sky.

Kay glanced at me. "What's that?"

"Planes. Gabb said the army was going to bomb up the jungle and try to knock out the Red terrorists who aren't there."

"Gabb's heading for the jungle."

I peered through the armor slit and saw three planes moving in a triangle across the hot blue sky toward the big hills and solid jungle.

The road was narrow, with the barbed wire of Silver Jubilee on our left. I kept the rifle between my legs; with the joggling and the distance between us there was no use in wasting any shots.

The jungle came in ahead of us, off in the distance. And then we saw dark smoke and green spray and a moment later the heavy explosions rocked us. The planes were circling and dropping their bombs. Gabb was still in sight barreling down the road. He must have forgotten about the planes. He must have figured he'd stand the best chance of getting loose in the jungle, but now it was too late to turn around if he wanted to. The road was too narrow.

The surface became more rutted and we were reaching the end of Silver Jubilee. The jungle rose up behind it in a towering wall of green. And suddenly the Mercury began to slow.

"What the hell," I muttered. "He's stopping."

"Maybe he's more afraid of the bombs up there than he is of us."

We gained fast now.

I pressed my eyes to the slit. I saw Gabb leave the car and start running. The river lay to the right of us, beyond the brush of lalang. Gabb was heading for the river, almost vanishing in the tall grass.

The bombing wasn't close enough to worry about. But as Kay slowed the car a new sound came to us—a wild, terrified trumpeting of elephants. And they were close.

We saw them almost at once breaking through the jungle wall. The ground shook as they thundered into the open, their ears cracking and their trunks raised. "The bombs have started a stampede!" I shouted. "I can't turn around!"

"What!"

"The road's too narrow!"

The jungle shivered and leaves flew in the air. I saw Gabb beating his way back through the lalang. The stampede was coming our way and he was trying to get back to the protection of the armored Mercury.

"Stop the car!" I yelled.

They came like a tidal wave and the din was earsplitting. There must have been forty mammoth hides shuffling down the road and tearing into the estate fencing. They bellowed and screamed, their backs laced with jungle vines and leaves and creepers. Their ears flapped and cracked like rifle shots. The lalang shook and the trumpeting and rumbling in the air turned your blood cold.

I opened my door and fired, hoping the explosion would turn them. The rifle sounded like a cap pistol against their heavy charge. I got back in the car and watched through the windshield slit. Gabb was still at least thirty yards from the Mercury. A trumpeting bull was charging through the lalang, the V of his mouth a pinkish white. He trotted between Gabb and the car, cutting him off. Within seconds the bull rumbled past us and I saw a tangle of orchids caught on its tusk. Gabb never reached the Mercury. The herd thundered around us like a gray-brown cloud and the car was buffeted like a toy. We held on and took it. Light came through the slits in flickers. We held on, and wondered how much the armor could take.

I was streaming sweat. The stampede thundered beyond us and we sat there bruised and still a little scared. Neither of us had anything to say. We sat there a long time.

"It must be a hell of a way to die," I said finally.

I opened the door. The lalang had been flattened as if by a steam roller. Gabb was somewhere under the matting and I didn't care about finding him any more.

I looked at the beat-up fenders. The armor still shone. I walked up the road to the Mercury. I got in and tried to start it. The starter whined, but the engine wouldn't fire. I looked at the gauge. It explained why Gabb had suddenly abandoned the car and cut out for the river. When I'd left the motor running behind Kay's bungalow I hadn't noticed how low the gas had been. I had burned most of what was left. Gabb had run out of gas.

I went back to Kay, and she moved over and I had a hell of a time getting the car jockied around. We limped back to Jade Tiger with the fenders scraping the tires.

Kay and I got married. Inspector Kris came over from Sumatra for the wedding, and he was still wearing a bandage above his left ear where Gabb had creased his skull with the chair. He wore his black fez as rakishly as before—on the other side of his head.

I was able to get my money out of Sumatra and I figured I'd have Jade Tiger back in shape within a few months.

Meanwhile, Kay kept calling me names.

She kept calling me Big Master.

THE END

Stark Houʌe Preʌʌ

1-933586-01-X **Benjamin Appel** Brain Guy / Plunder $19.95
1-933586-26-5 **Benjamin Appel** Sweet Money Girl / Life and Death of a Tough Guy $19.95
0-9749438-7-8 **Algernon Blackwood** Julian LeVallon / The Bright Messenger $21.95
1-933586-03-6 **Malcolm Braly** Shake Him Till He Rattles / It's Cold Out There $19.95
1-933586-10-9 **Gil Brewer** Wild to Possess / A Taste for Sin $19.95
1-933586-20-6 **Gil Brewer** A Devil for O'Shaugnessy / The Three-Way Split $14.95
1-933586-24-9 **W. R. Burnett** It's Always Four O'Clock / Iron Man $19.95
1-933586-31-1 **Catherine Butzen** Thief of Midnight $15.95
0-9667848-0-4 **Storm Constantine** The Oracle Lips/hb $45
1-933586-12-5 **A. S. Fleischman** Look Behind You Lady / The Venetian Blonde $19.95
0-9667848-7-1 **Elisabeth Sanxay Holding** Lady Killer / Miasma $19.95
0-9667848-9-8 **Elisabeth Sanxay Holding** The Death Wish / Net of Cobwebs $19.95
0-9749438-5-1 **Elisabeth Sanxay Holding** Strange Crime in Bermuda / Too Many Bottles $19.95
1-933586-16-8 **Elisabeth Sanxay Holding** The Old Battle Ax / Dark Power $19.95
1-933586-17-6 **Russell James** Underground / Collected Stories $14.95
0-9749438-8-6 **Day Keene** Framed in Guilt / My Flesh is Sweet $19.95
1-933586-21-4 **Mercedes Lambert** Dogtown / Soultown $14.95
1-933586-14-1 **Dan Marlowe/Fletcher Flora/Charles Runyon** Trio of Gold Medals $15.95
1-933586-02-8 **Stephen Marlowe** Violence is My Business / Turn Left for Murder $19.95
1-933586-07-9 **Ed by McCarthy & Gorman** Invasion of the Body Snatchers: A Tribute $17.95
1-933586-09-5 **Margaret Millar** An Air That Kills / Do Evil in Return $19.95
1-933586-23-0 **Wade Miller** The Killer / Devil on Two Sticks $17.95
0-9749438-0-0 **E. Phillips Oppenheim** Secrets & Sovereigns: Uncollected Stories $19.95
1-933586-27-3 **E. Phillips Oppenheim** The Amazing Judgment / Mr. Laxworthy's Adventures $19.95
0-9749438-3-5 **Vin Packer** Something in the Shadows / Intimate Victims $19.95
0-9749438-6-x **Vin Packer** Damnation of Adam Blessing / Alone at Night $19.95
1-933586-05-2 **Vin Packer** Whisper His Sin / The Evil Friendship $19.95
1-933586-18-4 **Richard Powell** A Shot in the Dark / Shell Game $14.95
1-933586-19-2 **Bill Pronzini** Snowbound / Games $14.95
0-9667848-8-x **Peter Rabe** The Box / Journey Into Terror $19.95
0-9749438-4-3 **Peter Rabe** Murder Me for Nickels / Benny Muscles In $19.95
1-933586-00-1 **Peter Rabe** Blood on the Desert / A House in Naples $19.95
1-933586-11-7 **Peter Rabe** My Lovely Executioner / Agreement to Kill $19.95
1-933586-22-2 **Peter Rabe** Anatomy of a Killer / A Shroud for Jesso $14.95
0-9749438-9-4 **Robert J. Randisi** The Ham Reporter / Disappearance of Penny $19.95
0-9749438-2-7 **Douglas Sanderson** Pure Sweet Hell / Catch a Fallen Starlet $19.95
1-933586-06-0 **Douglas Sanderson** The Deadly Dames / A Dum-Dum for the President $19.95
1-933586-29-x **Charlie Stella** Johnny Porno $15.95
1-933586-08-7 **Harry Whittington** A Night for Screaming / Any Woman He Wanted $19.95
1-933586-25-7 **Harry Whittington** To Find Cora / Like Mink Like Murder / Body and Passion $19.95

If you are interested in purchasing any of the above books, please send the cover price plus $3.00 U.S. for the 1st book and $1.00 U.S. for each additional book to:

STARK HOUSE PRESS

3190 1050128380   preʌʌ.com

Order 3 or more books and take a 10% discount. We accept PayPal payments.